Pretty Little Liars

VOLUMES 1 AND 2

Books by Sara Shepard:

PRETTY LITTLE LIARS NOVELS

Pretty Little Liars

+

Flawless

+

Perfect

+

Unbelievable

+

Wicked

+

Killer

+

Heartless

+

Wanted

+

Twisted

THE LYING GAME NOVELS

The Lying Game

Pretty Little Liars

VOLUME 1
PRETTY LITTLE LIARS

VOLUME 2
FLAWLESS

SARA SHEPARD

HARPER TEEN
An Imprint of HarperCollins*Publishers*

HarperTeen is an imprint of HarperCollins Publishers.

PRETTY LITTLE LIARS VOLUMES 1 AND 2

Pretty Little Liars
Copyright © 2006 by Alloy Entertainment and Sara Shepard

Flawless
Copyright © 2007 by Alloy Entertainment and Sara Shepard

All rights reserved. Printed in the United States of America.
No part of this book may be used or reproduced in any manner
whatsoever without written permission except in the case of brief
quotations embodied in critical articles and reviews. For information address
HarperCollins Children's Books, a division of HarperCollins Publishers,
10 East 53rd Street, New York, NY 10022.
www.harperteen.com

Produced by Alloy Entertainment
alloyentertainment 151 West 26th Street, New York, NY 10001

ISBN: 978-0-06-208791-1

Typography by Amy Trombat
11 12 13 14 15 CG/RRDH 1 2 3 4 5 6 7 8 9 10

CONTENTS

PRETTY LITTLE LIARS

For JSW

Three may keep a secret, if two of them are dead.

—BENJAMIN FRANKLIN

HOW IT ALL STARTED

Imagine it's a couple of years ago, the summer between seventh and eighth grade. You're tan from lying out next to your rock-lined pool, you've got on your new Juicy sweats (remember when everybody wore those?), and your mind's on your crush, the boy who goes to that other prep school whose name we won't mention and who folds jeans at Abercrombie in the mall. You're eating your Cocoa Krispies just how you like 'em—doused in skim milk—and you see this girl's face on the side of the milk carton. MISSING. She's cute—probably cuter than you—and has a feisty look in her eyes. You think, *Hmm, maybe* she *likes soggy Cocoa Krispies too*. And you bet she'd think Abercrombie boy was a hottie as well. You wonder how someone so . . . well, so much like you went missing. You thought only girls who entered beauty pageants ended up on the sides of milk cartons.

Well, think again.

Aria Montgomery burrowed her face in her best friend Alison DiLaurentis's lawn. "Delicious," she murmured.

"Are you smelling the grass?" Emily Fields called from behind her, pushing the door of her mom's Volvo wagon closed with her long, freckly arm.

"It smells good." Aria brushed away her pink-striped hair and breathed in the warm early-evening air. "Like summer."

Emily waved 'bye to her mom and pulled up the blah jeans that were hanging on her skinny hips. Emily had been a competitive swimmer since Tadpole League, and even though she looked great in a Speedo, she never wore anything tight or remotely cute like the rest of the girls in her seventh-grade class. That was because Emily's parents insisted that one built character from the inside out. (Although Emily was pretty certain that being forced to hide her IRISH GIRLS DO IT BETTER baby tee at the back of her underwear drawer wasn't exactly character enhancing.)

"You guys!" Alison pirouetted through the front yard. Her hair was bunched up in a messy ponytail, and she was still wearing her rolled-up field hockey kilt from the team's end-of-the-year party that afternoon. Alison was the only seventh grader to make the JV team and got rides home with the older Rosewood Day School girls, who blasted Jay-Z from their Cherokees and sprayed Alison with perfume before dropping her off so that she wouldn't smell like the cigarettes they'd all been smoking.

"What am I missing?" called Spencer Hastings, sliding through a gap in Ali's hedges to join the others. Spencer lived next door. She flipped her long, sleek dark-blond ponytail over her shoulder and took a swig from her purple Nalgene bottle. Spencer hadn't made the JV cut with Ali in the fall, and had to play on the seventh-grade team. She'd been on a year-long field hockey binge to perfect her game, and the girls *knew* she'd been practicing dribbling in the backyard before they arrived. Spencer hated when anyone was better at anything than she was. Especially Alison.

"Wait for me!"

They turned to see Hanna Marin climbing out of her mom's Mercedes. She stumbled over her tote bag and waved her chubby arms wildly. Ever since Hanna's parents had gotten a divorce last year, she'd been steadily putting on weight and outgrowing her old clothes. Even though Ali rolled her eyes, the rest of the girls pretended not to notice. That's just what best friends do.

Alison, Aria, Spencer, Emily, and Hanna bonded last year when their parents volunteered them to work Saturday afternoons at Rosewood Day School's charity drive—well, all except for Spencer, who volunteered herself. Whether or not Alison knew about the other four, the four knew about Alison. She was perfect. Beautiful, witty, smart. Popular. Boys wanted to kiss Alison, and girls—even older ones—wanted to *be* her. So the first time Ali laughed at one of Aria's jokes, asked Emily a question about swimming, told Hanna her shirt was adorable, or commented that Spencer's penmanship was *way* neater than her own, they couldn't help but be, well . . . dazzled. Before Ali, the girls had felt like pleated, high-waisted mom jeans—awkward and noticeable for all the wrong reasons—but then Ali made them feel like the most perfect-fitting Stella McCartneys that no one could afford.

Now, more than a year later, on the last day of seventh grade, they weren't just best friends, they were *the* girls of Rosewood Day. A lot had happened to make it that way. Every sleepover they had, every field trip, had been a new adventure. Even homeroom had been memorable when they were together. (Reading a steamy note from the varsity crew captain to his math tutor over the PA system was now a Rosewood Day legend.) But there were other things they all wanted to forget. And there was *one* secret they couldn't even bear to talk about. Ali said that secrets were what bonded their five-way best-friendship together for eternity. If that was true, they were going to be friends for life.

"I'm so glad this day is over." Alison moaned before gently pushing Spencer back through the gap in the hedges. "Your barn."

"I'm so glad seventh *grade* is over," Aria said as she, Emily, and Hanna followed Alison and Spencer toward the renovated barn-turned-guesthouse where Spencer's older sister, Melissa, had lived for her junior and senior years of high school. Fortunately, she'd just graduated and was headed to Prague this summer, so it was all theirs for the night.

Suddenly they heard a very squeaky voice. "Alison! Hey, Alison! Hey, Spencer!"

Alison turned to the street. "Not it," she whispered.

"Not it," Spencer, Emily, and Aria quickly followed.

Hanna frowned. "Shit."

It was this game Ali had stolen from her brother, Jason, who was a senior at Rosewood Day. Jason and his friends played it at inter-prep school field parties when scoping out girls. Being the last to call out "not it" meant you had to entertain the ugly girl for the night while your friends got to hook up with her hot friends—meaning, essentially, that you were as lame and unattractive as she was. In Ali's version, the girls called "not it" whenever there was anyone ugly, uncool, or unfortunate near them.

This time, "not it" was for Mona Vanderwaal—a dork from down the street whose favorite pastime was trying to befriend Spencer and Alison—and her two freaky friends, Chassey Bledsoe and Phi Templeton. Chassey was the girl who'd hacked into the school's computer system and then *told* the principal how to better secure it, and Phi Templeton went everywhere with a yo-yo—enough said. The three stared at the girls from the middle of the quiet, suburban road. Mona was perched on her Razor scooter, Chassey was on a black mountain bike, and Phi was on foot—with her yo-yo, of course.

"You guys want to come over and watch *Fear Factor*?" Mona called.

"Sorry," Alison simpered. "We're kind of busy."

Chassey frowned. "Don't you want to see when they eat the bugs?"

"Gross!" Spencer whispered to Aria, who then started pretending to eat invisible lice off Hanna's scalp like a monkey.

"Yeah, I wish we could." Alison tilted her head. "We've planned this sleepover for a while now. But maybe next time?"

Mona looked at the sidewalk. "Yeah, okay."

"See ya." Alison turned around, rolling her eyes, and the other girls did the same.

They crossed through Spencer's back gate. To their left was Ali's neighboring backyard, where her parents were building a twenty-seat gazebo for their lavish outdoor picnics. "Thank *God* the workers aren't here," Ali said, glancing at a yellow bulldozer.

Emily stiffened. "Have they been saying stuff to you again?"

"Easy there, Killer," Alison said. The others giggled. Sometimes they called Emily "Killer," as in Ali's personal pit bull. Emily used to find it funny, too, but lately she wasn't laughing along.

The barn was just ahead. It was small and cozy and had a big window that looked out on Spencer's large, rambling farm, which had its very own windmill. Here

in Rosewood, Pennsylvania, a little suburb about twenty miles from Philadelphia, you were more likely to live
in a twenty-five-room farmhouse with a mosaic-tiled
pool and hot tub, like Spencer's house, than in a prefab
McMansion. Rosewood smelled like lilacs and mown
grass in the summer and clean snow and wood stoves in
the winter. It was full of lush, tall pines, acres of rustic
family-run farms, and the cutest foxes and bunnies. It
had fabulous shopping and Colonial-era estates and
parks for birthday, graduation, and just-'cause-we-feel-
like-it fêtes. And Rosewood boys were gorgeous in that
glowing, healthy, just-stepped-out-of-an-Abercrombie-
catalog way. This was Philadelphia's Main Line. It was
full of old, noble bloodlines, older money, and practically
ancient scandals.

As they reached the barn, the girls heard giggles
coming from inside. Someone squealed, "I said, *stop* it!"

"Oh God," Spencer moaned. "What is she doing
here?"

As Spencer peeked through the keyhole, she could
see Melissa, her prim and proper, excellent-at-everything
older sister, and Ian Thomas, her tasty boyfriend, wrestling on the couch. Spencer kicked at the door with
the heel of her shoe, forcing it open. The barn smelled
like moss and slightly burned popcorn. Melissa turned
around.

"What the fu–?" she asked. Then she noticed the
others and smiled. "Oh, hey guys."

The girls eyed Spencer. She constantly complained that Melissa was a venomous super-bitch, so they were always taken aback when Melissa seemed friendly and sweet.

Ian stood up, stretched, and grinned at Spencer. "Hey."

"Hi, Ian," Spencer replied in a much brighter voice. "I didn't know you were here."

"Yeah you did." Ian smiled flirtatiously. "You were spying on us."

Melissa readjusted her long blond hair and black silk headband, staring at her sister. "So, what's up?" she asked, a little accusingly.

"It's just . . . I didn't mean to barge in . . . ," Spencer sputtered. "But we were supposed to have this place tonight."

Ian playfully hit Spencer on the arm. "I was just messing with you," he teased.

A patch of red crept up her neck. Ian had messy blond hair, sleepy-looking hazelnut-colored eyes, and totally gropeworthy stomach muscles.

"Wow," Ali said in a too-loud voice. All heads turned to her. "Melissa, you and Ian make the kuh-*yoo*-test couple. I've never told you, but I've always thought it. Don't you agree, Spence?"

Spencer blinked. "Um," she said quietly.

Melissa stared at Ali for a second, perplexed, and then turned back to Ian. "Can I talk to you outside?"

Ian downed his Corona as the girls watched. They only ever drank super-secretively from the bottles in their parents' liquor cabinets. He set the empty bottle down and offered them a parting grin as he followed Melissa outside. "Adieu, ladies." He winked before closing the door behind him.

Alison dusted her hands together. "Another problem solved by Ali D. Are you going to thank me now, Spence?"

Spencer didn't answer. She was too busy looking out the barn's front window. Lightning bugs had begun to light up the purplish sky.

Hanna walked over to the abandoned popcorn bowl and took a big handful. "Ian's *so* hot. He's, like, hotter than Sean." Sean Ackard was one of the cutest guys in their grade and the subject of Hanna's constant fantasies.

"You know what I heard?" Ali asked, flopping down on the couch. "Sean really likes girls who have good appetites."

Hanna brightened. "Really?"

"*No.*" Alison snorted.

Hanna slowly dropped the handful of popcorn back into the bowl.

"So, girls," Ali said. "I know the perfect thing we can do."

"I hope we're not streaking again." Emily giggled. They'd done that a month earlier—in the freezing frickin' cold—and although Hanna had refused to strip down to less than her undershirt and day-of-the-week panties, the rest of them had run through a nearby barren cornfield without a lick on.

"*You* loved that a little too much," Ali murmured. The smile faded from Emily's lips. "But no—I was leaving this for the last day of school. I learned how to hypnotize people."

"Hypnotize?" Spencer repeated.

"Matt's sister taught me," Ali answered, looking at the framed photos of Melissa and Ian on the mantel. Her boyfriend of the week, Matt, had the same sandy-colored hair as Ian.

"How do you do it?" Hanna asked.

"Sorry, she swore me to secrecy," Ali said, turning back around. "You want to see if it works?"

Aria frowned, taking a seat on a lavender floor pillow. "I don't know. . . ."

"Why not?" Ali's eyes flickered to a stuffed pig puppet that was peeking out of Aria's purple sweater-knit tote bag. Aria was always carrying around weird things—stuffed animals, random pages torn out of old novels, postcards of places she'd never visited.

"Doesn't hypnosis make you say stuff you don't want to say?" Aria asked.

"Is there something you can't tell us?" Ali responded. "And why do you still bring that pig puppet everywhere?" She pointed at it.

Aria shrugged and pulled the stuffed pig out of her bag. "My dad got me Pigtunia in Germany. She advises me on my love life." She stuck her hand into the puppet.

"You're shoving your hand up its butt!" Ali squealed and Emily started to giggle. "Besides, why do you want to carry around something your *dad* gave you?"

"It's not funny," Aria snapped, whipping her head around to face Emily.

Everyone was quiet for a few seconds, and the girls looked blankly at one another. This had been happening a lot lately: Someone—usually Ali—mentioned something, and someone else got upset, but everyone was too shy to ask what in the world was going on.

Spencer broke the silence. "Being hypnotized, um, does sound sort of sketch."

"*You* don't know anything about it," Alison said quickly. "C'mon. I could do it to you all at once."

Spencer picked at the waistband of her skirt. Emily blew air through her teeth. Aria and Hanna exchanged a look. Ali was always coming up with stuff for them to try—last summer, it was smoking dandelion seeds to see if they'd hallucinate, and this past fall they'd gone swimming in Pecks Pond, even though a dead body was once discovered there—but the thing was, they often didn't *want* to do the things that Alison made them do. They all loved Ali to death, but they sometimes hated her too—for bossing them around and for the spell she'd cast on them. Sometimes in Ali's presence, they didn't feel real, exactly. They felt kind of like dolls, with Ali arranging their every move. Each of them wished that, just once, she had the strength to tell Ali no.

"Puh-*leeeeeze*?" Ali asked. "Emily, you want to do it, right?"

"Um . . . " Emily's voice quivered. "Well . . . "

"I'll do it," Hanna butted in.

"Me too," Emily said quickly after.

Spencer and Aria reluctantly nodded. Satisfied, Alison shut off all the lights with a snap and lit several sweetly scented vanilla votive candles that were on the coffee table. Then she stood back and hummed.

"Okay, everyone, just relax," she chanted, and the girls arranged themselves in a circle on the rug. "Your heartbeat's slowing down. Think calm thoughts. I'm going to count down from one hundred, and as soon as I touch all of you, you'll be in my power."

"Spooky." Emily laughed shakily.

Alison began. "One hundred . . . ninety-nine . . . ninety-eight . . ."

Twenty-two . . .

Eleven . . .

Five . . .

Four . . .

Three . . .

She touched Aria's forehead with the fleshiest part

of her thumb. Spencer uncrossed her legs. Aria twitched her left foot.

"Two . . ." She slowly touched Hanna, then Emily, and then moved toward Spencer. "One."

Spencer's eyes sprang open before Alison could reach her. She jumped up and ran to the window.

"What're you doing?" Ali whispered. "You're ruining the moment."

"It's too dark in here." Spencer reached up and opened the curtains.

"No." Alison lowered her shoulders. "It's got to be dark. That's how it works."

"C'mon, no it doesn't." The blind stuck; Spencer grunted to wrench it free.

"No. It does."

Spencer put her hands on her hips. "I want it lighter. Maybe everyone does."

Alison looked at the others. They all still had their eyes closed.

Spencer wouldn't give in. "It doesn't always have to be the way you want it, you know, Ali?"

Alison barked out a laugh. "*Close* them!"

Spencer rolled her eyes. "God, take a pill."

"You think *I* should take a pill?" Alison demanded.

Spencer and Alison stared at each other for a few moments. It was one of those ridiculous fights that could have been about who saw the new Lacoste polo dress at Neiman Marcus first or whether honey-colored high-lights looked too brassy, but it was really about something else entirely. Something way bigger.

Finally, Spencer pointed at the door. "Leave."

"Fine." Alison strode outside.

"Good!" But after a few seconds passed, Spencer followed her. The bluish evening air was still, and there weren't any lights on in her family's main house. It was quiet, too—even the crickets were quiet—and Spencer could hear herself breathing. "Wait a second!" she cried after a moment, slamming the door behind her. "Alison!"

But Alison was gone.

When she heard the door slam, Aria opened her eyes. "Ali?" she called. "Guys?" No answer.

She looked around. Hanna and Emily sat like lumps on the carpet, and the door was open. Aria moved out to the porch. No one was there. She tiptoed to the edge of Ali's property. The woods spread out in front of her and everything was silent.

"Ali?" she whispered. Nothing. "Spencer?"

Inside, Hanna and Emily rubbed their eyes. "I just had the weirdest dream," Emily said. "I mean, I guess it was a dream. It was really quick. Alison fell down this really deep well, and there were all these giant plants."

"That was my dream too!" Hanna said.

"It *was*?" Emily asked.

Hanna nodded. "Well, kind of. There was a big plant in it. And I think I saw Alison too. It might've been her shadow—but it was definitely *her*."

"Whoa," Emily whispered. They stared at each other, their eyes wide.

"Guys?" Aria stepped back through the door. She looked very pale.

"Are you okay?" Emily asked.

"Where's Alison?" Aria creased her forehead. "And Spencer?"

"We don't know," Hanna said.

Just then, Spencer burst back into the house. All the girls jumped. "What?" she asked.

"Where's Ali?" Hanna asked quietly.

"I don't know," Spencer whispered. "I thought . . . I don't know."

The girls fell silent. All they could hear were the tree branches sliding across the windows. It sounded like someone scraping her long fingernails against a plate.

"I think I want to go home," Emily said.

The next morning, they still hadn't heard from Alison. The girls called one another to talk, a four-way call this time instead of five.

"Do you think she's mad at us?" Hanna asked. "She seemed weird all night."

"She's probably at Katy's," Spencer said. Katy was one of Ali's field hockey friends.

"Or maybe she's with Tiffany—that girl from camp?" Aria offered.

"I'm sure she's somewhere having fun," Emily said quietly.

One by one, they got calls from Mrs. DiLaurentis, asking if they'd heard from Ali. At first, the girls all covered for her. It was the unwritten rule: They'd covered for Emily when she snuck in after her 11 P.M. weekend curfew; they'd fudged the truth for Spencer when she borrowed Melissa's Ralph Lauren duffel coat and then accidentally left it on the seat of a SEPTA train; and so on. But as each one hung up with Mrs. DiLaurentis, a sour feeling swelled in her stomach. Something felt horribly wrong.

That afternoon, Mrs. DiLaurentis called again, this time in a panic. By that evening, the DiLaurentises had called the police, and the next morning there were cop cars and news vans camped out on the DiLaurentises' normally pristine front lawn. It was a local news channel's wet dream: a pretty rich girl, lost in one of the safest upper-class towns in the country.

Hanna called Emily after watching the first nightly Ali news report. "Did the police interview you today?"

"Yeah," Emily whispered.

"Me too. You didn't tell them about . . . " She paused. "About *The Jenna Thing*, did you?"

"No!" Emily gasped. "Why? Do you think they know something?"

"No . . . they couldn't," Hanna whispered after a second. "We're the only ones who know. The four of us . . . and Alison."

The police questioned the girls—along with practically everybody from Rosewood, from Ali's second-grade gymnastics instructor to the guy who'd once sold her Marlboros at Wawa. It was the summer before eighth grade and the girls were supposed to be flirting with older boys at pool parties, eating corn on the cob in one another's backyards, and shopping all day at the King James Mall. Instead they were crying alone in their canopied beds or staring blankly at their photo-covered walls. Spencer went on a room-cleaning binge, reviewing what her fight with Ali had *really* been about, and thinking of things she knew about Ali that none of the others did. Hanna spent hours on her bedroom floor, hiding emptied Cheetos bags under her mattress. Emily couldn't stop obsessing over a letter she'd sent to Ali before she disappeared. Had Ali ever gotten it? Aria sat at her desk with Pigtunia. Slowly, the girls began calling one another less frequently. The same thoughts haunted all four of them, but there wasn't anything left to say to one another.

The summer turned into the school year, which turned into the next summer. Still no Ali. The police continued to search—but quietly. The media lost interest, heading off to obsess over a Center City triple homicide. Even the DiLaurentises moved out of Rosewood almost two and a half years after Alison disappeared. As for Spencer, Aria, Emily, and Hanna, something shifted in them, too. Now if they passed Ali's old street and glanced at her house, they didn't go into insta-cry mode. Instead, they started to feel something else.

Relief.

Sure, Alison was *Alison*. She was the shoulder to cry on, the only one you'd ever want calling up your crush to find out how he felt about you, and the final word on whether your new jeans made your butt look big. But the girls were also afraid of her. Ali knew more about them than anyone else did, including the bad stuff they wanted to bury—just like a body. It was horrible to think Ali might be dead, but . . . if she was, at least their secrets were safe.

And they were. For three years, anyway.

1

ORANGES, PEACHES, AND LIMES, OH MY!

"Someone finally bought the DiLaurentises' old house," Emily Fields's mother said. It was Saturday afternoon, and Mrs. Fields sat at the kitchen table, bifocals perched on her nose, calmly doing her bills.

Emily felt the Vanilla Coke she was drinking fizz up her nose.

"I think another girl your age moved in," Mrs. Fields continued. "I was going to drop off that basket today. Maybe you want to do it instead?" She pointed to the cellophaned monstrosity on the counter.

"God, Mom, *no*," Emily replied. Since she'd retired from teaching elementary school last year, Emily's mom had become the unofficial Rosewood, Pennsylvania, Welcome Wagon lady. She assembled a million random things—dried fruit, those flat rubber thingies you use to get jars open, ceramic chickens (Emily's mom was chicken-obsessed), a guide to Rosewood inns, whatever—into a big wicker welcome basket. She was a prototypical suburban mom, minus the SUV. She thought they were ostentatious and gas-guzzling, so she drove an oh-so-practical Volvo wagon instead.

Mrs. Fields stood and ran her fingers through Emily's chlorine-damaged hair. "Would it upset you too much to go there, sweetie? Maybe I should send Carolyn?"

Emily glanced at her sister Carolyn, who was a year older and lounging comfortably on the La-Z-Boy in the den watching *Dr. Phil.* Emily shook her head. "No, it's fine. I'll do it."

Sure, Emily whined sometimes and occasionally rolled her eyes. But the truth was, if her mom asked, Emily would do whatever she was supposed to do. She was a nearly straight-A, four-time state champion butter-flyer and hyper-obedient daughter. Following rules and requests came easily to her.

Plus, deep down she kind of *wanted* a reason to see Alison's house again. While it seemed the rest of Rosewood had started to move on from Ali's disappearance three years, two months, and twelve days ago, Emily hadn't. Even now, she couldn't glance at her seventh-grade yearbook without wanting to curl up in a ball. Sometimes on rainy days, Emily still reread Ali's old notes, which she stored in a shell-top Adidas shoe box under her bed. She even kept a pair of Citizens corduroys Ali had let her borrow on a wooden hanger in her closet, even though they were now way too small on her. She'd spent the last few lonely years in Rosewood longing for another friend like Ali, but that probably wasn't going to happen. She hadn't been a perfect friend, but for all her flaws, Ali was pretty tough to replace.

Emily straightened up and grabbed the Volvo's keys from the hook next to the phone. "I'll be back in a little while," she called as she closed the front door behind her.

The first thing she saw when she pulled up to Alison's old Victorian home at the top of the leafy street was a huge pile of trash on the curb and a big sign marked, FREE! Squinting, she realized that some of it was Alison's stuff—she recognized Ali's old, overstuffed white corduroy bedroom chair. The DiLaurentises had moved away almost nine months ago. Apparently they'd left some things behind.

She parked behind a giant Bekins moving van and got out of the Volvo. "Whoa," she whispered, trying to keep her bottom lip from trembling. Under the chair, there were several piles of grimy books. Emily reached down and looked at the spines. *The Red Badge of Courage. The Prince and the Pauper.* She remembered reading them in Mr. Pierce's seventh-grade English class, talking about symbolism, metaphors, and denouement. There were more books underneath, including some that just looked like old notebooks. Boxes sat next to the books; they were marked ALISON'S CLOTHES and ALISON'S OLD PAPERS. Peeking out of a crate was a blue and red ribbon. Emily pulled at it a little. It was a sixth-grade swimming medal she'd left at Alison's house one day when they'd made up a game called Olympian Sex Goddesses.

"You want that?"

Emily shot up. She faced a tall, skinny girl with tawny-colored skin and wild, black-brown curly hair. The girl wore a yellow tank top whose strap had slid off her shoulder to reveal an orange and green bra strap. Emily wasn't certain, but she thought she had the same bra at home. It was from Victoria's Secret and had little oranges, peaches, and limes all over the, er, boob parts.

The swimming medal slid out of her hands and clattered to the ground. "Um, no," she said, scrambling to pick it up.

"You can take any of it. See the sign?"

"No, really, it's okay."

The girl stuck out her hand. "Maya St. Germain. Just moved here."

"I . . ." Emily's words clogged up in her throat. "I'm Emily," she finally managed, taking Maya's hand and shaking it. It felt really formal to shake a girl's hand—Emily wasn't sure she'd ever done that before. She felt a little fuzzy. Maybe she hadn't eaten enough Honey Nut Cheerios for breakfast?

Maya gestured to the stuff on the ground. "Can you

believe all this crap was in my new room? I had to move it all out myself. It sucked."

"Yeah, this all belonged to Alison," Emily practically whispered.

Maya stooped down to inspect some of the paperbacks. She shoved her tank top strap back onto her shoulder. "Is she a friend of yours?"

Emily paused. *Is?* Maybe Maya hadn't heard about Ali's disappearance? "Um, she *was*. A long time ago. Along with a bunch of other girls who live around here," Emily explained, leaving out the part about the kidnapping or murder or whatever might have happened that she couldn't bear to imagine. "In seventh grade. I'm going into eleventh now at Rosewood Day." School started after this weekend. So did fall swim practice, which meant three hours of lap swimming daily. Emily didn't even want to think about it.

"I'm going to Rosewood too!" Maya grinned. She sank down on Alison's old corduroy chair, and the springs squeaked. "All my parents talked about on the flight here was how lucky I am to have gotten into Rosewood and how different it will be from my school in California. Like, I bet you guys don't have Mexican food, right? Or, like, really *good* Mexican food, like Cali-Mexican food. We used to have it in our cafeteria and *mmm*, it was so good. I'm going to have to get used to Taco Bell. Their gorditas make me want to vomit."

"Oh." Emily smiled. This girl sure talked a lot. "Yeah, the food kind of sucks."

Maya sprang up from the chair. "This might be a weird question since I just met you, but would you mind helping me carry the rest of these boxes up to my room?" She motioned to a few Crate & Barrel boxes sitting at the base of the truck.

Emily's eyes widened. Go into Alison's old room? But it would be totally rude if she refused, wouldn't it? "Um, sure," she said shakily.

The foyer still smelled like Dove soap and potpourri—just as it had when the DiLaurentises lived here. Emily paused at the door and waited for Maya to give her instructions, even though she knew she could find Ali's old room at the end of the upstairs hall blindfolded. Moving boxes were everywhere, and two spindly Italian greyhounds yapped from behind a gate in the kitchen.

"Ignore them," Maya said, climbing the stairs to her room and shoving the door open with her terry-covered hip.

Wow, it looks the same, Emily thought as she entered the bedroom. But the thing was, it didn't: Maya had put her queen-size bed in a different corner, she had a huge, flat-screen computer monitor on her desk, and she'd put up posters everywhere, covering Alison's old flowered wallpaper. But *something* felt the same, as if Alison's presence was still floating here. Emily felt woozy and leaned against the wall for support.

"Put it anywhere," Maya said. Emily rallied herself to stand, set her box down at the foot of the bed, and looked around.

"I like your posters," she said. They were mostly of bands: M.I.A., Black Eyed Peas, Gwen Stefani in a cheer-leading uniform. "I love Gwen," she added.

"Yeah," Maya said. "My boyfriend's totally obsessed with her. His name's Justin. He's from San Fran, where I'm from."

"Oh. I've got a boyfriend too," Emily said. "His name's Ben."

"Yeah?" Maya sat down on her bed. "What's he like?"

Emily tried to conjure up Ben, her boyfriend of four months. She'd seen him two days ago—they'd watched the *Doom* DVD at her house. Emily's mom was in the other room, of course, randomly popping in, asking if they needed anything. They'd been good friends for a while, on the same year-round swim teams. All their teammates told them they should go out, so they did. "He's cool."

"So why aren't you friends with the girl who lived here anymore?" Maya asked.

Emily pushed her reddish-blond hair behind her ears. Wow. So Maya really *didn't* know about Alison. If Emily started talking about Ali, though, she might start crying—which would be weird. She hardly knew this Maya girl. "I grew apart from all my old seventh-grade friends. Everyone changed a lot, I guess."

That was an understatement. Of Emily's other best

friends, Spencer had become a more exaggerated version of her already hyper-perfect self; Aria's family had suddenly moved to Iceland the fall after Ali went missing; and dorky-but-lovable Hanna had become totally *un*dorky and *un*lovable and was now a total bitch. Hanna and her now best friend, Mona Vanderwaal, had completely transformed themselves the summer between eighth and ninth grade. Emily's mom had recently seen Hanna going into Wawa, the local convenience store, and told Emily that Hanna looked "sluttier than that Paris Hilton girl." Emily had never heard her mom use the word *slutty*.

"I know how growing apart is," Maya said, bouncing up and down on her bed as she sat. "Like my boyfriend? He's so scared I'm going to ditch him now that we're on different coasts. He's such a big baby."

"My boyfriend and I are on the swim team, so we see each other all the time," Emily replied, looking for a place to sit down too. *Maybe* too *much of the time*, she thought.

"You swim?" Maya asked. She looked Emily up and down, which made Emily feel a little weird. "I bet you're really good. You totally have the shoulders."

"Oh, I don't know." Emily blushed and leaned against Maya's white wooden desk.

"You do!" Maya smiled. "But . . . if you're a big jock, does that mean you'd kill me if I smoked a little weed?"

"What, right now?" Emily's eyes widened. "What about your parents?"

"They're at the grocery store. And my brother—he's here somewhere, but he won't care." Maya reached under her mattress for an Altoids tin. She hefted up the window, which was right next to her bed, pulled out a joint, and lit it. The smoke curled into the yard and made a hazy cloud around a large oak tree.

Maya brought the joint back inside. "Want a hit?"

Emily had never tried pot in her entire life—she always thought her parents would somehow *know*, like by smelling her hair or forcing her to pee in a cup or something. But as Maya pulled the joint gracefully from her cherry-frosted lips, it looked sexy. Emily wanted to look sexy like that too.

"Um, okay." Emily slid closer to Maya and took the joint from her. Their hands brushed and their eyes met. Maya's were green and a little yellow, like a cat's. Emily's hand trembled. She felt nervous, but she put the joint to her mouth and took a tiny drag, like she was sipping Vanilla Coke through a straw.

But it didn't taste like Vanilla Coke. It felt like she'd just inhaled a whole jar of rotten spices. She hacked an old man–ish cough.

"Whoa," Maya said, taking back the joint. "First time?"

Emily couldn't breathe and just shook her head, gasping. She wheezed some more, trying to get air into her chest. Finally she could feel air hitting her lungs again. As Maya turned her arm, Emily saw a long, white scar running lengthwise down her wrist. *Whoa.* It looked a little like an albino snake on her tan skin. God, she was probably high already.

Suddenly there was a loud clank. Emily jumped. Then she heard the clank again. "What is that?" she wheezed.

Maya took another drag and shook her head. "The workers. We're here for one day and my parents have already started on the renovations." She grinned. "You just totally freaked, like you thought the cops were coming. You been busted before?"

"No!" Emily burst out laughing; it was such a ridiculous thought.

Maya smiled and exhaled.

"I should go," Emily rasped.

Maya's face fell. "Why?"

Emily shuffled off the bed. "I told my mom I'd only stop over for a minute. But I'll see you in school Tuesday."

"Cool," Maya said. "Maybe you could show me around?"

Emily smiled. "Sure."

Maya grinned and waved good-bye with three fingers. "You know how to find your way out?"

"I think so." Emily took one more look around Ali's—er, *Maya's*—room, and then stomped down the all-too-familiar stairs.

It wasn't until Emily shook her head out in the open air, passed all of Alison's old stuff on the curb, and climbed back into her parents' car, that she saw the Welcome Wagon basket on the backseat. *Screw it*, she thought, wedging the basket between Alison's old chair and her boxes of books. *Who needs a guide to Rosewood's inns, anyway? Maya already lives here.*

And Emily was suddenly glad she did.

2

ICELANDIC (AND FINNISH)
GIRLS ARE EASY

"Omigod, *trees*. I'm so happy to see big fat *trees*."

Aria Montgomery's fifteen-year-old brother, Michelangelo, wagged his head out of the family's Outback window like a golden retriever. Aria; her
parents, Ella and Byron—they wanted their kids to call
them by their first names—and Mike were all driving
back from Philadelphia International Airport. They'd just
gotten off a flight from Reykjavík, Iceland. Aria's dad was
an art history professor, and the family had spent the last
two years in Iceland while he helped do research for a
TV documentary on Scandinavian art. Now that they
were back, Mike was marveling at the Pennsylvania cow-
country scenery. And that meant . . . Every. Single. Thing.
The 1700s-era stone inn that sold ornate ceramic vases;
the black cows staring dumbly at their car from behind
a wooden roadside fence; the New England village–style

mall that had sprung up since they'd been gone. Even the dingy twenty-five-year-old Dunkin' Donuts.

"Man, I can't *wait* to get a Coolata!" Mike gushed.

Aria groaned. Mike had spent a lonely couple of years in Iceland—he claimed that all Icelandic boys were "pussies who rode small, gay horses"—but Aria had blossomed. A new start had been just what she needed at the time, so she was happy when her dad made the announcement that her family was moving. It was the fall after Alison went missing, and her girls had grown far apart, leaving her with no real friends, just a school full of people she'd known forever.

Before she left for Europe, Aria would sometimes see boys look at her from afar, intrigued, but then look away. With her coltish, ballet-dancer frame, straight black hair, and pouty lips, Aria knew she was pretty. People were always saying so, but why didn't she have a date to the seventh-grade spring social, then? One of the last times she and Spencer had hung out—one of the awkward get-togethers that summer after Ali disappeared—Spencer told Aria she'd probably get a lot of dates if she just tried to fit in a little bit more.

But Aria didn't know how to fit in. Her parents had drilled it into her head that she was an individual, not a follower of the herd, and should be herself. Trouble was Aria wasn't sure who Aria was. Since turning eleven, she'd tried out punk Aria, artsy Aria, documentary film Aria, and, right before they moved, she'd even tried ideal

Rosewood girl Aria, the horse-riding, polo-shirt-wearing, Coach-satchel-toting girl who was everything Rosewood boys loved but everything Aria wasn't. Thankfully, they moved to Iceland two weeks into that disaster, and in Iceland, everything, everything, *everything* changed.

Her father got the job offer in Iceland just after Aria had started eighth grade, and the family packed up. She suspected they'd left so quickly because of a secret about her dad that only she—and Alison DiLaurentis—knew about. She'd vowed not to think about that again the minute the Icelandair plane took off, and after living in Reykjavík for a few months, Rosewood became a distant memory. Her parents seemed to fall back in love and even her totally provincial brother learned both Icelandic *and* French. And Aria fell in love . . . a few times, actually.

So what if Rosewood boys didn't get kooky Aria? Icelandic boys—rich, worldly, fascinating Icelandic boys—sure did. As soon as they moved there, she met a boy named Hallbjorn. He was seventeen, a DJ, and had three ponies and the most beautiful bone structure she'd ever seen. He offered to take her to Iceland's geysers, and then, when they saw one burble up and leave a big cloud of steam, he kissed her. After Hallbjorn was Lars, who liked to play with her old pig puppet, Pigtunia—the one who advised Aria on her love life—and took her to the best all-night dance parties by the harbor. She felt adorable and sexy in Iceland. There, she became Icelandic Aria, the best Aria yet. She found her style—a sort of bohemian-hipster-girl thing, with lots of layers, lace-up boots, and APC jeans, which she bought on a trip to Paris—read French philosophers, and traveled on the Eurail with just an outdated map and a change of underwear.

But now, every Rosewood sight outside the car window reminded her of the past she wanted to forget. There was Ferra's Cheesesteaks, where she spent hours with her friends in middle school. There was the stone-gated country club—her parents didn't belong, but she'd gone with Spencer, and once, feeling bold, Aria had walked up to her crush, Noel Kahn, and asked him if he wanted to share an ice-cream sandwich with her. He turned her down cold, of course.

And there was the sunny, tree-lined road where Alison DiLaurentis used to live. As the car paused at the four-way stop sign, Aria stared; she could see it, second house from the corner. There was a bunch of trash on the curb, but otherwise, the house was quiet and still. She could look for only so long before covering her eyes. In Iceland, days could go by when she could almost forget about Ali, their secrets, and what had happened. She'd been back in Rosewood for less than ten minutes, and Aria could practically hear Ali's voice at every bend in the road and see her reflection in every house's oversize bay window. She slumped down in her seat, trying not to cry.

Her father continued a few streets down and pulled up to their old house, a postmodern angry brown box with only one square window, right in the center—a huge letdown after their waterfront faded-blue Icelandic row house. Aria followed her parents inside and they bustled off into separate rooms. She heard Mike answer his cell phone outside and she swished her hands through the sparkly floating dust in the air.

"Mom!" Mike ran through the front door. "I just talked to Chad, and he said the first lacrosse tryouts are today."

"Lacrosse?" Ella emerged from the dining room. "Right now?"

"Yeah," Mike said. "I'm going!" He tore up the wrought-iron staircase to his old bedroom.

"Aria, honey?" Her mother's voice made her turn. "Can you drive him to practice?"

Aria let out a small laugh. "Um, Mom? I don't have my license."

"So? You drove all the time in Reykjavík. The lacrosse field's only a couple of miles away, isn't it? Worst thing, you'll hit a cow. Just wait for him until he's done."

Aria paused. Her mother already sounded frazzled. She heard her dad in the kitchen opening and closing cabinets and muttering under his breath. Would her parents love each other here like they had in Iceland? Or would things go back to the way they used to be?

"All right," she mumbled. She plopped her bags on the landing, grabbed the car keys, and slid into the wagon's front seat.

Her brother climbed in next to her, amazingly already dressed in his gear. He punched the netting on his stick enthusiastically and gave her an evil, knowing smile. "Happy to be back?"

Aria only sighed in response. The entire drive, Mike had his hands pressed up against the car's window, shouting things like, "There's Caleb's house! They tore down the skate ramp!" and "Cow poop still smells the same!" At the vast, well-mown practice field, she'd barely stopped the car when Mike opened the door and immediately bolted.

She slid back into the seat, stared up through the sunroof, and sighed. "*Thrilled* to be back," she murmured. A hot air balloon floated serenely through the clouds. It used to be such a delight to see them, but today she focused in on it, closed one eye, and pretended to crush the balloon between her thumb and pointer finger.

A bunch of boys in white Nike T-shirts, baggy shorts, and backward white baseball caps walked slowly past her car toward the field house. *See?* Every Rosewood boy was a carbon copy. Aria blinked. One of them was even wearing the same Nike University of Pennsylvania T-shirt that Noel Kahn, the ice-cream sandwich boy she loved in eighth grade, used to wear. She squinted at the boy's black wavy hair. Wait. Was that . . . *him*? Oh God. It was. Aria couldn't believe he was wearing the same T-shirt he wore when he was thirteen. He probably did it for luck or some other queer jock superstition.

Noel looked quizzically at her, then walked toward her car and knocked on her window. She rolled it down.

"You're that girl that went to the North Pole. Aria, right? You were Ali D's friend?" Noel continued.

Aria's stomach plummeted. "Um," she said.

"No, dude." James Freed, the second-hottest boy at Rosewood, came up behind Noel. "She didn't go to the North Pole, she went to Finland. You know, like where that model Svetlana is from. The one who looks like Hanna?"

Aria scratched the back of her head. Hanna? As in, Hanna *Marin*?

A whistle blew, and Noel reached into the car to touch Aria's arm. "You're going to stay and watch practice, aren't you, Finland?"

"Uh . . . *ja*," Aria said.

"What's that, a Finnish sex grunt?" James grinned.

Aria rolled her eyes. She was pretty sure *ja* was Finnish for *yes*, but of course these guys wouldn't know that. "Have fun playing with your balls." She smiled wearily.

The boys nudged each other, then ran off, flicking their lacrosse sticks to and fro even before they hit the field. Aria stared out the window. How ironic. This was the first time she'd ever been flirty with a boy in Rosewood—*especially* Noel—and she didn't even care.

Through the trees, she could just make out the spire that belonged to the chapel at Hollis College, the small liberal arts school where her dad taught. On Hollis's main street there was a bar, Snookers. She sat up straighter and checked her watch. Two-thirty. It might be open. She could go have a beer or two and find her own fun.

And hey, maybe beer goggles could make even Rosewood boys look good.

Where Reykjavík's bars smelled like freshly brewed lager, old wood, and French cigarettes, Snookers smelled like a mixture of dead bodies, festering hot dogs, and sweat. And Snookers, like everything else in Rosewood, carried memories: One Friday night, Alison DiLaurentis had dared Aria to go into Snookers and order a screaming orgasm. Aria had waited in line behind a bunch of preppie college boys, and when the bouncer at the door wouldn't let her in, she cried, "But my screaming orgasm is in there!" Then she realized what she'd said and fled back to her friends, who were crouching behind a car in the parking lot. They all laughed so hard they got the hiccups.

"Amstel," she said to the bartender after crossing through the glass-paneled front doors—apparently there was no need for bouncers at two-thirty on a Saturday. The bartender looked at her questioningly but then set a pint in front of her and turned away. Aria took a big sip. It tasted bland and watery. She spit it back into the glass.

"You all right there?"

Aria turned. Three stools down was a guy with messy, blondish hair and ice-blue, Siberian husky eyes. He was nursing something in a little tumbler.

Aria frowned. "Yeah, I forgot how beer tastes here. I've been in Europe for two years. Beer's better there."

"Europe?" The guy smiled. He had a very cute smile. "Where?"

Aria smiled back. "Iceland."

His eyes brightened. "I once spent a few nights in Reykjavík on my way to Amsterdam. There was this huge, awesome party in the harbor."

Aria cupped her hands around her pint glass. "Yeah," she said, smiling, "they have the best parties there."

"Were you there for the northern lights?"

"Of course," Aria replied. "And the midnight sun. We had these awesome raves in the summer . . . with the best music." She looked at his glass. "What are you drinking?"

"Scotch," he said, already signaling to the bartender. "Want one?"

She nodded. The guy moved three stools down next to her. He had nice hands with long fingers and slightly ragged fingernails. He wore a small button on his corduroy jacket that said, SMART WOMEN VOTE!

"So you lived in Iceland?" He smiled again. "Like for a junior year abroad?"

"Well, no," Aria said. The bartender set the Scotch down in front of her. She took a big, beer-size gulp. Her throat and chest immediately sizzled. "I was in Iceland because . . ."

She stopped herself. "Yeah, it was my, uh, year abroad." Let him think what he wanted.

"Cool." He nodded. "Where were you before that?"

She shrugged. "Um . . . back here in Rosewood." She smiled and quickly added, "But I liked it over there so much better."

He nodded. "I was really depressed to come back to the States after Amsterdam."

"I cried the whole way home," Aria admitted, feeling like herself–her new, improved Icelandic Aria self–for the first time since she'd been back. Not only was she talking to a cute, smart guy about Europe, but this might be the only guy in Rosewood who didn't know her as Rosewood Aria–the weirdo friend of the pretty girl who vanished. "So, do you go to school here?" she asked.

"Just graduated." He wiped his mouth off with a napkin and lit a Camel. He offered her one from the pack, but she shook her head. "I'm gonna do some teaching."

Aria took another sip of the Scotch and realized she'd finished it. Wow. "I'd like to teach, I think. Once I finish school. Either that or write plays."

"Yeah? Plays? What's your major?"

"Um, English?" The bartender set another Scotch in front of her.

"That's what I'm teaching!" the guy said. As he said it, he put his hand on Aria's knee. Aria was so surprised she flinched and nearly knocked over her drink. He pulled his hand away. She blushed.

"Sorry," he said, a little sheepishly. "I'm Ezra, by the way."

"Aria." Suddenly her name sounded hilarious. She giggled, off balance.

"Whoa." Ezra grabbed her arm to steady her.

Three Scotches later, Aria and Ezra had established that they'd both met the same old sailor bartender at the Borg bar in Reykjavík, loved the way bathing in the mineral-rich blue lagoon hot springs made them feel sleepy, and actually *liked* the rotten-egg sulfur smell of the geothermal hot spring water. Ezra's eyes were getting bluer by the second. Aria wanted to ask if he had a girlfriend. She felt warm inside, and she was pretty sure it wasn't just from the Scotch.

"I kind of have to go to the bathroom," Aria said woozily.

Ezra smiled. "Can I come?"

Well, that answered the girlfriend question.

"I mean, uh . . ." He rubbed the back of his neck. "Was that too forward of me?" he asked, looking up from under his knitted eyebrows.

Her brain buzzed. Hooking up with strangers wasn't really her thing, at least not in America. But hadn't she said she wanted to be Icelandic Aria?

She stood up and took his hand. They stared at each other the whole way to Snookers' women's bathroom. There was toilet paper all over the floor and it smelled even worse than the rest of the bar, but Aria didn't care. As Ezra hoisted her onto the sink and she wrapped her legs around his waist, all she could smell was his scent—a combination of Scotch, cinnamon, and sweat—and nothing had ever smelled sweeter.

As they said in Finland or wherever, *ja*.

3

HANNA'S FIRST TOGGLE

"And apparently they were having sex in Bethany's parents' bedroom!"

Hanna Marin stared at her best friend, Mona Vanderwaal, across the table. It was two days before school started and they were sitting in the King James Mall's terraced French-inspired café, Rive Gauche, drinking red wine, comparing *Vogue* to *Teen Vogue*, and gossiping. Mona always knew the best dirt on people. Hanna took another sip of wine and noticed a fortysomething guy staring lecherously at them. *A regular Humbert Humbert,* Hanna thought, but didn't say out loud. Mona wouldn't get the literary reference, but just because Hanna was the most sought-after girl at Rosewood Day didn't mean she was above sampling the books on Rosewood Day's recommended summer reading list now and then, especially when she was lying out next to her pool with nothing to do. Besides *Lolita* looked deliciously dirty.

Mona swiveled around to see who Hanna was looking at. Her lips twisted up into a naughty smile. "We should flash him."

"Count of three?" Hanna's amber eyes widened.

Mona nodded. On three, the girls slowly pulled up the hems of their already sky-high minis, revealing their panties. Humbert's eyes boggled and he knocked his glass of pinot noir into the crotch of his khakis. "Shit!" he yelled before he shot off to the bathroom.

"Nice," Mona said. They threw their napkins on their uneaten salads and stood to leave.

They'd become friends the summer between eighth and ninth grade, when they both got cut from Rosewood's freshman cheerleading tryouts. Vowing to make the squad the following year, they decided to lose tons of weight—so they could be the cute, perky girls that the boys tossed in the air. But once they got skinny and gorgeous, they decided cheerleading was passé and the cheerleaders were losers, so they never bothered trying out for the team again.

Since then, Hanna and Mona shared everything—well, almost everything. Hanna hadn't told Mona how she'd lost weight so quickly—it was too gross to talk about. While hard-core dieting was sexy and admirable, there was nothing, *nothing* glamorous about eating a ton of fatty, greasy, preferably cheese-filled crap and then puking it all up. But Hanna was over that bad little habit by now, so it didn't really matter.

"You know that guy had a boner," Mona whispered, gathering the magazines into a pile. "What's Sean gonna think?"

"He'll laugh," Hanna said.

"Uh, I don't think so."

Hanna shrugged. "He might."

Mona snorted. "Yeah, flashing strangers goes well with a virginity pledge."

Hanna looked down at her Michael Kors purple wedges. The virginity pledge. Hanna's incredibly popular, extraordinarily hot boyfriend, Sean Ackard—the boy she'd lusted over since seventh grade—was behaving a little strangely lately. He'd always been Mr. All-American Boy Scout—as in volunteering at the old-age home and serving turkey to the homeless on Thanksgiving—but last night, when Hanna, Sean, Mona, and a bunch of other kids were hanging out in Jim Freed's cedar hot tub, covertly drinking Coronas, Sean had taken All-American Boy Scout up a notch. He'd announced, a little proudly, that he'd signed a virginity "promise" and vowed not to have sex before marriage. Everyone, Hanna included, had been too stunned to respond.

"He's not serious," Hanna said confidently. How could he be? A bunch of kids signed the promise; Hanna figured it was just a passing trend, like those Lance Armstrong bracelets or Yogalates.

"You think?" Mona smirked, brushing her long bangs

out of her eyes. "Let's see what happens at Noel's party next Friday."

Hanna gritted her teeth. It seemed like Mona was laughing at her. "I want to go shopping," she said, standing up.

"How about Tiffany's?" Mona asked.

"Awesome."

They strolled through the brand-new luxe section of the King James Mall, which had a Burberry, a Tiffany's, a Gucci, and a Coach; smelled of the latest Michael Kors perfume; and was packed full of pretty back-to-prep-school girls with their beautiful moms. On a solo shopping trip a few weeks ago, Hanna had noticed her old friend Spencer Hastings slipping into the new Kate Spade, and remembered how she used to special-order an entire season's worth of nylon shoulder bags from New York.

Hanna felt funny knowing those sorts of details about someone she wasn't friends with anymore. And as she watched Spencer peruse Kate Spade's leather luggage, Hanna wondered if Spencer was thinking what she was thinking: that the mall's new wing was just the sort of place Ali DiLaurentis would have loved. Hanna often thought of all the things Ali had missed—last year's homecoming bonfire, Lauren Ryan's sweet sixteen karaoke party in her family's mansion, the return of round-toed shoes, Chanel's leather iPod nano holders . . . iPod nanos, in general. But the biggest thing Ali had missed? Hanna's makeover, of course—and it was *such* a bummer she had. Sometimes, when Hanna twirled around in front of her full-length mirror, she pretended that Ali was sitting behind her, critiquing her outfits the way she used to. Hanna had wasted so many years being a chubby, clingy loser, but things were *so* different now.

She and Mona strode into Tiffany's; it was full of glass, chrome, and white lights that made the flawless diamonds extra shimmery. Mona prowled around the cases and then raised her eyebrows at Hanna. "Maybe a necklace?"

"What about a charm bracelet?" Hanna whispered.

"Perfect."

They walked to the case and eyed the silver charm bracelet with the heart-shaped toggle. "So pretty," Mona breathed.

"Interested?" an elegant older saleswoman asked them.

"Oh, I don't know," Hanna said.

"It suits you." The woman unlocked the case and felt around for the bracelet. "It's in all the magazines."

Hanna nudged Mona. "You try it."

Mona slid it onto her wrist. "It's really beautiful." Then the woman turned to another customer. When she did, Mona slid the bracelet off her wrist and into her pocket. Just like that.

Hanna mashed her lips together and flagged down another saleswoman, a honey-blond girl who wore coral lipstick. "Can I try that bracelet there, with the round charm?"

"Sure!" The girl unlocked the case. "I have one of these myself."

"How about the matching earrings, too?" Hanna pointed to them.

"Of course."

Mona had moved over to the diamonds. Hanna held the earrings and the bracelet in her hands. Together, they were $350. Suddenly, a swarm of Japanese girls crowded around the counter, all pointing at another round-charm bracelet in the glass case. Hanna scanned the ceilings for cameras and the doors for detectors.

"Oh, Hanna, come look at the Lucida!" Mona called.

Hanna paused. Time slowed down. She slid the bracelet onto her wrist and then shoved it farther up her sleeve. She stuck the earrings in her Louis Vuitton cherry-monogrammed coin purse. Hanna's heart pounded. This was the best part of taking stuff: the feeling beforehand. She felt all buzzy and alive.

Mona waved a diamond ring at her. "Doesn't this look good on me?"

"C'mon." Hanna grabbed her arm. "Let's go to Coach."

"You don't want to try any on?" Mona pouted. She always stalled after she knew Hanna had done the job.

"Nah," Hanna said. "Purses are calling our names." She felt the bracelet's silver chain press gently into her arm. She had to get out of here while the Japanese girls were still bustling around the counter. The salesgirl hadn't even looked back in her direction.

"All right," Mona said dramatically. She handed the ring—holding it by its diamond, which even Hanna knew you weren't supposed to do—back to the saleswoman. "These diamonds are all too small," she said. "Sorry."

"We have others," the woman tried.

"Come on," Hanna said, grabbing Mona's arm.

Her heart hammered as they wove their way through Tiffany's. The charm tinkled on her wrist, but she kept her sleeve pulled down. Hanna was a seasoned pro at this—first it had been loose candy at the Wawa convenience store, then CDs from Tower, then baby tees from Ralph Lauren—and she felt bigger and more badass every time. She shut her eyes and crossed the threshold, bracing herself for the alarms to blare.

But nothing did. They were out.

Mona squeezed her hand. "Did you get one too?"

"Of course." She flashed the bracelet around her wrist. "And these." She opened the coin purse and showed Mona the earrings.

"Shit." Mona's eyes widened.

Hanna smiled. Sometimes it felt so good to one-up your best friend. Not wanting to jinx it, she walked quickly away from Tiffany's and listened for someone to come chasing after them. The only noise, though, was the burbling of the fountain and a Muzak version of "Oops! I Did It Again."

Oh yes, I did, Hanna thought.

4

SPENCER WALKS THE PLANK

"Honey, you're not supposed to eat mussels with your hands. It's not polite."

Spencer Hastings looked across the table at her mother, Veronica, who nervously ran her hands through her perfectly highlighted ash-blond hair. "Sorry," Spencer said, picking up the ridiculously small mussel-eating fork.

"I really don't think Melissa should be living in the town house with all that dust," Mrs. Hastings said to her husband, ignoring Spencer's apology.

Peter Hastings rolled his neck around. When he wasn't practicing law, he was furiously cycling all the back roads of Rosewood in tight, colorful spandex shirts and bike pants, shaking his fist at speeding cars. All that cycling gave him chronically sore shoulders.

"All that hammering! I don't know how she'll get *any* studying done," Mrs. Hastings went on.

Spencer and her parents were sitting at Moshulu, a restaurant aboard a clipper ship in the Philadelphia harbor, waiting for Spencer's sister, Melissa, to meet them for dinner. It was a big celebratory dinner because Melissa had graduated from U Penn undergrad a year early and had gotten into Penn's Wharton School of Business. The downtown Philly town house was being renovated as a gift from their parents to Melissa.

In just two days, Spencer was starting her junior year at Rosewood and would have to surrender herself to this year's jam-packed schedule: five APs, leadership training, charity drive organizing, yearbook editing, drama tryouts, hockey practice, and sending in summer program applications ASAP, since everyone knew that the best way to get into an Ivy was to get into one of their pre-college summer camps. But there was one thing Spencer had to look forward to this year: moving into the converted barn that sat at the back of her family's property. According to her parents, it was the perfect way to prepare for college—just look how well it had worked for Melissa! Barf. But Spencer was happy to follow in her sister's footsteps in this case, since they led out to the tranquil, light-flooded guesthouse where Spencer could escape her parents and their constantly barking labradoodles.

The sisters had a quiet yet long-standing rivalry and Spencer was always losing: Spencer had won the Presidential Physical Fitness Award four times in elementary school; Melissa had won it five. Spencer got second place in the seventh-grade geography bee; Melissa got first. Spencer was on the yearbook staff, in all of the school plays, and was taking five AP classes this year; Melissa did all those things her junior year plus worked at their mother's horse farm and trained for the Philadelphia marathon for leukemia research. No matter how high Spencer's GPA was or how many extra-curriculars she smashed into her schedule, she never quite reached Melissa's level of perfection.

Spencer picked up another mussel with her fingers and popped it into her mouth. Her dad loved this restaurant, with its dark wood paneling, thick oriental rugs, and the heady smells of butter, red wine, and salty air. Sitting among the masts and sails, it felt like you could jump right overboard into the harbor. Spencer gazed out across the Delaware River to the big bubbly aquarium in Camden, New Jersey. A giant party boat decorated with Christmas lights floated past them. Someone shot a yellow firework off the front deck. That boat was having way more fun than this one was having.

"What's Melissa's friend's name again?" her mother murmured.

"I think it's Wren," Spencer said. In her head she added, *As in scrawny bird.*

"She told me he's studying to be a doctor," her mother swooned. "At U Penn."

"Of course he is," Spencer quietly singsonged. She bit down hard on a piece of mussel shell and winced. Melissa was bringing her boyfriend of two months to dinner. The family hadn't met him yet—he'd been away visiting family or something—but Melissa's boyfriends were all the same: textbook handsome, well mannered, played golf. Melissa didn't have an ounce of creativity in her body and clearly looked for the same predictability in her boyfriends.

"Mom!" a familiar voice called from behind Spencer.

Melissa swooped to the other side of the table and gave each of her parents a huge kiss. Her look hadn't changed since high school: her ash-blond hair was cut bluntly to her chin, she wore no makeup except for a little foundation, and she wore a dowdy square-necked yellow dress, a pearl-buttoned pink cardigan, and semi-cute kitten-heeled shoes.

"Darling!" her mother cried.

"Mom, Dad, here's Wren." Melissa pulled in someone next to her.

Spencer tried to keep her mouth from dropping open. There was nothing scrawny, birdlike, or textbook about Wren. He was tall and lanky and wore a beautifully cut Thomas Pink shirt. His black hair was cut in a long, shaggy, messy style. He had beautiful skin, high cheekbones, and almond-shaped eyes.

Wren shook her parents' hands and sat down at the table. Melissa asked her mom a question about where to have the plumber's bill sent, while Spencer waited to be introduced. Wren pretended to be really interested in an oversize wineglass.

"I'm Spencer," she said finally. She wondered if her breath smelled like mussels. "The other daughter." Spencer nodded toward the other side of the table. "The one they keep in the basement."

"Oh." Wren grinned. "Cool."

Was that a British accent she heard? "Isn't it strange they haven't asked you a single thing about yourself?" Spencer gestured at her parents. Now they were talking about contractors and the best wood to use for the living room floor.

Wren shrugged, and then whispered, "Kinda." He winked.

Suddenly Melissa grabbed Wren's hand. "Oh, I see you've met her," she cooed.

"Yeah." He smiled. "You didn't tell me you had a sister."

Of course she hadn't.

"So Melissa," Mrs. Hastings said. "Daddy and I were talking about where you might be staying while all the renovations are happening. And I just thought of something. Why not just come back to Rosewood to live with us for a few months? You can commute to Penn; you know how easy it is."

Melissa wrinkled her nose. *Please say no, please say no,* Spencer willed.

"Well." Melissa adjusted the strap of her yellow dress. The more Spencer stared at it, the more the color made Melissa look like she had the flu. Melissa glanced at Wren. "The thing is . . . Wren and I are going to be moving into the town house . . . together."

"Oh!" Her mother smiled at both of them. "Well . . . I suppose Wren could stay with us too . . . what do you think, Peter?"

Spencer had to clutch her boobs to keep her heart from exploding out of her chest. They were moving *in* together? Her sister really had some balls. She could just imagine what would happen if *she* dropped a bomb like that. Mom really *would* make Spencer live in the basement—or maybe in the stable. She could set up shop next to the horses' companion goat.

"Well, I suppose that's all right," her father said. *Unbelievable!* "It'll certainly be quiet. Mom's in the stable most of the day, and of course Spencer will be in school."

"You're in school?" Wren asked. "Where?"

"She's in high school," Melissa butted in. She stared long at Spencer, as if she were sizing her up. From Spencer's tight ecru Lacoste tennis dress to her long, dark blond wavy hair to her two-carat diamond earrings. "Same high school I went to. I never asked, Spence—are you president of the class this year?"

"VP," Spencer mumbled. There was *no way* Melissa hadn't already known that.

"Oh, aren't you *so* happy it worked out that way?" Melissa asked.

"No," Spencer said flatly. She'd run for the spot last spring but had been beaten out and had to take the VP slot. She hated losing at anything.

Melissa shook her head. "You don't understand,

Spence—it's *soooooo* much work. When I was president, I barely had time for anything else!"

"You do have quite a few activities, Spencer," Mrs. Hastings murmured. "There's yearbook, and all those hockey games. . . . "

"Besides, Spence, you'll take over if the president, you know . . . dies." Melissa winked at her as if they were sharing this joke, which they weren't.

Melissa turned back to her parents. "Mom. I just got the best idea. What if Wren and I stayed in the barn? Then we'd be out of your hair."

Spencer felt as if someone had just kicked her in the ovaries. The *barn*?

Mrs. Hastings put her French-manicured finger to her perfectly lipsticked mouth. "Hmm," she started. She turned tentatively to Spencer. "Would you be able to wait a few months, honey? Then the barn will be all yours."

"Oh!" Melissa laid down her fork. "I didn't know you were going to move in there, Spence! I don't want to cause problems—"

"It's fine," Spencer interrupted, grabbing her glass of ice water and taking a hearty swallow. She willed herself not to throw a tantrum in front of her parents and Perfect Melissa. "I can wait."

"Seriously?" Melissa asked. "That's so sweet of you!"

Her mother pressed her cold, thin hand against Spencer's and beamed. "I *knew* you'd understand."

"Can you excuse me?" Spencer dizzily shoved her seat

back from the table and stood up. "I'll be right back." She walked across the boat's wooden floor, down the carpeted main stairs, and out the front entrance. She needed to get to dry land.

Out on the Penn's Landing walkway, the Philadelphia skyline glittered. Spencer sat down on a bench and breathed yoga fire breaths. Then she pulled out her wallet and started to organize her money. She turned all the ones, fives, and twenties in the same direction and alphabetized them according to the long letter-number combination printed in green in the corners. Doing this always made her feel better. When she finished, she gazed up at the ship's dining deck. Her parents faced the river, so they couldn't see her. She dug through her tan Hogan bag for her emergency pack of Marlboros and lit one.

She took drag after angry drag. Stealing the barn was evil enough, but doing it in such a polite way was *just* Melissa's style—Melissa had always been outwardly nice but inwardly horrid. And no one could see it but Spencer.

She'd gotten revenge on Melissa just once, a few weeks before the end of seventh grade. One evening, Melissa and her then-boyfriend, Ian Thomas, were studying for finals. When Ian left, Spencer cornered him outside by his SUV, which he'd parked behind her family's row of pine trees. She'd merely wanted to flirt—Ian was wasting all his hotness on her plain vanilla, goody-two-shoes sister—so she gave Ian a peck good-bye on the cheek. But when he pressed her up against his passenger door, she didn't try to run away. They only stopped kissing when his car alarm started to blare.

When Spencer told Alison about it, Ali said it was a pretty foul thing to do and that she should confess to Melissa. Spencer suspected Ali was just pissed because they'd had a running competition all year over who could hook up with the most older boys, and kissing Ian put Spencer in the lead.

Spencer inhaled sharply. She hated being reminded of that period of her life. But the DiLaurentises' old house was right next door to hers, and one of Ali's bedroom windows faced one of Spencer's—it was like Ali haunted her 24/7. All Spencer had to do was look out her window and there was seventh-grade Ali, hanging her JV hockey uniform right where Spencer could see it or strolling around her bedroom gossiping into her cell phone.

Spencer wanted to think she'd changed a lot since seventh grade. They'd all been so mean—especially Alison—but not *just* Alison. And the worst memory of all was *the thing* . . . The Jenna Thing. Thinking of that made Spencer feel so horrible, she wished she could erase it from her brain like they did in that movie *Eternal Sunshine of the Spotless Mind*.

"You shouldn't be smoking, you know."

She turned, and there was Wren, standing right next to her. Spencer looked at him, surprised. "What are you doing down here?"

"They were . . ." He opened and closed his hands at each other, like mouths yapping. "And I have a page." He pulled out a BlackBerry.

"Oh," Spencer said. "Is that from the hospital? I hear you're a big-time doctor."

"Well, no, actually, I'm only a first-year med student," Wren said, and then pointed at her cigarette. "You mind if I have a bit of that?"

Spencer twisted the corners of her mouth up wryly. "You just told me not to smoke," she said, handing it over to him.

"Yeah, well." Wren took a deep drag off the cigarette. "You all right?"

"Whatever." Spencer wasn't about to talk things over with her sister's new live-in boyfriend who'd just stolen her barn. "So where are you from?"

"North London. My Dad's Korean, though. He moved to England to go to Oxford and ended up staying. Everyone asks."

"Oh. I wasn't going to," Spencer replied, even though she *had* thought about it. "How'd you and my sister meet?"

"At Starbucks," he answered. "She was in line in front of me."

"Oh," Spencer said. How incredibly lame.

"She was buying a latte," Wren added, kicking at the stone curb.

"That's nice." Spencer fiddled with her pack of cigarettes.

"This was a few months ago." He raggedly took another drag, his hand shaking a little and his eyes darting around. "I fancied her before she got the town house."

"Right," Spencer said, realizing he seemed a little nervous. Maybe he was tense about meeting her parents. Or was it moving in with Melissa that had him on edge? If Spencer were a boy and had to move in with Melissa, she'd throw herself off Moshulu's crow's nest into the Delaware River.

He handed the cigarette back to her. "I hope it's okay that I'm going to be staying in your house."

"Um, yeah. Whatever."

Wren licked his lips. "Maybe I can get you to kick your smoking addiction."

Spencer stiffened. "I'm not addicted."

"Sure you're not," Wren answered, smiling.

Spencer shook her head emphatically. "No, I'd never let that happen." And it was true: Spencer hated feeling out of control.

Wren smiled. "Well, you certainly sound like you know what you're doing."

"I do."

"Are you that way with everything?" Wren asked, his eyes shining.

There was something about the light, teasing way he said it that made Spencer pause. Were they . . . flirting? They stared at each other for a few seconds until a big group of people came whooshing off the boat onto the street. Spencer lowered her eyes.

"So, do you think it's time we go back?" Wren asked.

Spencer hesitated and looked at the street, full of taxis, ready to take her wherever she wanted. She almost wanted to ask Wren to get in one of the cabs with her and go to a baseball game at Citizens Bank Park, where they could eat hot dogs, yell at the players, and count how many strikeouts the Phillies' starting pitcher racked up. She could use her dad's box seats—they mostly just went to waste, anyway—and she bet Wren would be into that. Why go back in, when her family was just going to continue to ignore them? A cab paused at the light, just a few feet from them. She looked at it, then back at Wren.

But no, that'd be wrong. And who would fill the vice president's post if he died and she was murdered by her own sister? "After you," Spencer said, and held the door open for him so they could climb back aboard.

5

STARTS AND FITZ

"Hey! Finland!"

On Tuesday, the first day of school, Aria walked quickly to her first-period English class. She turned to see Noel Kahn, in his Rosewood Day sweater vest and tie, jogging toward her. "Hey." Aria nodded. She kept going.

"You bolted from our practice the other day," Noel said, sidling up next to her.

"You expected me to watch?" Aria looked at him out of the corner of her eye. He looked flushed.

"Yeah. We scrimmaged. I scored three goals."

"Good for you," Aria deadpanned. Was she supposed to be impressed?

She continued down the Rosewood Day hallway, which she'd unfortunately dreamed about way too many times in Iceland. Above her were the same eggshell-white, vaulted ceilings. Below her were the same farmhouse-cozy wood floors. To her right and left were the usual framed photos of stuffy alums, and to her left, incongruous rows of dented metal lockers. Even the very same song, the *1812 Overture*, hummed through the PA speakers—Rosewood played between-classes music because it was "mentally stimulating." Sweeping by her were the exact same people Aria had known for a gazillion years . . . and all of them were staring.

Aria ducked her head. Since she'd moved to Iceland at the beginning of eighth grade, the last time everyone had seen her she was part of the grief-stricken group of girls whose best friend freakishly vanished. Back then, wherever she went, people were whispering about her.

Now, it felt like she'd never left. And it almost felt like Ali was still here. Aria's breath caught in her chest when she saw a flash of blond ponytail swishing around the corner to the gym. And when Aria rounded the corner past the pottery studio, where she and Ali used to meet between classes to trade gossip, she could almost hear Ali yelling, "Hey, wait up!" She pressed her hand to her forehead to see if she had a fever.

"So what class do you have first?" Noel asked, still keeping pace with her.

She looked at him, surprised, and then down at her schedule. "English."

"Me too. Mr. Fitz?"

"Yeah," she mumbled. "He any good?"

"Dunno. He's new. Heard he was a Fulbright Scholar, though."

Aria eyed him suspiciously. Since when did Noel Kahn care about a teacher's credentials? She turned around a corner and saw a girl standing in the English room doorway. She looked familiar and foreign all at the same time. This girl was model-thin, had long, red-brown hair, and wore a rolled-up blue plaid Rosewood uniform skirt, purple platform wedge-heels, and a Tiffany charm bracelet.

Aria's heart started to pound. She'd worried about how she might react when she saw her old friends again, and here was Hanna. What had *happened* to Hanna?

"Hey," Aria said softly.

Hanna turned and looked Aria up and down, from her long, shaggy haircut to her Rosewood Day white shirt and chunky Bakelite bracelets to her brown scuffed lace-up boots. A blank expression crossed her face, but then she smiled.

"Omigod!" Hanna said. At least it was still Hanna's same high-pitched voice. "How was . . . where were you? Czechoslovakia?"

"Um, yeah," Aria answered. Close enough.

"Cool!" Hanna gave Aria a tight smile.

"Kirsten looks like she's gone off South Beach," interrupted a girl next to Hanna. Aria turned her head sideways, trying to place her. Mona Vanderwaal? The last time Aria saw her, Mona had put a billion teensy braids in her hair and was riding her Razor scooter. Now, she looked even more glamorous than Hanna.

"Doesn't she?" Hanna agreed. She then gave Aria and Noel—who was *still* standing there—an apologetic shrug. "Sorry, guys, can you excuse us?"

Aria headed into the classroom and fell into the first desk she saw. She put her head down and took heaving, emotional breaths.

"*Hell is other people,*" she chanted. It was her favorite quote by the French philosopher Jean-Paul Sartre and a perfect mantra for Rosewood.

She rocked back and forth for a few seconds, in full freak-out mode. The only thing that made her feel better was the memory of Ezra, that guy she'd met at Snookers. At the bar, Ezra had followed her into the bathroom, grabbed her face, and kissed her. Their mouths fit perfectly together—they didn't bang teeth once. His hands floated all over the small of her back, her stomach, her legs. They'd had such a *connection.* And okay, fine, some might say it was just a . . . a tongue connection . . . but Aria knew it was more.

She'd felt so overcome thinking about it last night, she'd written a haiku about Ezra to express her feelings— haikus were her favorite kind of poem. Then, pleased with how it turned out, she'd keyed it into her phone and texted it to the number Ezra had given her.

Aria let out a tortured sigh and looked around the classroom. It smelled like books and Mop & Glo. The oversize, four-paned windows faced the south lawn and beyond that, green rolling hills. A few trees had started to turn yellow and orange. There was a great Shakespearean sayings poster next to the blackboard, and a MEAN PEOPLE SUCK sticker someone had stuck to the wall. It looked like the janitor had tried to scrape off the sticker but gave up halfway through.

Was it desperate to text Ezra at 2:30 A.M.? She still hadn't heard back from him. Aria felt for her phone in her bag and pulled it out. The screen read, NEW TEXT MESSAGE. Her stomach swooped, relieved and excited and nervous all at once. But as she clicked READ, a voice interrupted her.

"Excuse me. Um, you can't use your cell in school."

Aria covered her phone with her hands and looked up. Whoever had said it—the new teacher, she guessed—stood with his back to the rest of the room and was writing on the chalkboard. *Mr. Fitz* was all he'd written so far. He was holding a memo with Rosewood's insignia on the top. From the back, he looked young. A few of the other girls in the class gave him an appreciative once-over as they found seats. The now-fabulous Hanna even whistled.

"I know I'm the new guy," he went on, writing, *AP English,* under his name, "but I have this handout from the front office. Some stuff about no cell phones in school." Then he turned. The handout fluttered out of his hand and onto the linoleum floor.

Aria's mouth instantly went dry. Standing in front of the classroom was Ezra from the bar. Ezra, the recipient of her haiku. *Her* Ezra, looking lanky and adorable in a

Rosewood jacket and tie, his hair combed, his buttons buttoned correctly, and a leather-bound lesson planner under his left arm. Standing at the blackboard and writing . . . *Mr. Fitz, AP English.*

He stared at her, his face draining of color. "Holy shit."

The entire class turned around to see who he was looking at. Aria didn't want to stare back at them, so she looked down at her text message.

Aria: Surprise! I wonder what your pig puppet will have to say about this . . . —A

Holy shit, indeed.

6

EMILY'S FRENCH TOO!

Tuesday afternoon, Emily stood in front of her green metal locker after the final bell of the day had rung. The locker still had her old stickers from last year—USA Swimming, Liv Tyler as Arwen the elf, and a magnet that said, COED NAKED BUTTERFLY. Her boyfriend, Ben, hovered next to her.

"You want to hit Wawa?" he asked. His Rosewood swimming jacket hung loosely off his lanky, muscular body, and his blond hair was a little messy.

"Nah, I'm good," Emily answered. Because they had practice at three-thirty after school, the swimmers usually just stayed at Rosewood and sent someone off to Wawa so they could get their hoagie/iced tea/Cheats/Reese's Pieces fix before swimming a billion laps.

A bunch of boys stopped to slap Ben's hand as they headed toward the parking lot. Spencer Hastings, who was in Ben's history class last year, waved. Emily waved back before realizing Spencer was looking at Ben, not her. It was hard to believe that after everything they'd been through together and all the secrets they shared, they now acted like strangers.

After everyone passed, Ben turned back to her and frowned. "You've got your jacket on. You're not practicing?"

"Um." Emily shut her locker and gave the combination a spin. "You know that girl I've been showing around today? I'm walking her to her house 'cause this is her first day and all."

He smirked. "Well, aren't *you* sweet? Parents of prospective students pay for tours, but you're doing it for free."

"Come on." Emily smiled uneasily. "It's like a ten-minute walk."

Ben looked at her, vaguely nodding for a little while.

"What? I'm just trying to be nice!"

"That's cool," he said, and smiled. He took his eyes off her to wave at Casey Kirschner, the captain of the boys' varsity wrestling team.

Maya appeared a minute after Ben loped down the side stairs out to the student parking lot. She wore a white denim jacket over her Rosewood oxford shirt and Oakley flip-flops on her feet. Her toenails weren't painted. "Hey," she said.

"Hey." Emily tried to sound bright, but she felt uneasy. Maybe she should've just gone to practice with Ben. Was it weird to walk Maya home and walk right back?

"Ready?" Maya asked.

The girls walked through campus, which was basically a bunch of very old brick buildings off a twisty back road in Rosewood. There was even a Gothic clock tower that chimed out the hours. Earlier, Emily had shown Maya all the standard stuff that every private school has. She'd also shown her the cool things about Rosewood Day that you usually had to discover on your own, like the dangerous toilet in the girls' first-floor bathroom that sometimes spewed up geyser-style, the secret spot on the hill kids went when they cut gym class (not that Emily ever would), and the school's only vending machine that sold Vanilla Coke, her favorite. They'd even developed an inside joke about the prim, stick-up-her-butt model on the anti-smoking posters that hung outside the nurse's office. It felt good to have an inside joke again.

Now, as they cut through an unused cornfield to Maya's neighborhood, Emily took in every detail of her face, from her turned-up nose to her coffee-colored skin to the way her collar couldn't settle right around her neck. Their hands kept bumping against each other when they swung their arms.

"It's so different here," Maya said, sniffing the air. "It smells like Pine-Sol!" She took off her denim jacket and rolled up the sleeves of her button-down. Emily pulled at her hair, wishing it was dark and wavy, like Maya's, instead of chlorine-damaged and a slightly greenish shade of reddish blond. Emily also felt a little self-conscious about her body, which was strong, muscular, and not as slender as it used to be. She didn't usually feel so aware of herself, even when she was in her swimsuit, which was practically naked.

"Everyone has stuff they're really *into*," Maya continued. "Like this girl Sarah in my physics class. She's trying to form a band, and she asked me to be in it!"

"Really? What do you play?"

"Guitar," Maya said. "My dad taught me. My brother's actually a lot better, but whatever."

"Wow," Emily said. "That's cool."

"Omigod!" Maya grabbed Emily's arm. Emily flinched at first but then relaxed. "You should join the band too! How fun would that be? Sarah said we'd practice three days a week after school. She plays bass."

"But all I play is the flute," Emily said, realizing she sounded like Eeyore from *Winnie-the-Pooh*.

"The flute would be awesome!" Maya clapped her hands. "And drums!"

Emily sighed. "I really couldn't. I have swimming, like, every day after school."

"Hmm," Maya said. "Can't you skip a day? I bet you'd be so good at the drums."

"My parents would murder me." Emily tilted her head and stared at the old iron railroad bridge above them. Trains didn't use the bridge anymore, so now it was mostly a place for kids to go and get drunk without their parents knowing.

"Why?" Maya asked. "What's the big deal?"

Emily paused. What was she supposed to say? That her parents expected her to keep swimming because scouts from Stanford were already watching Carolyn's progress? That her older brother, Jake, and oldest sister, Beth, were now both at the University of Arizona on full swimming rides? That anything less than a swimming scholarship to somewhere top-notch would be a family failure? Maya wasn't afraid to smoke pot when her parents were buying groceries. Emily's parents, by comparison, seemed like old, conservative, controlling East Coast suburbanites. Which they were. But still.

"This is a shorter way home." Emily gestured across the street, to the large colonial house's lawn she and her friends used to cut through on winter days to get to Ali's house faster.

They started up through the grass, avoiding a sprinkler spraying the hydrangea bushes. As they pushed through the brambly tree branches to Maya's backyard, Emily stopped short. A small, guttural noise escaped her throat.

She hadn't been in this backyard—*Ali's* old backyard—in ages. There, across the lawn, was the teak deck where she and Ali had played countless games of Spit. There was the worn patch of grass where they'd hooked up Ali's thick white iPod to speakers and had dance parties. To her left was the familiar knotty oak tree. The tree house was gone, but carved in the bark on the trunk were the initials: *EF + AD*–Emily Fields + Alison DiLaurentis. Her face flushed. At the time, Emily hadn't known why she carved their names into the bark; she'd just wanted to show Ali how happy she was that they were friends.

Maya, who had walked on ahead of her, looked over her shoulder. "You okay?"

Emily shoved her hands into her jacket pockets. For a second, she considered telling Maya about Ali. But a hummingbird swept past her and she lost her nerve. "I'm fine," she said.

"Do you wanna come in?" Maya asked.

"No . . . I . . . I have to go back to school," Emily answered. "Swimming."

"Oh." Maya crinkled up her eyes. "You didn't have to walk me home, silly."

"Yeah, but I didn't want you to get lost."

"You're so cute." Maya looped her hands behind her back and swung her hips back and forth. Emily wondered what she meant by *cute*. Was that a California thing?

"So, well, have fun at swimming," Maya said. "And thanks for showing me around today."

"Sure." Emily stepped forward, and their bodies smushed together in a hug.

"*Mmm,*" Maya said, squeezing tighter. The girls stepped back and grinned at each other for a second. Then Maya leaned forward and kissed Emily on both cheeks. "Mwah, mwah!" she said. "Like the French."

"Well, then, I'll be French too." Emily giggled,

forgetting about Ali and the tree for a second. "Mwah!"
She kissed Maya's smooth left cheek.

Then Maya kissed her again, on her right cheek,
except now just a teensy bit closer to her mouth. There
was no *mwah* this time.

Maya's mouth smelled like banana bubble gum.
Emily jerked back and caught her swimming bag before
it slid off her shoulder. When she looked up, Maya was
grinning.

"I'll see ya," Maya said. "Be good."

Emily folded her towel into her swim bag after practice. The whole afternoon had been a blur. After Maya
skipped into her house, Emily jogged back to school—as
if running would untangle the jumble of feelings inside
her. As she slipped into the water and swam lap after lap,
she saw those haunting initials on the tree. When Coach
blew her whistle and they practiced starts and turns, she
smelled Maya's banana gum and heard her fun, easy
laugh. Standing at her locker, she was pretty sure she'd
shampooed her hair twice. Most of the other girls had
stayed in the communal showers for longer, gossiping,
but Emily was too spaced out to join them.

As she reached for her T-shirt and jeans, folded neatly
on the shelf in her locker, a note came fluttering out.
Emily's name was written on the front in plain, unfamiliar
handwriting, and she didn't recognize the graph notebook
paper. She picked it up off the cold, wet floor.

Hey Em,

Sob! I've been replaced! You found another friend to kiss!

—A

Emily curled her toes around the rubber locker room mat and stopped breathing for a second. She looked around. No one was looking at her.

Was this for real?

She stared at the note and tried to think rationally. She and Maya were out in the open, but no one was around.

And . . . *I've been replaced? Another friend to kiss?* Emily's hands trembled. She looked at the signature again. Laughter from the other swimmers echoed off the walls.

Emily had kissed just one other friend. It was two days after she carved their initials into that oak tree and just a week and a half before the end of seventh grade.

Alison.

7

SPENCER'S GOT A TIGHT POSTERIOR (DELTOID)

"Look at his butt!"

"Shut up!" Spencer knocked her friend Kirsten Cullen in the shin guard with her field hockey stick. They were supposed to be running defense drills, but they—along with the rest of the team—were too busy sizing up this year's new assistant coach. He was none other than Ian Thomas.

Spencer's skin prickled with adrenaline. Talk about weird; she remembered Melissa mentioning that Ian had moved to California. But then, a lot of people who you wouldn't expect ended up back in Rosewood.

"Your sister was so stupid to break up with him," Kirsten said. "He's so *hot*."

"*Shhh*," Spencer answered, giggling. "And anyway, my sister didn't break up with him. He broke up with her."

The whistle blew. "Get moving!" Ian called to them, jogging over. Spencer leaned over to tie her shoe, as if she didn't care. She felt his eyes on her.

"*Spencer?* Spencer Hastings?"

Spencer stood up slowly. "Oh. Ian, right?"

Ian's smile was so wide, Spencer was surprised his cheeks didn't rip. He still had that All-American, I'm-going-to-take-over-my-father's-company-at-twenty-five look, but now his curly hair was a little longer and messier. "You're all grown up!" he cried.

"I guess." Spencer shrugged.

Ian ran his hand against the back of his neck. "How's your sister these days?"

"Um, she's good. Graduated early. Going to Wharton."

Ian bent his head down. "And are her boyfriends still hitting on you?"

Spencer's mouth dropped open. Before she could answer, the head coach, Ms. Campbell, blew her whistle and called Ian over.

Kirsten grabbed Spencer's arm once his back was turned. "You *totally* hooked up with him, didn't you?"

"Shut *up!*" Spencer shot back.

As Ian jogged to center field, he glanced back at her over his shoulder. Spencer drew in her breath and leaned over to examine her cleat. She didn't want him to know she'd been staring.

By the time she got home from practice, every part of Spencer's body hurt, from her ass to her shoulders to her little toes. She'd spent the whole summer organizing committees, boning up on SAT words, and playing the lead in three different plays at Muesli, Rosewood's community theater—Miss Jean Brodie in *The Prime of Miss Jean Brodie*, Emily in *Our Town*, and Ophelia in *Hamlet*. With all that, she hadn't had time to keep in top shape for field hockey, and she was feeling it now.

All she wanted to do was go upstairs, crawl into bed, and not think about tomorrow and what another over-achieving day would hold: French club breakfast, reading the morning announcements, five AP classes, drama tryouts, a quick appearance at yearbook committee, and another grueling field hockey practice with Ian.

She opened the mailbox at the bottom of their private drive, hoping to find the scores for her PSATs. They were supposed to be in any day now, and she'd had a good feeling about them—a better feeling, in fact, than she'd ever had about any other test. Unfortunately, there were just a pile of bills, info from her dad's many investment accounts, and a brochure addressed to Ms. Spencer J (for *Jill*) Hastings from Appleboro College in Lancaster, Pennsylvania. Yeah, as if she'd go *there*.

Inside the house, she put the mail on the marble-topped kitchen island, rubbed her shoulder, and had a thought: *The backyard hot tub. A relaxing soak. Awww, yeah.*

She greeted Rufus and Beatrice, the family's two labradoodles, and threw a couple of King Kong toys out into the yard for them to chase. Then she dragged herself along the flagstone path toward the pool's changing room. Pausing at the door, ready to shower and change into her bikini, she realized, *Who cares?* She was too tired to change, and nobody was home. And the hot tub was surrounded by rose bushes. As she approached, it burbled, as if anticipating her arrival. She stripped down to her bra, undies, and tall field hockey socks, did a deep forward bend to loosen up her back, and climbed into the steaming tub. Now *that* was more like it.

"Oh."

Spencer turned. Wren stood next to the roses, naked to the waist, wearing the sexiest boxer brief Polo underwear she'd ever seen.

"Oops," he said, covering himself with a towel. "Sorry."

"You don't get here until tomorrow," she blurted, even though he was very clearly here, right now, which was obviously *today* and not tomorrow at all.

"We don't. But your sister and I were at Frou," Wren said, making a little face. Frou was this haughty store a few towns over that sold single pillowcases for about a thousand dollars. "She had to run another errand and told me to play with myself here."

Spencer hoped that was just some bizarre English expression. "Oh," she said.

"Did you just get home?"

"I was at field hockey," Spencer said, leaning back and relaxing a little. "First practice of the year."

Spencer glanced at her blurry body under the water. Oh God, she was still wearing her socks. And her high-waisted, sweaty panties and Champion sports bra! She kicked herself for not changing into the yellow Eres bikini she'd just bought but then realized how absurd that was.

"So, I was just planning to have a soak, but if you want to be alone, that's okay too," Wren said. "I'll just go inside and watch TV." He started to turn.

Spencer felt a tiny twinge of disappointment. "Um, no," she said. He stopped. "You can come in. I don't care." Quickly, while his back was turned, she yanked off her socks and threw them into the bushes. They landed with a soggy slap.

"If you're sure, Spencer," Wren said. Spencer loved the way he said her name with his British accent—Spen-*saah*.

He shyly slid into the tub. Spencer stayed very far on her side, curling her legs under her. Wren leaned his head back on the concrete deck and sighed. Spencer did the same and tried not to think about how her legs were getting really cramped and sore in this position. She stretched one tentatively and touched Wren's sinewy calf.

She jerked her leg away. "Sorry."

"No worries," Wren said. "So field hockey, huh? I rowed for Oxford."

"Really?" Spencer said, hoping she didn't sound too

gushy. Her favorite driving-into-Philadelphia sight was of the Penn and Temple men's crew teams rowing on the Schuylkill River.

"Yeah," he said. "I loved it. Do you love field hockey?"

"Um, not really." Spencer took her hair out of its ponytail and shook her head around but then wondered if Wren would find this really skanky and ridiculous. She'd probably imagined the spark between them outside Moshulu.

But then, Wren *had* gotten into the hot tub with her.

"So if you don't like field hockey, why do you play?" Wren asked.

"Because it looks good on a college application."

Now Wren sat up a little, making the water ripple. "It does?"

"Uh, *yeah*."

Spencer shifted and winced when her shoulder muscle cramped into her neck.

"You okay?" Wren asked.

"Yeah, it's nothing," Spencer said, and inexplicably felt an overwhelming wave of despair. It was only the first day of school, and she was already burned out. She thought of all the homework she had to do, lists she had to make, and lines she had to memorize. She was too busy to freak out, but that was the only thing keeping her from freaking out.

"Is it your shoulder?"

"I think," Spencer said, trying to rotate it. "In field hockey, you spend so much time bending over, and I don't know if I pulled it or what. . . ."

"I bet I could fix it for you."

Spencer stared at him. She suddenly had an urge to run her fingers through his shaggy hair. "That's okay. Thanks, though."

"Really," he said. "I'm not going to bite you."

Spencer hated when people said that.

"I'm a doctor," Wren continued. "I bet it's your posterior deltoid."

"Um, okay . . . "

"Your shoulder muscle." He motioned for her to come closer. "C'mere. Seriously. We just need to soften the muscle."

Spencer tried not to read into that. He was a doctor, after all. He was being doctorly. She drifted to him, and he pressed his hands into the middle of her back. His thumbs dug into the little muscles around her spine. Spencer closed her eyes.

"Wow. That's awesome," she murmured.

"You just have some fluid buildup in your bursa sac," he said. Spencer tried not to giggle at the word *sac*. When he reached under her sports bra strap to dig deeper, she swallowed hard. She tried to think about nonsexual things—her uncle Daniel's nose hair, the constipated look her mom got on her face when she rode a horse, the time her cat, Kitten, carried a dead mole from the creek out back and left it in her bedroom. *He's a doctor*, she told herself. *This is just what doctors do.*

"Your pectorals are a little tight too," Wren said, and, horrifyingly, moved his hand to the front of her body. He slid his fingers under her bra again, rubbing just above her chest, and suddenly the bra strap fell off her shoulder. Spencer breathed in but he didn't move away. *This is a doctor thing*, she reminded herself again. But then she realized: Wren was a first-year med student. *He* will *be a doctor*, she corrected herself. *One day. In about ten years.*

"Um, where's my sister?" she asked quietly.

"The store, I think? Wawa?"

"Wawa?" Spencer jerked away from Wren and pulled her bra strap back on her shoulder. "Wawa's only a mile away! If she's going there, she's just picking up cigarettes or something. She'll be back any minute!"

"I don't think she smokes," Wren said, tilting his head questioningly.

"You know what I mean!" Spencer stood up in the tub, grabbed her Ralph Lauren towel, and began violently drying her hair. She felt so hot. Her skin, bones—even her organs and nerves—felt like they'd been braised in the hot tub. She climbed out and fled to the house, in search of a giant glass of water.

"Spencer," Wren called after her. "I didn't mean to . . . I was just trying to help."

But Spencer didn't listen. She ran up to her room and

looked around. Her stuff was still in boxes, still packed up to move to the barn. Suddenly she wanted everything organized. Her jewelry box needed to be sorted by gemstone. Her computer was clogged with old English papers from two years ago, and even though they'd gotten A's back then they were probably embarrassingly bad and should be deleted. She stared at the books in the boxes. They needed to be arranged by subject matter, not by author. Obviously. She pulled them out and started shelving, starting with Adultery and *The Scarlet Letter*.

But by the time she got to Utopias Gone Wrong, she still didn't feel any better. So she switched on her computer and pressed her wireless mouse, which was comfortingly cool, to the back of her neck.

She clicked on her e-mail and saw an unopened letter. The subject line read, *SAT vocab*. Curious, she clicked on it.

Spencer,

Covet is an easy one. When someone covets something, they desire and lust after it. Usually it's something they can't have. You've always had that problem, though, haven't you? —A

Spencer's stomach seized. She looked around.
Who. The. Fuck. Could. Have. Seen?
She threw open her bedroom's biggest window, but the Hastingses' circular driveway was empty. Spencer looked around. A few cars swished past. The neighbors'

lawn service guy was trimming a hedge by their front gate. Her dogs were chasing each other around the side yard. Some birds flew to the top of a telephone pole.

Then, something caught her eye in the neighbor's upstairs window: a flash of blondish hair. But wasn't the new family black? An icy shiver crept up Spencer's spine. That was Ali's old window.

8

WHERE ARE THE DAMN GIRL SCOUTS WHEN YOU NEED THEM?

Hanna sank farther into the squishy cushions of her couch and tried to unbutton Sean's Paper Denim jeans.

"Whoa," Sean said. "We can't. . . . "

Hanna smiled mysteriously and put a finger to her lips. She started kissing Sean's neck. He smelled like Lever 2000 and, strangely, chocolate, and she loved how his recently buzzed haircut showed off all the sexy angles of his face. She'd loved him since sixth grade and he'd only gotten handsomer with each passing year.

As they kissed, Hanna's mother, Ashley, unlocked the front door and walked inside, chatting on her teensy LG flip phone.

Sean recoiled against the couch cushions. "She'll see!" he whispered, quickly tucking in his pale blue Lacoste polo.

Hanna shrugged. Her mom waved at them blankly and walked into the other room. Her mom paid more attention to her BlackBerry than she did to Hanna. Because of her work schedule, she and Hanna didn't bond much, aside from periodic checkups on homework, notes on which shops were running the best sales, and reminders that she should clean her room in case any of the execs coming to her cocktail party needed to use the upstairs bathroom. But Hanna was mostly okay with that. After all, her mom's job was what paid Hanna's AmEx bill—she wasn't *always* taking things—and her pricey tuition at Rosewood Day.

"I have to go," Sean murmured.

"You should come over on Saturday," Hanna purred. "My mom's going to be at the spa all day."

"I'll see you at Noel's party on Friday," Sean said. "And you know this is hard enough."

Hanna groaned. "It doesn't *have* to be so hard," she whined.

He leaned down to kiss her. "See you tomorrow."

After Sean let himself out, she buried her face in the couch pillow. Dating Sean still felt like a dream. Back when Hanna was chubby and lame, she'd adored how tall and athletic he was, how he was always really nice to teachers and kids who were less cool, and how he dressed well, not like a color-blind slob. She never stopped liking him, even after she shed her last few stubborn inches and discovered defrizzing hair products. So last school year, she casually whispered to James Freed in study hall that she liked Sean, and Colleen Rink told her three periods later that Sean was going to call Hanna on her cell that night after soccer. It was yet another moment Hanna was pissed Ali wasn't here to witness.

They'd been a couple for seven months and Hanna felt more in love with him than ever. She hadn't told him yet—she'd kept *that* to herself for years—but now, she was pretty sure he loved her too. And wasn't sex the best way to express love?

That was why the virginity pledge thing made no sense. It wasn't as if Sean's parents were overly religious, and it went against every preconceived notion Hanna had about guys. Despite how she used to look, Hanna had to hand it to herself: With her deep brown hair, curvy body, and flawless—we're talking no pimples, ever—skin, she was hot. Who wouldn't fall madly in love with her? Sometimes she wondered if Sean was gay—he *did* have a lot of nice clothes—or if he had a fear of vaginas.

Hanna called for her miniature pinscher, Dot, to hop up on the couch. "Did you miss me today?" she squealed as Dot licked her hand. Hanna had petitioned to let Dot come to school in her oversize Prada handbag—all the girls in Beverly Hills did it, after all—but Rosewood Day said no. So to prevent separation anxiety, Hanna had bought Dot the snuggliest Gucci bed money could buy and left QVC on her bedroom TV during the day.

Her mother strode into the living room, still in her

tailored tweed suit and brown kitten-heel slingbacks.
"There's sushi," Ms. Marin said.

Hanna looked up. "Toro rolls?"

"I don't know. I got a bunch of things."

Hanna strode into the kitchen, taking in her mom's
laptop and buzzing LG.

"What now?" Ms. Marin barked into the phone.

Dot's little claws *tick-ticked* behind Hanna. After
searching through the bag, she settled on one piece of
yellowtail sashimi, one eel roll, and a small bowl of miso
soup.

"Well, I talked to the client this morning," her mom
went on. "They were happy *then*."

Hanna daintily dipped her yellowtail roll into some
soy sauce and flipped breezily through a J. Crew catalog.
Her mom was second-in-command at the Philly advertising firm McManus & Tate, and her goal was to be the
firm's first woman president.

Besides being extremely successful and ambitious,
Ms. Marin was what most guys at Rosewood Day would
call a MILF—she had long, red-gold hair, smooth skin,
and an incredibly supple body, thanks to her daily
Vinyasa yoga ritual.

Hanna knew her mom wasn't perfect, but she still
didn't get why her parents had divorced four years ago,
or why her father quickly began dating an average-
looking ER nurse from Annapolis, Maryland, named
Isabel. Talk about trading down.

Isabel had a teenage daughter, Kate, and Mr. Marin had said Hanna would just *love* her. A few months after the divorce, he'd invited Hanna to Annapolis for the weekend. Nervous about meeting her quasi-stepsister, Hanna begged Ali to come along.

"Don't worry, Han," Ali assured her. "We'll outclass whoever this Kate girl is." When Hanna looked at her, unconvinced, she reminded Hanna of her signature phrase: "I'm Ali and I'm fabulous!" It sounded almost silly now, but back then Hanna could only imagine what it would feel like to be so confident. Having Ali there was like a security blanket—proof she wasn't a loser her dad just wanted to get away from.

The day had been a train wreck, anyway. Kate was the prettiest girl Hanna had ever met and her dad had basically called her a pig right in front of Kate. He'd quickly backpedaled and said it was only a joke, but that was the very last time she'd seen him . . . and the very first time she ever made herself throw up.

But Hanna hated thinking about stuff in the past, so she rarely did. Besides, now Hanna got to ogle her mom's dates in a not so will-you-be-my-new-father? way. And would her father let Hanna have a 2 A.M. curfew and drink wine, like her mom did? Doubtful.

Her mom snapped her phone shut and fastened her emerald green eyes on Hanna. "Those are your back-to-school shoes?"

Hanna stopped chewing. "Yeah."

Ms. Marin nodded. "Did you get a lot of compliments?"

Hanna turned her ankle to inspect her purple wedges. Too afraid to face the Saks security, she'd actually paid for them. "Yeah. I did."

"Mind if I borrow them?"

"Um, sure. If you wa—"

Her mom's phone rang again. She pounced on it. "Carson? Yes. I've been looking for you all night. . . . What the hell is going on there?"

Hanna blew at her side-swept bangs and fed Dot a tiny piece of eel. As Dot spit it out on the floor, the doorbell rang.

Her mother didn't even flinch. "They need it *tonight*," she said to the phone. "It's your project. Do I have to come down and hold your hand?"

The doorbell rang again. Dot started barking and her mother stood to get it. "It's probably those Girl Scouts again."

The Girl Scouts had come over three days in a row, trying to sell them cookies at dinnertime. They were rabid in this neighborhood.

Within seconds, she was back in the kitchen with a young, brown-haired, green-eyed police officer behind her. "This gentleman says he wants to speak with you." A gold pin on the breast pocket of his uniform read WILDEN.

"Me?" Hanna pointed at herself.

"You're Hanna Marin?" Wilden asked. The walkie-talkie on his belt made a noise.

Suddenly Hanna realized who this guy was: Darren Wilden. He'd been a senior at Rosewood when she was in seventh grade. The Darren Wilden she remembered allegedly slept with the whole girls' diving team and was almost kicked out of school for stealing the principal's vintage Ducati motorcycle. But this cop was definitely the same guy—those green eyes were hard to forget, even if it had been four years since she'd seen them. Hanna hoped he was a stripper that Mona had sent over as a joke.

"What's this all about?" Ms. Marin asked, looking longingly back at her cell phone. "Why are you interrupting us at dinner?"

"We received a call from Tiffany's," Wilden said. "They have you on tape shoplifting some items from their store. Tapes from various other mall security cameras tracked you out of the mall and to your car. We traced the license plate."

Hanna started pinching the inside of her palm with her fingernails, something she always did when she felt out of control.

"Hanna wouldn't do that," Ms. Marin barked. "Would you, Hanna?"

Hanna opened her mouth to respond but no words came out. Her heart was banging against her ribs.

"Look." Wilden crossed his arms over his chest.

Hanna noticed the gun on his belt. It looked like a toy. "I just need you to come to the station. Maybe it's nothing."

"I'm sure it's nothing!" Ms. Marin said. Then she took her Fendi wallet out of its matching purse. "What will it take for you to leave us alone to have our dinner?"

"Ma'am." Wilden sounded exasperated. "You should just come down with me. All right? It won't take all night. I promise." He smiled that sexy Darren Wilden smile that had probably kept him from getting expelled from Rosewood.

"Well," Hanna's mother said. She and Wilden looked at each other for a long moment. "Let me get my bag."

Wilden turned to Hanna. "I'm gonna have to cuff you."

Hanna gasped. "Cuff me?" Okay, now that was silly. It sounded fake, like something the six-year-old twins next door would say to each other. But Wilden pulled out real steel handcuffs and gently put them around her wrists. Hanna hoped he didn't notice that her hands were shaking.

If only this were the moment when Wilden tied her to a chair, put on that old '70s song "Hot Stuff," and stripped off all his clothes. Unfortunately, it wasn't.

The police station smelled like burned coffee and very old wood, because, like most of Rosewood's municipal buildings, it was a former railroad baron's mansion. Cops fluttered around her, taking phone calls, filling out forms, and sliding around on their little castor-wheel chairs. Hanna half expected to see Mona here, too, with her mom's Dior stole thrown over her wrists. But from the look of the empty bench, it seemed Mona hadn't been caught.

Ms. Marin sat very stiffly next to her. Hanna felt squirmy; her mom was usually really lenient, but then, Hanna had never been taken downtown and had the book thrown at her or whatever.

And then, very quietly, her mom leaned over. "What was it that you took?"

"Huh?" Hanna asked.

"That bracelet you're wearing?"

Hanna looked down. *Perfect.* She'd forgotten to take it off; the bracelet was circling her wrist in full view. She shoved it farther up her sleeve. She felt her ears for the earrings; yep, she'd worn them today too. Talk about stupid!

"Give it to me," her mother whispered.

"Huh?" Hanna squeaked.

Ms. Marin held out her palm. "Give it here. I can handle this."

Reluctantly, Hanna let her mom unfasten the bracelet from her wrist. Then, Hanna reached up and took off the earrings and handed them over too. Ms. Marin didn't even flinch. She simply dropped the jewelry in her purse and folded her hands over the metal clasp.

The blond Tiffany's girl who'd helped Hanna with the charm bracelet strode into the room. As soon as she saw Hanna, sitting dejectedly on the bench with the cuffs still on her hands, she nodded. "Yeah. That's her."

Darren Wilden glared at Hanna, and her mom stood up. "I think there's been a mistake." She walked over to Wilden's desk. "I misunderstood you at the house. I was with Hanna that day. We bought that stuff. I have a receipt for it at home."

The Tiffany's girl narrowed her eyes in disbelief. "Are you suggesting I'm lying?"

"No," Ms. Marin said sweetly, "I just think you're confused."

What was she *doing*? A gooey, uncomfortable, almost-guilty feeling washed over Hanna.

"How do you explain the surveillance tapes?" Wilden asked.

Her mom paused. Hanna saw a tiny muscle in her neck quiver. Then, before Hanna could stop her, she reached into her purse and took out the loot. "This was all my fault," she said. "Not Hanna's."

Ms. Marin turned back to Wilden. "Hanna and I had a fight about these items. I said she couldn't have them—I drove her to this. She'll never do it again. I'll make sure of it."

Hanna stared, stunned. She and her mom had never once discussed Tiffany's, let alone something she could or couldn't have.

Wilden shook his head. "Ma'am, I think your daughter may need to do some community service. That's usually the penalty."

Ms. Marin blinked, innocently. "Can't we let this slide? Please?"

Wilden looked at her for a long time, one corner of his mouth turned up almost devilishly. "Sit down," he said finally. "Let me see what I can do."

Hanna looked everywhere but in her mom's direction. Wilden hunched over his desk. He had a Chief Wiggum figurine from *The Simpsons* and a metal Slinky. He licked his pointer finger to turn the pages of the papers he was filling out. Hanna flinched. What sort of papers were they? Didn't the local newspapers report crimes? This was bad. Very bad.

Hanna jiggled her foot nervously, having a sudden urge for some Junior Mints. Or maybe cashews. Even the Slim Jims on Wilden's desk would do.

She could just see it: Everyone would find out, and she'd be instantaneously friendless and boyfriendless. From there, she'd recede back to dorky, seventh-grade Hanna in reverse evolution. She'd wake up and her hair would be a yucky, washed-out brown again. Then her teeth would go crooked and she'd get her braces back on. She wouldn't be able to fit into any of her jeans. The rest would happen spontaneously. She'd spend her life chubby, ugly, miserable, and overlooked, just the way she used to be.

"I have some lotion if those are chafing your wrists," Ms. Marin said, gesturing to the cuffs and rooting around in her purse.

"I'm okay," Hanna replied, brought back to the present.

Sighing, she pulled out her BlackBerry. It was tough because her hands were cuffed, but she wanted to convince Sean that he had to come over to her house this Saturday. She suddenly *really* wanted to know he would. As she stared blankly at the screen, an e-mail popped up in her inbox. She opened it.

Hey Hanna,

Since prison food makes you fat, you know what Sean's gonna say? Not it! —A

She was so startled that she stood up, thinking someone might be across the room, watching her. But there was no one. She closed her eyes, trying to think who might have seen the police car at her house.

Wilden looked up from his writing. "You all right?"

"Um," Hanna said. "Yeah." She slowly sat back down. *Not it?* What the hell? She checked the note's return address again, but it was just a mess of letters and numbers.

"Hanna," Ms. Marin murmured after a few moments. "No one needs to know about this."

Hanna blinked. "Oh. Yeah. I agree."

"Good."

Hanna swallowed hard. Except . . . someone *did* know.

9

NOT YOUR TYPICAL STUDENT-TEACHER CONFERENCE

Wednesday morning, Aria's father, Byron, rubbed his bushy black hair and hand-signaled out the Subaru window that he was making a left-hand turn. The turn signals had stopped working last night, so he was driving Aria and Mike to their second day of school and taking the car to the shop.

"You guys happy to be back in America?" Byron asked.

Mike, who sat next to Aria in the backseat, grinned. "America rocks." He went back to maniacally punching the tiny buttons of his PSP. It made a farting noise and Mike pumped one fist in the air.

Aria's father smiled and navigated across the single-lane stone bridge, waving to a neighbor as he passed. "Well, good. Now, *why* does it rock?"

"America rocks because it has lacrosse," Mike said,

not taking his eyes off his PSP. "And hotter chicks. And a Hooters in King of Prussia."

Aria laughed. Like Mike had been inside Hooters. Unless . . . Oh God, *had* he?

She shivered in her kelly green alpaca shrug and stared out the window at the thick fog. A woman wearing a long, red hooded stadium jacket that said, UPPER MAIN LINE SOCCER MOM, tried to stop her German shepherd from chasing a squirrel across the street. At the corner, two blondes with high-tech baby carriages stood together gossiping.

There was one word to describe yesterday's English class: *brutal*. After Ezra blurted out, "Holy shit," the whole class turned and stared at her. Hanna Marin, who sat in front of her, whispered in a not-so-quiet voice, "Did you sleep with the teacher?" Aria considered, for a half second, that maybe *Hanna* had written her the text message about Ezra—Hanna was one of the few people who knew about Pigtunia. But why would Hanna care?

Ezra—er, Mr. Fitz—had dispelled the laughing quickly, and come up with the lamest excuse for swearing in class. He said, and Aria quoted in her head, "I was afraid that a bee had flown into my pants, and I thought the bee was going to sting me, and so I yelled out in terror."

As Ezra then started talking about five-paragraph themes and the class's syllabus, Aria couldn't concentrate. *She* was the bee that had flown into his pants. She couldn't stop looking at his wolfish eyes and his sumptuous pink mouth. When he peeked in her direction out of the corner of his eye, her heart did two and a half somersaults off the high dive and landed in her stomach.

Ezra was the guy for her, and she was the girl for him—she just *knew* it. So what if he was her teacher? There *had* to be a way to make it work.

Her father pulled up to Rosewood's stone-gated entrance. In the distance, Aria noticed a vintage powder-blue Volkswagen beetle parked in the teacher's lot. She knew that car from Snooker's—it was Ezra's. She checked her watch. Fifteen minutes until homeroom.

Mike shot out of the car. Aria opened her door as well, but her father touched her forearm. "Hang on a sec," he said.

"But I have to . . . " She glanced longingly at Ezra's bug.

"Just for a minute." Her father turned down the radio volume. Aria slumped back in her seat. "You've seemed a little . . . " He flicked his wrist back and forth uncertainly. "You okay?"

Aria shrugged. "About what?"

Her father sighed. "Well . . . I don't know. Being back. And we haven't talked about . . . you know . . . in a while."

Aria fidgeted with her jacket's zipper. "What's there to talk about?"

Byron stuck a cigarette he'd rolled before they left into his mouth. "I can't imagine how hard it's been. Keeping quiet. But I love you. You know that, right?"

Aria looked out at the parking lot again. "Yeah, I know," she said. "I have to go. I'll see you at three."

Before he could answer, Aria shot out of the car, blood rushing in her ears. How was she supposed to be Icelandic Aria, who left her past behind, if one of her worst memories of Rosewood kept bubbling to the surface?

It had happened in May of seventh grade. Rosewood Day had dismissed the students early for teacher conferences, so Aria and Ali headed to Sparrow, Hollis campus's music store, to search for new CDs. As they cut through a back alley, Aria noticed her father's familiar beat-up brown Honda Civic in a far-off space in an empty parking lot. As Aria and Ali walked toward the car to leave a note, they realized there was someone inside. Actually, two someones: Aria's father, Byron, and a girl, about twenty years old, kissing his neck.

That's when Byron looked up and saw Aria. She sprinted away before she had to see any more and before he could stop her. Ali followed Aria all the way back to her house but didn't try to stop her when Aria said she wanted to be alone.

Later that night, Byron came up to Aria's room to explain. It wasn't what it looked like, he said. But Aria wasn't stupid. Every year her father invited his students over to their house for get-to-know-you cocktails, and Aria had seen that girl walk through her very door. Her name was Meredith, Aria remembered, because Meredith had gotten tipsy and spelled out her name on the refrigerator in plastic letter magnets. When Meredith left, instead of shaking her dad's hand as the other kids had, she gave him a lingering kiss on his cheek.

Byron begged Aria not to tell her mom. He promised her it would never happen again. She decided to believe him, and so she kept his secret. He'd never said so, but Aria believed Meredith was the reason her dad took his sabbatical when he did.

You promised yourself you wouldn't think about it, Aria thought, glancing back over her shoulder. Her father hand-signaled out of the Rosewood parking lot.

Aria walked into the narrow hallway of the faculty wing. Ezra's office was at the end of the hall, next to a small, cozy window seat. She stopped in the doorway and watched him as he typed something into his computer.

Finally, she knocked. Ezra's blue eyes widened when he saw her. He looked adorable in his button-down white shirt, blue Rosewood blazer, green cords, and beat-up black loafers. The corners of his mouth curled up into the tiniest, shyest smile.

"Hey," he said.

Aria hovered in the doorway. "Can I talk to you?" Aria asked. Her voice squeaked a little.

Ezra hesitated, pushing a lock of hair out of his eyes. Aria noticed a Snoopy Band-Aid wrapped around his left pinkie finger. "Sure," he said softly. "Come in."

She walked into his office and shut the door. It was empty, except for a wide, heavy wood desk, two folding chairs, and a computer. She sat down on the empty folding chair.

"So, um," Aria said. "Hey."

"Hey again," Ezra answered, grinning. He lowered his eyes and took a gulp from his Rosewood Day crest coffee mug. "Listen," he started.

"About yesterday," Aria said at the same time. They both laughed.

"Ladies first." Ezra smiled.

Aria scratched the back of her neck where her straight black hair was drawn up in a ponytail. "I, um, wanted to talk about . . . us."

Ezra nodded, but didn't say anything.

Aria wiggled in her chair. "Well, I guess it's shocking that I'm . . . um . . . your student, after, you know . . . Snooker's. But if you don't mind, I don't."

Ezra cupped his hand around his mug. Aria listened to the school-issued wall clock ticking off the seconds. "I . . . I don't think it's a good idea," he said softly. "You said you were older."

Aria laughed, not sure how serious he was. "I never told you how old I was." She lowered her eyes. "You just assumed."

"Yeah, but you shouldn't have implied it," Ezra responded.

"Everybody lies about their age," Aria said quietly.

Ezra ran his hand through his hair. "But . . . you're . . . " He met her eyes and sighed. "Look, I . . . I think you're amazing, Aria. I do. I met you in that bar, and I was like . . . wow, who *is* this? She's so unlike any other girl I've ever met."

Aria looked down, feeling both pleased and a little queasy.

Ezra reached across the desk and touched his hand to hers—it was warm, dry, and soothing—but then quickly pulled away. "But this isn't meant to be, you know? 'Cause, well, you're my student. I could get in a lot of trouble. You don't want me to get in trouble, do you?"

"No one would know," Aria said faintly, although she couldn't help but think about that bizarre text from yesterday, and that maybe someone *already* knew.

It took Ezra a long time to respond. It seemed to Aria that he was trying to make up his mind. She looked at him hopefully.

"I'm sorry, Aria," he finally mumbled. "But I think you should go."

Aria stood up, feeling her cheeks burn. "Of course." Aria wrapped her hands around the top of the chair. It felt like hot coals were bouncing around her insides.

"I'll see you in class," Ezra whispered.

She shut the door carefully. In the hall, teachers swarmed around her, rushing off to their homerooms. She decided to get to her locker by cutting through the commons—she needed some fresh air.

Outside, Aria heard a familiar girl's laugh. She froze for a second. When would she stop thinking she heard

Alison *everywhere*? She trudged not on the commons'
winding stone path, like you were supposed to, but
through the grass. The morning fog was so dense that
Aria could barely see her legs below her. Her footprints
vanished in the squishy grass as quickly as she made
them.

Good. This seemed like an appropriate time to
disappear completely.

10

SINGLE GIRLS HAVE
WAY MORE FUN

That afternoon, Emily was standing in the student parking lot, lost in thought, when someone threw their hands
over her eyes. Emily jumped, startled.

"Whoa, chill! It's just me!"

Emily turned and sighed with relief. It was only Maya.
Emily had been so distracted and paranoid since getting
that bizarre note yesterday. She'd been about to unlock
her car—her mom let her and Carolyn take it to school
on the condition they *drive carefully and call when they got
there*—and grab her swimming bag for practice.

"Sorry," Emily said. "I thought . . . never mind."

"I missed you today." Maya smiled.

"Me too." Emily smiled back. She'd tried calling
Maya this morning to offer her a ride to school, but
Maya's mom said she'd already left. "So, how are you?"

"Well, I could be better." Today, Maya had secured

her wild dark hair off her face with adorable iridescent pink butterfly clips.

"Oh yeah?" Emily tilted her head.

Maya pursed her lips together and slid one of her feet out of her Oakley sandals. Her second toe was longer than her big toe, just like Emily's. "I'd be better if you came somewhere with me. Right now."

"But I have swimming," Emily said, hearing Eeyore in her voice again.

Maya took her hand and swung it. "What if I told you that where we're going sort of *involves* swimming?"

Emily narrowed her eyes. "What do you mean?"

"You have to trust me."

Even though she'd been close to Hanna and Spencer and Aria, all of Emily's favorite memories were of hanging out alone with Ali. Like when they dressed up in bulky snow pants to sled down Bayberry Hill, talked about their ideal boyfriends, or cried about The Jenna Thing from sixth grade and comforted each other. When it was just the two of them, Emily saw a slightly less perfect Ali—which somehow made her seem even more perfect—and Emily felt she could be herself. It seemed like days, weeks, *years* had gone by where Emily hadn't been herself. And she thought that now, she could have something like that with Maya. She missed having a best friend.

Right now, Ben and all the other boys were probably changing into their suits, slapping one another's bare butts with wet towels. Coach Lauren was writing the practice sets on the big marker board and carrying out the appropriate fins, buoys, and paddles. And the girls on the team were complaining because they all had their periods at the same time. Did she dare miss the second day of practice?

Emily squeezed her plastic fish keychain. "I suppose I could tell Carolyn I had to tutor somebody in Spanish," she murmured. Emily knew Carolyn wouldn't buy that, but she probably wouldn't squeal on Emily, either.

Triple-checking the parking lot to see if anyone was watching, Emily smiled and unlocked the car.

"All right. Let's go."

"My brother and I checked out this spot this weekend," Maya said as Emily pulled into the gravel parking lot.

Emily stepped out of the car and stretched. "I forgot about this place." They were at the Marwyn trail, which was about five miles long and bordered a deep creek. She and her friends used to ride their bikes here all the time—Ali and Spencer would pedal furiously at the end and usually tie—and stop at the little snack bar by the swimming area for Butterfingers and Diet Cokes.

As she followed Maya up a muddy slope, Maya grabbed her arm. "Oh! I forgot to tell you. My mom said your mom stopped over yesterday while we were in school. She brought over brownies."

"Really?" Emily responded, confused. She wondered why her mother hadn't mentioned anything to her at dinner.

"The brownies were dee*lish*. My brother and I polished them off last night!"

They came to the dirt trail. A canopy of oaks sheltered them. The air had that fresh, woodsy smell and it felt about twenty degrees cooler.

"We're not there yet." Maya took her hand and led her down the path to a small stone bridge. Twenty feet beneath it, the stream widened. The calm water glittered in the late-afternoon sun.

Maya walked right up to the edge of the bridge and stripped down to her matching pale pink bra and undies. She threw her clothes in a pile, stuck her tongue out at Emily, and jumped off.

"Wait!" Emily rushed to the edge. Did Maya know how deep this was? A full *one-Mississippi, two-Mississippi* later, Emily heard a splash.

Maya's head popped back up out of the water. "Told you it involved swimming! C'mon, strip!"

Emily glanced at Maya's pile of clothes. She *really* hated undressing in front of people—even the swim team girls, who saw her every day. She slowly took off her pleated Rosewood skirt, crossing her legs over each other so Maya couldn't see her bare, muscular thighs, and then pulled at the tank top she wore under her uniform blouse. She decided to keep it on. She looked over the edge to the creek and, steeling herself, she jumped. A moment later, the water hugged her body. It was pleasantly warm and thick with mud, not cold and clean like the pool. The built-in shelf bra of her tank top puffed out with water.

"It's like a sauna in here," Maya said.

"Yeah." Emily paddled over to the shallower area, where Maya was standing. Emily realized she could see Maya's nipples straight through her bra, and cut her eyes away.

"I used to go cliff diving with Justin all the time back in Cali," Maya said. "He'd stand up at the top and, like, *think* about it for ten minutes before jumping. I like how you didn't even hesitate."

Emily floated on her back and smiled. She couldn't help it: she gobbled up Maya's compliments like cheese-cake.

Maya squirted Emily with water through her cupped hands. Some of it squirted right into her mouth. The creek water tasted gooey and almost metallic, nothing like chlorinated pool water. "I think me and Justin are going to break up," Maya said.

Emily swam closer to the edge and stood up. "Really? Why?"

"Yeah. The long-distance thing is too stressful. He calls me, like, *all* the time. I've only been gone for a few days, and he's already sent me two letters!"

"Huh," Emily answered, sifting her fingers through the murky water. Then something occurred to her. She turned to Maya. "Did you, um, put a note in my swim locker yesterday?"

Maya frowned. "What, after school? No . . . you walked me home, remember?"

"Right." She didn't really think Maya had written the note, but things would've been so much simpler if she had.

"What did the note say?"

Emily shook her head. "Never mind. It was nothing." She cleared her throat. "You know, I think I might break up with my boyfriend too."

Whoa. Emily wouldn't have been any more surprised if a bluebird had just flown out of her mouth.

"Really?" Maya said.

Emily blinked water out of her eyes. "I don't know. Maybe."

Maya stretched her arms over her head, and Emily caught sight of that scar on her wrist again. She looked away. "Well, fuck a moose," Maya said.

Emily smiled. "Huh?"

"It's this thing I say sometimes," Maya said. "It means . . . *screw it!*" She turned away and shrugged. "I guess it's silly."

"No, I like it," Emily said. "Fuck a moose." She giggled. She always felt funny swearing—as if her mom could hear her from their kitchen, ten miles away.

"You totally should break up with your boyfriend, though," Maya said. "Know why?"

"Why?"

"That would mean we'd both be single."

"And that means what?" Emily asked. The forest was very quiet and still.

Maya moved closer to her. "And that means . . . we . . . can . . . *have fun*!" She grabbed Emily by the shoulder and dunked her under the water.

"Hey!" Emily squealed. She splashed Maya back, ripping her whole arm through the water, creating a giant wave. Then she grabbed Maya by the leg and started tickling underneath her toes.

"Help!" Maya screamed. "Not my feet! I'm so ticklish!"

"I've found your weakness!" Emily crowed, maniacally dragging Maya over to the waterfall. Maya managed to wrench her foot away and pounced on Emily's shoulders from behind. Maya's hands drifted up Emily's sides, then down to her stomach, where she tickled her. Emily squealed. She finally pushed Maya into a small cave in the rocks.

"I hope there are no bats in here!" Maya squealed. Beams of sunlight pierced through the cave's tiny openings, making a halo around the top of Maya's sopping wet head.

"You have to come in here," Maya said. She held out her hand.

Emily stood next to her, feeling the cave's smooth, cool sides. The sounds of her breathing echoed off the narrow walls. They looked at each other and grinned.

Emily bit her lip. This was such a perfect friend moment, it made her feel kind of melancholy and nostalgic.

Maya's eyes turned down in concern. "What's wrong?"

Emily took a deep breath. "Well . . . you know that girl who lived in your house? Alison?"

"Yeah."

"She went missing. Right after seventh grade. She was never found."

Maya shivered slightly. "I heard something about that."

Emily hugged herself; she was getting cold, too. "We were really close."

Maya moved closer to Emily and put her arm around her. "I didn't realize."

"Yeah." Emily's chin wobbled. "I just wanted you to know."

"Thanks."

A few long moments passed; Emily and Maya continued to hug. Then, Maya backed off. "I kind of lied earlier. About why I want to break up with Justin."

Emily raised an eyebrow, curious.

"I'm . . . I'm not sure if I like guys," Maya said quietly. "It's weird. I think they're cute, but when I get alone with them, I don't want to be with them. I'd rather be with, like, someone more like me." She smiled crookedly. "You know?"

Emily ran her hands over her face and hair. Maya's gaze felt too close all of a sudden. "I . . . ," she started. No, she *didn't* know.

The bushes above them moved. Emily flinched. Her mom used to hate when she came to this trail—you never knew what kind of kidnappers or murderers hid in places like this. The woods were still for a moment, but then a flock of birds scattered wildly into the sky. Emily flattened herself up against the rock. Was someone watching them? Who was that laughing? The laugh sounded familiar. Then Emily heard heavy breathing. Goose bumps rose up on her arms and she peered out of the cave.

It was only a group of boys. Suddenly, they burst into the creek, wielding sticks like swords. Emily backed away from Maya and out of the waterfall.

"Where are you going?" Maya called.

Emily looked at Maya, and then at the boys, who had abandoned the sticks and were now throwing rocks at each other. One of them was Mike Montgomery, her old friend Aria's little brother. He'd grown up quite a bit since she last saw him. And wait—Mike went to Rosewood. Would he recognize her? Emily climbed out of the water and started scurrying up the hill.

She turned back to Maya. "I have to get back to school before Carolyn's done with swimming." She pulled on her skirt. "Do you want me to throw down your clothes?"

"Whatev." At that, she stepped out of the waterfall and waded through the water, her sheer underwear clinging to her butt. Maya climbed up the slope slowly, not once covering up her stomach or boobs with her hands. The freshmen boys stopped what they were doing and stared.

And even though Emily didn't want to, she couldn't help but stare too.

11

AT LEAST SWEET POTATOES
HAVE LOTS OF VITAMIN A

"Her. Definitely her," Hanna whispered, pointing.

"Nah. They're too small!" Mona whispered back.

"But look at the way they puff up at the top! Totally fake," Hanna countered.

"I think that woman over there has had her butt done."

"Gross." Hanna wrinkled her nose and ran her hands over the sides of her own toned, perfectly round butt to make sure it was still perfectly perfect. It was late afternoon on Wednesday, just two days until Noel Kahn's annual field party, and she and Mona were lounging on the outside terrace at Yam, the organic café at Mona's parents' country club. Below them, a bunch of Rosewood boys played a quick round of golf before dinner, but Hanna and Mona were playing another type of game: Spot the Fake Boobs. Or fake anything else, as there was lots of fake stuff around here.

"Yeah, it looks like her surgeon messed up," Mona murmured. "I think my mom plays tennis with her. I'll ask."

Hanna looked again at the pixieish, thirtysomething woman by the bar whose butt did look suspiciously extra-luscious for the rest of her toothpick-skinny figure. "I'd die before I got plastic surgery."

Mona played with the charm on her Tiffany bracelet— the one she, evidently, didn't have to give back. "Do you think Aria Montgomery had hers done?"

Hanna looked up, startled. "Why?"

"She's really thin, and they're like, too perfect," Mona said. "She went to Finland or wherever, right? I hear in Europe they can do your boobs for really cheap."

"I don't think they're fake," Hanna murmured.

"How do *you* know?"

Hanna chewed on her straw. Aria's boobs had always been there—she and Alison had been the only two of the friends who needed a bra in seventh grade. Ali always flaunted hers, but the only time Aria seemed to notice she even *had* boobs was when she knit everyone bras as Christmas gifts and had to make herself a larger size. "She just doesn't seem the type," Hanna answered. Talking to Mona about her old friends was awkward territory. Hanna still felt bad about how she and Ali and the others used to tease Mona back in seventh grade, but it always seemed too weird to bring up now.

Mona stared at her. "Are you all right? You look different today."

Hanna flinched. "I do? How?"

Mona gave her a tiny smirk. "Whoa! Somebody's jumpy!"

"I'm not jumpy," Hanna said quickly. But she was: Ever since the police station and that e-mail she had gotten last night, she'd been freaking. This morning, her eyes even seemed more dull brown than green, and her arms looked disturbingly puffy. She had this horrible sense that she really was going to spontaneously morph back into her seventh-grade self.

A blond, giraffelike waitress interrupted them. "Have you decided?"

Mona looked at the menu. "I'll have the Asian chicken salad, no dressing."

Hanna cleared her throat. "I want a garden salad with sprouts, no dressing, and an extra-large order of sweet potato fries. In a carry-out box, please."

As the waitress took their menus, Mona pushed her sunglasses down her nose. "Sweet potato fries?"

"For my mom," Hanna answered quickly. "She lives on them."

Down on the golf course, a group of older guys teed up, along with one young good-looking guy in fatigue shorts. He looked a little out of place with his messy brown hair, cargos, and . . . was that a . . . *Rosewood Police* polo? Oh no. It was.

Wilden scanned the terrace and coolly nodded when he saw Hanna. She ducked.

"Who is *that*?" Mona purred.

"Um . . . ," Hanna mumbled, half under the table. Darren Wilden was a *golfer*? Come *on*. Back in high school, he was the type to flick lit matches at the guys on Rosewood's golf team. Was the whole world out to get her?

Mona squinted. "Wait. Didn't he go to our school?" She grinned. "Oh my God. It's the girls' diving team guy. Hanna, you little bitch! How does he know *you*?"

"He's . . . " Hanna paused. She ran her hand along the waistband of her jeans. "I met him on the Marwyn trail a couple of days ago when I was running. We stopped at the water fountain at the same time."

"Nice," Mona said. "Does he work around here?"

Hanna paused again. She really wanted to avoid this. "Um . . . I think he said he was a cop," she said non-chalantly.

"You're kidding." Mona took out her Shu Uemura lip moisturizer from her blue leather hobo bag and lightly dabbed her bottom lip. "That guy's hot enough to be in a policeman's calendar. I could just see it: Mr. April. Let's ask if we can see his nightstick!"

"Shhh," Hanna hissed.

Their salads came. Hanna pushed the Styrofoam container of sweet potato fries to the side and took a bite of an undressed grape tomato.

Mona leaned closer. "I bet you could hook up with him."

"Who?"

"Mr. April! Who else?"

Hanna snorted. "Right."

"Totally. You should bring him to the Kahn party. I heard some cops came to the party last year. That's how they never get busted."

Hanna sat back. The Kahn party was a legendary Rosewood tradition. The Kahns lived on twenty-some acres of land, and the Kahn boys—Noel was the youngest—held a back-to-school party every year. The kids raided their parents' extremely well-stocked liquor supply in the basement, and there was *always* a scandal. Last year, Noel shot his best friend James in the bare ass with his BB gun because James had tried to make out with Noel's then-girlfriend, Alyssa Pennypacker. They were both so drunk they laughed the whole way to the ER and couldn't remember how or why it happened. The year before that, a bunch of stoners smoked too much and tried to get Mr. Kahn's Appaloosas to take hits from a bong.

"Nah." Hanna bit into another tomato. "I think I'm going with Sean."

Mona scrunched up her face. "Why waste a perfectly good party night on Sean? He took a virginity pledge! He probably won't even go."

"Just because you sign a virginity pledge doesn't mean you stop partying, too." Hanna took a big bite of her salad, crunching the dry, unappetizing vegetables in her mouth.

"Well, if you're not gonna ask Mr. April to Noel's, I will." Mona stood up.

Hanna grabbed her arm. "No!"

"Why not? C'mon. It'd be fun."

Hanna dug her fingernails into Mona's arm. "I said no."

Mona sat back down and stuck out her lip. "Why not?"

Hanna's heart galloped. "All right. You can't tell *any-one*, though." She took a deep breath. "I met him at the police station, not the trail. I was called in for questioning for the Tiffany's thing. But it's not a big deal. I'm not busted."

"Oh my *God*!" Mona yelled. Wilden looked up at them again.

"Shhh!" Hanna hissed.

"Are you all right? What happened? Tell me everything," Mona whispered back.

"There isn't much to tell." Hanna threw her napkin over her plate. "They brought me to the station, my mom came with me, and we sat for a while. They let me off with a warning. Whatever. The whole thing took like twenty minutes."

"Yikes." Mona gave Hanna an indeterminate look; Hanna wondered for a second if it was a look of pity.

"It wasn't, like, dramatic or anything," Hanna said defensively, her throat dry. "Not much happened. Most of the cops were on the phone. I text-messaged the whole time." She paused, considering whether she should tell Mona about that "not it" text message she'd received from A, whoever A was. But why waste her breath? It couldn't have actually meant anything, right?

Mona took a sip of her Perrier. "I thought you'd never get caught."

Hanna swallowed hard. "Yeah, well . . . "

"Did your mom totally kill you?"

Hanna looked away. On the drive home, her mom had asked Hanna if she'd meant to steal the bracelet and earrings. When Hanna said no, Ms. Marin answered, "Good. It's settled then." Then she flipped open her cell to make a call.

Hanna shrugged and stood up. "I just remembered–I gotta go walk Dot."

"Are you sure you're okay?" Mona asked. "Your face looks kind of splotchy."

"No biggie." She smacked her lips glamorously at Mona and turned for the door.

Hanna sauntered coolly out of the restaurant, but once she got to the parking lot, she broke into a run. She climbed inside her Toyota Prius–a car her mom had bought for herself last year but had recently handed off to Hanna because she'd grown tired of it–and checked her face in the rearview mirror. There were hideous bright red patches on her cheeks and forehead.

After her transformation, Hanna had been neurotically

careful about not only looking cool and perfect at all times, but *being* cool and perfect, too. Terrified that the tiniest mistake would send her spiraling back to dorkdom, she labored over every last detail, from little things like the perfect IM screen name and the right mix for her car's built-in iPod, to bigger stuff like the right combo of people to invite over before someone's party and choosing the perfect *it* boy to date—who, luckily, was the same boy she'd loved since seventh grade. Had getting caught for shoplifting just tarnished the perfect, controlled, über-cool Hanna everyone had come to know? She hadn't been able to read that look on Mona's face when she said "yikes." Had the look meant, *Yikes, but no big deal?* Or, *Yikes, what a loser?*

She wondered if maybe she shouldn't have told Mona at all. But then . . . someone else already knew. A.

Know what Sean's going to say? Not it!

Hanna's field of vision went blurry. She squeezed the steering wheel for a few seconds, then jammed the key into the ignition and rolled out of the country club parking lot to a gravelly, dead-end turn-off a few yards down the road. She could hear her heart pounding at her temples as she turned off the engine and took deep breaths. The wind smelled like hay and just-mown grass.

Hanna shut her eyes tight. When she opened them, she stared at the container of sweet potato fries. *Don't,* she thought. A car swished by on the main road.

Hanna wiped her hands on her jeans. She snuck another peek at the container. The fries smelled delicious. *Don't, don't, don't.*

She reached over for them and opened the lid. Their sweet, warm smell wafted into her face. Before she could stop herself, Hanna shoved handful after handful of fries into her mouth. The fries were still so hot that they burned her tongue, but she didn't care. It was such a relief; this was the only thing that made her feel better. She didn't stop until she'd eaten them all and even licked the sides of the container for the salt that had gathered at the bottom.

At first she felt much, much calmer. But by the time she pulled into her driveway, the old, familiar feelings of panic and shame had welled up inside her. Hanna was amazed how, even though it had been years since she'd done this, everything felt exactly the same. Her stomach ached, her pants felt tight, and all she wanted was to be rid of what was inside of her.

Ignoring Dot's excited cries from her bedroom, Hanna bolted to the upstairs bathroom, slammed the door, and collapsed onto the tiled floor. Thank God her mom wasn't home from work yet. At least she wouldn't hear what Hanna was about to do.

12

MMM, LOVE THAT
NEW-TEST-SCORE SMELL

Okay. Spencer had to calm down.

Wednesday night, she pulled her black Mercedes C-Class hatchback—her sister's castoff car, since she got the new, "practical" Mercedes SUV—into the circular driveway of her house. Her student council meeting had gone extra late and she'd been on edge driving through Rosewood's dark streets. All day, she'd felt like someone was watching her, like whoever had written that "covet" e-mail could jump out at her at any second.

Spencer kept thinking uneasily about that familiar ponytail in Alison's bedroom window. Her mind kept going back to Ali—all the things she knew about Spencer. But no, that was crazy. Alison had been gone—and most likely dead—for three years. Plus, a new family lived in her house now, right?

Spencer ran to the mailbox and pulled out a pile, tossing everything back that wasn't hers. Suddenly, she saw it. It was a long envelope, not too thick, not too thin, with Spencer's name typed neatly in the windowpane. The return address said, *The College Board*. It was here.

Spencer ripped open the envelope and scanned the page. She read the PSAT results six times before it sunk in.

She'd gotten a 2350 out of 2400.

"Yessssss!" she screamed, clutching the papers so tightly they wrinkled.

"Whoa! Someone's happy!" called a voice from the road.

Spencer looked up. Hanging out the driver's-side window of a black Mini Cooper was Andrew Campbell, the tall, freckly, long-haired boy that beat out Spencer for class president. They were number-one and number-two in the class in practically every subject. But before Spencer could brag about her score—telling Andrew about her PSATs would feel *so* good—he peeled away. *Freak.* Spencer turned back to her house.

As she excitedly scampered inside, something stopped her: she remembered her sister's near-perfect score and quickly converted it from the 1600-scale they used to use into the 2400-scale the College Board used nowadays. It was a full 100 points lower than Spencer's. And weren't they supposed to be harder these days, too?

Well, *now* who's the genius?

An hour later, Spencer sat at the kitchen table reading *Middlemarch*—a book on the English AP "suggested reading" list—when she began to sneeze.

"Melissa and Wren are here," Mrs. Hastings said to Spencer as she bustled into the kitchen, carrying in the mail Spencer had left in the box. "They've brought all of their luggage to move in!" She opened the oven a crack, checking on the rotisserie chicken and seven-grain rolls, and then bustled into the living room.

Spencer sneezed again. A cloud of Chanel No. 5 always preceded her mom—even though she spent the whole day working around horses—and Spencer was certain she was allergic. She considered announcing her PSAT news, but a twinkly voice from the foyer stopped her.

"Mom?" Melissa called. She and Wren strolled into the kitchen. Spencer pretended to study *Middlemarch*'s boring back cover.

"Hey," Wren said above her.

"Hey," she answered coolly.

"Whatcha reading?"

Spencer hesitated. It was better to steer clear of Wren, especially now that he was moving in.

Melissa brushed by without saying hello and began to unpack purple pillows from a Pottery Barn bag. "These are for the couch in the barn," she practically yelled.

Spencer cringed. Two could play at this game. "Oh,

Melissa!" Spencer cried. "I forgot to tell you! Guess who I ran into!"

Melissa continued to unpack the pillows. "Who?"

"Ian Thomas! He's coaching my field hockey team now!"

Melissa froze. "He . . . what? He is? He's *here*? Did he ask about me?"

Spencer shrugged and pretended to think. "No, I don't think so."

"Who's Ian Thomas?" Wren asked, leaning against the marble island counter.

"No one," Melissa snapped, turning back to the pillows. Spencer slapped her book shut and skipped off to the dining room. There. That felt better.

She sat down at the long, mission-style farmhouse table, running her finger around the stemless wineglass Candace, the family's housekeeper, had just filled with red wine. Her parents didn't care if their kids drank while they were at home as long as no one was driving, so she grabbed the glass with both hands and greedily took a large gulp. When she looked up, Wren was smirking at her from across the table, his spine very straight in his dining chair.

"Hey," he said. She raised her eyebrows in answer.

Melissa and Mrs. Hastings sat down, and Spencer's father adjusted the chandelier lights and took a seat as well. For a moment everyone was quiet. Spencer felt for the PSAT score papers in her pocket. "So guess what happened to me," she began.

"Wren and I are so happy you're letting us stay here!" Melissa said at the same time, grabbing Wren's hand.

Mrs. Hastings smiled at Melissa. "I'm always happy when the family's all here."

Spencer bit her lip, her stomach nervously gurgling. "So, Dad. I got my–"

"Uh-oh," Melissa interrupted, staring down at the plates Candace had just brought in from the kitchen. "Do we have anything other than chicken? Wren's trying not to eat meat."

"It's all right," Wren said hastily. "Chicken is perfect."

"Oh!" Mrs. Hastings stood up halfway. "You don't eat meat? I didn't know! I think we may have some pasta salad in the fridge, although it might have ham in it. . . ."

"Really, it's okay." Wren rubbed his head uncomfortably, making his messy black hair stand up in peaks.

"Oh, I feel terrible," Mrs. Hastings said. Spencer rolled her eyes. When the whole family was together, her mom wanted all meals–even sloppy cereal breakfasts–to be perfect.

Mr. Hastings eyed Wren suspiciously. "I'm a steak man, myself."

"Absolutely." Wren lifted his glass so forcefully that a little wine spilled on the tablecloth.

Spencer was considering a good segue into her big announcement when her father laid down his fork.

"I've got a brilliant idea. Since we're all here, why don't we play Star Power?"

"Oh, Daddy." Melissa grinned. "No."

Her father smiled. "Oh yes. I had a terrific day at work. I'm going to kick your butt."

"What's Star Power?" Wren asked, his eyebrows arched.

A nervous glow grew in Spencer's stomach. Star Power was a game her parents had made up when Spencer and Melissa were little kids that she'd always suspected they'd pilfered from some company power-retreat. It was simple: Everyone shared their biggest achievement of the day, and the family would select one Star. It was supposed to make people feel proud and accomplished, but in the Hastings family, people just got ruthlessly competitive.

But if there was one perfect way for Spencer to announce her PSAT results, Star Power was it.

"You'll catch on, Wren," Mr. Hastings said. "I'll start. Today, I prepared a defense so compelling for my client, he actually offered to pay me *more* money."

"Impressive," her mother said, taking a tiny bite of a golden beet. "Now me. This morning, I beat Eloise at tennis in straight sets."

"Eloise is tough!" her father cried before taking another sip of wine. Spencer peeked at Wren across the table. He was carefully peeling the skin off his chicken thigh, so she couldn't catch his eye.

Her mother dabbed her mouth with her napkin. "Melissa?"

Melissa laced her stubby-nailed fingers together.

"Well, hmm. I helped the builders tile the entire bath-room—the only way it'd be perfect is if I did it myself."

"Good for you, dear!" her father said.

Spencer jiggled her legs nervously.

Mr. Hastings finished sipping his wine. "Wren?"

Wren looked up, startled. "Yes?"

"It's your turn."

Wren fiddled with his wineglass. "I don't know what I should say. . . . "

"We're playing Star Power," Mrs. Hastings chirped, as if Star Power were as common a game as Scrabble. "What wonderful thing did you, Mr. Doctor, achieve today?"

"Oh." Wren blinked. "Well. Um, nothing, really. It was my day off from school and the hospital, so I went down to the pub with some hospital friends and watched the Phillies game."

Silence. Melissa shot Wren a disappointed look.

"I think that's awesome," Spencer offered. "The way they've been playing, it's a feat to watch the Phillies all day."

"I know, they're kind of crap, aren't they?" Wren smiled at her gratefully.

"Well, anyway," her mother interrupted. "Melissa, when do you start class?"

"Wait a minute," Spencer piped up. They were *not* about to forget her! "I have something for Star Power."

Her mother's salad fork hung in the air. "I'm sorry."

"Oops!" her father agreed jocularly. "Go ahead, Spence."

"I got my PSAT results," she said. "And, well . . . here."
She pulled out the scores and shoved them at her father.

As soon as he took them, she knew what would happen. They wouldn't care. What did PSATs matter, anyway? They'd go back to their Beaujolais and to Melissa and Wharton and that would be that. Her cheeks felt hot. Why did she even bother?

Then her dad put down his wineglass and studied the paper. "Wow." He motioned Mrs. Hastings over. When she saw the paper, she gasped.

"You can't get much higher than this, can you?" Mrs. Hastings said.

Melissa craned her neck to look too. Spencer could hardly breathe. Melissa glared at her over the lilac and peony centerpiece. It was a look that made Spencer think that maybe Melissa *had* written that creepy e-mail yesterday. But when Spencer met her eye, Melissa broke into a smile. "You really studied, didn't you?"

"It's a good score, yeah?" Wren asked, glancing at the page.

"It's a fantastic score!" Mr. Hastings bellowed.

"This is wonderful!" cried Mrs. Hastings. "How would you like to celebrate, Spencer? Dinner in the city? Is there something you've had your eye on?"

"When I got my SAT scores, you got me a Fitzgerald first edition at that estate auction, remember?" Melissa beamed.

"That's right!" Mrs. Hastings trilled.

Melissa turned to Wren. "You would've loved it. It was so amazing to bid."

"Well, why don't you give it some thought." Mrs. Hastings said to Spencer. "Try to think of something memorable, like what we got for Melissa."

Spencer slowly sat up. "Actually, there is something that I have in mind."

"What's that?" Her father leaned forward in his chair.

Here goes, Spencer thought. "Well, what I'd really, really, *really* love, right now, not a few months from now, would be to move into the barn."

"But—," Melissa started, before stopping herself.

Wren cleared his throat. Her father furrowed his brow. Spencer's stomach made a loud, hungry growl. She covered it with her hand.

"Is that what you *really* want?" her mother asked.

"Uh-huh," Spencer answered.

"Okay," Mrs. Hastings said, looking at her husband. "Well . . . "

Melissa loudly laid down her fork. "But, um, what about Wren and me?"

"Well, you said yourself the renovations wouldn't take too long." Mrs. Hastings put her hand to her chin. "You guys could stay in your old bedroom, I suppose."

"But it has a twin bed," Melissa said in an uncharacteristically childish voice.

"I don't mind," Wren said quickly. Melissa scowled sharply at him.

"We could move the queen bed from the barn to Melissa's room and put Spencer's bed out there," Mr. Hastings suggested.

Spencer couldn't believe her ears. "You would do that?"

Mrs. Hastings raised her eyebrows. "Melissa, you can survive, can't you?"

Melissa pushed her hair back from her face. "I guess," she said. "I mean, I personally got much more out of the auction and the first edition, but that's just me."

Wren discreetly took a sip of his wine. When Spencer caught his eye, he winked. Mr. Hastings turned to Spencer. "Done, then."

Spencer jumped up and hugged her parents. "Thank you, thank you, thank you!"

Her mother beamed. "You should move in tomorrow."

"Spencer, you're certainly the Star." Her father held up her scores, now slightly stained with red wine. "We should frame this as a memento!"

Spencer grinned. She didn't need to frame anything. She'd remember this day for as long as she lived.

13

ACT ONE: GIRL MAKES BOY WANT HER

"Want to come with me to an artist reception at the Chester Springs studio next Monday night?" Aria's mother, Ella, asked.

It was Thursday morning, and Ella was sitting across from Aria at the breakfast table, doing the *New York Times* crossword puzzle with a leaky black pen and eating a bowl of Cheerios. She had just returned to her part-time job at the Davis contemporary art gallery on Rosewood's main drag, and she was on the mailing list for all the benefits.

"Isn't Dad going to go with you?" Aria asked.

Her mom pursed her lips together. "He has a lot of work to do for his classes."

"Oh." Aria picked at a loose strand of wool on the fingerless gloves she'd knitted during a long train ride to Greece. Was that suspicion she detected in her mom's voice? Aria always worried Ella would find out about Meredith and never forgive her for keeping the secret.

Aria squeezed her eyes closed. *You're not thinking about it*, she thought. She poured some grapefruit juice into a glass. "Ella?" she asked. "I need some love advice."

"Love advice?" her mother teased, securing her jet-black bun with a take-out chopstick that had been lying on the table.

"Yeah," Aria said. "I like this guy, but he's kind of . . . unattainable. I'm out of ideas on how to convince him he should like me."

"Be yourself!" Ella said.

Aria groaned. "I've tried that."

"Go out with an attainable boy, then!"

Aria rolled her eyes. "Are you going to help or not?"

"Ooh, someone's sensitive!" Ella smiled, then snapped her fingers. "I just read this study in the paper." She held up the *Times*. "It was a survey about what men find most attractive in women. You know what was the number-one thing? Intelligence. Here, let me find it for you. . . . " She rifled through the paper and handed the page to Aria.

"Aria likes a guy?" Mike swept into the kitchen and grabbed a glazed donut from the box on the island.

"No!" Aria quickly responded.

"Well, someone likes *you*," Mike said. "Gross as that is." He made a barfing sound.

"Who?" Ella asked in an excited voice.

"Noel Kahn," Mike answered, talking with a huge,

chewed-up bite of donut in his mouth. "He asked about you at lacrosse practice."

"Noel Kahn?" Ella echoed, looking back and forth from Mike to Aria. "Which one is he? Was he here three years ago? Do I know him?"

Aria groaned and rolled her eyes. "He's nobody."

"Nobody?" Mike sounded disgusted. "He's, like, the coolest guy in your grade."

"Whatever," Aria said, kissing her mother on the top of her head. She headed to the hallway, staring at the newspaper clipping in her hands. So men liked brains? Well, Icelandic Aria could certainly be brainy.

"Why don't you like Noel Kahn?" Mike's voice made Aria jump. He stood a few feet away from Aria with a carton of orange juice in his hand. "He's the man."

Aria groaned. "If you like him so much, why don't *you* go out with him?"

Mike drank straight from the carton, wiped his mouth, and stared at her. "You've been acting freaky. Are you high? Can I have some if you are?"

Aria snorted. In Iceland, Mike had been constantly trying to score drugs and freaked when some guys at the harbor sold him a dime bag of pot. The stuff turned out to be skunky, but Mike proudly smoked it anyway.

Mike started stroking his chin. "I think I know why you're acting freaky."

Aria turned back to the closet. "You're full of crap."

"You think so?" Mike answered. "I don't. And you

know what? I'm going to find out if my suspicions are true."

"Good luck, Sherlock." Aria pulled at her jacket. Even though she knew Mike was probably full of shit, she hoped he hadn't noticed the quiver in her voice.

As the other kids filed into English—most of the boys sporting a few days' growth of stubble and most of the girls in copycat Mona-and-Hanna platform sandals and charm bracelets—Aria reviewed her just-scrawled stack of note cards. Today, they had to give an oral report about a play called *Waiting for Godot*. Aria adored oral reports—she had the perfect, sexy, gravelly voice for them—and she happened to know the play really well. Once, she'd spent a whole Sunday in a Reykjavík bar, vehemently arguing with an Adrien Brody look-alike about its theme . . . between swilling delicious apple vodka martinis and playing footsie with him under the table, that is. So not only was this an excellent day to become über student, it was also a great opportunity to show everyone how cool Icelandic Aria was.

Ezra strolled in, looking rumpled, bookish, and completely edible, and clapped his hands. "Okay, class," he said. "We have a lot of stuff to get through today. Quiet down."

Hanna Marin turned around and smirked at Aria. "What kind of underwear do you think he's wearing?"

Aria smiled blandly—striped cotton boxers, of course— but snapped her attention back to Ezra.

"All right." Ezra walked to the chalkboard. "Everyone did the reading, right? Everyone has a report? Who wants to go first?"

Aria's hand shot up. Ezra nodded at her. She walked to the podium at the front of the room, arranged her black hair around her shoulders so that it looked extra gorgeous, and made sure that her chunky coral necklace wasn't caught in the collar of her shirt. Quickly, she reread the first few scene-setting sentences on her index cards.

"Last year, I attended a performance of *Waiting for Godot* in Paris," she began.

She noticed Ezra raise his eyebrow just the tiniest bit.

"It was a small theater off the Seine, and the air smelled like the cheese brioche baking next door." She paused. "Picture the scene: a huge line of people waiting to go in, a woman toting her two little white poodles, the Eiffel Tower in the distance."

She briefly looked up. Everyone seemed so transfixed! "I could feel the energy, the excitement, the *passion* in the air. And it wasn't just the beer they were selling to *everyone*—even my little brother," she added.

"Nice!" Noel Kahn interjected.

Aria smiled. "The seats were very velvety and purple, and smelled like this type of butter in France that's sweeter than American butter. It's what makes the pastries so delicious."

"Aria," Ezra said.

"It's the kind of butter that even makes *escargot* taste good!"

"Aria!"

Aria stopped. Ezra leaned against the chalkboard with his arms crossed over his Rosewood blazer. "Yes?" She smiled.

"I have to stop you."

"But . . . I'm not even halfway done!"

"Well, I need less about velvet seats and pastries and more about the play itself."

The class snickered. Aria shuffled back to her seat and sat down. Didn't he know she was creating *ambiance*?

Noel Kahn raised his hand.

"Noel?" Ezra asked. "You want to go next?"

"No," Noel said. The class laughed. "I just wanted to say I thought Aria's report was good. I liked it."

"Thanks," Aria said quietly.

Noel swiveled around. "Is there really no drinking age?"

"Not really."

"I might go with my family to Italy this winter."

"Italy's amazing. You're going to love it."

"Are you two through?" Ezra asked. He shot Noel an exasperated look. Aria dug her hot-pink nails into the wood grain of her desk.

Noel turned back to her again. "Did they have absinthe?" he whispered.

She nodded, amazed Noel had even heard of absinthe.

"Mr. Kahn," Ezra interrupted sternly. A little too sternly. "That's enough."

Was this *jealousy* she detected?

"Damn," Hanna twisted around. "What crawled up his ass?"

Aria stifled a giggle. It seemed to her like a certain über student was making a certain teacher a little twitchy.

Ezra called on Devon Arliss next and she started her speech. As Ezra turned to the side and put his finger on his chin, listening, Aria throbbed. She wanted him so badly it made her whole body buzz.

No, wait. That was just her cell phone, which was nestled in her oversize lime-green tote next to her foot.

The thing kept buzzing. Aria slowly reached down and pulled it out. One new text message:

Aria,

Maybe he fools around with students all the time. A lot of teachers do. . . . Just ask your dad! —A

Aria quickly snapped her cell phone shut. But then she opened it and read the message again. And again. As she did, the little hairs on her arms stood straight up.

No one in the room had their phones out—not Hanna, not Noel, nobody. And no one was looking at her, either. She even looked up on the ceiling and out the classroom door, but nothing seemed out of place.

Everything was quiet and still.

"This can't be happening," Aria whispered.

The only person who knew about Aria's dad was . . . Alison. And she'd sworn *on her grave* she wouldn't tell a soul. Was she *back*?

14

THAT'LL TEACH YOU TO
GOOGLE-STALK WHEN YOU'RE
SUPPOSED TO BE STUDYING

During her free period Thursday afternoon, Spencer strode into the Rosewood Day reading room. With its ceiling-high stacks of reference books, giant pedestal globe in the corner, and stained-glass window on the far wall, it was her favorite place on campus. She stood in the middle of the empty room, closed her eyes, and inhaled the old, leather-bound book smell.

Everything had gone her way today: The unusual cold snap had allowed her to wear her brand-new Marc Jacobs pale blue wool coat, the Rosewood Day café barista had made her a perfect double skim latte, she'd just aced a French oral exam, and tonight she would be moving into the barn, while Melissa had to sleep in her old, cramped bedroom.

Despite all that, an uneasy haze hung over her. It was a cross between a bothersome feeling she sometimes had when she'd forgotten to do something and the sense that someone was . . . well, watching her. It was obvious why she was feeling so off: that creepy "covet" e-mail. The flash of blond hair in Ali's old window. The fact that only Ali knew about Ian . . .

Trying to shake it off, she sat down at the computer, adjusted the waistband of her navy blue Wolford patterned stockings, and logged on to the Internet. She began research for her upcoming AP bio project, but after scrolling through a list of Google results, she typed, *Wren Kim,* into the search engine.

Trolling through the results, she stifled a giggle. On a site called *Mill Hill School, London,* there was a photo of a longer-haired Wren standing next to a Bunsen burner and a bunch of test tubes. Another link was to Oxford University's Corpus Christi College student portal; there was a photo of Wren looking gorgeous in Shakespearean garb, holding a skull. She hadn't known Wren was into drama. As she tried to magnify the photo to check out the fit of his tights, someone tapped her on the shoulder.

"That your boyfriend?"

Spencer jumped, knocking her crystal-studded Sidekick cell phone to the floor. Andrew Campbell grinned awkwardly behind her.

She quickly closed the window. "Of course not!"

Andrew bent down to pick up her Sidekick, pushing a lock of straight, shoulder-length hair out of his eyes. Spencer noticed that he might actually have a chance at being cute if he cut off that lion's mane.

"Oops," he said, handing the Sidekick back to her. "I think a jewel thing fell off."

Spencer grabbed it from him. "You scared me."

"Sorry about that." Andrew smiled. "So your boyfriend's an actor?"

"I said he wasn't my boyfriend!"

Andrew stepped back. "Sorry. Just making conversation."

Spencer eyed him suspiciously.

"Anyway," Andrew went on, hefting his North Face backpack higher on his shoulder. "I was wondering. You going to Noel's tomorrow? I could give you a ride."

Spencer looked at him blankly and then remembered: Noel Kahn's field party. She'd gone to last year's. Kids did beer funnels, and practically every girl cheated on her boyfriend. This year would be more of the same. And what—Andrew seriously thought she'd ride with him in his Mini? Would they both even *fit*? "Doubt it," she said.

Andrew's face fell. "Yeah, I guess you're probably kind of busy."

Spencer furrowed her brow. "What's that supposed to mean?"

Andrew shrugged. "You seem to have a lot going on. Your sister's home, right?"

Spencer leaned back in her chair and drew her bottom lip into her mouth. "Yeah, she just got home last night. How'd you know tha—"

She stopped. Wait a *second*. Andrew drove his Mini up

and down her street all the time. She'd seen him just yesterday, when she was at the mailbox getting her test scores. . . .

She swallowed hard. Now that she thought about it, she might have seen his black Mini drive by the day she and Wren were in the hot tub together. He must've been driving it up and down her street a lot to notice Melissa was home. What if . . . what if *Andrew* was the one skulking around spying on her? What if Andrew wrote that creepy "covet" e-mail? Andrew was so competitive it seemed possible. Wouldn't sending threatening messages be a good way to throw someone off her game and make it easier to be reelected as next year's class president . . . or, *even better,* beat out his competition for valedictorian? And the long hair! Maybe she'd seen *him* in Ali's old window?

Unbelievable! Spencer stared at Andrew incredulously.

"Is something wrong?" Andrew asked, looking concerned.

"I have to go." She gathered up her books and walked out of the reading room.

"Wait," Andrew called.

Spencer kept going. But as she pushed through the library doors, she realized that she didn't feel enraged. Sure, it was bizarre that Andrew was spying on her, but if Andrew was A, Spencer was safe. Whatever Andrew *thought* he had on her, it was nothing . . . *nothing* . . . compared to what Alison knew.

She reached the door to the commons—coming in at the same time was Emily Fields.

"Hey," Emily said. A nervous look crossed her face.

"Hey," Spencer answered.

Emily readjusted her Nike backpack. Spencer pushed her bangs off her face. When was the last time she'd spoken to Emily?

"It got cold out, huh?" Emily asked.

Spencer nodded. "Yeah."

Emily smiled in that I-don't-know-what-to-say-to-you way. Then Tracey Reid, another swimmer, grabbed Emily's arm. "When is our swimsuit money due?" she asked.

As Emily answered, Spencer wiped some nonexistent dirt off her blazer and wondered if she could just walk away or if she had to say a formal good-bye. Then something on Emily's wrist caught her eye. Emily was still wearing her blue string bracelet from sixth grade. Alison had made them for everyone right after the accident—The Jenna Thing—happened.

Initially, they'd just wanted to get Jenna's brother, Toby; it was supposed to be a prank. After the five of them planned it, Ali went across the street to watch through Toby's tree house window, and then when it happened, it did something . . . *horrible* . . . to Jenna.

After the ambulance pulled away from Jenna's house, Spencer discovered something about the accident none of the other girls ever found out: Toby saw Ali, but Ali saw Toby doing something *just as bad*. He couldn't tell on her, because then she'd tell on *him*.

Not long after, Ali made everyone the bracelets to remind them they were best friends *forever* and now that they shared a secret like this, they had to protect one another *forever*. Spencer waited for Ali to tell the others that someone saw her, but she never did.

When the cops questioned Spencer after Ali went missing, they asked if Ali had any enemies, anyone who hated her so much they might want to hurt her. Spencer said that Ali was a popular girl, and like any popular girl, there were some girls who didn't like her, but it was just jealousy.

That, of course, was a bold-faced lie. There *were* people who hated Ali, and Spencer knew she should tell the police what Ali told her about The Jenna Thing . . . that maybe Toby wanted to hurt Ali . . . but how could she tell them that without telling them *why*? Spencer couldn't get through a day without passing Toby and Jenna's house on her street. But they'd been sent away to boarding school and hardly ever came home, so she thought their secret was safe. They were safe from Toby. And Spencer was safe from ever having to tell her best friends what she alone knew.

As Tracey Reid said good-bye, Emily turned around. She seemed surprised Spencer was still standing there. "I've got to get to class," she said. "Good to see you, though."

"'Bye," Spencer answered, and she and Emily exchanged one last awkward smile.

15

INSULTING HIS MASCULINITY
IS SUCH A DEAL BREAKER

"You guys are looking lazy. I want to see better form!"
Coach Lauren yelled at them from the deck.

On Thursday afternoon, Emily bobbed with the
other swimmers in the crystal blue water of Rosewood's
Anderson Memorial Natatorium, listening to their youngish, former-Olympian coach, Lauren Kinkaid, scream at
them. The pool was twenty-five yards wide, fifty yards
long, with a small diving well. Huge skylights mirrored
the length of the pool, so when you did backstrokes in the
evening, you could look up and see the stars.

Emily held on to the wall and pulled her cap over her
ears. Okay, better form. She needed to really concentrate
today.

Last night, after getting back from the creek with
Maya, she'd lain on her bed for a long time, flip-flopping
from feeling warm and happy about the fun she and

Maya had had . . . to feeling uneasy and antsy about Maya's confession. *I'm not sure I like guys. I think I'd like someone more like me.* Did Maya mean what Emily thought she meant?

Thinking about how giddy Maya had been at the waterfall—not to mention how much they'd tickled and touched each other—Emily felt nervous. After getting home last night, she'd rifled through her swimming bag for that note from A from the day before. She read it over and over again, picking apart every word until her eyes blurred.

By dinnertime, Emily decided she needed to throw herself back into swimming. No more skipped practices. No more slacking. From now on, she'd be the model swimmer girl.

Ben paddled over to her and put his hands on the wall. "I missed you yesterday."

"Mmmm." She should make a new start with Ben, too. With his freckles, piercing blue eyes, slightly stubbly jaw, and beautifully chiseled swimmer's body, he was hot, right? She tried to imagine Ben jumping off the Marwyn trail bridge. Would he laugh or think it was immature?

"So where were you?" Ben asked, blowing on his goggles to defog them.

"Tutoring for Spanish."

"Wanna come over to my house after practice? My parents won't be home till eight."

"I . . . I'm not sure if I can." Emily pushed away from

the wall and started to tread water. She stared down at her blurrily pumping legs and feet.

"Why not?" Ben pushed off the wall to join her.

"Because . . . " She couldn't come up with an excuse.

"You know you want to," Ben whispered. He took some water into his hands and began splashing her. Maya had done the same thing yesterday, but this time Emily jerked away.

Ben stopped splashing. "What?"

"Don't."

Ben put his hands around her waist. "No? You don't like to get splashed?" he asked in a baby voice.

She took his hands off her. *"Don't."*

He backed away. "Fine."

Sighing, Emily floated over to the other side of the lane. She liked Ben, she really did. Maybe she *should* just go over to Ben's after swimming. They'd watch TiVo'ed episodes of *American Chopper*, eat pizza delivered from DiSilvio's, and he'd feel underneath her unsexy sports bra. Suddenly tears sprang to her eyes. She really didn't want to sit on Ben's itchy blue basement couch, picking oregano spices out of her teeth and rolling her tongue around the inside of his mouth. She just *didn't*.

She wasn't the kind of girl who could fake things. But did that mean she wanted to break up? It was hard to make up your mind about a boy when he was right in your swimming lane, four feet away.

Her sister Carolyn, who was practicing in the lane

next to her, tapped Emily on the shoulder. "Everything all right?"

"Yeah," Emily mumbled, grabbing a blue kickboard.

"Okay." Carolyn looked as if she wanted to say more. After her trip with Maya to the creek yesterday, Emily had skidded the Volvo into the parking lot just in time to see Carolyn exiting the natatorium's double doors. When Carolyn asked where Emily had been, Emily had told her she had to tutor for Spanish. It seemed like Carolyn believed her, despite Emily's damp hair and the funny ticky noise the car was making—something it did only when it was cooling down from a drive.

Even though the sisters looked alike—both had broad freckles over their noses, chlorine-bleached reddish brown hair, and had to wear a lot of Maybelline Great Lash to lengthen their stubby lashes—and even though they shared a room, they weren't close. Carolyn was a quiet, demure, and obedient girl, and although Emily was all those things too, Carolyn seemed really satisfied to be that way.

Coach Lauren blew the whistle. "Kicking time! Line up!"

The swimmers lined up from fastest to slowest, kickboards in front of them. Ben was in front of Emily. He looked at her and raised an eyebrow.

"I can't come over tonight," she said quietly, so the other boy swimmers—who were crowded around behind her and laughing at Gemma Curran's fake tan gone wrong—couldn't hear. "Sorry."

Ben's mouth flattened into a straight line. "Yeah. As

if *that's* a surprise." Then, as Lauren blew the whistle, he pushed off the wall and began dolphin-kicking. Uneasy, Emily waited until Lauren blew the whistle again, and pushed off behind him.

As she swam, Emily stared at Ben's pumping legs. It was so dorky how he wore a cap over his already-short hair. He got so OCD before races, too, shaving off every hair on his body, including the ones on his arms and legs. Now, his feet made exaggeratedly huge splashes, which sprayed right into Emily's face. She glared at his head bobbing in front of her and pumped her legs harder.

Even though she'd left five seconds behind him, Emily reached the opposite wall at almost the same time Ben did. He turned to her, pissed. Swim team etiquette dictated that no matter how big a swimming star you were, if someone caught your feet on a set, you let them go ahead of you. But Ben just pushed back off the wall.

"Ben!" Emily called, the irritation in her voice showing.

He stood up in the shallow end and turned around. "What?"

"Let me go in front of you."

Ben rolled his eyes and ducked back underwater.

Emily shoved off the wall and kicked crazily until she caught up to him. He reached the wall and turned to face her.

"Would you stay off my ass?" he practically yelled.

Emily burst out laughing. "You're supposed to let me go!"

"Maybe if you didn't leave right on top of me you wouldn't *be* on top of me."

She snorted. "I can't help it if I'm faster than you."

Ben's mouth fell open. Oops.

Emily licked her lips. "Ben . . . "

"No." He held up his hand. "Just go swim really fast, okay?" He tossed his goggles onto the deck. They bounced awkwardly and landed back in the water, narrowly missing Gemma's fake-tanned shoulder.

"Ben . . . "

He glared at her, then turned and got out of the pool. "Whatever."

Emily watched him angrily push open the boys' locker room door.

She shook her head, watching the door slowly swing back and forth. Then she remembered the thing Maya said yesterday.

"Fuck a moose," she tried out quietly, and smiled.

16

NEVER TRUST AN INVITE
WITHOUT A RETURN ADDRESS

"So are you coming over tonight?" Hanna switched her BlackBerry to her other ear and waited for Sean's answer.

It was Thursday after school. She and Mona had just met for a quick cappuccino on campus, but Mona had to leave early to practice her drive for the mother/daughter golf tournament she was competing in this weekend. Now, Hanna sat on her front porch, talking to Sean and watching the six-year-old twins next door draw surprisingly anatomically correct naked boys in chalk all over their driveway.

"I can't," Sean answered. "I'm really sorry."

"But Thursday is *Nerve* night; you know that!"

Hanna and Sean were hooked on this reality show *Nerve*, which documented the lives of four couples who'd met online. Tonight's episode was extremely important, because their favorite two characters, Nate and Fiona, were about to do it. Hanna thought it might at least start a conversation.

"I . . . I have a meeting tonight."

"A meeting for what?"

"Um . . . V Club."

Hanna's mouth fell open. *V Club?* As in *Virginity Club?* "Can you skip it?"

He was quiet for a minute. "I can't."

"Well, are you at least coming to Noel's tomorrow?"

Another pause. "I don't know."

"Sean! You have to!" Her voice squeaked.

"All right," he answered. "I guess Noel would be kinda pissed if I didn't."

"*I* would be pissed too," Hanna added.

"I know. See you tomorrow."

"Sean, wait–" Hanna started. But he'd already hung up.

Hanna unlocked her house. Sean *had* to come to the party tomorrow. She'd hatched a foolproof, romantic plan: She'd take him to Noel's woods, they'd confess their love for each other, and then they'd have sex. V Club couldn't argue with having sex if you were in love, could it? Besides, the Kahn woods were legendary. They were known as the Manhood Woods, because so many guys at so many Kahn parties had lost their virginity there. It was rumored that the trees whispered sex secrets to new recruits.

She stopped at the mirror in the hallway and pulled

up her shirt to examine her taut stomach muscles. She swiveled sideways to investigate her small, round butt. Then she bent forward to look at her skin. Yesterday's blotchiness was gone. She bared her teeth. One bottom front tooth crossed over a canine. Had they always been that way?

She threw her thick-strapped, gold leather handbag onto the kitchen table and opened the freezer. Her mom didn't buy Ben & Jerry's, so Tofutti Cutie 50-percent-less sugar faux ice-cream sandwiches would have to do. She took out three and began to greedily unwrap the first one. As she took a bite, she felt that familiar tug to eat more.

"Here, Hanna, have another profiterole," Ali had whispered to her that day they visited her dad in Annapolis. Then Ali turned to Kate, her dad's girlfriend's daughter, and said, "Hanna's so lucky—she can eat anything and not gain an ounce!"

It wasn't true, of course. That's what made it so mean. Hanna was already chubby and seemed to be getting more so. Kate giggled, and Ali—who was supposed to be on Hanna's side—laughed too.

"I got you something."

Hanna jumped. Her mom sat at the little telephone table in a hot pink Champion sports bra and black flared-leg yoga pants. "Oh," Hanna said quietly.

Ms. Marin appraised Hanna, her eyes settling on the ice-cream sandwiches in her hands. "Do you really need *three*?"

Hanna looked down. She'd chomped through one sandwich in less than ten seconds, hardly even tasting it, and had already unwrapped the next.

She smiled faintly at her mom and quickly stuffed the remaining Cuties back into the freezer. When she turned back around, her mother set a little blue Tiffany bag on the table. Hanna looked at it questioningly. *"This?"*

"Open it."

Inside was a little blue Tiffany box, and inside that was the complete Tiffany toggle set—the charm bracelet, round silver earrings, plus the necklace. The very same kind she'd had to hand over to the Tiffany's woman at the police station. Hanna held them up, letting them sparkle in the overhead light. "Wow."

Ms. Marin shrugged. "You're welcome." Then, to signify that the conversation was finished, she retreated to the den, unrolled her purple yoga mat, and turned on her Power Yoga DVD.

Hanna slowly slid the earrings back in the bag, confused. Her mom was so *weird*. That was when she noticed a creamy, square card envelope sitting on the little telephone table. Hanna's name and address were typewritten in all caps. She smiled. An invite to a sweet party was just the thing she needed to cheer up.

Breathe in through your nose, out through your mouth, the soothing yogi instructed from the TV in the den. Ms. Marin stood with her arms placidly by her sides. She didn't even move when her BlackBerry started singing

Flight of the Bumblebee, which meant she had an e-mail. This was her Me time.

Hanna grabbed the envelope and climbed upstairs to her room. She sat down on her four-poster bed, felt the edges of her billion-thread-count sheets, and smiled at Dot, sleeping peacefully on his doggie bed.

"Come here, Dot," she whispered. He stretched and sleepily climbed into her arms. Hanna sighed. Maybe she just had PMS, and these jittery, uneasy, the-world-is-caving-in feelings would go away in a few days.

She sliced the envelope open with her fingernail and frowned. It wasn't an invitation, and the note didn't really make sense.

Hanna,
Even Daddy doesn't love you best! —A

What was that supposed to mean? But when she unfolded the accompanying page stuffed inside the envelope, she yelped.

It was a color printout from a private school's online newsletter. Hanna looked at the familiar people in the photo. The caption said, *Kate Randall was Barnbury School's student speaker at the benefit. Pictured here with her mother, Isabel Randall, and Ms. Randall's fiancé, Tom Marin.*

Hanna blinked quickly. Her father looked the same as when she'd last seen him. And although her heart stopped when she read the word *fiancé*–when had *that* happened?—it was the image of Kate that made her skin itch. Kate looked more perfect than ever. Her skin was glowing and her hair was perfect. She had her arms gleefully wrapped around her mom and Mr. Marin.

Hanna would never forget the moment she first saw Kate. Ali and Hanna had just gotten off Amtrak in Annapolis, and at first Hanna saw only her dad leaning up against the hood of his car. But then the car door opened, and Kate stepped out. Her long chestnut hair was straight and shiny, and she held herself like the kind of girl who'd taken ballet since she was two. Hanna's first instinct was to crouch behind a pole. She looked at her snug jeans and stretched-out cashmere sweater and tried not to hyperventilate. *This was why Dad left,* she thought. *He wanted a daughter who wouldn't embarrass him.*

"Oh my God," Hanna whispered, searching the envelope for a return address. Nothing. Something occurred to her. The only person who really knew about Kate was Alison. Her eyes moved to the *A* on the note.

The Tofutti Cutie burbled in her stomach. She ran for the bathroom and grabbed the extra toothbrush in the ceramic cup next to the sink. Then she knelt down over the toilet and waited. Tears dotted the corners of her eyes. *Don't start this again,* she told herself, gripping the toothbrush hard by her side. *You're better than this.*

Hanna stood up and stared in the mirror. Her face was flushed, her hair was strewn around her face, and her eyes were red and puffy. Slowly, she put the toothbrush back in the cup.

"I'm Hanna and I'm fabulous," she said to her reflection.

But it didn't sound convincing. Not at all.

17

DUCK, DUCK, GOOSE!

"Okay." Aria blew her long bangs out of her eyes. "In this scene, you have to wear this colander on your head and talk a lot about a baby we don't have."

Noel frowned and brought his thumb to his pink, bow-shaped lips. "Why do I have to wear a colander on my head, Finland?"

"Because," Aria answered. "It's an absurdist play. It's supposed to be, like, absurd."

"Gotcha." Noel grinned. It was Friday morning, and they were sitting on desks in English class. After yesterday's *Waiting for Godot* disaster, Ezra's next assignment had been for them to break up into groups and write their own existentialist plays. *Existentialist* was another way of saying, "silly and out there." And if anyone could do silly and out there, it was Aria.

"I know something really absurd we could do," Noel said. "We could have this character drive a Navigator and, like, after a couple of beers, crash it into his duck pond. But he's, like, fallen asleep at the wheel, so he doesn't notice he's in the duck pond until the next day. There could be ducks in the Navigator."

Aria frowned. "How could we stage all that? It sounds impossible."

"I don't know." Noel shrugged. "But that happened to me last year. And it was really absurd. And awesome."

Aria sighed. She hadn't exactly chosen Noel to be her partner because she thought he'd be a good cowriter. She looked around for Ezra, but he unfortunately wasn't watching them in fitful jealousy. "How about if we make one of the characters *think* he's a duck?" she suggested. "He could randomly quack."

"Um, sure." Noel wrote that down on a piece of lined paper with a gnawed-up Montblanc pen. "Hey, maybe we could shoot this with my dad's Canon DV camera? And have this as a movie instead of a boring play?"

Aria paused. "Actually, that would be kind of cool."

Noel smiled. "Then we could keep the Navigator scene!"

"I guess." Aria wondered if the Kahns really had a spare Navigator to crash. Probably.

Noel nudged Mason Byers, who was paired up with James Freed. "Dude. We're going to have a Navigator in our play! And pyrotechnics!"

"Wait. Pyrotechnics?" Aria asked.

"Nice!" Mason said.

Aria clamped her lips shut. Honestly, she didn't have the energy for this. Last night, she hardly slept. Plagued by yesterday's cryptic text message, she'd spent half the night thinking and furiously knitting a purple hat with earflaps.

It was awful to think that someone knew not only about her and Ezra, but also about that stuff with her dad. What if this A person sent her mom messages next? What if A already had? Aria didn't want her mom to find out—not now, and not that way.

Aria also couldn't shake the idea that the A message might actually be from *Alison*. There just weren't that many people who knew. A few faculty members maybe, and Meredith knew, obviously. But they didn't know Aria.

If the text was from Alison, that meant she was alive. Or . . . *not*. What if the texts were from Ali's ghost? A ghost could have easily slid between the cracks of the women's bathroom at Snooker's. And spirits from the dead sometimes contacted the living to make amends, right? It was like their final homework assignment before graduating to heaven.

If Ali needed to make amends, though, Aria could think of a more deserving candidate than her. Try Jenna. Aria put her hands over her eyes, blocking out the memory. Screw therapy that said you should face your demons: She tried to block out The Jenna Thing as much as she tried to block out her dad and Meredith.

Aria sighed. At times like this, she wished she hadn't drifted from her old friends. Like Hanna, a few desks over—if only Aria could walk up to Hanna and talk to her about this, ask her questions about Ali. But time really changed people. She wondered if it would be easier to talk to Spencer or Emily instead.

"Hey there."

Aria straightened up. Ezra was standing in front of her desk. "Hi," she squeaked.

She met his blue eyes and her heart ached.

Ezra tilted his hips awkwardly. "How are you?"

"Um, I'm . . . great. Really awesome." She sat up straight. On the plane back from Iceland, Aria had read in a *Seventeen* she found in her seat pocket that boys liked enthusiastic, positive girls. And since brilliant hadn't worked yesterday, why not try out peppy?

Ezra clicked and unclicked his Bic pen. "Listen, sorry to cut you off yesterday in the middle of your speech. Do you want to give me your index cards so I can take a look at them and grade you?"

"Okay." Huh. Would Ezra do that for the other students? "So . . . how are you?"

"Good." Ezra smiled. His lips twitched as if he wanted to say more. "What're you working on, there?" He placed his hands on her desk and leaned over to look at her notebook. Aria stared at his hands for a moment, then slid her pinkie finger up against his. She tried to make it look like an accident, but he didn't pull away. It felt like electricity was surging between their two pinkies.

"Mr. Fitz!" Devon Arliss's hand shot up in the back row. "I have a question."

"Be right there," Ezra said, straightening up.

Aria put the pinkie finger that had touched Ezra's into her mouth. She watched him for a few seconds, thinking he might come back to her, but he didn't.

Well then. Back to plan J, for *Jealous*. She turned to Noel. "I think our movie should have a sex scene in it."

She said it really loud, but Ezra was still bent over Devon's desk.

"Awesome," Noel said. "Does the guy who thinks he's a duck get some?"

"Yep. With a woman who kisses like a goose."

Noel laughed. "How does a goose kiss?"

Aria turned toward Devon's desk. Ezra was facing them now. Good.

"Like this." She leaned over and smacked Noel on the cheek with her lips. Surprisingly, Noel smelled pretty good. Like Kiehl's Blue Eagle shaving cream.

"Nice," Noel whispered.

The rest of the class burbled with activity, unaware of any goose kissing, but Ezra, still next to Devon's desk, stood absolutely still.

"So did you know I'm having a party tonight?" Noel put his hand on Aria's knee.

"Yeah, I heard something about that."

"You should totally come. We're going to have a lot of beer. And other things . . . like Scotch. Do you like Scotch? My dad has a collection, so . . . "

"I love Scotch." Aria felt Ezra's eyes burning into her back. Then she leaned over to Noel, and said: "I'll totally come to your party tonight."

By the way his pen fell out of his hand and clattered to the ground, it wasn't hard to guess whether or not Ezra had heard them.

18

WHERE'S OUR OLD EMILY AND WHAT HAVE YOU DONE WITH HER?

"Are you going to the Kahn party later?" Carolyn asked, steering the car into the Fieldses' driveway.

Emily ran a comb through her still-wet hair. "I don't know." Today at practice, she and Ben hadn't said two words to each other, so she wasn't exactly sure about going with him. "Are you?"

"I don't know. Topher and I might just go to Applebee's instead."

Of course Carolyn would have a hard time deciding between a Friday night field party and Applebee's.

They slammed the doors of the Volvo and walked up the stone path to the Fieldses' thirty-year-old colonial-style house. It wasn't nearly as big or flashy as most of the houses in Rosewood. The blue-painted shingles were chipping a little and some of the stones in the front path had disappeared. The deck furniture looked kind of outdated.

Their mother greeted them at the front door, holding the cordless phone. "Emily, I need to speak with you."

Emily glanced at Carolyn, who ducked her head and ran upstairs. Uh-oh. "What's up?"

Her mom smoothed her hands over her gray pleated slacks. "I was on the phone with Coach Lauren. She said your head seems to be somewhere else, not focused on swimming. And . . . you missed practice on Wednesday."

Emily swallowed hard. "I was tutoring some kids in Spanish."

"That's what Carolyn told me. So I called Ms. Hernandez."

Emily stared down at her green Vans. Ms. Hernandez was the Spanish teacher in charge of tutoring.

"Don't lie to me, Emily." Mrs. Fields frowned. "Where were you?"

Emily walked into the kitchen and slumped into a chair. Her mom was a rational person. They could discuss this.

She fiddled with the silver loop at the top of her ear. Years ago, Ali had asked Emily to come to the Piercing Palace with her when she got her belly button pierced, and they'd ended up getting matching piercings at the top of their ears, too. Emily still wore the same little silver hoop. Afterward, Ali bought Emily a pair of leopard-print earmuffs to hide the evidence. Emily still wore those earmuffs on the coldest days in the winter.

"Look," she finally said. "I was just hanging out with that new girl, Maya. She's really nice. We're friends."

Her mother looked confused. "Why didn't you just do something after practice, or on Saturday?"

"I don't see why it's such a big deal," Emily said. "I missed one day. I'll swim a double this weekend—I promise."

Her mother pursed her thin lips in a straight line and sat down. "But Emily . . . I just don't understand. When you signed up for swimming this year, you made a commitment. You can't go running off with friends if you're supposed to be swimming."

Emily stopped her. "*Signed up* for swimming? Like I had a choice?"

"What's going on with you? You're using a strange tone of voice; you're lying about where you've been." Her mother shook her head. "What's with this lying? You've never lied before."

"*Mom . . .* " Emily paused, feeling very tired. She wanted to point out that yes, she *had* lied, plenty. Even though she'd been the good girl of her seventh-grade friends, she'd done all kinds of stuff her mom never knew about.

Right after Ali went missing, Emily worried that Ali's disappearance was somehow . . . cosmically . . . her fault—as punishment, maybe, for how Emily had secretly disobeyed her parents. For getting that piercing. For The Jenna Thing. Since then, she'd tried to be perfect, to do everything her parents asked. She'd made herself into this model daughter, inside and out.

"I just like to know what's going on with you," her mother said.

Emily laid her hands on the place mat, remembering how she'd become this version of herself that wasn't *really* her. Ali wasn't gone because Emily had disobeyed her parents—she realized that now. And the same way she couldn't imagine sitting on Ben's itchy couch, feeling his slimy tongue on her neck, she also couldn't see herself spending the next two years of high school—and then the next four years of college—in a pool for hours every day. Why couldn't Emily just be . . . Emily? Couldn't her time be better served studying or—God forbid—having some fun?

"If you want to know what's going on with me," Emily started, pushing her hair out of her face. She took a deep breath. "I don't think I want to swim anymore."

Mrs. Fields's right eye twitched. Her lips parted slightly. Then she spun around to face the fridge, staring at all the chicken magnets on the freezer. She didn't speak, but her shoulders shook. Finally, she turned. Her eyes were slightly red, and her face looked saggy, as if she'd aged ten years in just a few moments. "I'm calling your father. He'll talk some sense into you."

"I've already made up my mind." As she said it, she realized she had.

"No you haven't. You don't know what's best for you."

"Mom!" Emily suddenly felt tears fill her eyes. It was scary and sad to have her mother angry with her. But now that she'd made the decision, she felt like she'd finally been allowed to take off a big goose down jacket in the middle of a heat wave.

Her mom's mouth trembled. "Is it because of that new friend of yours?"

Emily cringed and wiped her nose. "What? Who?"

Mrs. Fields sighed. "That girl who moved into the DiLaurentis house. She was the one you skipped practice to spend time with, right? What were you two doing?"

"We . . . we just went to the trail," Emily whispered. "And talked."

Her mother looked down. "I don't have a good feeling about girls . . . like that."

Wait. What? Emily stared at her mother. She . . . *knew*? But how? Her mom hadn't even met Maya. Unless you could look at her and just *know*?

"But Maya's really nice," Emily managed. "I forgot to tell you, but she said the brownies were great. She said thank you."

Her mother pinched her lips together. "I went over there. I was trying to be neighborly. But this . . . this is too much. She's not a good influence for you."

"I don't—"

"Please, Emily," her mom interrupted.

Emily's words stuck in her throat.

Her mom sighed. "There are just so many cultural differences with . . . her . . . and I just don't understand what you and Maya have in common, anyway. And who knows about her family? Who knows what they could be into?"

"Wait, *what*?" Emily stared at her mother. Maya's *family*? As far as Emily knew, Maya's father was a civic engineer and her mom worked as a nurse practitioner. Her brother was a senior at Rosewood and a tennis prodigy; they were building a tennis court for him in the backyard. What did her family have to do with anything?

"I just don't trust those people," her mother said. "I know that sounds really narrow-minded, but I don't."

Emily's mind screeched to a halt. *Her family. Cultural differences. Those people?* She went over everything her mother just said. Oh. My. God.

Mrs. Fields wasn't upset because she thought Maya was gay. She was upset because Maya—and the rest of her family—were *black*.

19

SPICY HOT

Friday evening, Spencer lay on her maple four-poster bed in the middle of her brand-new converted barn bedroom with Icy Hot slathered on her lower back, staring at the gorgeous beamed ceiling. You'd never guess that fifty years ago, cows slept in this barn. The room was huge, with four gigantic windows and a little patio. After dinner last night, she'd moved all of her boxes and furniture there. She'd organized all of her books and CDs according to author and artist, set up her surround-sound, and even reset TiVo to her preferences, including her brand-new favorite programs on BBC America. It was perfect.

Except, of course, for her throbbing back. Her body ached as if she'd gone bungee jumping without a ripcord. Ian had made them run three miles—at a sprint—followed by practice drills. All the girls had been talking about what they were wearing to Noel's party tonight, but after the hellish practice, Spencer was just as happy to stay home with some calc homework. Especially since home was now her very own little barn utopia.

Spencer reached for the jar of Icy Hot and realized it was empty. She sat up slowly, and put her hand on her back like an old woman. She'd just have to get some more from the main house. Spencer just *loved* that she could now call it *the main house*. It felt terribly grown up.

As she crossed her long, hilly lawn, she let her mind return to one of her favorite topics *du jour,* Andrew Campbell. Yes, it was a relief that A was Andrew and not Ali, and yes, she felt a billion times better and a zillion times less paranoid since yesterday, but still—what a horrible, meddling spy! How dare he ask such intrusive, gossipy questions in the reading room and write her a creepy e-mail! And everyone thought he was so sweet and innocent, with his perfectly knotted tie and his luminous skin—he was probably the type who brought Cetaphil to school and washed up after gym class. Weirdo.

Shutting the door of the upstairs bathroom, she found the jar of Icy Hot in the closet, pulled down her Nuala Puma warm-up pants, twisted around to see herself in the mirror, and started rubbing the balm all over her back and hamstrings. The Icy Hot's stinky menthol smell instantly wafted around the room, and she closed her eyes.

The door burst open. Spencer tried to pull her pants up as quickly as she could.

"Oh my God," Wren said, his eyes wide. "I . . . shit. I'm sorry."

"It's all right," Spencer said, scrambling to tie her waistband.

"I'm still confused about this house. . . . " Wren was wearing his blue hospital scrubs, which consisted of a V-neck draped top and tie-waist wide-leg pants. He looked all ready for bed. "I thought this was our bedroom."

"Happens all the time," Spencer said, even though it obviously didn't.

Wren paused in the doorway. Spencer felt him looking at her and quickly looked down to make sure her boob wasn't hanging out and there wasn't a glob of Icy Hot on her neck.

"So, um, how's the barn?" Wren asked.

Spencer grinned, then self-consciously covered her mouth. Last year, she'd had her teeth whitened at the dentist and they'd come out looking a little *too* white. She'd had to purposely dull them with tons of coffee. "Awesome. How's my sister's old bedroom?"

Wren smiled wryly. "Um. It's rather . . . pink."

"Yeah. All those frilly curtains," Spencer added.

"I found a disturbing CD, too."

"Oh yeah? What?"

"*Phantom of the Opera*." He grimaced.

"But aren't you into plays?" Spencer blurted out.

"Well, Shakespeare and stuff." Wren raised an eyebrow. "How'd you know that?"

Spencer paled. It might sound sort of weird if she told

Wren she'd Googled him. She shrugged and leaned back on the counter. A shooting pain exploded through her lower back, and she winced.

Wren hesitated. "What's the matter?"

"Um, you know." Spencer leaned against the sink. "Field hockey again."

"What'd you do this time?"

"Pulled something. See the Icy Hot?" Holding her towel in one hand, she reached for the jar, scooped some into her palm, and slid her hand down her pants to rub it into her hamstring. She groaned slightly, and hoped it was a sexy-sounding groan. Fine, so sue her for being a *teensy* bit dramatic.

"Do you need some help?"

Spencer hesitated. But Wren looked so concerned. And it *was* excruciating—well, painful, anyway—to twist her back that way, even if she was doing it on purpose.

"If you don't mind," she said softly. "Thanks."

Spencer nudged the door a little more closed with her foot. She smeared the Icy Hot goop from her hand onto his. Wren's large hands felt sexy all slimed up with balm. She caught sight of their figures in the mirror and shivered. They looked awesome together.

"So where's the damage?" Wren asked.

Spencer pointed. The muscle was right below her butt. "Hang on," she murmured. She grabbed a towel from the rack, wrapped it around herself, and then slid off her pants under the towel. She motioned to where it hurt, indicating that Wren reach below the towel. "But, um, try not to get too much on the towel," she said. "I begged my mom to order these special from France a couple years ago, and Icy Hot ruins them. You can't get the smell out in the wash."

She heard Wren stifle a laugh and stiffened. Had that come out way too uptight and Melissa-ish?

Wren slicked back his floppy hair with his goop-free hand and knelt down, slathering the Icy Hot on her skin. He reached his hands under her towel and began to rub slow, gentle circles across her muscles. Spencer relaxed and then leaned into him slightly. He stood but didn't back away from her. She felt his breath on her shoulder, and then on her ear. Her skin felt radiant and fiery.

"Feel better?" Wren murmured.

"Feels amazing." She might have said it in her head, she wasn't sure.

I should do it, Spencer thought. *I should kiss him.* He pressed his hands more firmly on her back, his nails digging in a little. Her chest fluttered.

In the hall, the phone rang.

"Wren, dear?" Spencer's mother called from downstairs. "Are you upstairs? Melissa's on the phone for you."

He sprang backward. Spencer jolted forward and pulled the towel around her. He quickly wiped the Icy Hot off his hands onto another towel. Spencer was too panicked to tell him not to. "Um," he murmured.

She looked away. "You should . . ."

"Yeah."

He pushed the door back open. "I hope that worked."

"Yeah, thanks," she murmured back, closing the door behind him. Then she draped herself over the sink and stared at her reflection.

Something flickered in the mirror, and for a second, she thought someone was by the shower. But it was only the flapping shower curtain, lifted by a breeze from the open window. Spencer turned back to the sink.

They'd spilled a few globs of Icy Hot on the counter. It was white and gooey, sort of like frosting. With her pointer finger, Spencer spelled out Wren's name. Then she drew a heart around it.

Spencer considered leaving it there. But when she heard Wren stomp down the hall and say, "Hey, love. Missed you," she frowned and rubbed it out with the heel of her hand.

20

ALL EMILY NEEDS IS A LIGHT SABER AND A BLACK HELMET

It was just getting dark as Emily slid into Ben's green Jeep Cherokee. "Thanks for convincing my parents that my punishment starts tomorrow."

"No prob," Ben answered. He didn't give her a hello kiss. And he was blasting Fall Out Boy, who he knew Emily hated.

"They're kinda pissed at me."

"I heard." He kept his eyes on the road.

Interesting that Ben didn't ask why. Maybe he already knew. Bizarrely, Emily's father had come into her room earlier and said, "Ben's going to pick you up in twenty minutes. Be ready." *Okay*. Emily had thought she was grounded for life for denouncing the Swimming Gods, but she had the feeling they actually *wanted* her to go out with Ben. Maybe he'd talk some sense into her.

Emily heaved a sigh. "Sorry about practice yesterday. I'm just under some stress."

Ben finally turned down the volume. "It's all right. You're just confused."

Emily licked her just-ChapSticked lips. *Confused? About what?*

"I'll forgive you this time," Ben added. He reached over and squeezed her hand.

Emily bristled. *This time?* And shouldn't he say he was sorry too? He had, after all, stormed off into the locker room like a baby.

They pulled through the Kahns' open wrought-iron gates. The property was set back from the road, so the driveway was half a mile long and surrounded by tall, thick pines. Even the air smelled cleaner. The redbrick house sat behind massive Doric columns. It had a portico with a little horse statue on top and a gorgeous all-glass sun room off to the side. Emily counted fourteen windows on the second floor, from one end to the other.

But the house didn't matter tonight. They were going to the field. It was set way off from the property by high, British-racing-green hedges and a stone wall and went on for acres. Half of it housed the Kahn horse farm; on the other side were a huge lawn and a duck pond. Surrounding the whole yard were thick woods.

As Ben parked the car in a makeshift grass parking lot, Emily climbed out, hearing The Killers blaring from the backyard. Familiar faces from Rosewood climbed out of their Jeeps, Escalades, and Saabs. A group of immaculately made-up girls took cigarette packs out of their little chain-link quilted bags and lit up, talking on their tiny cell phones. Emily looked down at her worn blue Converse All-Stars and touched her messy ponytail.

Ben caught up with her and they cut through the hedges and across a secluded stretch of woods and entered the party zone. There were a lot of kids Emily didn't know, but that was because the Kahns invited all the *it* kids from the area's other private schools, in addition to Rosewood. There were a keg and a drinks table by the bushes, and they'd set up a wooden dance floor, tiki lights, and tents in the middle of the field. On the other side of the field, near the woods, there was an old-school photo booth lit up with Christmas lights. The Kahns dragged it out of their basement for this party every year.

Noel greeted them. He wore a gray T-shirt that said WILL FLEX FOR FOOD, ripped-up faded blue jeans, and no shoes or socks. "What up." He handed them both a beer.

"Thanks, man." Ben took his cup and started drinking. The amber beer messily dribbled down his chin. "Nice party."

Someone tapped Emily on the shoulder.

Emily turned. It was Aria Montgomery, wearing a tight, faded red University of Iceland T-shirt, a frayed denim mini, and red John Fluevog cowboy boots. Her black hair was pulled back into a high ponytail.

"Wow, hi," Emily said. She'd heard Aria was back but she hadn't seen her yet. "How was Europe?"

"Awesome." Aria smiled. The girls looked at each other for a few seconds. Emily paused, wanting to tell Aria she was glad she'd ditched her fake nose ring and pink hair stripes but wondered if it would be weird to make a reference to their old friendship. She took a sip of her beer and pretended to be fascinated with the ridges on the cup.

Aria fidgeted. "Listen, I'm glad you're here. I've been wanting to talk to you."

"You have?" Emily met her eyes and then looked back down.

"Well . . . either you or Spencer."

"Really?" Emily felt her chest tighten. *Spencer?*

"So, promise me you won't think I'm crazy. I've been away for such a long time, and . . . " Aria made a puckered face that Emily remembered well. It meant she was considering her words carefully.

"And what?" Emily raised her eyebrows, waiting. Maybe Aria wanted all her old friends to have a reunion— of course, being away, she wouldn't know how far apart they'd grown. How uncomfortable would *that* be?

"Well . . ." Aria looked around warily. "Was there any more news about Ali's disappearance while I was away?"

Emily jerked back, hearing Ali's name come out of her old friend's mouth. "Her disappearance? What do you mean?"

"Like, did they ever find out who took her? Did she ever come back?"

"Um . . . no . . . " Emily chewed on her thumbnail uncomfortably.

Aria leaned into Emily. "Do you think she's dead?"

Emily's eyes widened. "I . . . I don't know. *Why?*"

Aria set her jaw. She looked deep in thought.

"What's this about?" Emily asked, her heart pounding.

"Nothing."

Then Aria's eyes focused on someone behind her. She clamped her mouth shut.

"Hey," said a gravelly voice behind Emily.

Emily turned. Maya. "Hey," she answered, nearly dropping her cup. "I . . . I didn't know you were coming."

"I didn't either," Maya said. "But my brother wanted to. He's here somewhere."

Emily turned to introduce Aria, but she was gone.

"So is this Maya?" Ben reappeared next to them. "The girl that's turned Emily to the dark side?"

"Dark side?" Emily squeaked. "What dark side?"

"Quitting swimming," Ben answered. He turned to Maya. "You know she's quitting, right?"

"*You are?*" Maya turned to Emily and grinned excitedly.

Emily shot Ben a look. "Maya didn't have anything to do with that. And we don't have to talk about it now."

Ben took another big sip of beer. "Why not? Isn't it your big news?"

"I don't know. . . . "

"Whatever." He clapped his heavy hand on her shoulder a little roughly. "I'm going to get another beer. You want another?"

Emily nodded, even though she only ever drank one beer at parties, max. Ben didn't ask Maya if she wanted a drink. As he walked away, she noticed his saggy jeans. Yuck.

Maya took Emily's hand and squeezed. "How's it feel?"

Emily stared at their entwined hands, blushed, but kept holding on. "Good." Or scary. Or, at some moments, like a bad movie. "Confusing, but good."

"I have just the thing to celebrate with," Maya whispered. She reached into her Manhattan Portage knapsack and showed Emily the top of a Jack Daniel's bottle. "Stole it from the liquor table. Wanna help kill it with me?"

Emily gazed at Maya. Her hair was pulled off her face, and she wore a simple black sleeveless shirt and an army green cargo skirt. She looked effervescent and fun—way more fun than Ben in his saggy-butt jeans.

"Why not?" she answered, and followed Maya toward the woods.

21

HOT GIRLS—THEY'RE
JUST LIKE US!

Hanna took a sip of her vodka lemonade and lit another cigarette. She hadn't seen Sean since they parked his car on the Kahns' lawn two hours ago, and even Mona had vanished. Now she was stuck talking to Noel's best friend, James Freed, Zelda Millings—a beautiful blond girl who only wore clothes and shoes made out of hemp—and a bunch of squeally, cliquey girls from Doringbell Friends, the ultra-hip Quaker school in the next town over. The girls had come to Noel's party last year and even though Hanna had hung out with them then, she couldn't remember any of their names.

James stubbed out his Marlboro on the heel of his Adidas shell-tops and took a swig of beer. "I heard Noel's brother has a ton of pot."

"Eric?" asked Zelda. "Where's he at?"

"Photo booth," James answered.

Suddenly, Sean darted through the pines. Hanna

stood up, adjusted her hopefully slimming BCBG slip dress, and tied the straps of her brand-new pale blue Christian Louboutin sandals back around her ankles. As she ran to catch up with him, her heel sunk into the dewy grass. She flailed her arms, dropped her drink, and suddenly she was on her butt.

"And she's down!" James called out drunkenly. The Doringbell girls all laughed.

Hanna quickly scrambled up, pinching her palm to keep herself from crying. This was the biggest party of the year, but she felt way off her game: Her dress felt snug around her hips, she hadn't been able to get Sean to crack a smile during the car ride over here—despite the fact that he'd scored his dad's BMW 760i for the night—and she was on her third calorie-laden vodka lemonade and it was only nine-thirty.

Sean held out his hand to help her up. "Are you okay?"

Hanna hesitated. Sean was dressed in a plain white T-shirt that accentuated his strong-from-soccer chest and flat-from-good-genes stomach, dark blue Paper Denim jeans that made his butt look awesome, and ragged black Pumas. His blondish brown hair was messily styled, his brown eyes looked extra soulful, and his pink lips extra kissable. For the past hour, she'd watched Sean bond with every guy there and carefully avoid her.

"I'm fine," she said, sticking her lip out in a Hanna-patented pout.

"What's the matter?"

She tried to balance in her shoes. "Can we . . . go somewhere private for a while? Maybe the woods? To talk?"

Sean shrugged. "Okay."

Yes.

Hanna led Sean down a path to the Manhood Woods, the trees casting long, dark shadows across their bodies. The only other time Hanna had ever been here was in seventh grade, when her friends had a secret rendezvous with Noel Kahn and James Freed. Ali made out with Noel, Spencer made out with James, and she, Emily, and Aria sat on logs, shared cigarettes, and miserably waited for them to finish. Tonight, she vowed, would be different.

She sat down on a thick patch of grass and pulled Sean down with her. "You having fun?" She passed her drink to Sean.

"Yeah, it's cool." Sean took a small sip. "You?"

Hanna hesitated. Sean's skin shone in the moonlight. His shirt had a tiny smear of dirt on it near the collar. "I guess."

All right, chatting time was over. Hanna took the drink out of Sean's hand and grabbed his sweet, square jaw and started to kiss him. *There.* It sort of sucked that the world was kind of spinning, and that instead of tasting the inside of Sean's mouth, she tasted Mike's Hard Lemonade, but whatever.

After a minute of kissing, she felt Sean pulling away. Maybe this called for upping the ante a little. She hiked up her navy dress, exposing her legs and tiny lavender Cosabella lace thong. The woodsy air was cold. A mosquito landed on her upper thigh.

"Hanna," Sean said gently, reaching to pull her dress back down. "This isn't . . . "

He wasn't fast enough, though; Hanna had already torn the dress over her head. Sean's eyes canvassed her whole body. Amazingly, this was only the second time he'd seen her in her underwear—unless you counted the week they spent at his parents' place in Avalon on the Jersey Shore, when she was in her bikini. But that was different.

"You don't *really* want to stop, do you?" She reached toward him, hoping she looked smoldering yet wholesome.

"Yeah." Sean caught her hand. "I do."

Hanna wrapped herself up in her dress as best she could. She probably had a hundred mosquito bites already. Her lip trembled. "But . . . I don't get it. Don't you love me?" The words felt very small and frail coming out of her mouth.

Sean took a long time to respond. Hanna heard another couple from the party giggling nearby. "I don't know," he answered.

"Jesus," Hanna said, rolling away from him. The vodka lemonades sloshed in her stomach. "Are you *gay*?" It came out a little meaner than she meant it to.

"No!" Sean sounded hurt.

"Well then what? Am I not hot enough?"

"Of course not!" Sean said, sounding shocked. He thought for a moment. "You're one of the prettiest girls I know, Hanna. Why don't *you* know that?"

"What are you talking about?" Hanna asked, disgusted.

"I just . . . ," Sean started. "I just think that maybe if you could have a little more respect for yourself—"

"I have plenty of self-respect!" Hanna shouted at him. She shifted onto her butt, rolling onto a pine cone.

Sean stood up. He looked deflated and sad. "Look at you." His eyes traveled from her shoes to the top of her head. "I'm just trying to help you, Hanna—I *care* about you."

Hanna felt tears gathering at the corners of her eyes and tried to choke them back down. She would not cry right now. "I respect myself," she repeated. "I just wanted to . . . to . . . show you how I feel."

"I'm just trying to be choosy about sex." He sounded not kind, but not mean, either. Just . . . detached. "I want it to be at the right time with the right person. And it doesn't look like that's going to be you." Sean sighed and took a step away from her. "I'm sorry." Then he pushed through the trees and was gone.

Hanna was so embarrassed and angry, she couldn't speak. She tried to stand up to follow Sean, but her heel caught again and she fell over. She splayed her arms out and stared up at the stars, holding her thumbs over her eyes, so tears wouldn't pour out of them.

"She looks like she might puke."

Hanna opened one eye and saw two freshman boys—most likely crashers—hovering over her as if she were a girl they'd created on their computers.

"Fuck off, pervs," she said to the ogling freshmen as she stood up. Across the lawn, she could see Sean running after Mason Byers, wielding a yellow croquet mallet. Hanna sniffed as she brushed herself off and headed back toward the party. Didn't *anyone* care about her? She thought of the letter she'd gotten yesterday. *Even Daddy doesn't love you best!*

Hanna wished, suddenly, that she had her dad's number, her mind flashing back to that day she'd met her dad and Isabel and Kate with Ali.

Although it had been February, the weather in Annapolis had been freakishly warm, and Hanna, Ali, and Kate had been sitting outside on the porch, trying to get tan. Ali and Kate were bonding over their favorite shades of MAC nail polish, but Hanna couldn't get into it. She felt heavy and awkward. She'd seen Kate's relieved expression when she and Ali first emerged from the train—surprise at how gorgeous Ali was, and then relief when she laid eyes on Hanna. It was as if Kate was thinking, *Well, I don't need to worry about her!*

Without realizing it, Hanna had eaten the entire bowl of cheese popcorn that was on the table. And six of the profiteroles. And some of the Brie wedge that was meant for Isabel and her dad. She clutched her bloated stomach, gazed at Ali's and Kate's flat six-packs, and groaned out loud, without meaning to.

"Little piggy doesn't feel good?" Hanna's dad asked, squeezing her small toe.

Hanna shuddered at the memory and touched her now-slim stomach. A—whoever A was—was totally right. Her dad *didn't* love her best.

"Everyone in the pond!" Noel shouted, snapping Hanna out of her thoughts.

Across the field, Hanna watched Sean pull off his T-shirt and run toward the water. Noel, James, Mason, and some other boys threw off their shirts, but Hanna didn't even care. Of all the nights to see Rosewood's hottest boys without their shirts on . . .

"They're all so gorgeous," murmured Felicity McDowell, who was mixing tequila with Fanta Grape, next to her. "Aren't they?"

"Mmm," she muttered.

Hanna ground her teeth together. Fuck her happy father and his perfect soon-to-be stepdaughter, and fuck Sean and his choosiness! She grabbed a bottle of Ketel One from the table and drank straight from it. She put the bottle back down but at the last second decided to bring it to the pond with her. Sean wasn't going to get away with dumping her, insulting her, and then straight-up ignoring her. No way.

She stopped at a pile of clothes that were no doubt Sean's—the jeans were neatly folded, and he'd anally stuffed his little white socks into his Pumas. Making sure no one was looking, she balled up the jeans in her hands and started backing away from the pond. What would the V Club say if they caught him driving home in his boxers?

As she walked toward the trees with Sean's jeans, something fell and bounced off her foot. Hanna picked it up and stared at it for a moment, waiting for her vision to un-double.

The key to the BMW.

"Sweet," she whispered, stroking the alarm button with her finger. Then she dropped the jeans back on the ground and shoved the keys into her blue quilted Moschino bag.

It was a gorgeous night for a drive.

22

BEER BATHS ARE GOOD
FOR THE PORES

"Check it out," Maya whispered excitedly. "There used to be one of these in my favorite café back in Cali!"

Emily and Maya stared at the old-school photo booth at the perimeter of Noel's yard and the woods. A long, orange extension cord wound its way to the booth from Noel's house across the lawn. As they admired it, Noel's older brother, Eric, and a very-giddy Mona Vanderwaal fell out of the booth, grabbed their photos, and skipped away.

Maya glanced at Emily. "Wanna try it?"

Emily nodded. Before they ducked inside, she quickly glanced around the party. Some kids were gathered around the keg and a lot of other people held their red plastic cups in the air as they danced. Noel and a bunch of boys were swimming in the duck pond in their boxers. Ben was nowhere to be seen.

Emily sat beside Maya on the photo booth's little orange seat and closed the curtain. They were so squeezed together, their shoulders and thighs touched.

"Here." Maya handed her the Jack Daniel's bottle and hit the green start button. Emily did a shot, then held it up triumphantly as the camera snapped the first picture. Then they squished their faces together and donned huge grins. Emily rolled her eyes back into her head, and Maya puffed her cheeks out like a monkey for the third picture. Then the camera caught them looking seminormal, if maybe a bit nervous.

"Let's go see how they look," Emily said.

But as she stood up, Maya grabbed her sleeve. "Can we stay in here a sec? This is such a great hiding spot."

"Um, sure." Emily sat back down. She swallowed loudly, without meaning to.

"So, how have you been?" Maya asked, pushing hair out of Emily's eyes.

Emily sighed, trying to get comfy on the cramped seat. *Confused. Upset at my possibly racist parents. Afraid I made the wrong decision about swimming. Kinda freaked that I'm sitting so close to you.*

"I'm all right," she said finally.

Maya snorted and took a swig of whiskey. "I don't believe that for one second."

Emily paused. Maya seemed like the only person who actually understood her. "Yeah, I guess not," she said.

"Well, what's going on?"

But suddenly, Emily didn't want to talk about swimming or Ben or her parents. She wanted to talk about . . . something else completely. Something that had been slowly dawning on her. Maybe seeing Aria had triggered it. Or maybe finally having a real friend again had brought the feeling back. Emily thought Maya would understand.

She took a deep breath. "So, you know that girl Alison, the one who used to live in your house?"

"Yeah."

"We were really close and I, like, really loved her. Like, everything about her."

She heard Maya breathe out and nervously took another sip of Jack Daniel's from the bottle.

"We were best friends," Emily said, rubbing her fingers between the ratty blue fabric of the photo booth curtain. "I cared about her so much. So this one day, sort of out of the blue, I did it."

"Did what?"

"Well, Ali and I were in this tree house in her backyard—we went there a lot to talk. We were sitting up there, talking about this guy that she liked, some older boy whose name she wouldn't say, and I just felt like I couldn't hold any of it in anymore. So I leaned over . . . and kissed her."

Maya made a small sniffing noise.

"She wasn't into it, though. She was even kind of distant and said, like, 'Well, now I know why you get so quiet when we're changing for gym!'"

"God," Maya said.

Emily took another sip of whiskey and felt dizzy. She'd never had this much to drink. And here was one of her biggest secrets, hanging out like granny underwear on a clothesline. "Ali said she didn't think best friends should kiss," she went on. "So I tried to play it off as a joke. But when I went home, I realized how I really felt. So I wrote her this letter, telling her that I loved her. I don't think she ever got it, though. If she did, she never said anything."

A tear plopped on Emily's bare knee. Maya noticed it, and smeared it with her finger.

"I still think about her a lot." Emily sighed. "I'd sort of pushed that memory back, told myself it was just about her being my very best friend but not anything, you know . . . *else* . . . but now I don't know."

They sat there for a few minutes. The party sounds filtered in. Every few seconds, Emily heard the rough flicker of someone's Zippo lighting a cigarette. She wasn't that surprised about what she'd just said about Ali. It was scary, of course—but it was also the truth. In a way, it felt good to have finally figured it out.

"Since we're sharing," Maya said quietly, "I have something to tell you, too."

She turned her forearm over to show Emily the white, raised scar on her wrist. "You might have seen this."

"Yeah," Emily whispered, squinting at it in the pale, semidarkness of the booth.

"It's from one of the times I cut myself with a razor blade. I didn't know it was going to go so deep. There was so much blood. My parents took me to the emergency room."

"You cut yourself on purpose?" Emily whispered.

"Um . . . yeah. I mean, I don't really do it anymore. I try not to."

"Why do you do that?"

"I don't know," Maya said. "Sometimes I just . . . feel like I need to. You can touch it, if you want."

Emily did. It was puckered and smooth, not like real skin at all. Touching it felt like the most intimate thing Emily had ever done. She reached over to hug Maya.

Maya's body shook. She buried her head in Emily's neck. Like before, she smelled like artificial bananas. Emily pressed herself to Maya's slight chest. What was it like to cut yourself, to watch yourself bleed like that? Emily had her fair share of baggage, but even in the wake of her absolute worst memories—like of when Ali rejected her, or of The Jenna Thing—she'd felt guilty and horrible and strange, but she'd *never* wanted to hurt herself.

Maya raised her head and met Emily's eyes. Then smiling a little sadly, she kissed Emily's lips. Emily blinked at her, surprised.

"Sometimes best friends *do* kiss," Maya said. "See?"

They hung apart, nose practically touching nose. Outside, the crickets sawed away furiously.

Then Maya reached for her. Emily melted into her lips. Their mouths were open and she felt Maya's soft tongue. Emily's chest clenched up excitedly as she raked her hands through Maya's rough hair, then down to her shoulders, then her back. Maya stuck her hands under Emily's polo shirt and pressed her fingers flat against her belly. Emily self-consciously flinched but then relaxed. This felt a zillion times different than kissing Ben.

Maya's hands traveled up her body and felt over her bra. Emily shut her eyes. Maya's mouth tasted delicious, like Jack Daniel's and licorice. Next, Maya kissed Emily's chest and shoulders. Emily threw her head back. Someone had painted a moon and a bunch of stars on the photo booth's ceiling.

Suddenly, the curtain started to open. Emily jumped, but it was too late—someone had torn the curtain back completely. Then Emily saw who it was. "Oh my God," she sputtered.

"Shit," Maya echoed. The Jack Daniel's bottle swished onto the floor.

Ben held two cups of beer, one in each hand. "Well. This explains things."

"Ben . . . I . . . " Emily scrambled out of the booth, bumping her head on the door.

"Don't get up for me," Ben said in a horrible, mocking, angry-yet-hurt voice Emily had never heard before.

"No . . . ," Emily squeaked. "You don't understand."

She climbed out of the booth completely. So did Maya. Out of the corner of her eye, Emily noticed Maya pick up their strip of photos and stuff it into her pocket.

"Don't even talk," Ben spat. Then he turned and threw one of the cups of beer at her. It splashed warmly all over Emily's legs, her shoes, and her shorts. The cup bounced crazily into the bushes.

"Ben!" Emily cried.

Ben hesitated, then threw the other one more directly at Maya. It splashed her face and hair. Maya screamed.

"Stop it!" Emily gasped.

"You fucking dykes," Ben said. She heard the crackly tears in his voice. Then he turned and ran crookedly into the darkness.

23

ICELANDIC ARIA GETS
WHAT SHE WANTS

"Finland! I've been looking everywhere for you!"

It was an hour later, and Aria was just stepping out of the photo booth. Noel Kahn stood in front of her, naked except for his Calvin Klein boxers, which were wet and clingy. He was holding a yellow plastic cup of beer and her just-developed strip of pictures. Noel shook his hair around a little, and water from his hair sprayed onto her APC miniskirt.

"Why are you all wet?" Aria asked.

"We were playing water polo."

Aria glanced at the pond. The boys were batting one another in the heads with pink fun-noodles. On the banks, girls in nearly identical Alberta Ferrari minidresses huddled together, gossiping. Over by the hedges, not that far from them, she spied her brother, Mike. He was with a petite girl in a plaid micromini and platform heels.

Noel followed her gaze. "That's one of those Quaker school girls," he murmured. "Those chicks are nuts."

Mike glanced up and saw Aria and Noel together. He gave Aria an approving nod.

Noel tapped Aria's photo strip with his thumb. "These are gorgeous."

Aria looked at them. Bored out of her skull, she'd been taking pictures of herself in the booth for twenty minutes. This round, she'd made sultry, sex-kitten expressions.

Très sigh. She'd come here thinking that Ezra, jealous and lustful, would come and whisk her away. But, duh, he was a teacher, and a teacher wouldn't go to a students' party.

"Noel!" James Freed called from across the lawn. "Keg's tapped!"

"Shit," Noel said. He gave Aria a wet kiss on her cheek. "This beer's for you. Don't leave."

"Uh-huh," Aria said drolly, watching him scamper away, his boxers slowly sliding down to reveal his pale, defined-from-running butt.

"He really likes you, you know."

Aria turned. Mona Vanderwaal sat on the ground a few feet away. Her blond hair was in coils around her face and her gold-rimmed bug-eye sunglasses had slid down her nose. Noel's older brother, Eric, had his head in her lap.

Mona blinked slowly. "Noel's awesome. He'd make such a good friendboy."

Eric burst out laughing. "What?" Mona bent down to him. "What's so funny?"

"She's so stoned," Eric said to Aria.

As Aria scoured her brain for something to say, her Treo beeped. She wrenched it out of her purse and looked at the number. Ezra. *Oh my God, oh my God!*

"Um, hello?" she answered quietly.

"Hey. Um, Aria?"

"Oh. Hey! What's up?" She tried to sound as controlled and cool as possible.

"I'm at home, having a Scotch, thinking about you."

Aria paused, closed her eyes, and a glow passed through her. "Really?"

"Yep. You at that big party?"

"Uh-huh."

"You bored?"

She laughed. "A little."

"Wanna come by?"

"Okay." Ezra started to give her directions, but Aria already knew where it was. She'd looked up his address on MapQuest and Google Earth, but she couldn't exactly tell *him* that.

"Cool," she said. "See you soon."

Aria shoved the phone back into her purse as calmly as she could, and then banged the rubbery soles of her boots together. *Yessss!!!*

"Hey, I know where I know you from."

Aria looked over. Noel's brother, Eric, was squinting

at her while Mona kissed his neck. "You're the friend of that chick who disappeared, right?"

Aria looked at him and pushed her hair out of her eyes. "I don't know who you're talking about," she said, and walked away.

A lot of Rosewood was gated estates and renovated fifty-acre horse farms, but near the college there was a series of rambling, cobblestone streets lined with falling-to-pieces Victorian houses. The houses in Old Hollis were painted crazy colors like purple, pink, and teal and were usually split into apartments and leased to students. Aria's family had lived in an Old Hollis house until Aria was five, which was when her dad got his first teaching job at the college.

As Aria drove slowly down Ezra's street, she noticed one house with Greek letters mounted onto its siding. Toilet paper wound through its trees. Another house had a half-finished painting on an easel in the front yard.

She pulled up to Ezra's house. After parking, she climbed up the stone front steps and rang the bell. The door flung open, and there he was.

"Wow," he said. "Hey." His mouth spread into a wiggly smile.

"Hi," Aria answered, smiling back at him in the same way.

Ezra laughed. "I . . . um, you're here. Wow."

"You already said wow," Aria teased.

They entered into a hallway. Ahead of her, a creaky staircase with a different swatch of carpet on each step wound its way upstairs. On the right, a door was ajar. "This apartment's mine."

Aria walked in and noticed a claw-foot bathtub in the middle of Ezra's living room. She pointed at it.

"It's too heavy to move," Ezra said sheepishly. "So I store books in there."

"Cool." Aria looked around, taking in Ezra's gigantic bay window, dusty built-in bookshelves, and yellow crushed velvet sofa. It smelled faintly of macaroni and cheese but there was a crystal chandelier hanging from the ceiling, a funky mosaic tile around the mantel, and real logs in the fireplace. This was so much more Aria's style than the Kahns' million-dollar duck pond and twenty-seven-room estate.

"I totally want to live here," Aria said.

"I can't stop thinking about you," Ezra said at the same time.

Aria looked over her shoulder. "Really?"

Ezra came up behind her and put his hands on her waist. Aria leaned slightly into him. They stood there for a moment, and then Aria turned. She stared at his clean-shaven face, at the bump at the edge of his nose, the green flecks in his eyes. She touched a mole on his earlobe and felt him shudder.

"I just . . . couldn't ignore you in class," he whispered. "It was torture. When you were giving that report . . . "

"You touched my hand today," Aria teased. "You were looking at my notebook."

"You kissed Noel," Ezra said back. "I was so jealous."

"Then it worked," Aria whispered.

Ezra sighed and wrapped his arms around her. She met his mouth with hers and they kissed feverishly, their hands crawling up each other's backs. They backed up for a second, breathlessly staring into each other's eyes.

"No more talk about class," Ezra said.

"Deal."

He guided her into a tiny back bedroom that had clothes all over the floor and an open bag of Lay's on the nightstand. They sat down on his bed. The mattress was barely bigger than a twin, and even though the comforter was made of stiff denim and the mattress probably had potato chip crumbs in the cracks, Aria had never felt anything so perfect in her life.

Aria was still on the bed, staring up at a crack in the ceiling. The streetlight outside the window cast long shadows across everything, turning Aria's bare skin a weird shade of pink. A stiff, chilly breeze from the open window blew out the sandalwood candle next to the bed. She heard Ezra turn on the faucet in the bathroom.

Wow. Wow wow *wow*!

She felt alive. She and Ezra had nearly had sex . . . but then, at exactly the same time, they'd agreed that they should wait. So then they'd snuggled up to each other, naked, and started to talk. Ezra told her about the time he was six and sculpted a red squirrel out of clay, only to have his brother squash it. How he used to smoke a lot of pot after his parents got divorced. About the time he had to take the family's fox terrier to the vet to have her put to sleep. Aria told him about how when she was little, she kept a can of split pea soup named Pee as a pet and cried when her mom tried to cook Pee for dinner. She told him about her furious knitting habit and promised to knit him a sweater.

It was easy to talk to Ezra—so easy she could imagine doing it forever. They could travel together to faraway places. Brazil would be amazing. . . . They could sleep in a tree and eat nothing but plantains and write plays for the rest of their lives. . . .

Her Treo beeped. *Ugh.* It was probably Noel, wondering what happened to her. She hugged one of Ezra's pillows close to her—mmm, it smelled just like him—and waited for him to come out of the bathroom and kiss her some more.

Then it beeped again. And again and again.

"Jesus," Aria groaned, leaning her naked body off the bed to pull it out of her bag. Seven new text messages. More kept beeping in.

Opening her inbox, Aria frowned. The messages all had the same title: STUDENT-TEACHER CONFERENCE! Her stomach turned as she opened the first one.

Aria,

That's some kind of extra credit!

Love ya, A

P.S. Wonder what your mom would think if she found out about your dad's little, uh, study buddy . . . and that you knew!

Aria read the next text message and the next and the next. *All the messages said the same thing.* She dropped the Treo on the floor. She had to sit down.

No. She had to get out of here.

"Ezra?" She frantically peered out Ezra's windows. Was she watching, right this second? What did she want? Was it really *her*? "Ezra, I have to go. It's an emergency."

"What?" Ezra called from behind the bathroom door. "You're leaving?"

Aria couldn't quite believe it, either. She yanked her shirt over her head. "I'll call you, okay? I just have to go do something."

"Wait. What?" he asked, opening the bathroom door.

Aria grabbed her bag and tore out the door and across the yard. She needed to get away. Now.

24

THERE'S MORE THAN JUST SHOES AND JEANS IN SPENCER'S CLOSET

"The limit of x is . . . ," Spencer murmured to herself. She propped herself up on one elbow on her bed and stared at her brand-new, just-covered-with-a-brown-bag calculus book. Her lower back still burned with Icy Hot.

She checked her watch: It was after midnight. Was she crazy to stress over her calc homework on the school year's first Friday night? The Spencer of last year would've whizzed over to the Kahns' in her Mercedes, drunk bad keg beer, and maybe made out with Mason Byers or some other cute lax boy. But not the Spencer of now. She was the Star, and the Star had homework to do. Tomorrow, the Star was visiting home design stores with her mom to properly accessorize the barn. She might even hit Main Line Bikes with her dad in the afternoon—he'd pored over some bicycling catalogues with her during dinner, asking her which Orbea frame she liked better. He'd never asked her opinion about bikes before.

She cocked her head. Was that a tiny, tentative knock at the door? Putting down her mechanical pencil, Spencer gazed out the barn's large front window. The moon was silvery and full, and the windows of the main house blazed a warm yellow. There was the knock again. She padded over to the heavy wooden door and opened it a crack.

"Hey," Wren whispered. "Am I interrupting?"

"Of course not." Spencer opened the door wider. Wren was barefoot, in a slim-fitting white T-shirt that said, UNIVERSITY OF PENNSYLVANIA MEDICAL, and baggy khaki shorts. She looked down at her black French Connection baby tee, short track-star gray sweat shorts from Villanova, and bare legs. Her hair was pulled back in a low, messy ponytail; wisps hanging around her face. It was a completely different look from her everyday Thomas Pink striped button-down and Citizens jeans. That look said, *I'm sophisticated and sexy*, this look said, *I'm studying . . . but still sexy*.

Okay, so maybe she'd planned for the off chance this would happen. But it goes to show you shouldn't just throw on your high-waisted underwear and old, ratty I HEART PERSIAN CATS T-shirt.

"How's it going?" she asked. A warm breeze lifted the wispy ends of her hair. A pine cone fell out of a nearby tree with a thump.

Wren hovered in the doorway. "Shouldn't you be out partying? I heard there was a huge field party some-where."

Spencer shrugged. "Not into it."

Wren met her eyes. "No?"

Spencer's mouth felt cottony. "Um . . . where's Melissa?"

"She's sleeping. Too much renovating, I guess. So I thought maybe you could give me a tour of this fabulous barn I don't get to live in. I never even got to see it!"

Spencer frowned. "Do you have a housewarming gift?"

Wren paled. "Oh. I . . . "

"I'm kidding." She opened the door. "Enter the Spencer Hastings barn."

She'd spent some of the night daydreaming about all the potential scenarios of being alone with Wren, but nothing compared to actually having him right here, next to her.

Wren strolled over to her Thom Yorke poster and stretched his hands behind his head. "You like Radiohead?"

"Love."

Wren's face lit up. "I've seen them like twenty times in London. Every show gets better."

She smoothed down the duvet on her bed. "Lucky. I've never seen them live."

"We have to remedy that," he said, leaning against her couch. "If they come to Philly, we're going."

Spencer paused. "But I don't think . . . " Then she stopped. She was about to say *I don't think Melissa likes them*, but . . . maybe Melissa wasn't invited.

She led him to the walk-in closet. "This is my, um, closet," she said, accidentally bumping into the doorjamb. "It used to be a milking station."

"Oh yeah?"

"Yep. This is where the farmers squeezed the cow's nipples or whatever."

He laughed. "Don't you mean *udders?*"

"Uh, yeah." Spencer blushed. Oops. "You don't have to look in there to be polite. I mean, I know closets aren't that interesting to guys."

"Oh no." Wren grinned. "I've come all this way; I absolutely want to see what Spencer Hastings has in her closet."

"As you wish." Spencer flicked on the closet light. The closet smelled like leather, mothballs, and Clinique Happy. She'd stashed all her undies, bras, nightgowns, and grubby hockey clothes in wicker pull-out baskets, and her shirts hung in neat rows, arranged according to color.

Wren chuckled. "It's like being in a shop!"

"Yeah," Spencer said bashfully, running her hands against her shirts.

"I've never heard of a window in a closet." Wren pointed to the open window on the far wall. "Seems funny."

"It was part of the original barn," Spencer explained.

"You like people watching you naked?"

"There are *blinds*," Spencer said.

"Too bad," Wren said softly. "You looked so beautiful in the bathroom. . . . I hoped I'd get to see you . . . like that . . . again."

When Spencer whirled around—*what* did he just say?—Wren was staring at her. He rubbed his fingers over the cuff of a hung-up pair of Joseph trousers. She slid her Tiffany Elsa Peretti heart ring up and down her finger, afraid to speak. Wren took a step forward, then another, until he was right next to her. Spencer could see the light smattering of freckles over his nose. The well-behaved Spencer of a parallel universe would have ducked around him and shown him the rest of the barn. But Wren kept staring at her with his huge, gorgeous brown eyes. The Spencer who was here now rubbed her lips together, afraid to speak, yet dying to do . . . something.

So then she did. She closed her eyes, reached up, and kissed him right on the lips.

Wren didn't hesitate. He kissed her back, then held on to the back of her neck and kissed her harder. His mouth was soft, and he tasted a tiny bit like cigarettes.

Spencer sank back into her wall of shirts. Wren followed. A few slipped off the hangers, but Spencer didn't care.

They sank down onto the soft carpeted floor. Spencer kicked her field hockey cleats out of the way. Wren rolled on top of her, groaning slightly. Spencer grabbed fistfuls of his worn T-shirt in her hands and pulled it over his head. He took hers off next and ran his feet up and down her legs. They rolled over and now Spencer was on top of him. A huge, overwhelming surge of—well, she didn't know what—overcame her. Whatever it was, it was so intense it didn't occur to her to feel guilty. She paused over him, breathing hard.

He reached up and kissed her again, then kissed her nose and her neck. Then he pushed himself up. "I'll be right back."

"Why?"

He motioned his eyes to his left, the direction of her bathroom.

As soon as she heard Wren shut the door, Spencer threw her head back onto the floor and stared dizzily up at her clothes. Then she scrambled up and examined herself in the three-way mirror. Her hair had come out of its ponytail and cascaded over her shoulders. Her bare skin looked luminous, and her face was slightly flushed. She grinned at the three Spencers in the mirror. This. Was. *Unbelievable*.

That was when the reflection of her computer screen, directly opposite her closet, caught her eye.

It was flashing. She turned around and squinted. It looked like she had hundreds of instant messages, piled one on top of the other. Another IM popped on the screen, this time written in 72-point font. Spencer blinked.

A A A A A A: I already told you: Kissing your sister's boy-friend is WRONG.

Spencer ran up to her computer screen and read the IM again. She turned and glanced toward the bathroom; a tiny strip of light shone from underneath the door.

A was definitely not Andrew Campbell.

When she kissed Ian back in seventh grade, she told Alison about it, hoping for some advice. Ali examined her French-manicured toenails for a long moment before she finally said, "You know, I've been in your corner when it comes to Melissa. But this is different. I think you should tell her."

"Tell her?" Spencer shot back. "No way. She'd kill me."

"What, do you think Ian's going to go out with you?" Ali said nastily.

"I don't know," Spencer said. "Why not?"

Ali snorted. "If you don't tell her, maybe I will."

"No you won't!"

"Oh yeah?"

"If you tell Melissa," Spencer said after a moment, her heart pounding wildly, "I'll tell everyone about The Jenna Thing."

Ali barked out a laugh. "You're just as guilty as I am."

Spencer stared at Ali long and hard. "But no one saw *me*."

She turned to Spencer and gave her a fierce, angry look—scarier than any look she'd ever given any of the girls before. "You know I took care of that."

Then there was that sleepover in the barn on the last day of seventh grade. When Ali said how cute Ian and Melissa were together, Spencer realized Ali really might tell on her. Then, strangely, a light, free feeling swept over her. *Let her,* Spencer thought. She suddenly didn't care anymore. And even though it sounded horrible to say now, the truth was, Spencer wanted to be free of Ali, right then and there.

Now Spencer felt nauseous. She heard the toilet flush. Wren strode out and stood in the closet's doorway. "Now, where were we?" he cooed.

But Spencer still had her eyes on her computer screen. Something on it—a flicker of red—just moved. It looked like . . . a reflection.

"What's the matter?" Wren asked.

"Shh," Spencer said. Her eyes focused. It *was* a reflection. She spun around. There was someone outside her window.

"Holy shit," Spencer said. She held her T-shirt up against her naked chest.

"What is it?" Wren asked.

Spencer stepped back. Her throat was dry. "Oh," she croaked.

"Oh," Wren echoed.

Melissa stood outside the window, her hair messy and Medusa-like, her face absolutely expressionless. A cigarette shook in her tiny, usually steady fingers.

"I didn't know you smoked," Spencer finally said.

Melissa didn't answer. Instead, she took one more drag, threw the butt in the dewy grass, and turned back toward the main house.

"You coming, Wren?" Melissa called frostily over her shoulder.

25

STUDENT DRIVERS THESE DAYS!

Mona's mouth dropped open when she came around the corner to Noel's front lawn. "Holy shit."

Hanna leaned out the window of Sean's father's BMW and grinned at Mona. "You love it?"

Mona's eyes lit up. "I'm speechless."

Hanna smiled gratefully and took a swig from the Ketel One bottle she'd swiped from the booze table. Two minutes ago, she'd texted Mona a picture of the BMW with the message, *I'm all lubed up and out front. Come ride me.*

Mona opened the heavy passenger door and slid into the seat. She leaned over and stared intensely at the BMW insignia on the steering wheel. "It's so beautiful. . . . " She traced the little blue and white triangles with her pinkie.

Hanna flicked her hand off. "Get stoned much?"

Mona raised her chin and appraised Hanna's dirty hair, crooked dress, and tear-stained face. "Things didn't go well with Sean?"

Hanna looked down and jammed the key into the ignition.

Mona moved to hug her. "Oh Han, I'm sorry. . . . What happened?"

"Nothing. Whatever." Hanna jerked away and put on her sunglasses—which made it a little hard to see, but who cared?—and started the car. It burst into action, all of the BMW's dashboard lights switching on.

"Pretty!" Mona cried. "It's like the lights at Club Shampoo!"

Hanna slammed the gear into reverse and the tires rolled through the thick grass. Then she jerked it into drive, cut the wheel, and off they went. Hanna was too keyed up to worry about the fact that the double lines on the road were quadrupling in her vision.

"*Yee haw,*" Mona whooped. She rolled down the window to let her long, blond hair flutter behind her. Hanna lit a Parliament and swiveled the Sirius radio dial until she found a retro rap station playing "Baby Got Back." She turned the volume up and the cabin throbbed—of *course* the car had the best bass money could buy.

"That's more like it," Mona said.

"Hells yeah," Hanna answered.

As she navigated a sharp turn a little too quickly, something in the back of her mind made a *ping*.

It's not gonna be you.

Ouch.

Even Daddy doesn't love you best!

Double ouch.

Well, fuck it. Hanna pressed down on the gas and nearly took out someone's dog-shaped mailbox.

"We've got to go somewhere and show this bitch off." Mona put her Miu Miu heels up on the dashboard, smearing bits of grass and dirt on it. "How 'bout Wawa? I'm jonesing for some Tastykake."

Hanna giggled and took another swig of Ketel One. "You must be super-baked."

"I'm not just baked, I'm broiled!"

They parked crookedly in the Wawa lot and sang, "*I like big BUTTS and I cannot lie!*" as they stumbled into the store. A couple of grubby delivery guys, holding 64-ounce cups of coffee and leaning against their trucks, stared with their mouths open.

"Can I have your hat?" Mona asked the skinnier of the two, pointing to his mesh ball cap that said WAWA FARMS. Without a word, the guy gave it to her.

"Ew," Hanna whispered. "That thing is germy!" But Mona had already put it on her head.

In the store, Mona bought sixteen Tastykake Butterscotch Krimpets, a copy of *Us Weekly*, and a huge bottle of Tahitian Treat; Hanna bought a Tootsie Pop for ten cents. When Mona wasn't looking, she shoved a Snickers and a pack of M&M's into her purse.

"I can hear the car," Mona said dreamily as they paid. "It's screaming."

It was true. In her drunken haze, Hanna had activated the alarm on the keychain. "Oops." She giggled.

Hooting with laughter, they ran back to the car and slid inside. They stopped at a red light, heads bobbing. The supermarket strip mall to their left was empty except for some loose shopping carts. The store's neon signs glowed vacantly; even the Outback Steakhouse bar was dead.

"People in Rosewood are such losers." Hanna gestured to the darkness.

The highway was barren too, so Hanna let out a startled, "Eep!" when a car stealthily rolled up in the lane next to her. It was a silver, pointy-nosed Porsche with tinted windows and those creepy blue headlights.

"Check that out," Mona said, Krimpet crumbs falling out of her mouth.

As they stared, the car revved its engine.

"It wants to race," Mona whispered.

"Bull," Hanna answered. She couldn't make out who was inside the car—only the red, glowing tip of a lit cigarette. An uneasy feeling washed over her.

The car revved its engine again—impatiently, this time—and she could finally see a vague outline of the driver. He revved his engine again.

Hanna raised an eyebrow at Mona, feeling drunk, hyped, and completely invincible.

"Do it," Mona whispered, pulling down the brim of the Wawa milk hat.

Hanna swallowed hard. The light turned green. As

Hanna hit the gas, the car launched forward. The Porsche growled ahead of her.

"You pussy, don't let him beat you!" Mona cried.

Hanna stepped down on the gas pedal and the engine roared. She pulled alongside the Porsche. They were doing 80, then 90, then 100. Driving this fast felt better than stealing.

"Kick his ass!" Mona screamed.

Heart pounding, Hanna pressed the pedal to the floor. She could hardly hear what Mona was saying over the engine noise. As they rounded a turn, a deer stepped into their lane. It came out of nowhere.

"Shit!" Hanna screamed. The deer stood dumbly still. She gripped the wheel tightly, hit the brakes, and swerved right, and the deer jumped out of the way. Quickly, she wrenched the wheel to straighten it out, but the car began to skid. The tires caught on a patch of gravel on the side of the road, and suddenly, they were spinning.

The car spun around and around, and then they hit something. All at once, there was a crunch, splintering glass and . . . darkness.

A split second later, the only sound in the car was a vigorous hissing noise from under the hood.

Slowly, Hanna felt her face. It was okay; nothing had hit it. And her legs could move. She pushed herself up through a bunch of folded, puffy fabric—the airbag. She checked on Mona. Her long legs kicked wildly from behind her airbag.

Hanna wiped tears from the corners of her eyes. "You okay?"

"Get this thing off me!"

Hanna got out of the car and then pulled Mona out. They stood on the side of the highway, breathing hard. Across the street were the SEPTA tracks and the dark Rosewood station. They could see far up the highway: There was no sign of the Porsche—or the deer that they'd missed. Ahead of them, the stoplights swung, turning from yellow to red.

"That was something," Mona said, her voice quivering.

Hanna nodded. "You sure you're all right?" She looked at the car.

The whole front end had crumpled into a telephone pole. The bumper hung off the car, touching the ground. One of the headlights had twisted around to a crooked angle; the other flashed crazily. Stinky steam poured out of the hood.

"You don't think it's gonna blow up, do you?" Mona asked.

Hanna giggled. This shouldn't have been funny, but it was. "What should we do?"

"We should bolt," Mona said. "We can walk home from here."

Hanna swallowed more giggles. "Oh my God. Sean's gonna shit!"

Then both girls started to laugh. Hiccupping, Hanna turned around on the empty road and spread her arms out. There was something empowering about standing in the middle of an empty four-lane highway. She felt like she owned Rosewood. She also felt like she was spinning, but maybe that was because she was still wasted. She tossed the key ring next to the car. It hit the pavement hard, and the alarm started wailing again.

Hanna quickly bent down and hit the deactivate button. The alarm stopped. "Does it have to be so *loud*?" she complained.

"Totally." Mona put her sunglasses back on. "Sean's dad should really get that fixed."

26

DO U LOVE ME? Y OR N?

The grandfather clock in the hall rang at 9 A.M. on Saturday morning as Emily padded quietly down the stairs to the kitchen. She never got up this early on the weekends, but this morning, she couldn't sleep.

Someone had made coffee, and there were sticky buns sitting out on a chicken-print plate on the table. It looked as if her parents had gone out for their never-fail, rain-or-shine Saturday crack-of-dawn walk. If they did their two loops around the neighborhood, Emily could get out of here without anybody noticing.

Last night, after Ben caught her and Maya in the photo booth, Emily had bolted from the party—without saying good-bye to Maya. Emily had called Carolyn—who *was* at Applebee's—and asked for a ride, pronto. Carolyn and Topher, her boyfriend, came, no questions asked, although her sister gave Emily—who stank of whiskey—a stern, parental look when she climbed in the backseat. At home, she'd hidden under her covers so she wouldn't have to talk to Carolyn and dropped off into a deep sleep. But this morning, she felt worse than ever.

She didn't know what to think about what happened at the party. It was all a blur. She wanted to believe that kissing Maya had been a mistake, and that she could explain everything to Ben and it would be okay. But Emily kept returning to how everything felt. It was like . . . before last night, she'd never been kissed before.

But there was nothing, *nothing* about Emily that said lesbian. She bought girly hot-oil treatments for her chlorine-damaged hair. She had a poster of the hot Australian swimmer Ian Thorpe on her wall. She giggled with the other swimmer girls about the boys in their Speedos. She'd only kissed one other girl, years ago, and that didn't count. Even if it did, it didn't mean anything, right?

She broke a Danish in half and stuffed a piece in her mouth. Her head throbbed. She wanted things to go back to the way they were. To throw a fresh towel in her duffel and head to practice, to happily make goofy pig faces into someone's digital camera on the away-meet bus. To be content with herself and her life and to not be an emotional yo-yo.

So that was it. Maya was awesome and all, but they were just confused—and sad, for their own reasons. But not gay. Right?

She needed some air.

It was desolate outside. The birds were chirping

noisily, and someone's dog kept barking, but everything was still. Freshly delivered papers were still waiting on front lawns, wrapped in blue plastic.

Her old, red Trek mountain bike was propped up against the side of the toolshed. Emily jerked it upright, hoping she'd be coordinated enough to handle a bike after last night's whiskey. She pushed off to the street, but her bike's front wheel made a flapping noise.

Emily bent down. There was something caught in the wheel. A piece of notebook paper was woven through the spokes. She pulled it out and read a few lines. Wait. This was her own handwriting.

. . . I love staring at the back of your head in class, I love how you chew gum whenever we're talking on the phone together, and I love that when you jiggle your Skechers during class when Mrs. Hat starts talking about famous American court cases, I know you're totally bored.

Emily's eyes darted around her empty front yard. Was this what she thought it was? She nervously skimmed down to the bottom, her mouth dry.

. . . and I've done a lot of thinking about why I kissed you the other day. I realized: It wasn't a joke, Ali. I think I love you. I can understand if you never want to speak to me again, but I just had to tell you. —Em

There was something else written on the other side of the paper. She flipped it over.

Thought you might want this back.
Love, A

Emily let her bike clatter to the ground.

This was *the* letter to Ali, the very one Emily had sent right after the kiss. The one she'd wondered if Ali had ever gotten.

Calm down, Emily told herself, realizing her hands were trembling. *There's a logical explanation for this.*

It had to be Maya. She lived in Ali's old room. Emily had told Maya about Alison and the letter last night. Maybe she was just giving it back?

But then . . . *Love, A.* Maya wouldn't write that.

Emily didn't know what to do or who to talk to. Suddenly, she thought of Aria. So much had happened last night after Emily ran into her, she'd forgotten their conversation. What had all Aria's bizarre Alison questions been about? And there was something about her expression last night. Aria seemed . . . nervous.

Emily sat on the ground and looked at the "Thought you might want this back" message again. If Emily recalled correctly, Aria had spiky handwriting that looked a lot like this.

In the last days before Ali had gone missing, she'd held the kiss over Emily's head, forcing Emily to go along with whatever she wanted to do. It hadn't occurred to Emily that maybe Ali had told the rest of their friends. But maybe . . .

"Honey?"

Emily jumped. Her parents stood above her, dressed in sensible white sneakers, high-waisted shorts, and preppy pastel golf shirts. Her father had a red fanny pack, and her mom swung turquoise arm weights back and forth.

"Hey," Emily croaked.

"Going for a bike ride?" her mother asked.

"Uh-huh."

"You're supposed to be grounded." Her father put on his glasses, as if he needed to see Emily to scold her. "We only let you out last night because you were going with Ben. We hoped he'd get through to you. But bike rides are off limits."

"Well," Emily groaned, standing up. If only she didn't have to explain things to her parents. But then . . . whatever. She wouldn't. Not now. She threw her leg over the bar and sat on her seat.

"I have somewhere to go," she mumbled, pedaling down the driveway.

"Emily, come back here," her father yelled gruffly.

But Emily, for the first time in her life, just kept pedaling.

27

DON'T MIND ME, I'M JUST DEAD!

Aria awoke to her doorbell ringing. Except it wasn't her family's normal doorbell chime, it was "American Idiot," by Green Day. Huh—when had her parents changed that?

She threw back her duvet, slid on the blue-flowered, fur-lined clogs she'd bought in Amsterdam, and clomped down the spiral staircase to see who it was.

When she opened the door, she gasped. It was Alison. She was taller and her blond hair was cut in long shaggy layers. Her face looked more glamorous and angular than it had in seventh grade.

"Ta-*daa*!" Ali grinned and spread out her arms. "I'm back!"

"Holy . . . " Aria choked on her words, blinking furiously a couple of times. "*Wh*-where have you been?"

Ali rolled her eyes. "My stupid parents," she said. "Remember my aunt Camille, the really cool one who was born in France and married my uncle Jeff when we

were in seventh? I went to visit her in Miami that summer. Then, I liked it so much that I just stayed. I totally
told my parents about all of it, but I guess they forgot to
tell everyone else."

Aria rubbed her eyes. "So, wait. You've been in . . .
Miami? You're *okay*?"

Ali twirled around a little. "I look more than okay,
don't I? Hey, did you like my texts?"

Aria's smile faded. "Um . . . no, actually."

Ali looked hurt. "Why not? That one about your
mom was *so* funny."

Aria stared at her.

"God, you're sensitive." Ali narrowed her eyes. "Are
you going to blow me off again?"

"Wait, what?" Aria stammered.

Alison gave Aria a long look, and a black, gelatinous
substance began dripping out her nostrils. "I told the others, you know. About your dad. I told them everything."

"Your . . . nose . . . " Aria pointed. Suddenly it started
seeping out of Ali's eyeballs. Like she was crying oil. It
was dripping from her fingernails, too.

"Oh, I'm just rotting." Ali smiled.

Aria jerked up in bed. Sweat drenched the back of
her neck. The sun streamed in through her window, and
she heard "American Idiot" on her brother's stereo next
door. She checked her hands for black goo, but they were
squeaky clean.

Whoa.

"Morning, honey."

Aria staggered down her spiral staircase to see her father, dressed only in thin, tartan plaid boxer shorts and a sleeveless T-shirt, reading the *Philadelphia Inquirer*. "Hey," she murmured back.

Shuffling to the espresso machine, she stared for a long time at her father's pale, randomly hairy shoulders. He jiggled his feet and made *hmmm* noises at the paper.

"Dad?" Her voice cracked slightly.

"Mmm?"

Aria leaned against the stone-topped island. "Can ghosts send text messages?"

Her father looked up, surprised and confused. "What's a text message?"

She stuck her hand into an open box of Frosted Mini Wheats and pulled out a handful. "Never mind."

"You sure?" Byron asked.

She chewed nervously. What did she want to ask? *Is a ghost sending me texts?* But c'mon, she knew better. Anyway, she didn't know why Ali's ghost would come back and do this to her. It was as if she wanted revenge, but was that possible?

Ali had been great the day they caught her dad in the car. Aria had fled around the corner and ran until she had to start walking. She kept walking all the way home, not sure what else to do with herself. Ali hugged her for a long time. "I won't tell," she whispered.

But the next day, the questions started. *Do you know that girl? Is she a student? Is your dad going to tell your mom? Do you think he's doing it with lots of students?* Usually, Aria could take Ali's inquisitiveness and even her teasing—she was okay with being the "weird kid" of the group. But this was different. This *hurt*.

So the last few days of school, before she disappeared, Aria avoided Alison. She didn't send her "I'm bored" texts during health class or help her clean out her locker. And she certainly didn't talk about what happened. She was mad that Ali was prying—as if it was some celebrity gossip in *Star* and not her life. She was mad that Ali knew. Period.

Now, three years later, Aria wondered who she'd really been mad at. It wasn't really Ali. It was her dad.

"Really, never mind," Aria answered her father, who'd been waiting patiently, sipping his coffee. "I'm just sleepy."

"Okay," Byron answered incredulously.

The doorbell rang. It wasn't the Green Day song but their normal *bong, bong* chime. Her father looked up. "I wonder if that's for Mike," he said. "Did you know that some girl from the Quaker school came by here at eight-thirty, looking for him?"

"I'll get it," Aria said.

She tentatively pulled open the front door, but it was only Emily Fields on the other side, her reddish-blond hair messy and her eyes swollen.

"Hey," Emily croaked.

"Hey," Aria answered.

Emily puffed up her cheeks with air—her old nervous habit. She stood there for a moment. Then she said, "I should go." She started to turn.

"Wait." Aria caught her arm. "What? What's going on?"

Emily paused. "Um. Okay. But . . . this is going to sound weird."

"That's okay." Aria's heart started to pound.

"I was thinking about what you were saying yesterday at the party. About Ali. I was wondering . . . did Ali ever tell you guys something about me?"

Emily said it very quietly. Aria pushed her hair out of her eyes.

"What?" Aria whispered. "Recently?"

Emily's eyes widened. "What do you mean, *recently*?"

"I—"

"In seventh grade," Emily interrupted. "Did she tell you . . . like . . . something about me in seventh grade? Was she telling everybody?"

Aria blinked. At the party yesterday, when she'd seen Emily, she'd wanted more than anything to tell her about the texts. "No," Aria answered slowly. "She never talked behind your back."

"Oh." Emily stared at the ground. "But I—" she started.

"I've been getting these—" Aria said at the same time. Then Emily looked past her and her eyes grew still.

"Miss Emily Fields! Hello!"

Aria turned. In the living room stood Byron. At least he'd thrown on a striped bathrobe. "I haven't seen you in ages!" Byron boomed.

"Yeah." Emily puffed out her cheeks again. "How are you, Mr. Montgomery?"

He frowned. "Please. You're old enough to call me Byron." He scratched his chin with the top edge of his coffee cup. "How's your life? Good?"

"Absolutely." Emily looked like she was about to cry.

"Do you need something to eat?" Byron asked. "You look hungry."

"Oh. No. Thanks. I, um, I guess I didn't really sleep well."

"You girls." He shook his head. "You never sleep! I always tell Aria she needs eleven hours—she needs to bank sleep for when she gets to college and parties all night!" He began climbing the stairs to the second floor.

As soon as he was out of sight, Aria whirled back around. "He's so—" she started. But then she realized Emily was halfway across her lawn, on the way to her bike. "Hey!" she called. "Where are you going?"

Emily picked her bike up off the ground. "I shouldn't have come."

"Wait! Come back! I . . . I need to talk to you!" Aria called out.

Emily paused and looked up. Aria felt all of her words swarming like bees in her mouth. Emily seemed terrified.

But suddenly Aria was too afraid to ask. How would she talk about the texts from A without mentioning her secret? She still didn't want anyone to know. Especially with her mom just upstairs.

Then she thought of Byron in his bathrobe and how uncomfortable Emily seemed around him just now. Emily had asked, *Did Alison tell you something about me in seventh grade?* Why would she ask that?

Unless . . .

Aria bit her pinkie nail. What if Emily already *knew* Aria's secret? Aria clamped her mouth shut, paralyzed.

Emily shook her head. "I'll see you later," she mumbled, and before Aria could compose herself, Emily was biking furiously away.

28

BRAD AND ANGELINA ACTUALLY MET AT THE ROSEWOOD POLICE STATION

"Ladies, discover yourselves!"

As Oprah's audience clapped wildly, Hanna sank into her coffee-colored leather couch cushions, balancing the TiVo remote on her bare stomach. She could use a little self-discovery on this crisp Saturday morning.

Last night was pretty blurry—like she'd gone through the night without her contacts in—and her head was throbbing. Had it involved some sort of animal? She'd found some empty candy wrappers in her purse. Had she eaten them? *All* of them? Her stomach hurt, after all, and it looked a little puffy. And why did she have a distinct memory of a Wawa dairy truck? It felt like piecing together a puzzle, except Hanna was too impatient for puzzles—she always jammed pieces together that didn't actually fit.

The doorbell rang. Hanna groaned, then rolled off the couch, not bothering to fix her army-green ribbed tank top, which was turned around and practically exposing her boob. She cracked the oak door and then slammed it shut again.

Whoa. It was that cop, Mr. April. Er, Darren Wilden.

"Open up, Hanna."

She checked him out through the peephole. He stood with his arms crossed, seeming all business, but then his hair was a mess and she didn't see his gun anywhere. And what kind of cop worked at 10 A.M. on a cloudless Saturday morning like this?

Hanna glanced at her reflection in the round mirror across the room. Jesus. Sleep marks from the pillow? Yes. Puffy eyes, lips in need of gloss? Absolutely. She quickly ran her hands over her face, pushed her hair into a ponytail, and put on her round Chanel sunglasses. Then she flung open the door.

"Hey!" she said brightly. "How are you?"

"Is your mom home?" he asked.

"Nope," Hanna said flirtatiously. "She's out all morning."

Wilden pursed his lips together, looking stressed. Hanna noticed Wilden had a little clear Band-Aid right above his eyebrow. "What, did your girlfriend deck you?" she asked, pointing at it.

"No . . . " Wilden touched the Band-Aid. "I banged it on my medicine cabinet when I was washing my face."

He rolled his eyes. "I'm not the most graceful person in the morning."

Hanna smiled. "Join the club. I fell on my ass last night. It was so random."

Wilden's kind expression was suddenly grim. "Was that before or after you stole the car?"

Hanna stood back. "What?"

Why was Wilden looking at her as if she were the love child of space aliens? "There was an anonymous tip that you stole a car," he enunciated slowly.

Hanna's mouth fell open. "I . . . *what*?"

"A black BMW? Belonging to a Mr. Edwin Ackard? You crashed it into a phone pole? After you drank a bottle of Ketel One? Any of this sound familiar?"

Hanna shoved her sunglasses up her nose. Wait, *that* was what happened? "I wasn't drunk last night," she lied.

"We found a vodka bottle on the driver's-side floor in the car," Wilden said. "So, *someone* was drunk."

"But–" Hanna started.

"I have to bring you into the station," Wilden interrupted, sounding a little disappointed.

"I didn't steal it," Hanna squeaked. "Sean–his son–said I could take it!"

Wilden raised an eyebrow. "So you admit you were driving it?"

"I–" Hanna started. *Shit*. She took a step back into the house. "But my mom's not even here. She won't know what happened to me." Embarrassingly, tears rushed to her eyes. She turned away, trying to get her shit together.

Wilden shifted his weight uncomfortably. It seemed like he didn't know what to do with his hands—first he put them in his pockets, then they hovered near Hanna, then he wrung them together. "Listen, we can call your mom at the station, all right?" he said. "And I won't cuff you. And you can ride up front with me." He walked back to his car and opened the passenger door for her.

An hour later, she sat on the police station's same yellow plastic bucket seats, staring at the same *Chester County's Most Wanted* poster, fighting back the urge to start crying again. She'd just been given a blood test to see if she was still drunk from last night. Hanna wasn't sure if she was—did alcohol stay in your body for that long? Now Wilden was hunching over his same desk, which held the same Bic pens and a metallic Slinky. She pinched her palm with her fingernails and swallowed.

Unfortunately, the events of last night had coalesced in her head. The Porsche, the deer, the airbag. *Had* Sean said she could take the car? She doubted it; the last thing she could remember was his little self-esteem speech before he'd ditched her in the woods.

"Hey, were you at the Swarthmore battle of the bands last night?"

A college-age guy with a buzz cut and a uni-brow sat next to her. He wore a ripped flannel surfer's shirt, paint-spattered jeans, and no shoes. His hands were cuffed. "Um, no," Hanna muttered.

He leaned close to her, and Hanna could smell his beery breath. "Oh. I thought I saw you there. I was and I drank too much and started terrorizing someone's cows. That's why I'm here! I was trespassing!"

"Good for you," she answered frostily.

"What's your name?" He jingled his cuffs.

"Um, Angelina." Like hell she was giving him her real name.

"Hey, Angelina," he said. "I'm Brad!"

Hanna cracked a smile at how lame that line was.

Just then, the station's front door opened. Hanna jerked back in her seat and pushed her sunglasses up her nose. Great. It was her mom.

"I came as soon as I heard," Ms. Marin said to Wilden.

This morning, Ms. Marin wore a simple white boat-neck tee, low-waisted James jeans, Gucci slingbacks, and the exact same Chanel shades that Hanna was wearing. Her skin radiated—she'd been at the spa all morning—and her red-gold hair was pulled back into a simple ponytail. Hanna squinted. Had her mom stuffed her bra? Her boobs looked like they belonged to someone else.

"I'll talk to her," Ms. Marin said to Wilden in a low voice. Then she walked over to Hanna. She smelled of seaweed body wrap. Hanna, certain that she smelled of Ketel One and Eggo waffles, tried to shrink in her seat.

"I'm sorry," Hanna squeaked.

"Did they make you take a blood test?" she hissed.

She nodded miserably.

"What else did you tell them?"

"N-n-nothing," she stuttered.

Ms. Marin laced her French-manicured hands together. "Okay. I'll handle this. Just be quiet."

"What are you going to do?" she whispered back. "Are you going to call Sean's dad?"

"I said I'll *handle* it, Hanna."

Her mother rose up from the plastic bucket seats and leaned over Wilden's desk. Hanna tore through her purse for her emergency pack of Twizzlers Pull-n-Peel. She'd just have a couple, not the whole pack. It had to be in here somewhere.

As she pulled out the Twizzlers, she felt her BlackBerry buzzing. Hanna hesitated. What if it was Sean, chewing her out via voice mail? What if it was Mona? Where the hell *was* Mona? Had they actually let her go to the golf tourney? She hadn't stolen the car, but she'd come along for the ride. That had to count for something.

Her BlackBerry had a few missed calls. Sean . . . six times. Mona, twice, at 8 A.M. and 8:03. There were also some new text messages: a bunch from kids at the party, unrelated, and then one from a cell number she didn't know. Hanna's stomach knotted.

Hanna: Remember the KATE toothbrush? Thought so! —A

Hanna blinked. A cold, clammy sweat gathered on the back of her neck. She felt dizzy. *The Kate toothbrush?* "Come on," she said shakily, trying to laugh. She glanced up at her mother, but she was still bent over Wilden's desk, talking.

When she was in Annapolis, after her father told Hanna that she was, essentially, a pig, Hanna shot up from the table and ran inside. She ducked into the powder room, shut the door, and sat down on the toilet.

She took deep breaths, trying to calm down. Why couldn't she be beautiful and graceful and perfect like Ali or Kate? Why did she have to be who she was, dumpy and clumsy and a wreck? And she wasn't sure who she was angriest at—her dad, Kate, herself, or . . . Alison.

As Hanna choked on hot, angry tears, she noticed the three framed pictures on the wall across from the toilet. All three were close-ups of someone's eyes. She recognized her father's squinty, expressive eyes right away. And there were Isabel's small, almond-shaped ones. The third pair of eyes were large, intoxicating. They looked like they were straight out of a Chanel mascara ad. They were obviously Kate's.

They were all watching her.

Hanna stared at herself in the mirror. A peal of laughter floated in from outside. Her stomach felt like it was bursting from all the popcorn everyone had watched her eat. She felt so sick, she just wanted it *out* of there, but when she leaned over the toilet, nothing happened. Tears spilled down her cheeks. As she reached for a Kleenex, she noticed a green toothbrush sitting in a little porcelain cup. It gave her an idea.

It took her ten minutes to work up the nerve to put it into her throat, but when she did, she felt worse—but also better. She started crying even harder, but she also wanted to do it again. As she eased the toothbrush back in her mouth, the bathroom door burst open.

It was Alison. Her eyes swept over Hanna kneeling on the floor, the toothbrush in her hand. "Whoa," she said.

"Please go away," Hanna whispered.

Alison took a step into the bathroom. "Do you want to talk about it?"

Hanna looked at her desperately. "At least close the door!"

Ali shut the door and sat on the side of the tub. "How long have you been doing this for?"

Hanna's lip quivered. "Doing what?"

Ali paused, looking at the toothbrush. Her eyes widened. Hanna looked at it too. She hadn't noticed before, but KATE was printed on the side in white letters.

A phone rang loudly in the police station and Hanna flinched. *Remember the Kate toothbrush?* Someone else might have known about Hanna's eating problem, or might have seen her going into the police station, or might even know about Kate. But the *green toothbrush*? There was only one person who knew about that.

Hanna liked to believe that if Ali were alive, she'd be rooting for her, now that her life was so perfect. That was the scene she replayed in her mind constantly—Ali impressed by her size 2 jeans. Ali oohing over her Chanel lip gloss. Ali congratulating Hanna on how she'd planned the perfect pool party.

With shaking hands, Hanna typed, *Is this Alison?*

"Wilden," a cop shouted. "We need you in the back."

Hanna looked up. Darren Wilden rose from his desk, excusing himself from Hanna's mom. Within seconds, the whole precinct burst into action. A cop car flew out of the parking lot; three more followed. Phones rang maniacally; four cops sprinted through the room.

"It looks like something big," said Brad, the drunk trespasser sitting next to her. Hanna flinched—she'd forgotten he was there.

"A donut shortage?" she asked, trying to laugh.

"Bigger." He jiggled his handcuffed hands excitedly. "Looks like something *very* big."

29

GOOD MORNING, WE HATE YOU

The sun streamed in through the barn's window, and for the first time in Spencer's life, she was awakened by the chirping of high-on-life sparrows instead of the frightening '90s techno mix her dad blasted from the main house's exercise room. But could she enjoy it? Nope.

Although she hadn't drunk a drop last night, her body felt achy, chilled, and hungover. There was zero sleep in her fuel tank. After Wren left, she'd tried to sleep, but her mind spun. The way Wren held her felt so . . . different. Spencer had never felt anything remotely like that before.

But then that IM. And Melissa's calm, spooky expression. And . . .

As the night wore on, the barn creaked and groaned, and Spencer pulled the covers up to her nose, shaking. She chided herself for feeling paranoid and immature, but she couldn't help it. She kept thinking of the possibilities.

Eventually, she'd gotten up and rebooted her computer. For a few hours, she searched the Internet. First she looked at technical websites, searching for answers on how to trace IMs. No luck. Then she tried to find where that first e-mail—the one titled "covet"—had come from. She wanted, desperately, for the trail to end at Andrew Campbell.

She found that Andrew had a blog, but after scouring the whole thing, she found nothing. The entries were all about the books Andrew liked to read, dorky boy philosophizing, a couple of melancholy passages about an unrequited crush on some girl he never named. She thought he might slip up and give himself away, but he didn't.

Finally, she plugged in the key words *missing persons* and *Alison DiLaurentis*.

She found the same stuff from three years ago—the reports on CNN and in the *Philadelphia Inquirer*, search groups, and kooky sites, like one showing what Ali might look like with different hairstyles. Spencer stared at the school picture they'd used; she hadn't seen a photo of Ali in a long time. Would she recognize Ali if she had, for instance, a short, black bob? She certainly looked different in this picture they'd created.

The main house's screen door squeaked as she nervously pushed through it. Inside, she smelled freshly brewed coffee, which was odd, because usually her mom was already at the stables by now and her dad was riding or at the golf course. She wondered what had happened between Melissa and Wren after last night, praying she wouldn't have to face them.

"We've been waiting for you."

Spencer jumped. At the kitchen table were her parents and Melissa. Her mother's face was pale and drained and her dad's cheeks were beet red. Melissa's eyes were red-rimmed and puffy. Even the two dogs didn't jump up to greet her as they normally did.

Spencer swallowed hard. So much for praying.

"Sit down, please," her father said quietly.

Spencer scraped back a wooden chair and sat next to her mother. The room was so still and silent, she could hear her stomach, nervously on spin cycle.

"I don't even know what to say," her mother croaked. "How *could* you?"

Spencer's stomach dropped. She opened her mouth, but her mother held up her hand. "You have no right to talk right now."

Spencer clamped her mouth shut and lowered her eyes.

"Honestly," her father said, "I am so mortified you're my daughter right now. I thought we raised you better."

Spencer picked at a rough cuticle on her thumb and tried to stop her chin from wobbling.

"What were you thinking?" her mother asked. "That was her *boyfriend*. They were planning to move *in* together. Do you realize what you've done?"

"I–" Spencer started.

"I mean . . . ," her mother interrupted, then wrung her hands and looked down.

"You're under eighteen, which means we're legally responsible for you," her father said. "But if it were up to me, I'd lock you out of this house right now."

"I wish I never had to see you again," Melissa spat.

Spencer felt faint. She half-expected them to set down their coffee cups and tell her they were just kidding, that everything was all right. But they couldn't even *look* at her. Her dad's words stung in her ears: *I am so mortified you're my daughter.* No one had ever said anything like that to her before.

"One thing's for certain; Melissa will be moving into the barn," her mother continued. "I want all of your stuff out and back into your old bedroom. And once her town house is ready, I'm turning the barn into a pottery studio."

Spencer balled up her fists under the table, willing herself not to cry. She didn't care about the barn, not really. It was what came with the barn that mattered. It was that her dad was going to build shelves for her. Her mom was going to help her pick out new curtains. They'd said she could get a kitten and they'd all spent a few minutes thinking up funny names for it. They were excited for her. They *cared*.

She reached out for her mother's arm. "I'm sorry–"

Her mother slid her body away. "Spencer, don't."

Spencer couldn't manage to swallow her sob. Tears started running down her cheeks.

"It's not me you need to apologize to, anyway," her mother said in a low voice.

Spencer looked at Melissa, sniveling across the table. She wiped her nose. As much as she hated Melissa, she'd never seen her sister this miserable—not since Ian broke up with her back in high school. It was wrong to flirt with Wren, but Spencer hadn't thought it would go as far as it did. She tried to put herself in Melissa's place—if she'd met Wren first, and Melissa had kissed him, she'd be shattered too. Her heart softened. "I'm sorry," she whispered.

Melissa shuddered. "Rot in hell," she spat.

Spencer bit the inside of her mouth so hard she tasted blood.

"Just get your things out of the barn." Her mother sighed. "Then get out of our sight."

Spencer's eyes widened. "But—" she squeaked.

Her father gave her a withering look.

"It's just so despicable," her mother murmured.

"You're such a bitch," Melissa threw in.

Spencer nodded—perhaps if she agreed with them, they would stop. She wanted to shrivel up into a tiny ball and evaporate. Instead, she mumbled, "I'll go do it now."

"Good." Her father took another sip of coffee and left the table.

Melissa made a small squeak and pushed back her chair. She sobbed the whole way up the stairs and slammed her bedroom door.

"Wren left last night," Mr. Hastings said as he paused in the doorway. "We won't be hearing from him, ever again. And if you know what's best for you, *you* won't talk about him ever again."

"Of course," Spencer mumbled, and set her head down on the cool oak table.

"Good."

Spencer kept her head firmly on the table, breathing yoga fire breaths and waiting for someone to come back and tell her that everything would be okay. Nobody did. Outside, she heard an ambulance siren screaming in the distance. It sounded like it was coming toward the house.

Spencer sat up. *Oh God.* What if Melissa had . . . hurt herself? She wouldn't, would she? The sirens howled, coming closer. Spencer shoved back her chair.

Holy shit. What had she done?

"Melissa!" she yelled, running to the stairs.

"You're a whore!" came a voice. "You're a fucking whore!"

Spencer slumped back against the railing. Well, then. It seemed Melissa was just fine, after all.

30

THE CIRCUS IS BACK IN TOWN

Emily biked furiously away from Aria's house, narrowly missing a jogger on the side of the road. "Watch it!" he yelled.

As she passed a neighbor walking two huge Great Danes, Emily made a decision. She had to go to Maya's. It was the only answer. Maybe Maya had meant it in a nice way, like she was just returning the note after Emily told her about Alison last night. Maybe Maya wanted to mention the letter last night but, for whatever reason, she didn't. Maybe the *A* was really an *M*?

Besides, she and Maya had tons of other stuff to talk about—besides the note. Try everything that happened at the party. Emily closed her eyes, remembering. She could practically smell Maya's banana gum and feel the soft contours of her mouth. Opening her eyes, she swerved away from the curb.

Okay, they definitely needed to work that out. But what did Emily want to say?

I loved it.

No. Of course she wouldn't say that. She would say, *We should just be friends.* She was going back to Ben, after all. If he'd have her. She wanted to rewind time, to go back to being the Emily who was happy with her life, who her parents were happy with. The Emily who only worried about her breaststroke reach and her algebra homework.

Emily pedaled past Myer Park, where she and Ali used to swing for hours. They tried to pump together in unison, and when they were completely even, Ali always called out, "We're married!" Then they'd squeal and jump off at the same time.

But what if Maya hadn't put that note on her bike? When Emily asked Aria if Ali had told her Emily's secret, Aria had replied, "What, recently?" Why would Aria say that? Unless . . . unless Aria knew something. Unless Ali was back.

Was that possible?

Emily skidded through the gravel. No, that was crazy. Her mother still exchanged holiday cards with Mrs. DiLaurentis; she would've heard if Ali had returned. Back when Ali vanished, it was on the news 24/7. These days, her parents usually had on CNN while they ate breakfast. It would surely be a top story again.

Still, it was thrilling to consider. Every night for almost a year after Ali's disappearance, Emily had asked her Magic 8 Ball if Alison would come back. Although it sometimes said, *Wait and see*, it never, ever said, *No*. She made bets with herself, too: *If two kids get on the school bus today wearing red shirts*, she would whisper to herself, *Ali is okay. If they're serving pizza at lunch, Ali's not dead. If Coach makes us practice starts and turns, Ali will come back*. Nine times out of ten, according to Emily's little superstitions, Ali was on her way back to them.

Maybe she'd been right all along.

She pumped uphill and around a sharp turn, narrowly avoiding a stone Revolutionary War battle memorial sign. If Ali was back, what would that mean for Emily's friendship with Maya? She sort of doubted she could have two best friends . . . two best friends she felt so similarly about. She wondered what Ali would even think of Maya. What if they hated each other?

I loved it.

We should just be friends.

She swept past the beautiful farmhouses, crumbling stone inns, and gardeners' pickups parked on the road's shoulder. She used to bike this exact route to Ali's house; the last time, in fact, had been before the kiss. Emily hadn't planned to kiss Ali before she came; something had come over her in the heat of the moment. She would never forget how soft Ali's lips were or the stunned look on Ali's face when she pulled back. "What did you do that for?" she'd asked.

Suddenly, a siren wailed behind her. Emily barely had time to move to the edge of the road again before a Rosewood ambulance screamed past. A gust of wind kicked up, blowing dust into her face. She wiped her eyes and stared as the ambulance got to the top of the hill and paused at Alison's street.

Now it was turning onto Alison's street. Fear seized Emily. Ali's street was . . . Maya's street. She gripped the rubber handles of her bike.

With all the craziness, she'd forgotten the secret Maya had told her last night. The cutting. The hospital. That huge, jagged scar. *Sometimes I just feel like I need to,* Maya had said.

"Oh my God," Emily whispered.

She pedaled furiously and skidded around the corner. *If the ambulance sirens stop by the time I get around the corner,* she thought, *Maya will be okay.*

But then the ambulance pulled to a stop in front of Maya's house. The sirens were still roaring. Police cars were everywhere.

"No," Emily whispered. White-coated medics got out of the vehicle and ran for the house. A ton of people littered Maya's yard, some with cameras. Emily threw her bike at the curb and ran crookedly toward the house.

"Emily!"

Maya burst through the crowd. Emily gasped, then ran into Maya's arms, tears messily running down her face.

"You're okay." Emily sobbed. "I was afraid—"

"I'm fine," Maya said.

But there was something in her voice that was clearly *not* fine. Emily stood back. Maya's eyes were red and watery. Her mouth was drawn down nervously.

"What is it?" Emily asked. "What's going on?"

Maya swallowed. "They found your friend."

"What?" Emily stared at her, then at the scene on Maya's lawn. It was all so eerily familiar: the ambulance, the cop cars, the crowds of people, the long-lensed cameras. A news helicopter hovered overhead. This was exactly the same scene as three years ago, when Ali went missing.

Emily stepped back out of Maya's arms, grinning in disbelief. She *had* been right!

Alison was back at her house, like nothing had ever happened. "I knew it!" she whispered.

Maya took Emily's hand. "They were digging for our tennis court. My mom was there. She . . . saw her. I heard her scream from my bedroom."

Emily dropped her hand. "Wait. What?"

"I tried to call you," Maya added.

Emily wrinkled her brow and stared back at Maya. Then she looked at the twenty-strong team of cops.

At Mrs. St. Germain sobbing by the tire swing. At the POLICE LINE, DO NOT CROSS tape loops around the backyard. And then at the van parked in the driveway. It said, ROSEWOOD PD MORGUE. She had to read it six times for it to make sense. Her heart sped up and suddenly she couldn't breathe.

"I don't . . . understand," Emily sputtered, taking another step back. "Who did they find?"

Maya looked at her sympathetically, her eyes shiny with tears. "Your friend Alison," she whispered. "They just found her body."

31

HELL IS OTHER PEOPLE

Byron Montgomery took a big sip of coffee and shakily lit his pipe. "They found her when they were excavating the concrete slab in the DiLaurentises' old backyard to put in a tennis court."

"She was under the concrete," Ella jumped in. "They knew it was her from the ring she was wearing. But they're doing DNA tests to make sure."

It felt like a fist was pummeling Aria's stomach. She remembered Ali's white-gold initialed ring. Ali's parents had gotten it for her at Tiffany's when she was ten after she got her tonsils out. Ali liked to wear it on her pinkie.

"Why did they have to do DNA tests?" Mike asked. "Was she all decomposed?"

"Michelangelo!" Byron frowned. "That's not a very sensitive thing to say in front of your sister."

Mike shrugged and jammed a piece of sour green-apple Bubble Tape into his mouth. Aria sat opposite him, tears quietly running down her cheeks, absentmind-edly unraveling the edge of a rattan place mat. It was 2 P.M., and they were sitting around the kitchen table.

"I can handle it." Aria's throat constricted. "*Was* she decomposed?"

Her parents looked at each other. "Well, yes," her father said, scratching his chest through a little hole in his shirt. "Bodies break down pretty fast."

"Sick," Mike whispered.

Aria shut her eyes. Alison was dead. Her body was rotted. Someone had probably killed her.

"Sweetheart?" Ella asked quietly, cupping her hand over Aria's. "Honey, are you all right?"

"I don't know," Aria murmured, trying not to start bawling all over again.

"Would you like a Xanax?" Byron asked.

Aria shook her head.

"*I'll* take a Xanax," Mike said quickly.

Aria nervously picked at the side of her thumb. Her body felt hot and then cold. She didn't know what to do or think. The only person who she thought might make her feel better was Ezra; she thought she could explain all of her feelings to him. At the very least, he would let her curl up on his denim futon and cry.

Scraping back her chair, she started for her room. Byron and Ella exchanged glances and followed her to the spiral staircase.

"Sweetie?" Ella asked. "What can we do?"

But Aria ignored them and pushed through her bedroom door. Her room was a disaster. Aria hadn't cleaned since she'd moved back from Iceland, and she wasn't the neatest girl in the world to start with. Her clothes were all over the floor in unorganized piles. On her bed were CDs, sequins she was using to make a beaded hat, poster paints, playing cards, Pigtunia, line drawings of Ezra's profile, several skeins of yarn. The carpet had a big, red candle wax stain on it. She searched in the covers of her bed and on the surface of her desk for her Treo—she needed it to call Ezra. But it wasn't there. She checked the green bag she'd taken to the party last night, but her phone wasn't in that, either.

Then she remembered. After she received that text, she'd dropped the phone like it was poisonous. She must have left it behind.

She stormed down the stairs. Her parents were still on the landing.

"I'm taking the car," she mumbled, grabbing the keys off the ring by the foyer table.

"Okay," her father said.

"Take your time," her mother added.

Someone had propped the front door to Ezra's house open with a large metal sculpture of a terrier. Aria stepped around it and walked inside the hallway. She knocked on Ezra's door. She had the same feeling she did when she had to pee really badly—it might be torture, but you knew that very soon, you were going to feel a whole hell of a lot better.

Ezra flung open the door. As soon as he saw her, he tried to shut it again.

"Wait," Aria squeaked, her voice still filled with tears. Ezra retreated into his kitchen, his back to her. She followed him in.

Ezra whirled around to face her. He was unshaven and looked exhausted. "What are you doing here?"

Aria chewed on her lip. "I'm here to see you. I got some news. . . . " Her Treo sat on his sideboard. She picked it up. "Thanks. You found it."

Ezra glared at the Treo. "Okay, you got it. Can you leave now?"

"What's going on?" She walked toward him. "I got this news. I had to see—"

"Yeah, I got some news too," he interrupted. Ezra moved away from her. "Seriously, Aria. I can't . . . I can't even look at you."

Tears sprang to her eyes. *What?* Aria stared at him, confused.

Ezra lowered his eyes. "I found what you said about me on your cell phone."

Aria wrinkled her eyebrows. "My cell phone?"

Ezra raised his head. His eyes flashed with anger. "Do you think I'm stupid? Was this all just a game? A *dare?*"

"What are you . . . ?"

Ezra sighed angrily. "Well, you know what? You got

me. Okay? I'm the brunt of your big joke. You happy?
Now get out."

"I don't understand," Aria said loudly.

Ezra slapped his palm against the wall. The force of it made
Aria jump. "Don't play dumb! I'm not some boy, Aria!"

Aria's whole body started to tremble. "I swear to God,
I don't know what you're talking about. Can you explain,
please? I'm kind of falling apart here!"

Ezra took his hand off the wall and started to pace
around the tiny room. "Fine. After you left, I tried to sleep.
There was this . . . this *beeping*. You know what it was?" He
pointed to the Treo. "Your cell phone thing. The only way
to shut it up was to open your *text messages*."

Aria wiped her eyes.

Ezra crossed his arms over his chest. "Shall I *quote*
them for you?"

Then Aria realized. The text messages. "Wait! No!
You don't understand!"

Ezra trembled. "*Student-teacher conference? Extra credit?*
This sound familiar?"

"No, Ezra," Aria stammered. "You don't understand."
The world was spinning. Aria gripped the edge of Ezra's
kitchen table.

"I'm waiting," Ezra said.

"This friend of mine was killed," she began. "They just
found her body." Aria opened her mouth to say more, but
couldn't find the words. Ezra stood at the farthest point in
the room from her, behind the bathtub.

"It's all so silly," Aria said. "Can you please come over here? Can you at least hug me?"

Ezra crossed his arms over his chest and looked down. He stood that way for what felt like a long time. "I *really* liked you," he finally said, his voice thick.

Aria choked back a sob. "I really like you, too. . . . " She walked over to him.

But Ezra stepped away. "No. You have to get out of here."

"But . . . "

Ezra clapped his hand over her mouth. "Please," he said a little desperately. "*Please* leave."

Aria widened her eyes and her heart started to pound. Alarms went off in her head. This felt . . . *wrong*. On impulse, she bit down into Ezra's hand.

"What the *fuck*?" he shrieked, pulling away.

Aria stood back, dazed. Blood dripped out of Ezra's hand onto the floor.

"You're insane!" Ezra cried.

Aria breathed heavily. She couldn't speak even if she wanted to. So she turned and ran for the door. As her hand turned the doorknob, something screamed past her, bounced off the wall, and landed next to her foot. It was a copy of *Being and Nothingness*, by Jean-Paul Sartre. Aria turned back to Ezra, her mouth open in shock.

"Get *out*!" Ezra boomed.

Aria slammed the door behind her. She tore down across the lawn as fast as her legs would carry her.

32

A FALLEN STAR

The next day, Spencer stood at her old bedroom window, smoking a Marlboro and looking across her lawn into Alison's old bedroom. It was dark and empty. Then, her eyes moved to the DiLaurentises' yard. The flashing lights hadn't stopped since they found her.

The police had put up DO NOT CROSS tape all around the concrete area of Alison's old backyard, even though they had already removed her body from the ground. They'd put huge tents around the area while doing that, too, so Spencer hadn't seen anything. Not that she'd have wanted to. It was beyond awful to think that Ali's body had been next door to her, rotting in the ground for three years. Spencer remembered the construction before Ali disappeared. They dug the hole right around the night she went missing. She knew, too, that they'd filled it after Ali disappeared but wasn't sure when. Someone had just *dumped* her there.

She stubbed out her Marlboro in the brick siding of her house and turned back to *Lucky* magazine. She'd hardly exchanged a word with her family since yesterday's confrontation and she'd been trying to calm herself down by going methodically through it and marking everything she wanted to buy with the magazine's little YES stickers. As she looked at a page on tweed blazers, though, her eyes glazed over.

She couldn't even talk to her parents about this. Yesterday, after they confronted her at breakfast, Spencer had wandered outside to see what the sirens were all about—ambulances still made her nervous, from both The Jenna Thing and Ali's disappearance. As she walked across her lawn to the DiLaurentis house, she sensed something and turned back. Her parents had come out to see what was going on too. When they saw her turn, they quickly looked away. The police told her to stand back, that this area was off limits. Then Spencer saw the morgue van. One of the policeman's walkie-talkies crackled, "Alison."

Her body had grown very cold. The world spun. Spencer slumped down on the grass. Someone spoke to her, but she couldn't understand him. "You're in shock," she finally heard. "Just try to calm down." Spencer's field of vision was so narrow, she wasn't sure who it was—only that it wasn't her mom or dad. The guy came back with a blanket and told her to sit there for a while and keep warm.

Once Spencer felt well enough to get up, whoever

had helped her was gone. Her parents had left too. They hadn't even bothered to see if she was okay.

She'd spent the rest of Saturday and most of Sunday in her room, only going out into the hall to the bathroom when she knew no one else was around. She hoped someone would come up and check on her, but when she heard a small, tentative knock on her door earlier this afternoon, Spencer didn't answer. She wasn't sure why. She listened to whoever it was sigh and pad back down the hall.

And then, only a half hour ago, Spencer had watched her dad's Jaguar back out of the driveway and turn toward the main road. Her mom was in the passenger seat; Melissa was in the back. She had no idea where they were going.

She slumped down in her computer chair and pulled up that first e-mail from A, the one talking about coveting things she couldn't have. After reading it a few times, she clicked REPLY. Slowly she typed, *Are you Alison?*

She hesitated before hitting SEND. Were all the police lights making her trippy? Dead girls didn't have Hotmail accounts. Nor did they have Instant Messenger screen names. Spencer had to get a grip—someone was pretending to be Ali. But who?

She stared up at the Mondrian mobile she'd bought last year at the Philadelphia Art Museum. Then she heard a *plink* sound. There it was again.

Plink.

It sounded really close, actually. Like at her window. Spencer sat up just as a pebble hit her window again. Someone was throwing rocks.

A?

As another rock hit, she went to the window—and gasped. On the lawn was Wren. The blue and red lights from the police cars kept making streaky shadows across his cheeks. When he saw her, he broke into a huge smile. Immediately, she bolted downstairs, not caring how horrible her hair looked or that she was wearing marinara-stained Kate Spade pajama pants. Wren ran for her as she came out the door. He threw his arms around her and kissed her scruffy head.

"You're not supposed to be here," she murmured.

"I know." He stood back. "But I noticed your parents' car was gone, so . . . "

She pushed her hand through his soft hair. Wren looked exhausted. What if he had to sleep in his little Toyota last night?

"How did you know I'd be back in my old room?"

He shrugged. "A hunch. I also thought I saw your face at the window. I wanted to come earlier, but there was . . . all that." He gestured to the police cars and random news vans next door. "You okay?"

"Yeah," Spencer answered. She tilted her head up to Wren's mouth and bit her chapped lip to keep from crying. "Are *you* okay?"

"Me? Sure."

"Do you have somewhere to live?"

"I can stay on a friend's couch until I find something. Not a big deal."

If only Spencer could stay on a friend's couch too. Then something occurred to her. "Are you and Melissa over?"

Wren cupped her face in his hand and sighed. "Of course," he said softly. "It was kind of obvious. With Melissa, it wasn't like . . . "

He trailed off, but Spencer thought she knew what he was going to say. *It wasn't like being with you.* She smiled shakily and laid her head against his chest. His heart thumped in her ear.

She looked over at the DiLaurentis house. Someone had started a little shrine to Alison on the curb, complete with pictures and Virgin Mary candles. In the center were little alphabet magnet letters that spelled *Ali*. Spencer herself had propped up a smiling picture of Alison in a tight blue Von Dutch T-shirt and spanking new Sevens. She remembered when she'd taken that picture: They were in sixth grade, and it was the night of the Rosewood Winter Formal. The five of them had spied on Melissa as Ian picked her up. Spencer had gotten hiccups from laughing when Melissa, trying to make a grand entrance, tripped down the Hastingses' front walk on the way to the tacky rented Hummer limo. It was probably their last really fun, carefree memory. The Jenna Thing happened not too long after. Spencer glanced at Toby and Jenna's house. No one was home, as usual, but it still made her shiver.

As she blotted her eyes with the back of her pale, thin hand, one of the news vans drove by slowly, and a guy in a red Phillies cap stared at her. She ducked. Now would not be the time to capture some emotional-girl-breaks-down-at-the-tragedy footage.

"You'd better go." She sniffed and turned back to Wren. "It's so crazy here. And I don't know when my parents will be back."

"All right." He tilted her head up. "But can we see each other again?"

Spencer swallowed, and tried to smile. As she did, Wren bent down and kissed her, wrapping one hand around the back of her neck and the other around the very spot on her lower back that, just Friday, hurt like hell.

Spencer broke away from him. "I don't even have your number."

"Don't worry," Wren whispered. "I'll call you."

Spencer stood out on the edge of her vast yard for a moment, watching Wren walk to his car. As he drove away, her eyes stung with tears again. If only she had someone to talk to—someone who wasn't banned from her house. She glanced back at the Ali shrine and wondered how her old friends were dealing with this.

As Wren pulled to the end of her street, Spencer noticed another car's headlights turn in. She froze. Was that her parents? Had they seen Wren?

The headlights inched closer. Suddenly, Spencer realized who it was. The sky was a dark purple, but she could just make out Andrew Campbell's longish hair.

She gasped, ducking behind her mother's rosebushes. Andrew slowly pulled his Mini up to her mailbox, opened it, slid something in, and neatly closed it again. He drove away.

She waited until he was gone before sprinting out to the curb and wrenching open the mailbox. Andrew had left her a folded-up piece of notepaper.

Hey, Spencer. I didn't know if you were taking any calls. I'm really sorry about Alison. I hope my blanket helped you yesterday. —Andrew

Spencer turned up her driveway, reading and rereading the note. She stared at the slanty boy handwriting. *Blanket? What blanket?*

Then she realized. It was *Andrew* who helped her?

She crumpled up the note in her hands and started sobbing all over again.

33

ROSEWOOD'S FINEST

"Police have reopened the DiLaurentis case, and are in the process of questioning witnesses," a newscaster on the eleven-o'clock news reported. *"The DiLaurentis family, now living in Maryland, will have to face something they've tried to put behind them. Except now, there is closure."*

Newscasters were such drama queens, Hanna thought angrily as she shoved another handful of Cheez-Its in her mouth. Only the news could find a way to make a horrible story worse. The camera stayed focused on the Ali shrine, as they called it, the candles, Beanie Babies, wilted flowers people no doubt just picked out of neighbors' gardens, marshmallow Peeps—Ali's favorite candy—and of course photos.

The camera cut to Alison's mother, whom Hanna hadn't seen in a while. Besides her teary face, Mrs. DiLaurentis looked pretty—with a shaggy haircut and dangly chandelier earrings.

"We've decided to have a service for Alison in Rosewood, which was the only home Ali knew," Mrs. DiLaurentis said in a controlled voice. "We want to thank all of those who helped search for our daughter three years ago for their enduring support."

The newscaster came back on the screen. *"A memorial will be held tomorrow at the Rosewood Abbey and will be open to the public."*

Hanna clicked off the TV. It was Sunday night. She sat on her living room couch, dressed in her rattiest C&C T-shirt and a pair of Calvin Klein boxer briefs she'd pilfered out of Sean's top drawer. Her long brown hair was messy and strawlike around her face and she was pretty sure she had a pimple on her forehead. A huge bowl of Cheez-Its rested in her lap, an empty Klondike wrapper was crumpled up on the coffee table, and a bottle of pinot noir was wedged snugly at her side. She'd been trying all night *not* to eat like this but, well, her willpower just wasn't very strong today.

She clicked the TV back on, wishing she had someone to talk to . . . about the police, about A, and mostly about Alison. Sean was out, for obvious reasons. Her mom—who was on a date right now—was her usual useless self. After the hubbub of activity at the police station yesterday, Wilden told Hanna and her mother to go home; they'd deal with her later, since the police had more important things to attend to at the moment.

Neither Hanna nor her mom knew what was happening at the station, only that it involved a murder.

On the drive home, instead of Ms. Marin reprimanding Hanna for, oh, *stealing a car and driving piss-drunk*, she told Hanna that she "was taking care of it." Hanna didn't have a clue what that meant. Last year, a cop had spoken at a Rosewood Day assembly about how Pennsylvania had a "zero tolerance" rule for drunk drivers under twenty-one. At the time, Hanna had paid attention only because she thought the cop was sort of hot, but now his words haunted her.

Hanna couldn't rely on Mona, either: She was still at that golf tournament in Florida. They'd spoken briefly on the phone, and Mona had admitted the police had called her about Sean's car, but she'd played dumb, saying she'd been at the party the whole time and Hanna had been too. And the lucky bitch: They'd gotten the back of her head on the Wawa surveillance tape, but not her face, since she'd been wearing that disgusting delivery hat. That was yesterday, though, after Hanna got back from the police station. She and Mona hadn't talked today, and they hadn't discussed Alison yet.

And then . . . there was A. Or if A was Alison, would A be gone now? But the police said Alison had been dead for years. . . .

As Hanna scanned the guide feature on TV for what else was on, her eyelids swollen with tears, she considered calling her father—this story might be on the Annapolis-area news, too. Or maybe he'd call her? She picked up the silent phone to make sure it was still working.

She sighed. The problem with being Mona's best friend was that they had no other friends. Watching all this Ali footage made her think of her old group of friends. They'd had their rocky, horrible moments together, but they used to have a lot of fun, too. In a parallel universe, they'd all be together now, remembering Ali and laughing even though they were crying, too. But in this dimension, they'd grown too far apart.

They'd split up for valid reasons, of course—things had started to go rotten way before Ali went missing. In the beginning, when they were doing that charity drive stuff, it was wonderful. But then, after The Jenna Thing happened, things got tense. They were all so afraid that what happened to Jenna could be linked to them. Hanna remembered being jumpy even when she was on the bus and a cop car would pass by them, going in the other direction. Then, that next winter and spring, whole topics were suddenly off-limits. Someone was always saying, "Shhh!" and then they all fell into an uncomfortable silence.

The eleven-o'clock newscasters signed off and *The Simpsons* came on. Hanna picked up her BlackBerry. She still knew Spencer's number by heart, and it probably wouldn't be too late to call. As she dialed the second digit, she cocked her ear, her Tiffany earrings jangling. There was a scratching noise at the door.

Dot, who had been lying by her feet, picked up his head and growled. Hanna took the Cheez-It bowl off her lap and stood.

Was it . . . A?

Knees shaking, Hanna crept into the hall. There were long, dark shadows at the back door, and the scratching noise had grown louder. "Oh my God," Hanna whispered, her chin trembling. *Someone was trying to get in!*

Hanna looked around. There was a round jade paperweight on the little hall table. It had to weigh at least twenty pounds. She heaved it up and took three tentative steps for the kitchen door.

Suddenly, the door burst open. Hanna jumped back. A woman stumbled through the entranceway. Her tasteful, gray pleated skirt was up around her waist. Hanna held up the paperweight, about to throw it.

Then she realized. It was her mom.

Ms. Marin bumped into the telephone table as if she were wasted. Some guy was behind her, trying to unzip her skirt and kiss her at the same time. Hanna's eyes widened.

Darren Wilden. Mr. April.

So *that* was what her mom meant by "taking care of it"?

Hanna's stomach clenched. No doubt she looked a little insane, tenaciously clutching the paperweight. Ms. Marin gave Hanna a very long look, not even bothering to turn away from Wilden.

Her mother's eyes said, *I'm doing this for you.*

34

FANCY MEETING YOU HERE

On Monday morning, instead of sitting in first-period bio, Emily stood next to her parents in the high-ceilinged, marble-floored nave of Rosewood Abbey. She tugged uncomfortably at the black, pleated, too-short Gap skirt she'd found in the back of her closet and tried to smile. Mrs. DiLaurentis stood in the doorway, clad in a cowl-neck black dress, heels, and tiny freshwater pearls. She walked up to Emily and engulfed her in a hug.

"Oh, Emily," Mrs. DiLaurentis sobbed.

"I'm so sorry," Emily whispered back, her own eyes watering. Mrs. DiLaurentis still wore the same perfume— Coco Chanel. It instantly brought back all kinds of memories: A million rides to and from the mall in Mrs. DiLaurentis's Infiniti, sneaking into her bathroom to steal TrimSpa tablets and to experiment with her expensive La Prairie makeup, going through her enormous, walk-in closet and trying on all her sexy size-2 black Dior cocktail dresses.

Other kids from Rosewood streamed around them, trying to find seats in the high-backed wooden pews. Emily hadn't known what to expect at Alison's memorial service. The abbey smelled like incense and wood. Simple cylinder-shaped lamps hung from the ceiling, and the altar was covered with a billion white tulips. Tulips were Alison's favorite flower. Emily remembered Ali helped her mom plant rows of them in their front yard every year.

Alison's mom finally stood back and wiped her eyes. "I want you to sit up in the front, with all of Ali's friends. Is that okay, Kathleen?"

Emily's mom nodded. "Of course." ❧

Emily listened to every click of Mrs. DiLaurentis's heels and the shuffling of her own chunky loafers as they walked down the aisle. Suddenly it hit Emily why she was here again. Ali was *dead*.

Emily clutched Mrs. DiLaurentis's arm. "Oh my God." Her field of vision narrowed, and she heard a *waaaah* noise in her ears, the sign that she was about to faint.

Mrs. DiLaurentis held her upright. "It's okay. Come on. Sit down here."

Dizzily, Emily slid into the pew. "Put your head between your legs," she heard a familiar voice say.

Then another familiar voice snorted. "Say it louder, so *all* the boys can hear."

Emily looked up. Next to her were Aria and Hanna. Aria wore a blue, purple, and fuchsia-striped cotton boat-neck dress, a navy velvet jacket, and cowboy boots. It was so Aria—she was the type who thought wearing some color to funerals celebrated the living. Hanna, on the other hand, wore a skimpy black V-neck dress and black stockings.

"Dear, can you move over?"

Above her, Mrs. DiLaurentis stood with Spencer Hastings, who wore a charcoal suit and ballet flats.

"Hey, guys," Spencer said to all of them, in that buttery voice Emily had missed. She sat down next to Emily.

"So, we meet again," Aria said, smiling.

Silence. Emily peeked at all of them out of the corner of her eye. Aria was fidgeting with a silver ring on her thumb, Hanna was fumbling around in her purse, and Spencer was sitting very still, staring at the altar.

"Poor Ali," Spencer murmured.

The girls sat quietly for a few minutes. Emily wracked her brain for something to say. Her ears filled with the *waaaah* sound again.

She twisted around to scan the crowd for Maya, and her eyes landed square on Ben's. He was sitting in the second-to-last row with the rest of the swimmers. Emily lifted her hand in a tiny wave. Next to this, the party stuff seemed petty.

But instead of waving back, Ben glared at her, his thin mouth in a stubborn, straight line. Then he looked away. *Okay.*

Emily swung back around. Rage filled her body. *My old best friend was just found murdered,* she wanted to scream. *And we're in a church, for God's sake! What about forgiveness?*

Then it hit her. She didn't want him to take her back. Not one bit.

Aria tapped her on the leg. "You okay after Saturday morning? I mean, you didn't even know yet, right?"

"No, it was something else, but I'm okay," Emily answered, even though that wasn't true.

"Spencer." Hanna's head popped up. "I, um, I saw you at the mall recently."

Spencer looked at Hanna. "Huh?"

"You were . . . you were going into Kate Spade." Hanna looked down. "I don't know. I was going to say hi. But, um, I'm glad you don't have to order those purses from New York anymore." She put her head down and blushed, as if she'd said too much.

Emily was startled—she hadn't seen Hanna make that expression in years.

Spencer's brow crinkled. Then, a sad, tender look came over her face. She swallowed hard and looked down. "Thanks," she murmured. Her shoulders started to shake and she squeezed her eyes shut. Emily felt her own throat choking up. She'd never actually seen Spencer cry.

Aria put her hand on Spencer's shoulder. "It's okay," she said.

"Sorry," Spencer said, wiping her eyes with her sleeve. "I just . . . " She glanced around at all of them and then started crying even harder.

Emily hugged her. It felt a little awkward, but by the way Spencer squeezed her hand, Emily could tell she appreciated it.

When they sat back, Hanna pulled a tiny silver flask out of her bag and reached over Emily to pass it to Spencer. "Here," she whispered.

Without even smelling it or asking what it was, Spencer took a huge swallow. She winced but said, "Thanks."

She passed the flask back to Hanna, who drank and handed it to Emily. Emily took a sip, which burned in her chest, then passed it to Aria. Before drinking, Aria pulled on Spencer's sleeve.

"This'll make you feel better too." Aria tugged down the shoulder of her dress to reveal a white knitted bra strap. Emily immediately recognized it—Aria had knitted heavy woolen bras for all the girls in seventh grade. "I wore it for old time's sake," Aria whispered. "It's itching like hell."

Spencer sputtered out a laugh. "Oh my God."

"You're such a spaz," Hanna added, grinning.

"I could never wear mine, remember?" Emily chimed in. "My mom thought it was too sexy for school!"

"Yeah." Spencer giggled. "If you can call scratching your boobs all day sexy."

The girls snickered. Suddenly, Aria's cell phone buzzed. She reached into her bag and looked at the phone's screen.

"What?" Aria looked up, realizing they were all staring at her.

Hanna fiddled with her charm bracelet. "Did you, um, just get a text message?"

"Yeah. So?"

"Who was it?"

"It was my mom," Aria answered slowly. "Why?"

Low pipe organ music began to lilt through the church. Behind them, more kids shuffled in quietly. Spencer glanced nervously at Emily. Emily's heart started to pound.

"Never mind," Hanna said. "That was nosy."

Aria licked her lips. "Wait. Seriously. *Why?*"

Hanna's adam's apple rose with a nervous swallow. "I . . . I just thought maybe strange things had been happening to you, too."

Aria's mouth fell open. "Strange is an understatement."

Emily clutched her arms around herself.

"Wait. You guys, too?" Spencer whispered.

Hanna nodded. "Texts?"

"E-mails," Spencer said.

"About . . . stuff from seventh?" Aria whispered.

"Are you guys *serious*?" Emily squeaked.

The friends stared at each other. But before anyone could say anything else, the somber-sounding pipe organ filled the room.

Emily turned around. A bunch of people were walking slowly up the center aisle. It was Ali's mom and dad, her brother, her grandparents, and some others who must've been relatives. Two redheaded boys were the last to come down the aisle; Emily recognized them as Sam and Russell, Ali's cousins. They used to visit Ali's family every summer. Emily hadn't seen them in years, and wondered if they were still as gullible as they used to be.

The family members slid into the front row and waited for the music to stop.

As Emily stared at them, she noticed movement. One of the pimply, redheaded cousins was staring at them. Emily was pretty sure it was the one named Sam—he'd been the geekier of the two. He stared at all the girls and then slowly and flirtatiously raised an eyebrow. Emily quickly looked away.

She felt Hanna jab her in the ribs. "Not it," Hanna whispered to the girls.

Emily looked at her, puzzled, but then Hanna motioned with her eyes to the two gangly cousins.

All the girls caught on at the same time. "Not it," Emily, Spencer, and Aria said at once.

They all giggled. But then Emily paused, considering what "not it" really meant. She'd never thought about it before, but it was kind of mean. When she looked around, she noticed her friends had stopped laughing too. They all exchanged a look.

"I guess it was funnier back then," Hanna said quietly.

Emily sat back. Maybe Ali didn't know everything. Yes, this might have been the worst day of her life, and she was horribly devastated about Ali, and completely freaked about A. But for a moment, she felt okay. Sitting here with her old friends seemed like the tiny beginning of something.

35

JUST YOU WAIT

The organ started up again with its dreary music, and Ali's brother and the others filed out of the church. Spencer, tipsy from a few slugs of whiskey, noticed that her three old friends had stood up and were filing out of the pew, and she figured she should go, too.

Everyone from Rosewood Day hung out at the back of the church, from the lacrosse boys to the video game-obsessed geeks who Ali no doubt would have teased back in seventh. Old Mr. Yew—the one in charge of the Rosewood Day charity drive—stood in the corner, talking quietly to Mr. Kaplan, who taught art. Even Ali's older JV field hockey friends had returned from their respective colleges; they stood in a teary huddle near the door. Spencer scanned the familiar faces, remembering all the people she used to know and didn't anymore. And then, she saw a dog—a seeing-eye dog.

Oh my God.

Spencer grabbed Aria's arm. "By the exit," she hissed.

Aria squinted. "Is that . . . ?"

"Jenna," Hanna murmured.

"And Toby," Spencer added.

Emily turned pale. "What are they doing here?"

Spencer was too stunned to answer. They looked the same but totally different. His hair was long now, and she was . . . gorgeous, with long black hair and wearing big Gucci sunglasses.

Toby, Jenna's brother, caught Spencer staring. A sour, disgusted look settled over his face. Spencer quickly jerked her eyes away.

"I can't believe he showed up," she whispered, too quietly for the others to hear.

By the time the girls reached the heavy wooden doors that led to the church's crumbling stone steps, Toby and Jenna were gone. Spencer squinted in the sunlight of the brilliant, perfectly blue sky. It was one of those lovely early-fall days with no humidity, where you were dying to skip school, lie in a field, and not think about your responsibilities. Why was it always on days like this that something horrible happened?

Someone touched her shoulder and Spencer jumped. It was a blond burly cop. She motioned for Hanna, Aria, and Emily to go on without her.

"Are you Spencer Hastings?" he asked.

She nodded dumbly.

The cop wrung his enormous hands together. "I'm

very sorry for your loss," he said. "You were good friends with Ms. DiLaurentis, right?"

"Thanks. Yeah, I was."

"I'm going to need to talk with you." The cop reached into his pocket. "Here's my card. We're reopening the case. Since you were friends, you might be able to help us. Is it okay if I come by in a couple of days?"

"Um, sure," Spencer stammered. "Whatever I can do."

Zombielike, she caught up with her old friends, who'd gathered under a weeping willow. "What did he want?" Aria asked.

"They want to talk to me, too," Emily said quickly. "It's not a big deal though, is it?"

"I'm sure it's the same old stuff," Hanna said.

"He couldn't be wondering about . . . ," Aria started. She looked nervously to the church's front door, where Toby, Jenna, and her dog had stood.

"No," Emily said quickly. "We couldn't get in trouble for that now, could we?"

They all glanced at each other worriedly.

"Of course not," Hanna finally said.

Spencer looked around at everyone talking quietly on the lawn. She felt sick after seeing Toby, and she hadn't seen Jenna since the accident. But it was a coincidence that the cop had spoken to her right after she'd seen them, right? Spencer quickly pulled out her emergency cigarettes and lit up. She needed something to do with her hands.

I'll tell everyone about The Jenna Thing.

You're just as guilty as I am.

But no one saw me.

Spencer nervously exhaled and scanned the crowd. *There wasn't any proof.* End of story. Unless . . .

"This has been the worst week of my life," Aria said suddenly.

"Mine too." Hanna nodded.

"I guess we can look on the bright side," Emily said, her voice high-pitched and jittery. "It can't get any worse than this."

As they followed the procession out to the gravel parking lot, Spencer stopped. Her old friends stopped too. Spencer wanted to say something to them—not about Ali or A or Jenna or Toby or the police, but instead, more than anything, she wanted to tell them that she'd missed them all these years.

But before she could say it, Aria's phone rang.

"Hang on . . . ," Aria muttered, rooting around in her bag for her phone. "It's probably my mom again."

Then, Spencer's Sidekick vibrated. And rang. And chirped. It wasn't just her phone, but her friends' phones too. The sudden, high-pitched noises sounded even louder against the sober, silent funeral procession. The other mourners shot them dirty looks. Aria held hers up to silence it; Emily struggled to operate her Nokia. Spencer wrenched her phone out of her clutch's pocket.

Hanna read her screen. "I have one new message."

"I do too," Aria whispered.

"Same," Emily echoed.

Spencer saw she did, too. Everyone hit READ. A moment of stunned silence passed.

"Oh my God," Aria whispered.

"It's from . . . ," Hanna squeaked.

Aria murmured, "Do you think she means . . . "

Spencer swallowed hard. In tandem, the girls read their texts out loud. Each said the exact same thing:

I'm still here, bitches. And I know everything. —A

ACKNOWLEDGMENTS

I owe a lot to a great group of people at Alloy Entertainment. I've known them for years and without them, this book could never have happened. Josh Bank, for being hilarious, magnetic, and brilliant . . . and for giving me a chance years ago despite the fact that I so rudely crashed his company Christmas party. Ben Schrank, for encouraging me to do this project in the first place and for his invaluable writing advice. Of course Les Morgenstein, for believing in me. And my fantastic editor, Sara Shandler, for her friendship and dedicated help in shaping this novel.

I'm grateful to Elise Howard and Kristin Marang at HarperCollins for their support, insight, and enthusiasm. And huge thanks to Jennifer Rudolph Walsh at William Morris for all the magical things she made happen.

Thanks also to Doug and Fran Wilkens for a great summer in Pennsylvania. I'm grateful to Colleen

McGarry, for reminding me of our junior high and high school inside jokes, especially those about our fictitious band whose name I won't mention. Thanks to my parents, Bob and Mindy Shepard, for their help with sticky plot points and for encouraging me to be myself, however weird that might be. And I don't know what I'd do without my sister, Ali, who agrees that Icelandic boys are pussies who ride small, gay horses and is okay with a certain character in this book being named after her.

And finally, thanks to my husband, Joel, for being loving, silly, and patient, and also for reading every draft of this book (happily!) and offering good advice—proof that boys might just understand more about girls' inner struggles than we think.

WHAT HAPPENS NEXT . . .

I bet you thought I was Alison, didn't you? Well, sorry, but I'm not. Duh. She's dead.

Nope, I'm very much alive . . . and I'm very, very close. And for a certain clique of four pretty girls, the fun has just started. Why? 'Cause I say so.

Naughty behavior deserves punishment, after all. And Rosewood's finest deserve to know that Aria's been doing some extra-credit smooching with her English teacher, don't they? Not to mention the nasty family secret she's been hiding for years. The girl is a train wreck.

While I'm at it, I really ought to tip Emily's parents off to the reason she's been acting funny lately. Hey there, Mr. and Mrs. Fields, nice weather, huh? And by the way, your daughter likes kissing girls.

Then there's Hanna. Poor Hanna. Just free-falling into dorkdom. She may try to claw her way back to the top, but don't worry—I'll be there waiting to knock her rapidly growing behind back into a pair of stonewashed mom-jeans.

Oh my god, I almost forgot Spencer. She's a total mess! After all, her family thinks she's a completely worthless skank. That's gotta suck. And just between us, it's about to get much worse. Spencer's keeping a deep, dark secret that could pretty much ruin all four of their lives. But who would tell such an awful secret? Oh, I don't know. Take a wild guess.

Bingo.

Life's so much fun when you know everything.

Just how do I know so much? You're probably dying to know, aren't you? Well, relax. All in due time.

Believe me, I'd love to tell you. But what's the fun in that?

I'll be watching. —A

FLAWLESS

For MDS and RNS

An eye for an eye and the whole world goes blind.

—GANDHI

HOW IT REALLY BEGAN

You know that boy who lives a few doors down from you who's just the creepiest person alive? When you're on your front porch, about to kiss your boyfriend good night, you might glimpse him across the street, just standing there. He'll randomly appear when you're gossiping with your best friends—except maybe it's not so random at all. He's the black cat who seems to know your route. If he rides by your house, you think, I'm going to fail my bio exam. If he looks at you funny, watch your back.

Every town has a black-cat boy. In Rosewood, his name was Toby Cavanaugh.

"I think she needs more blush." Spencer Hastings leaned back and examined one of her best friends, Emily Fields. "I can still see her freckles."

"I've got some Clinique concealer." Alison DiLaurentis sprang up and ran to her blue corduroy makeup bag.

Emily looked at herself in the mirror propped up on Alison's living room coffee table. She tilted her face one way, then another, and puckered her pink lips. "My mom would kill me if she saw me with all this stuff on."

"Yeah, but we'll kill you if you take it off," warned Aria Montgomery, who was, for her own Aria reasons, prancing around the room in a pink mohair bra she'd recently knitted.

"Yeah, Em, you look awesome," Hanna Marin agreed. Hanna sat cross-legged on the floor and kept swiveling around to check that her crack wasn't sticking out of her low-rise, slightly-too-small Blue Cult jeans.

It was a Friday night in April, and Ali, Aria, Emily, Spencer, and Hanna were having one of their typical sixth-grade sleepovers: putting way too much makeup on one another, chowing on salt-and-vinegar kettle chips, and half-watching MTV *Cribs* on Ali's flat-screen TV. Tonight there was the added clutter of everyone's clothes spread out on the carpet, since they'd decided to swap clothes for the rest of their sixth-grade school year.

Spencer held up a lemon-yellow cashmere cardigan to her slender torso.

"Take it," Ali told her. "It'll look cute on you."

Hanna pulled an olive corduroy skirt of Ali's around her hips, turned to Ali, and struck a pose. "What do you think? Would Sean like it?"

Ali groaned and smacked Hanna with a pillow. Ever since they'd become friends in September, all Hanna could talk about was how much she *looooved* Sean Ackard, a boy in their class at the Rosewood Day School, where most of them had been going since kindergarten. In fifth grade, Sean had been just another short, freckled guy in their class, but over the summer, he'd grown a couple inches and lost his baby fat. Now, pretty much every girl wanted to kiss him.

It was amazing how much could change in a year.

The girls—everyone but Ali—knew *that* all too well. Last year, they were just . . . *there*. Spencer was the über-anal girl who sat at the front of the class and raised her hand at every question. Aria was the slightly freaky girl who made up dance routines instead of playing soccer like everyone else. Emily was the shy, state-ranked swimmer who had a lot going on under the surface—if you just got to know her. And Hanna might've been klutzy and bumbling, but she studied *Vogue* and *Teen Vogue*, and every once in a while she'd blurt out something totally random about fashion that no one else knew.

There was something special about all of them, sure, but they lived in Rosewood, Pennsylvania, a suburb twenty miles outside Philadelphia, and *everything* was special in Rosewood. Flowers smelled sweeter, water tasted better, houses were just plain bigger. People joked that the squirrels spent their nights cleaning up litter and weeding errant dandelions from the cobblestone sidewalks so Rosewood would look perfect for its demanding residents. In a place where everything looked so flawless, it was hard to stand out.

But somehow Ali did. With her long blond hair, heart-shaped face, and huge blue eyes, she was the most stunning girl around. After Ali united them in friendship—sometimes it felt like she'd *discovered* them—the girls were definitely more than just there. Suddenly, they had an all-access pass to do things they'd never dared to before. Like changing into short skirts in the Rosewood Day girls' bathroom after they got off the bus in the morning. Or passing boys ChapStick-kissed notes in class. Or walking down the Rosewood Day hallway in an intimidating line, ignoring all the losers.

Ali grabbed a tube of shimmery purple lipstick and smeared it all over her lips. "Who am I?" The others groaned—Ali was imitating Imogen Smith, a girl in their class who was a little bit too in love with her Nars lipstick.

"No, wait." Spencer pursed her bow-shaped lips and handed Ali a pillow. "Put this up your shirt."

"Nice." Ali stuffed it under her pink polo, and everyone giggled some more. The rumor was that Imogen had gone all the way with Jeffrey Klein, a tenth grader, and she was having his baby.

"You guys are awful." Emily blushed. She was the most demure of the group, maybe because of her super-strict upbringing—her parents thought anything fun was evil.

"What, Em?" Ali linked her arm through Emily's.

"Imogen's looking awfully fat—she should *hope* she's pregnant."

The girls laughed again, but a little uneasily. Ali had a talent for finding a girl's weakness, and even if she was right about Imogen, the girls all sometimes wondered if Ali was ever ripping on *them* when they weren't around. Sometimes it was hard to know for sure.

They settled back into sorting through one another's clothes. Aria fell in love with an ultra-preppy Fred Perry dress of Spencer's. Emily slid a denim miniskirt up her skinny legs and asked everyone if it was too short. Ali declared a pair of Hanna's Joe's jeans too bell-bottomy and slid them off, revealing her candy-pink velour boy shorts. As she walked past the window to the stereo, she froze.

"Oh my God!" she screamed, running behind the blackberry-colored velvet couch.

The girls wheeled around. At the window was Toby Cavanaugh. He was just . . . *standing there*. Staring at them.

"Ew, ew, ew!" Aria covered up her chest—she had taken off Spencer's dress and was again in her knitted bra. Spencer, who was clothed, ran up to the window. "Get away from us, perv!" she cried. Toby smirked before he turned and ran away.

When most people saw Toby, they crossed to the other side of the street. He was a year older than the girls, pale, tall, and skinny, and was always wandering around the neighborhood alone, seemingly spying on everyone. They'd heard rumors about him: that he'd been caught French-kissing his dog. That he was such a good swimmer because he had fish gills instead of lungs. That he slept in a coffin in his backyard tree house every night.

There was only one person Toby spoke to: his stepsister, Jenna, who was in their grade. Jenna was a hopeless dork as well, although far less creepy—at least she spoke in complete sentences. And she was pretty in an irksome way, with her thick, dark hair, huge, earnest green eyes, and pursed red lips.

"I feel, like, *violated*." Aria wriggled her naturally thin body as if it were covered in E. coli. They'd just learned about it in science class. "How dare he scare us?"

Ali's face blazed red with fury. "We have to get him back."

"How?" Hanna widened her light brown eyes.

Ali thought for a minute. "We should give him a taste of his own medicine."

The thing to do, she explained, was to scare Toby. When Toby wasn't skulking around the neighborhood, spying on people, he was guaranteed to be in his tree house. He spent every other waking second there, playing with his Game Boy or, who knows, building a giant robot to nuke Rosewood Day. But since the tree house was, obviously, up in a tree—and because Toby pulled up the rope ladder so no one could follow him—they couldn't just peek in and say boo. "So we

need fireworks. Luckily, we know just where they are."
Ali grinned.

Toby was obsessed with fireworks; he kept a stash of
bottle rockets at the base of the tree and often set them off
through his tree house's skylight. "We sneak over there,
steal one, and light it at his window," Ali explained. "It'll
totally freak him out."

The girls looked at the Cavanaugh house across the
street. Although most of the lights were already out,
it wasn't that late—only ten-thirty. "I don't know,"
Spencer said.

"Yeah," Aria agreed. "What if something goes wrong?"

Ali sighed dramatically. "C'mon, guys."

Everyone was quiet. Then Hanna cleared her throat.
"Sounds good to me."

"All right." Spencer caved. Emily and Aria shrugged
in agreement.

Ali clapped her hands and gestured to the couch by
the window. "I'll go do it. You can watch from here."

The girls scrambled over to the great room's big bay
window and watched Ali slip across the street. Toby's
house was kitty-corner to the DiLaurentises' and built in
the same impressive Victorian style, but neither house was
as big as Spencer's family's farm, which bordered Ali's
backyard. The Hastings compound had its own windmill,
eight bedrooms, a five-car detached garage, a rock-lined
pool, and a separate barn apartment.

Ali ran around to the Cavanaughs' side yard and right

up to Toby's tree house. It was partially obscured by tall elms and pines, but the streetlight illuminated it just enough for them to see its vague outline. A minute later, they were pretty sure they saw Ali holding a cone-shaped firework in her hands, stepping about twenty feet back, far enough so that she had a clear view into the tree house's flickering blue window.

"Do you think she's really going to do it?" Emily whispered. A car slid past, brightening Toby's house.

"Nah," Spencer said, nervously twirling the diamond studs her parents had bought her for getting straight A's on her last report card. "She's bluffing."

Aria put the tip of one of her black braids in her mouth. "Totally."

"How do we know Toby's even in there?" Hanna asked.

They fell into an edgy silence. They'd been in on their fair share of Ali's pranks, but those had been innocent— sneaking into the saltwater hot tub at Fermata spa when they didn't have appointments, putting droplets of black dye into Spencer's sister's shampoo, sending fake secret admirer letters from Principal Appleton to dorky Mona Vanderwaal in their grade. But something about this made them all just a little . . . uneasy.

Boom!

Emily and Aria jumped back. Spencer and Hanna pressed their faces against the window. It was still dark across the street. A brighter light flickered from the tree house window, but that was all.

Hanna squinted. "Maybe that wasn't the firework."

"What else could it have been?" Spencer said sarcastically. "A gun?"

Then the Cavanaughs' German shepherd started to bark. The girls grabbed one another's arms. The side patio light snapped on. There were loud voices, and Mr. Cavanaugh burst out the side door. Suddenly, little fingers of fire leapt up from the tree house window. The fire started to spread. It looked like the video Emily's parents made her watch every year at Christmas. Then came the sirens.

Aria looked at the others. "What's going on?"

"Do you think . . . ?" Spencer whispered.

"What if Ali–" Hanna started.

"Guys." A voice came from behind them. Ali stood in the great room doorway. Her arms were at her sides and her face was pale–paler than they'd ever seen it before.

"What happened?" everyone said at once.

Ali looked worried. "I don't know. But it wasn't my fault."

The siren got closer and closer . . . until an ambulance wailed into the Cavanaugh driveway. Paramedics poured out and rushed to the tree house. The rope had been lowered down.

"What happened, Ali?" Spencer turned, heading out the door. "You've got to tell us what happened."

Ali started after her. "Spence, no."

Hanna and Aria looked at each other; they were too afraid to follow. Someone might see them.

Spencer crouched behind a bush and looked across the street. That was when she saw the ugly, jagged hole in Toby's tree house window. She felt someone creeping up behind her. "It's me," Ali said.

"What—" Spencer started, but before she could finish, a paramedic began climbing back down the tree house, and he had someone in his arms. Was Toby *hurt*? Was he . . . *dead*?

All the girls, inside and out, craned to see. Their hearts began to beat faster. Then, for just a second, they stopped.

It wasn't Toby. It was Jenna.

Several minutes later, Ali and Spencer came back inside. Ali told them all what happened with an almost-eerie calmness: the firework had gone through the window and hit Jenna. No one had seen her light it, so they were safe, as long as they all kept quiet. It was, after all, Toby's firework. If the cops would blame anyone, it would be him.

All night, they cried and hugged and went in and out of sleep. Spencer was so shell-shocked, she spent hours curled in a ball, wordlessly flicking from E! to the Cartoon Network to Animal Planet. When they awoke the next day, the news was all over the neighborhood: someone had confessed.

Toby.

The girls thought it was a joke, but the local paper confirmed that Toby had admitted to playing with a lit firework in his tree house, accidentally sending one at his sister's face . . . and the firework had *blinded* her. Ali read it out loud as they all gathered around her kitchen table, holding hands. They knew they should be relieved, except . . . they knew the truth.

The few days that Jenna was in the hospital, she was hysterical—and confused. Everyone asked her what had happened, but she didn't seem to remember. She said she couldn't recall anything that happened right before the accident, either. Doctors said it was probably post-traumatic stress.

Rosewood Day held a don't-play-with-fireworks assembly in Jenna's honor, followed by a benefit dance and a bake sale. The girls, especially Spencer, participated overzealously, although of course they pretended not to know anything about what had happened. If anyone asked, they said that Jenna was a sweet girl and one of their closest pals. A lot of girls who'd never spoken to Jenna were saying the exact same thing. As for Jenna, she never came back to Rosewood Day. She went to a special school for the blind in Philadelphia, and no one saw her after that night.

Bad things in Rosewood were all eventually gently nudged out of sight, and Toby was no exception. His parents homeschooled him for the remainder of the year. The summer passed, and the next school year Toby went to a reform school in Maine. He left unceremoniously one clear day in mid-August. His father drove him to the SEPTA station, where he took the train to the airport alone. The girls watched as his family tore down the tree house that afternoon. It was like they wanted to erase as much of Toby's existence as possible.

Two days after Toby left, Ali's parents took the girls on a camping trip to the Pocono Mountains. The five of them went white-water rafting and rock-climbing, and tanned on the banks of the lake. At night, when their conversation turned to Toby and Jenna—as it often did that summer—Ali reminded them that they could never, *ever* tell *anyone*. They'd all keep the secret forever . . . and it would bond their friendship into eternity. That night, when they zipped themselves into their five-girl tent, J. Crew cashmere hoodies up around their heads, Ali gave each of them a brightly colored string bracelet to symbolize the bond. She tied the bracelets on each of their wrists and told them to repeat after her: "I promise not to tell, until the day I die."

They went around in a circle, Spencer to Hanna to Emily to Aria, saying exactly that. Ali tied on her bracelet last. "Until the day I die," she whispered after making the knot, her hands clasped over her heart. Each of the girls squeezed hands. Despite the dreadfulness of the situation, they felt lucky to have each other.

The girls wore their bracelets through showers, spring break trips to D.C. and Colonial Williamsburg—or, in Spencer's case, to Bermuda—through grubby hockey practices and messy bouts with the flu. Ali managed to keep her bracelet the cleanest of everyone's, as if getting it dirty would cloud its purpose. Sometimes, they would touch their fingers to the bracelet and whisper, "Until the day I die," to remind themselves of how close they all were. It became their code; they all knew what it meant. In fact, Ali said it less than a year later, the very last day of seventh grade, as the girls were starting their summer-kickoff sleepover. No one knew that in just a few short hours, Ali would disappear.

Or that it would be the day she died.

1

AND WE THOUGHT
WE WERE FRIENDS

Spencer Hastings stood on the apple-green lawn of the Rosewood Abbey with her three ex–best friends, Hanna Marin, Aria Montgomery, and Emily Fields. The girls had stopped speaking more than three years ago, not long after Alison DiLaurentis mysteriously went missing, but they'd been brought back together today for Alison's memorial service. Two days ago, construction workers had found Ali's body under a concrete slab behind what used to be her house.

Spencer looked again at the text message she'd just received on her Sidekick.

I'm still here, bitches. And I know everything. —A

"Oh my God," Hanna whispered. Her BlackBerry's screen read the same thing. So did Aria's Treo and Emily's Nokia. Over the past week, each of them had gotten e-mails, texts, and IMs from someone who went by the initial *A*. The notes had mostly been about stuff from seventh grade, the year Ali went missing, but they'd also mentioned new secrets . . . stuff that was happening *now*.

Spencer thought A might have been Alison—that somehow she was back—except that was out of the question now, right? Ali's body had decayed under the concrete. She'd been . . . dead . . . for a long, long time.

"Do you think this means . . . The Jenna Thing?" Aria whispered, running her hand over her angular jaw.

Spencer slid her phone back in her tweed Kate Spade bag. "We shouldn't talk about this here. Someone might hear us." She glanced nervously at the abbey's steps, where Toby and Jenna Cavanaugh had stood just a moment before. Spencer hadn't seen Toby since before Ali even went missing, and the last time she saw Jenna was the night of her accident, limp in the arms of the paramedic who'd carried her down.

"The swings?" Aria whispered, meaning the Rosewood Day Elementary playground. It was their old special meeting place.

"Perfect," Spencer said, pushing through a crowd of mourners. "Meet you there."

It was the late afternoon on a crystal-clear fall day. The air smelled like apples and wood smoke. A hot-air balloon floated overhead. It was a fitting day for a memorial service for one of the most beautiful girls in Rosewood.

I know everything.

Spencer shivered. It had to be a bluff. Whoever this A was, A couldn't know *everything*. Not about The Jenna Thing . . . and certainly not about the secret only Spencer and Ali shared. The night of Jenna's accident, Spencer had witnessed something that her friends hadn't, but Ali had made her keep it a secret, even from Emily, Aria, and Hanna. Spencer had wanted to tell them, but when she couldn't, she pushed it aside and pretended that it hadn't happened.

But . . . it had.

That fresh, springy April night in sixth grade, just after Ali shot the firework into the tree house window, Spencer ran outside. The air smelled like burning hair. She saw the paramedics bringing Jenna down the tree house's shaky rope ladder.

Ali was next to her. "Did you do that on purpose?" Spencer demanded, terrified.

"No!" Ali clutched Spencer's arm. "It was—"

For years, Spencer had tried to block out what had come next: Toby Cavanaugh coming straight for them. His hair was matted to his head, and his goth-pale face was flushed. He walked right up to Ali.

"*I saw you.*" Toby was so angry he was shaking. He glanced toward his driveway, where a police car had pulled in. "I'm going to tell."

Spencer gasped. The ambulance doors slammed shut and its sirens screamed away from the house. Ali was calm. "Yeah, but I saw *you*, Toby," she said. "And if you tell, I'll tell, too. Your *parents*."

Toby took a step back. "No."

"*Yes*," Ali countered. Although she was only five-three, suddenly she seemed much taller. "*You* lit the firework. You hurt your sister."

Spencer grabbed her arm. What was she doing? But Ali shook her off.

"Stepsister," Toby mumbled, almost inaudibly. He glanced at his tree house and then toward the end of the street. Another police car slowly rolled up to the Cavanaugh house. "I'll get you," he growled to Ali. "You just wait."

Then he disappeared.

Spencer grabbed Ali's arm. "What are we going to do?"

"Nothing," Ali said, almost lightly. "We're fine."

"Alison . . ." Spencer blinked in disbelief. "Didn't you hear him? He said he saw what you did. He's going to tell the police right now."

"I don't think so." Ali smiled. "Not with what I've got on him." And then she leaned over and whispered what she'd seen Toby do. It was something so disgusting Ali had forgotten she was holding the lit firework until it shot out of her hands and through the tree house window.

Ali made Spencer promise not to tell the others about any of it, and warned that if Spencer *did* tell them, she'd figure out a way for Spencer—and only Spencer—to take the heat. Terrified at what Ali might do, Spencer kept her mouth shut. She worried that Jenna might say something—surely Jenna remembered that Toby hadn't done it—but Jenna had been confused and delirious . . . she'd said that night was a blank.

Then, a year later, Ali went missing.

The police questioned everyone, including Spencer, asking if there was anyone who wanted to hurt Ali. *Toby*, Spencer thought immediately. She couldn't forget the moment when he'd said: *I'll get you.* Except naming Toby meant telling the cops the truth about Jenna's accident—that she was partially responsible. That she'd known the truth all this time and hadn't told anyone. It also meant telling her friends the secret she'd been keeping for more than a year. So Spencer said nothing.

Spencer lit another Parliament and turned out of the Rosewood Abbey parking lot. *See?* A couldn't possibly know everything, like the text had said. Unless, that was, A was Toby Cavanaugh . . . But that didn't make sense. A's notes to Spencer were about a secret that only Ali knew: back in seventh grade, Spencer had kissed Ian, her sister Melissa's boyfriend. Spencer had admitted what she'd done to Ali—but no one else. And A also knew about Wren, her sister's now-ex, whom Spencer had done more than just kiss last week.

But the Cavanaughs *did* live on Spencer's street. With binoculars, Toby might be able to see in her window. And Toby *was* in Rosewood, even though it was September. Shouldn't he be at boarding school?

Spencer pulled into the brick-paved driveway of the

Rosewood Day School. Her friends were already there, huddling by the elementary school jungle gym. It was a beautiful wooden castle, complete with turrets, flags, and a dragon-shaped slide. The parking lot was deserted, the brick walkways were empty, and the practice fields were silent; the whole school had the day off in Ali's memory.

"So we all got texts from this A person?" Hanna asked as Spencer approached. Everyone had her cell phone out and was staring at the *I know everything* note.

"I got two others," Emily said tentatively. "I thought they were from Ali."

"I did too!" Hanna gasped, slapping her hand on the climbing dome. Aria and Spencer nodded as well. They all looked at one another with wide, nervous eyes.

"What did yours say?" Spencer looked at Emily.

Emily pushed a lock of blondish-red hair out of her eye. "It's . . . personal."

Spencer was so surprised, she laughed aloud. "You don't have any secrets, Em!" Emily was the purest, sweetest girl on the planet.

Emily looked offended. "Yeah, well, I do."

"Oh." Spencer plopped down on one of the slide's steps. She breathed in, expecting to smell mulch and sawdust. Instead she caught a whiff of burning hair—just like the night of Jenna's accident. "How about you, Hanna?"

Hanna wrinkled her pert little nose. "If Emily's not talking about hers, I don't want to talk about mine. It was something only Ali knew."

"Same with mine," Aria said quickly. She lowered her eyes. "Sorry."

Spencer felt her stomach clench up. "So everyone has secrets only *Ali* knew?"

Everyone nodded. Spencer snorted nastily. "I thought we were best friends."

Aria turned to Spencer and frowned. "So what did yours say, then?"

Spencer didn't feel like her Ian secret was all that juicy. It was nothing compared to what else she knew about The Jenna Thing. But now she felt too proud to tell. "It's a secret Ali knew, same as yours." She pushed her long dirty-blond hair behind her ears. "But A also e-mailed me about something that's happening now. It felt like someone was *spying* on me."

Aria's ice-blue eyes widened. "Same here."

"So there's someone watching all of us," Emily said. A ladybug landed delicately on her shoulder, and she shook it off as though it were something much scarier.

Spencer stood up. "Do you think it could be . . . Toby?"

Everyone looked surprised. "Why?" Aria asked.

"He's part of The Jenna Thing," Spencer said carefully. "What if he knows?"

Aria pointed to the text on her Treo. "You really think this is about . . . The Jenna Thing?"

Spencer licked her lips. *Tell them.* "We still don't know why Toby took the blame," she suggested, testing to see what the others would say.

Hanna thought for a moment. "The only way Toby could know what we did is if one of us told." She looked at the others distrustfully. "*I* didn't tell."

"Me neither," Aria and Emily quickly piped up.

"What if Toby found out another way?" Spencer asked.

"You mean if someone else saw Ali that night and told him?" Aria asked. "Or if he saw Ali?"

"No . . . I mean . . . I don't know," Spencer said. "I'm just throwing it out there."

Tell them, Spencer thought again, but she couldn't. Everyone seemed wary of one another, sort of like it had been right after Ali went missing, when their friendship disintegrated. If Spencer told them the truth about Toby, they'd hate her for not having told the police when Ali disappeared. Maybe they'd even blame her for Ali's death. Maybe they should. What if Toby really had . . . done it? "It was just a thought," she heard herself saying. "I'm probably wrong."

"Ali said no one knew except for us." Emily's eyes looked wet. "She *swore* to us. Remember?"

"Besides," Hanna added, "how could Toby know that much about us? I could see it being one of Ali's old hockey friends, or her brother, or someone she actually spoke to. But she hated Toby's guts. We all did."

Spencer shrugged. "You're probably right." As soon as she said it, she relaxed. She was obsessing over nothing.

Everything was quiet. Maybe too quiet. A tree branch

snapped close by, and Spencer whirled around sharply. The swings swayed back and forth, as if someone had just jumped off. A brown bird perched atop the Rosewood Day Elementary roof glared at them, as if it knew things, too.

"I think someone's just trying to mess with us," Aria whispered.

"Yeah," Emily agreed, but she sounded just as unconvinced.

"So, what if we get another note?" Hanna tugged her short black dress over her slender thighs. "We should at least figure out who it is."

"How about, if we get another note, we call each other," Spencer suggested. "We could try to put the pieces together. But I don't think we should do anything, like, crazy. We should try not to worry."

"I'm not worried," Hanna said quickly.

"Me neither," Aria and Emily said at the same time. But when a horn honked on the main road, everyone jumped.

"Hanna!" Mona Vanderwaal, Hanna's best friend, poked her pale blond head out the window of a yellow Hummer H3. She wore large, pink-tinted aviator sunglasses.

Hanna looked at the others unapologetically. "I've gotta go," she murmured, and ran up the hill.

Over the last few years, Hanna had reinvented herself into one of the most popular girls at Rosewood Day. She'd lost weight, dyed her hair a sexy dark auburn, got a whole new designer wardrobe, and now she and Mona Vanderwaal–also a transformed dork–pranced around school, too good for everyone else. Spencer wondered what Hanna's big secret could be.

"I should go too." Aria pushed her slouchy purple purse higher on her shoulder. "So . . . I'll call you guys." She headed for her Subaru.

Spencer lingered by the swings. So did Emily, whose normally cheerful face looked drawn and tired. Spencer put a hand on Emily's freckled arm. "You all right?"

Emily shook her head. "Ali. She's–"

"I know."

They awkwardly hugged, then Emily broke away for the woods, saying she was going to take the shortcut home. For years, Spencer, Emily, Aria, and Hanna hadn't spoken, even if they sat behind one another in history class or were alone together in the girls' bathroom. Yet Spencer knew things about all of them–intricate parts of their personalities only a close friend could know. Like, of course Emily was taking Ali's death the hardest. They used to call Emily "Killer" because she defended Ali like a possessive Rottweiler.

Back in her car, Spencer sank into the leather seat and turned on the radio. She spun the dial and found 610 AM, Philly's sports radio station. Something about over-testosteroned guys barking about Phillies and Sixers stats calmed her. She'd hoped talking to her old friends might clear some things up, but now things just felt even . . . *ickier*. Even with Spencer's massive SAT vocabulary, she couldn't think of a better word to describe it than that.

When her cell phone buzzed in her pocket, she pulled it out, thinking it was probably Emily or Aria. Maybe even Hanna. Spencer frowned and opened her inbox.

Spence, I don't blame you for not telling them our little secret about Toby. The truth can be dangerous—and you don't want them getting hurt, do you? —A

2

HANNA 2.0

Mona Vanderwaal put her parents' Hummer into park but left the engine running. She tossed her cell phone into her oversize, cognac-colored Lauren Merkin tote and grinned at her best friend, Hanna. "I've been trying to call you."

Hanna stood cautiously on the pavement. "Why are you here?"

"What are you talking about?"

"Well, I didn't ask you for a ride." Trembling, Hanna pointed to her Toyota Prius in the parking lot. "My car's right there. Did someone tell you I was here, or . . . ?"

Mona wound a long, white-blond strand of hair around her finger. "I'm on my way home from the church, nut job. I saw you, I pulled over." She let out a little laugh. "You take one of your mom's Valiums? You seem sort of messed up."

Hanna pulled a Camel Ultra Light out of the pack in

her black Prada hobo bag and lit up. Of course she was messed up. Her old best friend had been murdered, and she'd been receiving terrifying text messages from someone named A all week. Every moment of today—getting ready for Ali's funeral, buying Diet Coke at Wawa, merging onto the highway toward the Rosewood Abbey—she felt sure someone was watching her. "I didn't see you at the church," she murmured.

Mona took her sunglasses off to reveal her round blue eyes. "You looked right at me. I waved at you. Any of this sound familiar?"

Hanna shrugged. "I . . . don't remember."

"Well, I guess you were busy with your old friends," Mona shot back.

Hanna bristled. Her old friends were a sticky subject between them—back a million years ago, Mona was one of the girls Ali, Hanna, and the others teased. She became *the* girl to rag on, after Jenna got hurt. "Sorry. It was crowded."

"It's not like I was hiding." Mona sounded hurt. "I was sitting behind Sean."

Hanna inhaled sharply. *Sean.*

Sean Ackard was her now ex-boyfriend; their relationship had imploded at Noel Kahn's welcome-back-to-school field party last Friday night. Hanna had made the decision that Friday was going to be the night she lost her virginity, but when she started to put the moves on Sean, he dumped her and gave her a sermon about respecting her body. In revenge, Hanna took the Ackard family's BMW out for a joyride with Mona and wrapped it around a telephone pole in front of a Home Depot.

Mona pressed her peep-toe heel on the Hummer's gas pedal, revving the car's billion-cylinder engine. "So listen. We have an emergency—we don't have dates yet."

"To what?" Hanna blinked.

Mona raised a perfectly waxed blond eyebrow. "Hello, Hanna? To Foxy! It's this weekend. Now that you dumped Sean, you can ask someone cool."

Hanna stared at the little dandelions growing out of the cracks in the sidewalk. Foxy was the annual charity ball for "the young members of Rosewood society," sponsored by the Rosewood Foxhunting League, hence the name. A $250 donation to the league's choice of charity got you dinner, dancing, a chance to see your picture in the *Philadelphia Inquirer* and on glam-R5.com—the area's society blog—and it was a good excuse to dress up, drink up, and hook up with someone else's boyfriend. Hanna had paid for her ticket in July, thinking she'd go with Sean. "I don't know if I'm even going," she mumbled gloomily.

"Of course you're going." Mona rolled her blue eyes and heaved a sigh. "Listen, just call me when they've reversed your lobotomy." And then she put the car back into drive and zoomed off.

Hanna walked slowly back to her Prius. Her friends had gone, and her silver car looked lonely in the empty parking lot. An uneasy feeling nagged at her. Mona was her best friend, but there were tons of things Hanna wasn't telling her right now. Like about A's messages. Or how she'd gotten arrested Saturday morning for stealing Mr. Ackard's car. Or that Sean dumped *her*, and not the other way around. Sean was so diplomatic, he'd only told his friends they'd "decided to see other people." Hanna figured she could work the story to her advantage so no one would ever know the truth.

But if she told Mona any of that, it would show her that Hanna's life was spiraling out of control. Hanna and Mona had re-created themselves together, and the rule was that as co-divas of the school, they had to be perfect. That meant staying swizzle-stick thin, getting skinny Paige jeans before anyone else, and never losing control. Any cracks in their armor could send them back to unfashionable dorkdom, and they never wanted to go back there. Ever. So Hanna had to pretend none of the horror of the past week had happened, even though it definitely had.

Hanna had never known anyone who had died, much less someone who was murdered. And the fact that it was *Ali*—in combination with the notes from A—was even spookier. If someone really knew about The Jenna Thing . . . and could tell . . . *and* if that someone had something to do with Ali's death, Hanna's life was definitely not in her control.

Hanna pulled up to her house, a massive brick

Georgian that overlooked Mt. Kale. When she glanced at herself in the car's rearview mirror, she was horrified to see that her skin was blotchy and oily and her pores looked *enormous*. She leaned closer to the mirror, and then suddenly . . . her skin was clear. Hanna took a few long, ragged breaths before getting out of the car. She'd been having a lot of hallucinations like this lately.

Shaken, she slid into her house and headed for her kitchen. When she strode through the French doors, she froze.

Hanna's mother sat at the kitchen table with a plate of cheese and crackers in front of her. Her dark auburn hair was in a chignon, and her diamond-encrusted Chopard watch glinted in the afternoon sun. Her Motorola wireless headset hung from her ear.

And next to her . . . was Hanna's father.

"We've been waiting for you," her dad said.

Hanna took a step back. There was more gray in his hair, and he wore new wire-rimmed glasses, but otherwise he looked the same: tall, crinkly eyes, blue polo. His voice was the same, too—deep and calm, like an NPR commentator. Hanna hadn't seen or spoken to him in almost four years. "What are you *doing* here?" she blurted.

"I've been doing some work in Philly," Mr. Marin said, his voice squeaking nervously on *work*. He picked up his Doberman coffee cup. It was the mug her dad used faithfully when he'd lived with them; Hanna wondered if he'd rooted through the cupboard to find it.

"Your mom called and told me about Alison. I'm so sorry, Hanna."

"Yeah," Hanna sounded out. She felt dizzy.

"Do you need to talk about anything?" Her mom nibbled on a piece of cheddar.

Hanna tilted her head, confused. Ms. Marin and Hanna's relationship was more boss/intern than mother/daughter. Ashley Marin had clawed her way up the executive ladder at the Philly advertising firm McManus & Tate, and she treated everyone like her employee. Hanna couldn't remember the last time her mom had asked her a touchy-feely question. Possibly never. "Um, that's okay. But thanks," she added, a little snottily.

Could they really blame her for being a tad bitter? After her parents divorced, her dad moved to Annapolis, started dating a woman named Isabel, and inherited a gorgeous quasi-stepdaughter, Kate. Her father made his new life so unwelcoming, Hanna visited him just once. Her dad hadn't tried to call her, e-mail her, anything, in years. He didn't even send birthday presents anymore—just checks.

Her father sighed. "This probably isn't the best day to talk things over."

Hanna eyed him. "Talk what over?"

Mr. Marin cleared his throat. "Well, your mom called me for another reason, too." He lowered his eyes. "The car."

Hanna frowned. Car? What car? *Oh.*

"It's bad enough you stole Mr. Ackard's car," her father said. "But you left the scene of the accident?"

Hanna looked at her mom. "I thought this was taken care of."

"Nothing is taken care of." Ms. Marin glared at her.

Could've fooled me, Hanna wanted to say. When the cops let her go on Saturday, her mother mysteriously told Hanna she'd "worked things out" so Hanna wouldn't be in trouble. The mystery was solved when Hanna found her mom and one of the young officers, Darren Wilden, practically doing it in her kitchen the next night.

"I'm serious," Ms. Marin said, and Hanna stopped smirking. "The police have agreed to drop the case, yes, but it doesn't change what's going on with *you*, Hanna. First you steal from Tiffany, now this. I didn't know what to do. So I called your father."

Hanna stared at the plate of cheese, too weirded out to look either of them in the eye. Her mom had told her dad that she'd gotten caught shoplifting at Tiffany too?

Mr. Marin cleared his throat. "Although the case was dropped with the police, Mr. Ackard wants to settle it privately, out of court."

Hanna bit the inside of her mouth. "Doesn't insurance pay for those things?"

"That's not it exactly," Mr. Marin answered. "Mr. Ackard made your mother an offer."

"Sean's father is a plastic surgeon," her mother explained, "but his pet project is a rehabilitation clinic for burn victims. He wants you to report there at three-thirty tomorrow."

Hanna wrinkled her nose. "Why can't we just give him the money?"

Ms. Marin's tiny LG cell phone started to ring. "I think this will be a good lesson for you. To do some good for the community. To understand what you've done."

"But I *do* understand!" Hanna Marin did not want to give her free time away to a burn clinic. If she *had* to volunteer, why couldn't it be somewhere chic? Like at the UN, with Nicole and Angelina?

"It's already settled," Ms. Marin said brusquely. Then she shouted into her phone, "Carson? Did you do the mock-ups?"

Hanna sat with her fingernails pressed into her fists. Frankly, she wished she could go upstairs, change out of her funeral dress—was it making her thighs look huge, or was that just her reflection in the patio doors?—redo her makeup, lose five pounds, and do a shot of vodka. Then she would come back down and reintroduce herself.

When she glanced at her father, he gave her a very small smile. Hanna's heart jumped. His lips parted as if he were going to speak, but then his cell phone rang, too. He held up one finger to Hanna to hold on. "Kate?" he answered.

Hanna's heart sank. *Kate.* The gorgeous, perfect quasi-stepdaughter.

Her father tucked the phone under his chin. "Hey!

How was the cross-country meet?" He paused, then beamed. "Under eighteen minutes? That's *awesome.*"

Hanna grabbed a hunk of cheddar from the cheese plate. When she'd visited Annapolis, Kate wouldn't look at her. She and Ali, who'd come with Hanna for moral support, had formed an insta–pretty girl bond, excluding Hanna entirely. It drove Hanna to wolf down every snack within a one-mile radius—this was back when she was chubby and ugly and ate and ate. When she clutched her stomach in binged-out agony, her father had wiggled her toe and said, "Little piggy not feeling so good?" In front of *everyone.* And then Hanna had fled to the bathroom and forced a toothbrush down her throat.

The hunk of cheddar hovered in front of Hanna's mouth. Taking a deep breath, she stuffed it into a napkin instead and threw it in the trash. All that stuff happened a long time ago . . . when she was a very different Hanna. One only Ali knew about, and one Hanna had buried.

3

IS THERE AN AMISH SIGN-UP
SHEET SOMEWHERE?

Emily Fields stood in front of the Gray Horse Inn, a crumbling stone building that was once a Revolutionary War hospital. The current-day innkeeper had converted its upper floors into an inn for rich out-of-town guests and ran an organic café in the parlor. Emily peered through the café's windows to see some of her classmates and their families eating smoked-salmon bagels, pressed Italian sandwiches, and enormous Cobb salads. Everyone must have had the same post-funeral brunch craving.

"You made it."

Emily swung around to see Maya St. Germain leaning against a terra-cotta pot full of peonies. Maya had called as Emily was leaving the Rosewood Day swings, asking that she meet her here. Like Emily, Maya still had on her funeral outfit—a short, pleated black corduroy skirt, black boots, and a black sleeveless sweater with delicate lace stitching around the neck. And also like Emily, it seemed that Maya had scrounged to find black and mournful-looking stuff from the back of her closet.

Emily smiled sadly. The St. Germains had moved into Ali's old house. When workers started to dig up the DiLaurentises' half-finished gazebo to make way for the St. Germains' tennis court, they uncovered Ali's decayed body underneath the concrete. Ever since then, news vans, police cars, and curiosity seekers had gathered around the property 24/7. Maya's family was taking refuge here at the inn until things died down.

"Hey." Emily looked around. "Are your folks having brunch?"

Maya shook her thick brownish-black curls. "They went to Lancaster. To get back to nature or something. Honestly, I think they've been in shock, so maybe the simple life will do them some good." Emily smiled, thinking of Maya's parents trying to commune with the Amish in the small township west of Rosewood.

"You wanna come up to my room?" Maya asked, raising an eyebrow.

Emily pulled at her skirt—her legs were looking beefy from swimming—and paused. If Maya's family wasn't here, they'd be alone. In a room. With a bed.

When Emily first met Maya, she'd been psyched. She'd been pining for a friend who could replace Ali. Ali and Maya were really similar in a lot of ways—they were both fearless and fun, and they seemed to be the only two people in the world who understood the real Emily. They had something else in common: Emily felt something *different* around them.

"C'mon." Maya turned to go inside. Emily, not sure what else to do, followed.

She trailed Maya up the creaky, twisty stairs of the inn to her 1776-themed bedroom. It smelled like wet wool. It had slanted pine floors, a shaky, queen-size four-poster bed with a giant crazy quilt on top, and a puzzling contraption in the corner that looked like a butter churn. "My parents got my brother and me separate rooms." Maya sat down on the bed with a squeak.

"That's nice," Emily answered, perching on the edge of a rickety chair that had probably once belonged to George Washington.

"So, how *are* you?" Maya leaned toward her. "God, I saw you at the funeral. You looked . . . devastated."

Emily's hazel eyes filled with tears. She *was* devastated about Ali. Emily had spent the past three-and-a-half years hoping Ali would show up on her porch one day, as healthy and glowing as ever. And when she started receiving the A notes, she was sure Ali was back. Who else could have known? But now, Emily knew for certain that Ali was really gone. Forever. On top of that, someone knew her squirmiest secret—that she'd been in love with Ali—*and* that she felt the same way about Maya. And maybe that same someone knew the truth about what they'd done to Jenna, too.

Emily felt bad, refusing to tell her old friends what her notes from A said. It was just . . . she *couldn't*. One of A's notes was written on an old love letter that she'd sent to Ali. The ironic thing was that she *could* talk to Maya about what the notes said, but she was afraid to tell Maya about A. "I think I'm still pretty shook up," she finally answered, feeling a headache coming on. "But, also . . . I'm just tired."

Maya kicked off her boots. "Why don't you take a nap? You aren't going to feel any better sitting in that torture contraption of a chair."

Emily wrapped her hands around the chair's arms. "I—"

Maya patted the bed. "You look like you need a hug."

A hug *would* feel good. Emily pushed her reddish-blond hair out of her face and sat down on the bed next to Maya. Their bodies melted into each other. Emily could feel Maya's ribs through the fabric of her shirt. She was so petite, Emily could probably pick her up and spin her around.

They pulled away, pausing a few inches from each other's faces. Maya's eyelashes were coal black, and there were tiny flecks of gold in her irises. Slowly, Maya tilted Emily's chin up. She kissed her gently at first. Then harder.

Emily felt the familiar whoosh of excitement as Maya's hand grazed the edge of Emily's skirt. Suddenly, she reached underneath it. Her hands felt cold and surprising. Emily eyes shot open and she pulled away.

The frilly white curtains in Maya's room were open wide, and Emily could see the Escalades, Mercedes wagons, and Lexus Hybrids in the parking lot. Sarah Isling and Taryn Orr, two girls in Emily's grade, sauntered out of the restaurant exit, followed by their parents. Emily ducked.

Maya sat back. "What's wrong?"

"What are you *doing?*" Emily covered her unbuttoned skirt with her hand.

"What do you think I'm doing?" Maya grinned.

Emily glanced at the window again. Sarah and Taryn were gone.

Maya jiggled up and down on the bed's creaky mattress. "Did you know there's a charity party this Saturday called Foxy?"

"Yeah." Emily's whole body throbbed.

"I think we should go," Maya continued. "It sounds fun."

Emily frowned. "The tickets are $250. You have to be invited."

"My brother scored tickets. Enough for both of us." Maya inched closer to Emily. "Will you be my date?"

Emily shot off the bed. "I . . ." She took a step backward, stumbling on the slippery hooked rug. Lots of people from Rosewood Day went to Foxy. All the popular kids, all the jocks . . . everyone. "I have to go to the bathroom."

Maya looked confused. "It's over there."

Emily shut the crooked bathroom door. She sat on

the toilet and stared at the print on the wall of an Amish woman wearing a bonnet and an ankle-length dress. Perhaps it was a sign. Emily was always looking for signs to help her make decisions—in her horoscope, in fortune cookies, in random things like this. Maybe this picture meant, *Be like the Amish*. Weren't they chaste for life? Weren't their lives maddeningly simple? Didn't they burn girls at the stake for liking other girls?

And then her cell phone rang.

Emily pulled it out of her pocket, wondering if it was her mother wanting to know where Emily was. Mrs. Fields was less than pleased that Emily and Maya had become friends—for disturbing, possibly racist reasons. Imagine if her mom knew what they were up to now.

Emily's Nokia blinked, *One new text message*. She clicked READ.

Em! Still enjoying the same kinds of *activities* with your best friends, I see. Even though most of us have totally changed, it's nice to know you're still the same! Gonna tell everyone about your new love? Or shall I? —A

"No," Emily whispered.

There was a sudden whoosh behind her. She jumped, bumping her hip on the sink. It was only someone flushing the toilet in the next guest room. Then there was some whispering and giggling. It sounded like it was coming from the sink drain.

"Emily?" Maya called. "Everything okay?"

"Uh . . . fine." Emily croaked. She stared at herself in the mirror. Her eyes were wide and hollow, and her reddish-blonde hair was disheveled. When she finally emerged from the bathroom, the bedroom lights were off and the shades were drawn.

"*Psssst,*" Maya called from the bed. She'd laid seductively on her side.

Emily looked around. She was pretty sure Maya hadn't even locked the door. All those Rosewood kids were eating brunch downstairs. . . .

"I can't do this," Emily blurted out.

"What?" Maya's dazzlingly white teeth glowed in the dimness.

"We're friends." Emily plastered herself against the wall. "I like you."

"I like you, too." Maya ran a hand over one bare arm.

"But that's all I can be right now," Emily clarified. "Friends."

Maya's smile disappeared in the dark.

"Sorry." Emily shoved on her loafers fast, putting her right shoe on her left foot.

"It doesn't mean you have to leave," Maya said quietly.

Emily looked at her as she reached for the doorknob. Her eyes were already adjusting to the dim light, and she could see that Maya looked disappointed and confused and . . . and beautiful. "I should go," Emily mumbled. "I'm late."

"Late for what?"

Emily didn't answer. She turned for the door. Just as she suspected, Maya hadn't bothered to lock it.

4

THERE'S TRUTH IN WINE . . . OR, IN ARIA'S CASE, AMSTEL

As Aria Montgomery slipped into her family's boxy, avant-garde house—which stuck out on their typical Rosewood street of neoclassical Victorians—she heard her parents talking quietly in the kitchen.

"But I don't understand," her mother, Ella—her parents liked Aria to call them by their first names—was saying. "You told me you could make it to the artists' dinner last week. It's important. I think Jason might buy some of the paintings I did in Reykjavík."

"It's just that I'm already behind on my papers," her father, Byron, answered. "I haven't gotten back into the swing of grading yet."

Ella sighed. "How is it they have papers and you've only had two days of class?"

"I gave them their first assignment before the semester

started." Byron sounded distracted. "I'll make it up to you, I promise. How about Otto's? Saturday night?"

Aria shifted her weight in the foyer. Her family had just returned from two years in Reykjavík, Iceland, where her dad had been on sabbatical from teaching at Hollis, Rosewood's liberal arts college. It had been a perfect reprieve for all of them—Aria needed the escape after Ali went missing, her brother, Mike, needed some culture and discipline, and Ella and Byron, who'd begun to go days without speaking, seemed to fall back in love in Iceland. But now that they were back home, everyone was reverting back to their dysfunctional ways.

Aria passed the kitchen. Her dad was gone, and her mom was standing over the island, her head in her hands. When she saw Aria, she brightened. "How you doing, pumpkin?" Ella asked carefully, fingering the memorial card they'd received from Ali's service.

"I'm all right," Aria mumbled.

"You want to talk about it?"

Aria shook her head. "Later, maybe." She scuttled into the living room, feeling spastic and distracted, as though she'd drunk six cans of Red Bull. And it wasn't just from Ali's funeral.

Last week A had taunted Aria about one of her darkest secrets: In seventh grade, Aria caught her father kissing one of his students, a girl named Meredith. Byron had asked Aria not to tell her mother, and Aria never had, although she always felt guilty about it. When A threatened to tell Ella the whole ugly truth, Aria had assumed A was Alison. It was Ali who'd been with Aria when she caught Bryon and Meredith together, and Aria had never told anyone else.

But now Aria knew A couldn't be Alison, but A's threat was still out there, promising to ruin Aria's family. She knew she should tell Ella before A got to her—but she couldn't make herself do it.

Aria walked to the back porch, winding her fingers through her long black hair. A flash of white zoomed by. It was her brother, Mike, racing around the yard with his lacrosse stick. "Hey," she called, getting an idea. When Mike didn't answer, she walked out onto the lawn and stood in his path. "I'm going downtown. Wanna come?"

Mike made a face. "Downtown's full of dirty hippies. Besides, I'm practicing."

Aria rolled her eyes. Mike was so obsessed with making the Rosewood Day varsity lacrosse team, he hadn't even bothered to change out of his charcoal gray funeral suit before starting drills. Her brother was so cookie-cutter Rosewood—dirty white baseball cap, obsessed with PlayStation, saving up for a hunter-green Jeep Cherokee as soon as he turned sixteen. Unfortunately, there was no question they shared the same gene pool—both Aria and her brother were tall and had blue-black hair and unforgettable angular faces.

"Well, I'm going to get bombed," she told him. "You *sure* you want to practice?"

Mike narrowed his grayish-blue eyes at her, processing this. "You're not secretly dragging me to a poetry reading?"

She shook her head. "We'll go to the skankiest college bar we can find."

Mike shrugged and laid down his lacrosse stick. "Let's go," he said.

Mike fell into a booth. "This place rocks."

They were at the Victory Brewery—indeed the skankiest bar they could find. It was flanked by a piercing parlor and a store called Hippie Gypsy that sold "hydroponic seeds"—nudge, nudge. There was a puke stain on the sidewalk out front, and a half-blind, three-hundred-pound bouncer had waved them right through, too engrossed in *Dubs* magazine to card them.

Inside, the bar was dark and grubby, with a dingy Ping-Pong table in the back. This place was pretty much like Snooker's, Hollis's other grimy student bar, but Aria had vowed to never set foot in Snooker's again. She'd met a sexy boy named Ezra at Snooker's two weeks ago, but then he wound up being less of a boy and more of an AP English teacher—*her* AP English teacher. A sent Aria taunting texts about Ezra, and when Ezra accidentally saw what A had written, he assumed that Aria was telling the whole school about them. So ended Aria's Rosewood faculty romance.

A waitress with enormous boobs and Heidi braids

came up to their booth and looked at Mike suspiciously. "Are you twenty-one?"

"Oh, yeah," Mike said, folding his hands on the table. "I'm actually twenty-five."

"We'll have a pitcher of Amstel," Aria interrupted, kicking Mike under the table.

"And," Mike added, "I want a shot. Of Jaeger."

Heidi Braids looked pained, but she came back with the pitcher and the shot. Mike downed the Jaeger and made a puckered, girlish face. He slammed the shot glass on the chipped wooden table and eyed Aria. "I think I've cracked why you've become so loco." Mike had announced last week that he thought Aria was acting even freakier than usual, and he'd vowed to figure out why.

"I'm dying to know," Aria said dryly.

Mike pushed his fingers together in a steeple, a professorly gesture their father often made. "I think you're secretly dancing at Turbulence."

Aria laughed so forcefully, beer flew up her nasal passages. Turbulence was a strip club two towns over, next to a one-strip airport.

"A couple of guys said they saw a girl going in there who looked *just* like you," Mike said. "You don't have to keep it a secret from me. I'm cool."

Aria pulled discreetly at her knitted mohair bra. She'd made one for herself, Ali, and her old friends in sixth grade, and had worn hers to Ali's memorial as a tribute. Unfortunately, in sixth grade, Aria's measurements were about a cup size smaller, and the mohair itched like hell. "You mean you don't think I'm acting strange because a) we're back in Rosewood and I hate it here, and b) my old best friend is dead?"

Mike shrugged. "I thought you didn't really like that girl."

Aria turned away. There had been moments when she really didn't like Ali, that was true. Especially when Ali didn't take her very seriously, or when she hounded Aria for details about Byron and Meredith. "That's not true," she lied.

Mike poured more beer into his glass. "Isn't it messed up that she was, like, dumped in the ground? And, like, concrete was poured on top of her?"

Aria winced and shut her eyes. Her brother had zero tact.

"So you think someone killed her?" Mike asked.

Aria shrugged. It was a question that had been haunting her—a question no one else had asked. At Ali's memorial, no one came out and said Ali had been *murdered*, only that she'd been *found*. But what else could it have been but murder? One minute, Ali was at their sleepover. The next, she was gone. Three years later, her body showed up in a hole in her backyard.

Aria wondered if A and Ali's killer were linked—and if the affair was tangled up in The Jenna Thing. When Jenna's accident happened, Aria thought she saw someone *besides* Ali at the base of Toby's tree house. Later that night, Aria was startled awake by the vision and decided she needed to ask Ali about it. She'd found her and Spencer whispering behind the closed bathroom door, but when Aria asked to come in, Ali told her to go back to sleep. By morning, Toby had confessed.

"I bet the killer's, like, someone out of left field," Mike said. "Like . . . someone you'd never guess in a trillion years." His eyes lit up. "How about Mrs. Craycroft?"

Mrs. Craycroft was their elderly neighbor to the right. She'd once saved up $5,000 worth of coins in Poland Spring jugs and tried to redeem them for cash at a nearby Coinstar. The local news did a story on her and everything. "Yep, you cracked the case," Aria deadpanned.

"Well, someone like that." Mike drummed his knobby fingers on the table. "Now that I know what's going on with *you*, I can focus my attention on Ali D."

"Go for it." If the cops weren't adept enough to find Ali in her own backyard, Mike might as well try his hand at it.

"So I'm thinking we need to play some beer-pong," Mike said, and before Aria could answer, he had already collected some Ping-Pong balls and an empty pint glass. "This is Noel Kahn's favorite game."

Aria smirked. Noel Kahn was one of the richest kids at school and *the* quintessential Rosewood boy, which basically made him Mike's idol. And, irony of all ironies, he seemed to have a thing for Aria, which she was trying her hardest to squelch.

"Wish me luck," Mike said, holding the Ping-Pong

ball ready. He missed the glass, sending the ball rolling off the table onto the floor.

"Chug it down," Aria singsonged, and her brother wrapped his hands around his beer and poured the whole thing down his throat.

Mike tried for the second time to get the Ping-Pong ball in Aria's glass but missed again. "You suck!" Aria teased, the beer beginning to make her feel a little buzzy.

"Like you're any better," Mike shot back.

"You wanna bet?"

Mike snorted. "If you don't make it, you have to get me into Turbulence. Me *and* Noel. But not while you're working," he added hastily.

"If I make it, you have to be my slave for a week. That means *during* school, too."

"Deal," Mike said. "You're not going to make it, so it doesn't matter."

She moved the glass to Mike's side of the table and took aim. The ball careened off one of the table's many dents and landed cleanly in the glass, not even bumping its sides on the way in. "Ha!" Aria cried. "You are *so* going down!"

Mike looked stunned. "That was just a lucky shot."

"Whatever!" Aria snickered gleefully. "So, I wonder . . . should I make you crawl on all fours behind me at school? Or wear mom's *faldur*?" She giggled. Ella's *faldur* was a traditional Icelandic pointed cap that made the wearer look like a deranged elf.

"Screw you." Mike grabbed the Ping-Pong ball out of his glass. It slipped out of his hands and bounced away from them.

"I'll get it," Aria offered. She stood, feeling pleasantly tipsy. The ball had rolled all the way to the front of the bar, and Aria bent down on the floor to get it. A couple swept past her, squeezing into the discreet, partially blocked seats in the corner. Aria noticed that the girl had long dark hair and a pink spiderweb tattoo on her wrist.

That tattoo was familiar. *Very* familiar. And when she whispered something to the guy she was with, he started coughing maniacally. Aria straightened up.

It was her father. And Meredith.

Aria bolted back to Mike. "We have to go."

Mike rolled his eyes. "But I just asked for a second shot of Jaeger."

"Too bad." Aria grabbed her jacket. "We're leaving. Now." She threw forty bucks on the table and pulled on Mike's arm until he stood. He was a little wobbly, but she managed to push him toward the door.

Unfortunately, Byron chose that very moment to let out one of his very distinctive laughs, which Aria always said sounded like a dying whale. Mike froze, recognizing it too. Their father's face was turned to the side, and he was touching Meredith's hand across the table.

Aria watched Mike recognize Byron. He knitted his brow. "Wait," he squeaked, looking confusedly at Aria. She willed her face to look unworried, but instead, she felt the corners of her mouth wiggle down. She knew she was making the same face Ella did when she tried to protect Aria or Mike from things that might hurt them.

Mike narrowed his eyes at her, then looked back at their father and Meredith. He opened his mouth to say something, then closed it, taking a step toward them. Aria reached out to stop him—she didn't want this happening right now. She didn't want this happening *ever*. Then Mike steeled his jaw, turned away from their dad, and stormed out of Victory, bumping into their waitress as he went.

Aria pushed through the door after him. She squinted in the bright afternoon light of the parking lot, looking back and forth for Mike. But her brother was gone.

5

A HOUSE DIVIDED

Spencer awoke on the floor of her upstairs bathroom with no idea how she'd gotten there. The clock on the shower radio said 6:45 P.M., and out the window, the evening sun cast long shadows on their yard. It was still Monday, the day of Ali's funeral. She must have fallen asleep . . . and sleepwalked. She used to be a chronic sleepwalker—it got so bad that in seventh grade, she had to spend a night at the University of Pennsylvania Sleep Evaluation Clinic with her brain hooked up to electrodes. The doctors said it was just stress.

She stood up and ran cold water over her face, looking at herself in the mirror: long blond hair, emerald-green eyes, pointed chin. Her skin was flawless and her teeth were radiantly white. It was preposterous that she didn't look as wrecked as the felt.

She ran the equation over again in her head: A knew about Toby and The Jenna Thing. Toby was back.

Therefore, Toby *had* to be A. And he was telling Spencer to keep her mouth shut. It was the same torture from sixth grade, all over again.

She went back to her bedroom and pressed her forehead to the window. To her left was her family's own private windmill—it had long since stopped working, but her parents loved how it gave their property such a rustic, authentic look. To her right, the Do Not Cross tape was still all over the DiLaurentises' lawn. The Ali shrine, which consisted of flowers, candles, photos, and other knickknacks in Ali's honor, had grown larger, swallowing the whole cul-de-sac.

Across the street from that was the Cavanaughs' house. Two cars in the driveway, a basketball in the yard, the little red flag up on the mailbox. From the outside, everything seemed so normal. But *inside* . . .

Spencer closed her eyes, remembering May of seventh grade, a year after The Jenna Thing. She had boarded the Philadelphia-bound SEPTA train to meet Ali in the city to go shopping. She was so busy texting Ali on her spanking-new Sidekick that it was five or six stops before she noticed there was someone across the aisle. It was *Toby*. Staring.

Her hands started shaking. Toby had been at boarding school all year, so Spencer hadn't seen him in months. As usual, his hair hung over his eyes and he wore enormous headphones, but something about him that day seemed . . . stronger. *Scarier.*

All of the guilty, anxious feelings about The Jenna Thing that Spencer had tried to bury flooded back. *I'll get you.* She didn't want to be in the same train car as him. She slid one leg into the aisle, then the other, but the conductor abruptly stepped in her way. "You going to Thirtieth Street or Market East?" he boomed.

Spencer shrank back. "Thirtieth," she whispered. When the conductor passed, she glanced at Toby again. His face bloomed into a huge, sinister smile. A split second later, his mouth became impassive again, but his eyes said, *Just. You. Wait.*

Spencer shot up and moved to another car. Ali was waiting for her on the platform at Thirtieth Street, and when they glanced back at the train, Toby was looking straight at them.

"I see someone's been let out of his little prison," Ali said with a smirk.

"Yeah." Spencer tried to laugh it off. "And he's still a loser with a capital *L*."

But a few weeks later, Ali went missing. And then it wasn't so funny.

A slide-whistle noise coming from Spencer's computer made her jump. It was her new e-mail alert. She paced over to her computer nervously and double-clicked the new message.

Hi, love. Haven't spoken to you in two days, and I'm going crazy missing you. —Wren.

Spencer sighed, a nervous sensation fluttering through her. The moment she'd laid eyes on Wren—her sister had brought him to meet their parents at a family dinner—something had happened to her. It was like . . . like he'd put a hex on her the second he sat down at Moshulu, took a sip of red wine, and met her eyes. He was British, exotic, witty, and smart, and liked the same indie bands Spencer did. He was just so wrong for her milquetoast, prim-and-perfect sister Melissa. But he was *so* right for Spencer. *She* knew it . . . and apparently he did too.

Before Melissa caught them making out Friday night, she and Wren experienced an unbelievable twenty minutes of passion. But because Melissa tattled, and because Spencer's parents *always* took her side, they banned Spencer from seeing Wren ever again. She was going crazy missing him, too, but what was she supposed to do?

Feeling groggy and unsettled, she walked down the stairs and passed the long, narrow gallery hall where her mother displayed the Thomas Cole landscapes she'd inherited from her grandfather. She stepped into her family's spacious kitchen. Her parents had restored it to look just like it had in the 1800s—except with updated countertops and state-of-the-art appliances. Her family was gathered at the kitchen table around Thai takeout containers.

Spencer hesitated in the doorway. She hadn't spoken to them since before Ali's funeral—she'd driven there alone and had barely seen them afterward on the lawn.

Actually, she hadn't spoken to her family since they reprimanded her about Wren two days ago, and now they'd shunned her again by starting dinner without her. And they had company. Ian Thomas, Melissa's old boyfriend—and the first of Melissa's exes that Spencer had kissed—was sitting in what should've been Spencer's seat.

"Oh," she squeaked.

Ian was the only one who looked up. "Hey, Spence! How are you?" he asked, as if he ate in the Hastingses' kitchen every day. It was hard enough for Spencer that Ian was coaching her field hockey team at Rosewood— but this was bizarre.

"I'm . . . fine," Spencer said, looking shiftily at the rest of her family, but no one was looking at her . . . or explaining why Ian was scarfing down Thai food in their kitchen. Spencer pulled up a chair to the corner of the table and started to spoon some lemongrass chicken onto her plate. "So, um, Ian. You're having dinner with us?"

Mrs. Hastings looked at her sharply. Spencer shut her mouth, a hot, clammy feeling coursing through her.

"We ran into each other at the, um, memorial," Ian explained. A siren interrupted him, and Ian dropped his fork. The noise was most likely coming from the DiLaurentises' house. Police cars had been there non-stop. "Pretty crazy, huh?" Ian said, running a hand through his curly blond hair. "I didn't know so many cop cars would still be here."

Melissa elbowed him lightly. "You get a big police

record, living out there in dangerous California?" Melissa and Ian had broken up because he'd moved across the country to go to college at Berkeley.

"Nah," Ian said. Before he could go on, Melissa, in typical Melissa fashion, had moved on to something else: herself. She turned to Mrs. Hastings. "So, Mom, the flowers at the service were the exact color I want to paint my living room walls."

Melissa reached for a *Martha Stewart Living* magazine and opened it to a marked page. She was constantly talking about home renovations; she was redecorating the Philadelphia town house their parents bought her as a reward for getting into U Penn's Wharton School of Business. They'd never do anything like that for Spencer.

Mrs. Hastings leaned in to see. "Lovely."

"Really nice," Ian agreed.

A disbelieving laugh escaped from Spencer's mouth. Alison DiLaurentis's *memorial service* was today, and all they could think to talk about was paint colors?

Melissa turned to Spencer. "What was that?"

"Well . . . I mean . . ." Spencer stuttered. Melissa looked offended, as if Spencer had just said something really rude. She nervously twirled her fork. "Forget it."

There was another silence. Even Ian seemed to be wary of her now. Her dad took a hearty sip of wine. "Veronica, did you see Liz there?"

"Yes, I spoke with her for a while," said Spencer's mother. "I thought she looked fantastic . . . considering." By

Liz, Spencer assumed they meant Elizabeth DiLaurentis, Ali's youngish aunt who lived in the area.

"It must be awful for her," Melissa said solemnly. "I can't imagine."

Ian made an empathetic *mmm*. Spencer felt her lower lip quiver. *Hello, what about me?* she wanted to scream. *Don't you guys remember? I was Ali's best friend!*

With every minute of silence, Spencer felt more unwelcome. She waited for someone to ask how she was holding up, offer her a piece of fried tempura, or at least to say, *Bless you*, when she sneezed. But they were still punishing her for kissing Wren. Even though today was . . . *today*.

A lump formed in her throat. She was used to being everyone's favorite: her teachers', her hockey coaches', her yearbook editor's. Even her colorist, Uri, said she was his favorite client because her hair took color so nicely. She'd won tons of school awards and had 370 MySpace friends, not counting bands. And while she might not ever be her parents' favorite—it was impossible to eclipse Melissa—she couldn't bear them hating her. Especially not now, when everything else in her life was so unstable.

When Ian got up and excused himself to make a phone call, Spencer took a deep breath. "Melissa?" Her voice cracked.

Melissa looked up, then went back to pushing her pad Thai around her plate.

Spencer cleared her throat. "Will you please talk to me?"

Melissa barely shrugged.

"I mean, I can't . . . I can't have you hate me. You were completely right. About . . . you know." Her hands shook so badly, she kept them wedged under her thighs. Apologizing made her nervous.

Melissa folded her hands over her magazines. "Sorry," she said. "I think that's out of the question." She stood and carried her plate to the sink.

"But . . ." Spencer was shocked. She looked to her parents. "I'm really sorry, guys. . . ." She felt tears brimming at her eyes.

Her father's face bore the tiniest glimmer of sympathy, but he quickly looked away. Her mother spooned the remaining lemongrass chicken into a Tupperware container. She shrugged. "You made your bed, Spencer," she said, rising and carrying the leftovers to the massive stainless-steel fridge.

"But—"

"Spencer." Mr. Hastings used his *stop talking* voice.

Spencer clamped her mouth shut. Ian loped back into the room, a big, stupid grin on his face. He sensed the tension and his smile wilted.

"Come on." Melissa stood and took his arm. "Let's go out for dessert."

"Sure." Ian clapped a hand on Spencer's shoulder. "Spence? Want to come?"

Spencer didn't really want to—and by the way Melissa nudged him, it seemed she didn't want her to, either, but she didn't have the chance to respond. Mrs. Hastings quickly said, "No, Ian, Spencer is *not* getting dessert." Her tone of voice was the same one she used when reprimanding the dogs.

"Thanks anyway," Spencer said, biting back tears. To steel herself, she shoved an enormous bite of mango curry into her mouth. But it slid down her throat before she could swallow, the thick sauce burning as it went down. Finally, after making a series of horrible noises, Spencer spit it up into her napkin. But when the tears cleared from her eyes, she saw that her parents hadn't approached to make sure she wasn't choking. They'd simply left the room.

Spencer wiped her eyes and stared at the nasty gob of chewed-up, spit-out mango in her napkin. It looked exactly the way she felt inside.

6

CHARITY ISN'T SO SWEET

Tuesday afternoon, Hanna adjusted the cream-colored camisole and slouchy cashmere cardigan she'd changed into after school and strolled purposefully up the steps of the William Atlantic Plastic Surgery and Burn Rehabilitation Clinic. If you were going in for burn treatment, you called it the William Atlantic. If you were having lipo, you called it Bill Beach.

The building was set back in the woods, and just the teensiest bit of blue sky peeked out from the majestic, overpowering trees. The whole world smelled like wildflowers. It was the perfect early fall afternoon to lie out at the country club pool and watch boys play tennis. It was the perfect afternoon to take a six-mile run to work off the box of Cheez-Its she'd binged on last night, freaked out by the surprise visit from her dad. It might even be the perfect afternoon to look at an anthill or baby-sit the bratty six-year-old twins next door. Anything would be better than what she *was* doing today: volunteering at a burn clinic.

Volunteering was a four-letter word to Hanna. Her last attempt at it was at the Rosewood Day School Charity Fashion Show in seventh grade. Rosewood Day girls dressed up in designer clothes and paraded across the stage; people bid on their outfits, and the money went to charity. Ali wore a stunning Calvin Klein sheath and some size-zero dowager bid it up to $1,000. Hanna, on the other hand, got stuck with a frilly, neon-colored monstrosity by Betsey Johnson, which made her look even fatter than she was. The only person to bid on her outfit was her dad. A week later, her parents announced they were getting divorced.

And now her dad was back. Sort of.

When Hanna thought of her dad's visit yesterday, she felt giddy, anxious, and angry all at the same time. Since her transformation, she'd dreamed about the moment she'd see him again. She'd be thin, popular, and poised. In her dream he always came back with Kate, who'd gotten fat and zitty, and Hanna looked even more beautiful in comparison.

"Oof," she cried. Someone had come out the door just as she was going in.

"Watch it," the person mumbled. Then Hanna looked up. She was standing at the double-glass doors, next to a stone ashtray and a large potted primrose plant. Coming out the door was . . . Mona.

Hanna's mouth fell open. The same surprised look passed over Mona's face. They considered each other. "What are you doing here?" Hanna asked.

"Visiting a friend of my mom's. Boob job." Mona tossed her pale blond hair over her freckled shoulder. "You?"

"Um, same." Hanna eyed Mona carefully. Hanna's bullshit-radar told her that Mona might be lying. But then, maybe Mona could sense the exact same thing about her.

"Well, I'm off." Mona tugged on her burgundy tote. "I'll call you later."

"Okay," Hanna croaked. They walked in opposite directions. Hanna turned back and glanced at Mona, only to see that Mona was looking over her shoulder at her.

"Now, pay attention," said Ingrid, the portly, stoic, German head nurse. They were in an examination room, and Ingrid was teaching Hanna how to change out the trash cans. As if it was hard.

Each exam room was painted a guacamole green, and the only posters on the wall were grim pictures of skin diseases. Ingrid assigned Hanna to the outpatient checkup rooms; some day, if Hanna did well, she might be allowed to clean the inpatient rooms instead—where serious burn victims stayed. Lucky her.

Ingrid pulled out the trash bag. "This goes in the blue Dumpster out back. And you must empty the infectious waste bins, too." She gestured to an identical-looking trash can. "They need to be kept separate from the regular trash at all times. And you need to wear these." She handed Hanna a pair of latex gloves. Hanna looked at them as if *they* were covered in infectious waste.

Next, Ingrid pointed her down the hall. "There are ten other rooms here," she explained. "Clean the trash and wipe down the counters in each, then see me."

Trying not to breathe—she despised the antiseptic, sick-person way hospitals smelled—Hanna trudged to the utility closet to get more trash bags. She looked down the hall, wondering where the inpatient rooms were. Jenna had been an inpatient here. A lot of things had made her think of The Jenna Thing in the past day, although she kept trying to shove it out of her mind. The idea that someone knew—and could tell—was something she couldn't even comprehend.

Although The Jenna Thing had been an accident, Hanna sometimes felt like it wasn't *exactly*. Ali had given Jenna a nickname: Snow, as in Snow White, because Jenna had an annoying resemblance to the Disney character. Hanna thought Jenna looked like Snow White, too—but in a good way. Jenna wasn't as polished as Ali, but there was something oddly pretty about her. It had once occurred to Hanna that the only character she looked like from *Snow White* was Dopey Dwarf.

Still, Jenna was one of Ali's favorite targets, so back in sixth grade Hanna scrawled a rumor about Jenna's boobs just below the paper-towel dispenser in the girls' bathroom. She spilled water on Jenna's seat in algebra so Jenna would get a fake pee stain on her pants. She poked fun at the way Jenna put on a fake French accent in French II. . . . So when the paramedics carried Jenna out of the tree house, Hanna felt sick. She'd been the one to agree to pranking Toby first. And in her head, she'd thought, *Maybe if we prank Toby, we can prank Jenna, too.* It was like she'd willed this to happen.

The automatic doors swished open at the end of the hall, breaking Hanna out of her thoughts. She froze, heart pounding, wishing for the new arrival to be Sean, but it wasn't. Frustrated, she pulled her BlackBerry out of her cardigan pocket and dialed his number. It went to voice mail, and Hanna hung up. She redialed, thinking maybe he was just fumbling for his phone and hadn't gotten it in time, but it went to voice mail again.

"Hey, Sean," Hanna chirped after the beep, trying to sound carefree. "Hanna again. I'd really like to talk, so, um, you know where to find me!"

She'd left him three messages today saying she'd be here this afternoon, but Sean hadn't responded. She wondered if he was at a V Club meeting—he'd recently signed a virginity pledge, vowing not to have sex, like, *ever.* Maybe he'd call her when he was done. Or . . . maybe he wouldn't. Hanna swallowed, trying to shove that possibility out of her mind.

She sighed and walked to the employee closet/supply

room. Ingrid had hung Hanna's pewter Ferragamo hobo bag on a hook next to a striped vinyl thing from the Gap, and she suppressed the urge to shudder. She dropped her phone into her bag, grabbed a roll of paper towels and a spray bottle, and found an empty exam room. Maybe actually doing her job would keep her mind off stressing about Sean and A.

As she finished sponging off the sink, she accidentally bumped open a metal cabinet right next to it. Inside were shelves of cardboard containers all emblazoned with familiar names. Tylenol 3. Vicodin. Percocet. Hanna peeked inside. There were thousands of drug samples. Just . . . just sitting there. Without a lock.

Jackpot.

Hanna quickly shoved a few handfuls of Percocet into the surprisingly deep pockets of her cardigan. At least she could get a fun weekend with Mona out of this.

Then someone placed a hand on Hanna's shoulder. Hanna jumped back and whirled around, knocking the Fantastik-soaked paper towels and a jar full of cotton swabs onto the floor.

"Why are you only on room two?" Ingrid frowned. She had a face like a grumpy pug.

"I . . . I was just trying to be thorough." Hanna quickly tossed the paper towels in the trash and hoped the Percocet would stay in her pockets. Her neck burned where Ingrid had touched it.

"Well, come with me," Ingrid said. "There's something in your bag that's making a noise. It's disturbing the patients."

"Are you sure it's *my* bag?" Hanna asked. "I was just at my bag, and—"

Ingrid led Hanna back into the closet. Sure enough, there was a tinkling sound coming from her purse's inside pocket. "It's just my cell phone." Hanna's spirits jumped. Maybe Sean *had* called!

"Well, please make it quiet." Ingrid sighed. "And then get back to work."

Hanna pulled out her BlackBerry to see who was calling. She had a new text.

> Hannakins: Mopping the floors at Bill Beach won't help you get your life back. Not even you could clean up this mess. And besides, I know something about you that'll guarantee you'll never be Rosewood Day's it girl— ever again. —A

Hanna looked around the coatroom, confused. She read the note again, her throat dry and sticky. What could A know that could guarantee *that*?

Jenna.

If A knew that . . .

Hanna quickly typed a response on her phone's keypad: *You don't know anything.* She hit SEND. Within seconds, A responded:

> I know it all. I could RUIN YOU.

7

O CAPTAIN, MY CAPTAIN

Tuesday afternoon, Emily hovered in Coach Lauren's office doorway. "Can I talk to you?"

"Well, I only have a couple minutes until I have to give this to the officials," Lauren said, holding up her meet roster. Today was the Rosewood Tank, the first swim meet of the season. It was supposed to be a friendly exhibition meet—all the area prep schools were invited and there was no scoring—but Emily usually shaved down and got pre-meet jitters all the same. Except not this time. "What's up, Fieldsy?" Lauren asked.

Lauren Kinkaid was in her early thirties, had perma-chlorine-damaged blondish hair, and lived in T-shirts with motivational swimming slogans like EAT OUR BUB-BLES and I PUT THE STYLE IN FREESTYLE. She had been Emily's swim coach for six years. First at Tadpole League, then at long-course, and now Rosewood Day. Not very many people knew Emily so well—not well enough to call her "Fieldsy," to know that her favorite pre-swim meet dinner was pepper steak from China Rose, or to know that when Emily's butterfly times were three-tenths of a second faster, it meant she had her period. Which made what Emily was about to say that much harder.

"I want to quit," Emily blurted out.

Lauren blinked. She looked stunned, like someone had just told her the pool was filled with electric eels. "W-Why?"

Emily stared at the checkerboard linoleum floor. "It's not fun anymore."

Lauren blew air out of her cheeks. "Well, it isn't always fun. Sometimes it's work."

"I know. But . . . I just don't want to do it anymore."

"Are you *sure*?"

Emily sighed. She thought she was sure. Last week she was sure. She'd been swimming for years, not asking herself whether she liked it or not. With Maya's help, Emily had mustered up the courage to admit to herself—and to her parents—that she wanted to quit.

Of course, that was before . . . everything. Now, she felt more like a yo-yo than ever. One minute, she wanted to quit. The next, she wanted her normal, good-girl life back, the life where she went to swimming, hung out with her sister Carolyn on the weekends, and spent hours goofing off on the bus with her teammates and reading from the birthday horoscope book. And then she wanted the freedom to pursue her own interests all over again. Except . . . what were her interests, aside from swimming?

"I feel really burnt out," Emily finally offered, attempting to explain.

Lauren propped her head up with her hand. "I was going to make you captain."

Emily gaped. "Captain?"

"Well, yeah." Lauren clicked and unclicked her pen. "I thought you deserved it. You're a real team player, you know? But if you don't want to swim, then . . ."

Not even her older siblings Jake and Beth, who had swum all four years of high school and gotten college scholarships, had been captain.

Lauren wound her whistle around her finger. "How about I go easy on you for a bit?" She took Emily's hand. "I know it's been hard. With your friend . . ."

"Yeah." Emily stared at Lauren's Michael Phelps poster, hoping she wouldn't start crying again. Every time someone mentioned Ali—which was about once every ten minutes—her nose and eyes got twitchy.

"What do you say?" Lauren coaxed.

Emily ran her tongue over the back of her teeth. Captain. Sure, she was state champion in the 100-meter butterfly, but Rosewood Day had a freakishly good swim team—Lanie Iler got fifth in the 500 freestyle at Junior Nationals, and Stanford had already promised Jenny Kestler a full ride next year. That Lauren chose Emily over Lanie or Jenny *meant* something. Maybe it was a sign that her yo-yoing life was supposed to go back to normal.

"All right," she heard herself saying.

"Awesome." Lauren patted her hand. She reached into one of her many cardboard boxes of T-shirts and handed one to Emily. "For you. A start-of-the-season present."

Emily opened it up. It said, GAY GIRLS: SLIPPERY WHEN WET. She looked at Lauren, her throat cottony dry. Lauren *knew*?

Lauren cocked her head. "It's in reference to the stroke," she said slowly. "You know, butterfly?"

Emily looked at the shirt again. It didn't say *gay* girls. It said *fly* girls. "Oh," she croaked, folding the T-shirt. "Thanks."

She left Lauren's office and walked through the natatorium lobby on shaky legs. The room was crammed full of swimmers, all here for the Tank. Then she paused, suddenly aware that someone was looking at her. Across the room, she saw Ben, her ex-boyfriend, leaning up against the trophy case. His stare was so intense, he didn't blink. Emily's skin prickled and heat rose to her cheeks. Ben smirked and turned to whisper something to his best friend, Seth Cardiff. Seth laughed, glanced again at Emily, and whispered something back to Ben. Then they both snickered.

Emily hid behind a crowd of kids from St. Anthony's.

This was another reason why she wanted to quit swimming—so she wouldn't have to spend every day after school with her ex-boyfriend, who *did* know. He'd caught Maya and Emily in a more-than-just-friends moment at Noel's party on Friday.

She pushed into the empty hallway that led to the girls' and boys' locker rooms, thinking again about A's latest note. It was weird, but when Emily read the text in Maya's hotel bathroom, it was almost like she could *hear* Ali's voice. Except that was impossible, right? Besides, Ben was the only person who knew about Maya. Maybe he'd somehow found out that Emily had tried to kiss Ali. Could . . . could Ben be A?

"Where are you going?"

Emily whirled around. Ben had followed her into the hall. "Hey." Emily tried to smile. "What's up?"

Ben was wearing his shredded Champion sweats—he thought they brought him good luck, so he wore them to every meet. He'd re-buzzed his hair over the weekend. It made his already angular face look severe. "Nothing's *up*," he answered nastily, his voice echoing off the tile walls. "I thought you were quitting."

Emily shrugged. "Yeah, well, I guess I changed my mind."

"Really? You were so into it Friday. Your girlfriend seemed so proud of you."

Emily looked away. "We were drunk."

"Right." He took a step toward her.

"Think what you want." She turned for her locker room. "And that text you sent didn't scare me."

Ben furrowed his eyebrows. "What text?"

She stopped. "The text that says you're going to tell everyone," she said, testing him.

"I didn't write you any texts." Ben tilted his chin. "But . . . I *might* tell everyone. You being a dyke is a juicy little story."

"I'm not gay," Emily said through her teeth.

"Oh yeah?" Ben took a step closer. His nostrils flared in and out. "Prove it."

Emily barked out a laugh. This was *Ben*. But then he lunged forward, wrapped his hand around Emily's wrist, and pushed her against the water fountain.

She breathed in sharply. Ben's breath was hot on her neck and smelled like grape Gatorade. "Stop it," she whispered, trying to squirm away.

Ben needed just one strong arm to hold her down. He pressed his body up against hers. "I said, *prove it.*"

"Ben, stop." Frightened tears came to her eyes. She swatted at him tentatively, but his movements just became more forceful. He ran his hand up her chest. A small squeak escaped her throat.

"There a problem?"

Ben stepped back suddenly. Behind them on the far side of the hall stood a boy in a Tate Prep warm-up jacket. Emily squinted. Was that . . . ?

"It's none of your business, man," Ben said loudly.

"What isn't any of my business?" The boy stepped closer. It was.

Toby Cavanaugh.

"Dude." Ben twisted around.

Toby's eyes moved down to Ben's hand on Emily's wrist. He nudged his chin up at Ben. "What's the deal?"

Ben glared at Emily, then let go of her. She shot away from him, and Ben used his shoulder to shove open the boys' locker room door. Then, silence.

"You all right?" Toby asked.

Emily nodded, her head down. "I think so."

"You sure?"

Emily sneaked a peek at Toby. He was really tall now, and his face was no longer rodentlike and guarded but, well, high-cheekboned and dark-eyed gorgeous. It made her think of the other part of A's note. *Although most of us have totally changed . . .*

Her knees felt wobbly. It couldn't be . . . *could it?*

"I have to go," she mumbled, and ran, her arms outstretched, into the girls' locker room.

8

EVEN TYPICAL ROSEWOOD BOYS SOUL-SEARCH

Tuesday afternoon as Aria was driving home from school, she passed the lacrosse field and recognized the lone figure sprinting around the goal area, his lacrosse stick cradled in front of his face. He kept switching directions and sliding in the wet, muddy grass. Ominous gray clouds had gathered overhead, and now it was starting to sprinkle.

Aria pulled over. "Mike." She hadn't seen her brother since he'd stormed out of the Victory yesterday. A few hours afterward, he'd called home saying he was having dinner at his friend Theo's house. Then, later, he called to say he was staying overnight.

Her brother looked up from across the field and frowned. "What?"

"Come here."

Mike trudged across the close-cropped, not-a-weed-insight grass. "Get in," Aria commanded.

"I'm practicing."

"You can't avoid this forever. We have to talk about it."

"Talk about what?"

She raised a perfectly arched eyebrow. "Um, what we saw yesterday? At the bar?"

Mike picked at one of the rawhide straps on his lacrosse stick. Raindrops bounced off the canvas top of his Brine cap. "I don't know what you're talking about."

"What?" Aria narrowed her eyes. But Mike wouldn't even look at her.

"Fine." She shifted into reverse. "Be a wuss."

Then Mike wrapped his hand around the window frame. "I . . . I don't know what I'll do," he said quietly.

Aria pressed the brake. "What?"

"If they get divorced, I don't know what I'll do," Mike repeated. The vulnerable, embarrassed expression on his face made him look as if he were about ten years old. "Blow myself up, maybe."

Tears came to her eyes. "It's not going to happen," she said shakily. "I promise."

Mike sniffed. She reached out for him, but he jerked away and ran down the field.

Aria decided to go, slowly rolling down the twisty, wet road. Rain was her favorite kind of weather. It reminded her of rainy days, back when she was nine. She'd sneak over to her neighbor's parked sailboat, climb under the tarp, and snuggle into one of the cabins, listening to the sound of the rain hitting the canvas and writing entries in her Hello Kitty diary.

She felt like she could do her best thinking on rainy days, and she definitely needed to think now. She could have dealt with A telling Ella about Meredith if it had been in the past. Her parents could talk through it, Byron could say it would never happen again, yadda yadda yadda. But now that Meredith was back, well, that changed everything. Last night, her father hadn't come home for dinner—because of the, um, papers he had to grade—and Aria and her mom had sat on the couch in front of *Jeopardy!* with bowls of soup in their laps. They were both totally silent. The thing was, she didn't know what she'd do if her parents divorced, either.

Climbing a particularly steep hill, Aria gunned the engine—the Subaru always needed an extra push on inclines. But instead of revving forward, the interior lights flickered out. The car began to roll backward down the hill. "Shit," Aria whispered, jerking up the e-brake. When she tried the ignition again, the car wouldn't even start.

She looked down the empty, two-lane country road. Thunder broke overhead, and the rain started to hurtle down from the sky. Aria searched through her bag, figuring she needed to call a tow truck or her parents to come get her, but after rooting around the bottom, she realized she'd left her Treo at home. The rain was falling so violently, the windshield and windows blurred. "Oh God," Aria whispered, feeling claustrophobic. Spots formed in front of her eyes.

Aria knew this anxious feeling: It was a panic attack. She'd had them a few times before. One was after The Jenna Thing, one was after Ali went missing, and one was when she was walking down Laugavegur Street in Reykjavík and saw a girl on a billboard that looked exactly like Meredith.

Calm down, she told herself. *It's just rain.* She took two cleansing breaths, stuck her fingers in her ears, and started singing "Frère Jacques"—for some reason, the French version did the trick. After she went through three rounds, the spots began to disappear. The rain had let up from hurricane-force to merely torrential. What she needed to do was walk back to the farmhouse she'd passed and ask to use their phone. She thrust open the car door, held her Rosewood Day blazer over her head, and started to run. A gust of wind blew up her miniskirt, and she stepped in an enormous, muddy puddle. The water seeped right through the gauzy straps of her stacked-heel sandals. "Damn it," she muttered.

She was only a hundred feet from the farmhouse when a navy-colored Audi passed. It splashed a wave of puddle water at Aria, then stopped at the dead Subaru. It slowly backed up until it was right next to her. The driver's window glided down. "You okay?"

Aria squinted, raindrops dripping off the tip of her nose. Hanging out the driver's side was Sean Ackard, a boy in her class. He was a typical Rosewood boy: crisp polo, moisturized skin, All-American features, expensive car. Only he played soccer, not lacrosse. *Not* the kind of person she wanted to see right now. "I'm fine," she yelled.

"Actually, you're soaked. Need a ride?"

Aria was so wet, she felt like her face was pruning. Sean's car looked dry and snuggly. So she slid into the passenger seat and shut the door.

Sean told her to throw her soaked blazer into the back. Then he reached over and turned up the heat. "Where to?"

Aria pushed her matted-down, fringey black bangs off her forehead. "Actually, I'll just use your cell phone and then be out of your way."

"All right." Sean dug through his backpack to find it.

Aria sat back and looked around. Sean hadn't plastered his car with band stickers like some guys did, and the interior didn't reek of boy sweat. Instead, it smelled like some combination of bread and a freshly shampooed dog. Two books sat on the passenger-side floor: *Zen and the Art of Motorcycle Maintenance* and *The Tao of Pooh*.

"You like philosophy?" Aria moved her legs so she wouldn't get them wet.

Sean ducked his head. "Well, yeah." He sounded embarrassed.

"I read those books, too," Aria said. "I also got really into French philosophers this summer, when I was in Iceland." She paused. She'd never really spoken to Sean. Before she left, Rosewood boys terrified her—which was probably partly why she hated them. "I, um, was in Iceland for a while. My dad was on sabbatical."

"I know." Sean gave her a crooked smile.

Aria stared at her hands. "Oh." There was an awkward pause. The only sound was the hurtling rain and the windshield wipers' rhythmic *whaps*.

"So you read, like, Camus and stuff?" Sean asked. When Aria nodded, he smirked. "I read *The Stranger* this summer."

"Really?" Aria jutted her chin into the air, certain he hadn't understood it. What would a typical Rosewood boy want with deep philosophy books, anyway? If this were an SAT analogy, it would be "typical Rosewood boy: reading French philosophers :: American tourists in Iceland: eating anywhere but McDonald's." It just didn't happen.

When Sean didn't answer, she dialed her home number into his cell phone. It rang and rang, not going to voice mail—they hadn't set up the answering machine yet. Next she dialed her dad's number at school—it was almost five, and he had posted his 3:30–5:30 office hours on the refrigerator. It rang and rang too.

The spots started to flash in front of Aria's eyes again as she imagined where he could be . . . or who he could be with. She leaned forward over her bare legs, trying to breathe deeper. *Frère Jacques,* she chanted silently.

"Whoa," Sean said, his voice sounding very far away.

"I'm all right," Aria called, her voice muffled in her legs. "I just have to . . ."

She heard Sean fumbling around. Then he pressed a Burger King bag into her hands. "Breathe into this. I think there were some fries in there. Sorry about that."

Aria put the bag over her mouth and slowly inflated and deflated it. She felt Sean's warm hand on the middle of her back. Slowly, the dizziness started to fade. When she raised her head, Sean was looking at her anxiously.

"Panic attacks?" he asked. "My stepmom gets them. The bag always works."

Aria crumpled the bag in her lap. "Thanks."

"Something bothering you?"

Aria shook her head quickly. "No, I'm cool."

"C'mon," Sean said. "Isn't that, like, why people get panic attacks?"

Aria pressed her lips together. "It's complicated." *Besides,* she wanted to say, *since when are typical Rosewood boys interested in weird girls' problems?*

Sean shrugged. "You were friends with Alison DiLaurentis, right?"

Aria nodded.

"It's weird, isn't it?"

"Yeah." She cleared her throat. "Although, um, it's not weird in the way you might think. I mean, it *is* weird in that way, but it's weird in other ways, too."

"Like how?"

She shifted; her wet underwear was starting to itch. Today at school it had felt like everyone was speaking to her in babyish whispers. Did they think that if they spoke in normal-person volume, Aria would have an insta-breakdown?

"I just wish everyone would leave me alone," she managed. "Like last week."

Sean flicked the pine tree air freshener that hung from the rearview mirror, making it swing. "I know what you mean. When my mom died, everyone thought that if I had a second to myself, I'd lose it."

Aria sat up straighter. "Your mom died?"

Sean looked at her. "Yeah. It was a long time ago. Fourth grade."

"Oh." Aria tried to remember Sean from fourth grade. He had been one of the shortest kids in the class, and they'd been on the same kickball team a bunch of times, but that was it. She felt bad for being so oblivious. "I'm sorry."

A silence passed. Aria crossed and uncrossed her bare legs. The car had begun to smell like her skirt's wet wool. "It was tough," Sean said. "My dad went through all these girlfriends. I didn't even like my stepmom at first. I got used to her, though."

Aria felt her eyes well up with tears. She didn't want to get used to *her* family changing. She let out a loud sniff.

Sean leaned forward. "You sure you can't talk about it?"

Aria shrugged. "It's supposed to be a secret."

"Tell you what. How about if you tell me your secret, I'll tell you mine?"

"All right," Aria quickly agreed. The truth was, she was dying to talk about this. She would've admitted it to her old friends, but they were so tight-lipped about their own A secrets, it made Aria feel even weirder about revealing hers. "But you can't say anything."

"Absolutely."

And then Aria told him about Byron and Ella, Meredith, and what she and Mike had seen at the bar yesterday. It all just came spilling out. "I don't know what to do," she finished. "I feel like I'm the one who has to keep everyone together."

Sean was quiet, and Aria was afraid he'd stopped listening. But then he raised his head. "Your dad shouldn't be putting you in that position."

"Yeah, well." Aria glanced at Sean. If you got past his tucked-in shirt and khaki shorts, he was actually pretty cute. He had really pink lips and knobby, imperfect fingers. From the way his polo shirt fit snugly against his chest, she guessed he was in tip-top soccer boy shape. She suddenly felt incredibly self-conscious. "You're easy to talk to," Aria said shyly, staring at her naked knees. She'd missed a few hairs on her knees when shaving. It usually didn't matter, but it sort of did now. "So, um, thanks."

"Sure." When Sean smiled, his eyes got crinkly and warm.

"This definitely isn't how I imagined spending my afternoon," Aria added. The rain was still pelting the windshield, but the car had gotten really warm while she'd been talking.

"Me neither." Sean looked out the window. The rain had started to subside. "But . . . I don't know. It's kind of cool, right?"

Aria shrugged. Then she remembered. "Hey, you promised me a secret! It better be good."

"Well, I don't know if it's *good*." Sean leaned toward Aria, and she scooted closer. For a crazy second, she thought they might kiss.

"So, I'm in this thing called V Club," Sean whispered. His breath smelled like Altoids. "Do you know what that is?"

"I guess." Aria tried to keep her lips from wriggling into a smirk. "It's the no-sex-till-marriage thing, right?"

"Right." Sean leaned back. "So . . . I'm a virgin. Except . . . I don't know if I want to be one anymore."

9

SOMEONE'S ALLOWANCE JUST GOT A WHOLE LOT SMALLER

On Wednesday afternoon, Mr. McAdam, Spencer's AP economics teacher, strolled up and down the aisles, peeling papers off a stack and putting them facedown on each student's desk. He was a tall man with bulging eyes, a sloped nose, and a paunchy face. A few years ago, one of his top students had remarked that he looked like Squidward from *SpongeBob SquarePants*, and the name stuck. "A lot of these quizzes were very good," he murmured.

Spencer straightened up. She did what she always did when she wasn't sure how she'd done on a test: She thought of the rock-bottom grade she could get, a grade that would still ensure she had an A for the class. Usually, the grade in her mind was so low—although low for Spencer was a B plus or, at the very worst, a B—that she ended up being pleasantly surprised. *B plus*, she told herself now, as Squidward put the test on her desk. *That's rock-bottom*. Then she turned it over.

B *minus*.

Spencer dropped the paper to her desk as if it were on fire. She scanned the quiz for answers that Squidward had graded incorrectly, but she didn't know the answers to the questions that had big red X marks next to them.

Okay, so maybe she hadn't studied enough.

When they'd taken the quizzes yesterday, all she'd been able to think about while filling in the multiple choice bubbles were a) Wren and how she could never see him, b) her parents and Melissa and how she could get them to love her again, c) Ali, and d), e), f), and g), her festering Toby secret.

The Toby torture was insane. But what could she do—go to the cops? And tell them . . . what? *Some kid said, I'll get you, to me four years ago, and I think he killed Ali and I think he's going to kill me? I got a text that said my friends and I were in danger?* The cops would laugh and say she'd been snorting too much Ritalin. She was afraid, too, to tell her friends what was going on. What if A was serious and something happened to them if she did?

"How'd you do?" a voice whispered.

Spencer jumped. Andrew Campbell sat next to her. He was as big an overachiever as she was. He and Spencer were ranked number one and number two in the class, and they were always switching positions. His quiz was proudly faceup on his desk. A big red A plus was at the top of it.

Spencer pulled her own quiz to her chest. "Fine."

"Cool." A lock of Andrew's long lion's mane of blond hair fell in his face.

Spencer gritted her teeth. Andrew was notoriously nosy. She'd always thought it was just a symptom of his über-competitiveness, and then last week, she wondered if he might be A. But while Andrew's earnest interest in the minutiae of Spencer's life was suspect, she didn't think he had it in him. Andrew had helped Spencer the day the workers discovered Ali's body, covering her up with a blanket when she was in shock. A wouldn't do something like that.

As Squidward gave them their homework assignment, Spencer looked at her notes. Her handwriting, which was normally squeezed neatly in the lines, had wavered all over the page. She began to quickly recopy the notes, but the bell interrupted her, and Spencer sheepishly rose to leave. B *minus*.

"Miss Hastings?"

She looked up. Squidward was gesturing her toward his desk. She walked over, straightening her navy Rosewood Day blazer and taking extra caution not to trip in her caramel-colored kidskin riding boots. "You're Melissa Hastings's sister, yes?"

Spencer felt her insides wilt. "Uh-huh." It was obvious what was coming next.

"This is quite a treat for me, then." He tapped his mechanical pencil on his desk. "It was such a pleasure to have Melissa in class."

I'm sure, Spencer growled to herself.

"Where is Melissa now?"

Spencer gritted her teeth. *At home, hogging up all our parents' love and attention.* "She's at Wharton. Getting her MBA."

Squidward smiled. "I always knew she'd go to Wharton." Then he gave Spencer a long look. "The first set of essay questions is due next Monday," he said. "And I'll give you a hint: the supplemental books I've mentioned on the syllabus will help."

"Oh." Spencer felt self-conscious. Was he giving her a tip because she'd gotten a B minus and he felt sorry for her, or because she was Melissa's sister? She squared her shoulders. "I was planning to get them anyway."

Squidward looked at her evenly. "Well, good."

Spencer trudged into the hall, feeling unhinged. Normally, she could kiss ass with the best of them, but Squidward made her feel like she was at the bottom of the class.

It was the end of the day. Rosewood students were bustling around their lockers, dragging books into their bags, making plans on their cell phones, or getting their gear for sports practice. Spencer had field hockey at three, but she wanted to hit Wordsmith's for Squidward's books first. Then, after that, she had to check in with the yearbook staff, see what was up with the Habitat for

Humanity volunteer list, and say hi to the drama club advisor. She might be a couple minutes late to hockey, but what could she do?

As she pushed through the door of Wordsmith's Books, she instantly felt calmer. The store was always quiet, with no obsequious salespeople shooing you out. After Ali disappeared, Spencer used to come in here and read *Calvin and Hobbes* comic books just to be alone. The staff didn't get pissy when cell phones rang, either, which was exactly what Spencer's was doing right now. Her heart pounded . . . and then pounded in a different way when she saw who it was.

"Wren," she whispered into her phone, sinking against the travel shelf.

"Did you get my e-mail?" he asked in his sexy British accent when she answered.

"Um . . . yeah," Spencer responded. "But . . . I don't think you should be calling me."

"So you want me to hang up?"

Spencer looked around cagily, eyeing two freshman dorks giggling by the self-help sex books and an old woman who was leafing through a Philadelphia Streetwise map. "No," she whispered.

"Well, I'm dying to see you, Spence. Can we meet somewhere?"

Spencer paused. It ached how much she wanted to say yes. "I'm not sure if that's a good idea right now."

"What do you mean, you're not sure?" Wren laughed. "C'mon, Spence. It was hard enough to wait this long before calling."

Spencer shook her head. "I . . . I can't," she decided. "I'm sorry. My family . . . they hardly even look at me. I mean, maybe we could try this in . . . in a couple months?"

Wren was quiet for a moment. "You're serious."

Spencer sniffed uncertainly in response.

"I just thought . . . I don't know." Wren's voice sounded tight. "Are you sure?"

She pushed her hand through her hair and looked out Wordsmith's big front windows. Mason Byers and Penelope Waites, two kids from her class, were kissing outside Ferra's, the cheesesteak place across the street. She hated them. "I'm sure," she said to Wren, the words choked in her throat. "I'm sorry." She hung up.

She heaved a sigh. Suddenly, the bookstore felt too quiet. The classical CD had stopped. The hair on the back of her neck rose. A could have heard her conversation.

Shaking, she walked to the economics section, suspiciously eyeing a guy as he paused at the World War II shelf and a woman as she thumbed through a bulldog-of-the-month calendar. Could one of them be A? How did A know *everything*?

She quickly found the books on Squidward's list, walked to the counter, and handed over her credit card, nervously fidgeting with the silver buttons on her navy blue school blazer. She so didn't want to go to her activities and hockey after this. She just wanted to go home and hide.

"Hmm." The checkout girl, who had three eyebrow rings, held up Spencer's Visa. "Something's wrong with this card."

"That's impossible," Spencer snapped. Then she fished out her MasterCard.

The salesgirl ran it through, but the card machine made the same disapproving beep. "This one's doing the same thing."

The salesgirl made a quick phone call, nodded a few times, then hung up. "These cards have been canceled," she said quietly, her heavily lined eyes wide. "I'm supposed to cut them up, but . . ." She shrugged meekly and handed them back to Spencer.

Spencer snatched the cards from her. "Your machine must be broken. Those cards, they're . . . " She was about to say, *They're linked to my parents' bank account.*

Then it hit her. Her parents had canceled them.

"Do you want to pay with cash?" the salesgirl asked.

Her parents had *canceled* her credit cards. What was next, putting a lock on the refrigerator? Cutting off the A/C to her bedroom? Limiting her use of oxygen?

Spencer pushed her way out of the store. She'd used her Visa to buy a slice of soy-cheese pizza on her way home from Ali's memorial. It had worked then.

Yesterday morning, she had apologized to her family, and now her cards were no good. It was a slap in the face.

Rage filled her body. So that was how they felt about her.

Spencer stared sadly at her two credit cards. They'd gotten so much use, the signature strip was almost worn off. Setting her jaw, she slapped her wallet shut and whipped out her Sidekick, scrolling through her received calls list for Wren's number. He answered on the first ring.

"What's your address?" she asked. "I changed my mind."

10

ABSTINENCE MAKES THE
HEART GROW FONDER

That same Wednesday afternoon, Hanna stood at the entrance of the Rosewood YMCA, a restored, Colonial-style mansion. The façade was redbrick, it had two-story-high white pillars, and the moldings around the eaves and the windows looked like they belonged on a ginger-bread house. The Briggses, a legendary eccentric, wealthy family, built the place in 1886, populating it with ten Briggs family members, three live-in guests, two parrots, and twelve standard poodles. Most of the building's historical details had been torn down to make way for the Y's six-lane swimming pool, fitness center, and "meeting" rooms. Hanna wondered what the Briggses would think about some of the groups that now met in their mansion. Like the Virginity Club.

Hanna threw her shoulders back and walked down the slanted wood hall to room 204, where V Club was meeting. Sean still wasn't returning her calls. All she wanted to say was that she was sorry, *God*. How were they supposed to get back together if she couldn't apologize to him? The one place she knew Sean went—and Sean thought she'd *never* be—was Virginity Club.

So maybe it was a violation of Sean's personal space, but it was for a worthy cause. She missed Sean, especially with everything that was happening with A.

"Hanna?"

Hanna whirled around. Naomi Zeigler was on an elliptical trainer in the exercise room. She was dressed in dark red Adidas terry-cloth short-shorts, a tight-fitting pink sports bra, and matching pink socks. A coordinated red hair tie held her perfect blond ponytail in place.

Hanna fake-smiled, but inside she was wincing. Naomi and her best friend, Riley Wolfe, hated Hanna and Mona. Last spring, Naomi stole Mona's crush, Jason Ryder, and then dumped him two weeks later. At last year's prom, Riley learned that Hanna was wearing a sea-foam-green Calvin Klein dress . . . and bought the exact same dress, except in lipstick red.

"What are you doing here?" Naomi yelled, still cycling. Hanna noticed that the elliptical's LED screen said Naomi had burned 876 calories. Bitch.

"I'm just meeting someone," Hanna mumbled. She pressed her hand against room 204's door, trying to seem casual, only she didn't realize the door was ajar. It tipped open, and Hanna lost her balance and toppled halfway over. Everyone inside turned to look at her.

"Yoo-hoo?" A woman in a hideous plaid knockoff Burberry jacket called. She stuck her head out the door and noticed Hanna. "Are you here for the meeting?"

"Uh," Hanna sputtered. When she glanced back at the elliptical, Naomi was gone.

"Don't be afraid." Hanna didn't know what else to do, so she followed the woman inside and took a seat.

The room was wood-paneled, dark, and airless. Kids sat on high-backed wooden chairs. Most of them looked normal, if a bit on the goody-goody side. The boys were either too pudgy or too scrawny. She didn't recognize anyone from Rosewood Day except for Sean. He was sitting across the room next to two wholesome-looking blond girls, staring at Hanna in alarm. She gave him a tiny wave, but he didn't react.

"I'm Candace," the woman who'd come to the door said. "And you are . . ."

"Hanna. Hanna Marin."

"Well! Welcome, Hanna," Candace said. She was in her mid-forties, had short blondish hair, and had drowned herself in Chloé Narcisse perfume—ironic, since Hanna had spritzed herself with Narcisse last Friday night, when she was supposed to do it with Sean. "What brings you here?"

Hanna paused. "I guess I've come to . . . to hear more about it."

"Well, the first thing I want you to know is, this is a safe space." Candace curled her hands around the back of a blond girl's chair. "Whatever you tell us is in the strictest confidence, so feel free to say anything. But you have to promise not to repeat anything anyone else says, too."

"Oh, I promise," Hanna said quickly. There was no way she'd repeat what anyone said. That would mean telling someone she'd come here in the first place.

"Is there anything you'd like to know?" Candace asked.

"Well, um, I'm not sure," Hanna stuttered.

"Is there anything you'd like to say?"

Hanna sneaked a peek at Sean. He gave her a look that seemed to say, *Yes, what* would *you like to say?*

She straightened up. "I've been thinking a lot about sex. Um, I mean, I was really curious about it. But now . . . I don't know." She took a deep breath and tried to imagine what Sean would want to hear. "I think it should be with the right person."

"The right person you *love*," Candace corrected. "And marry."

"Yes," Hanna added quickly.

"It's hard, though." Candace strolled around the room. "Does anyone have any thoughts for Hanna? Any experiences they want to share?"

A blond boy in camo cargo pants who was almost cute—if you squinted—raised his hand, then changed his mind and put it down. A brown-haired girl who wore a pink Dubble Bubble T-shirt raised two tentative fingers in the air and said, "I thought a lot about sex, too. My boyfriend threatened to break up with me if I wouldn't do it. For a while, I was considering giving in, but I'm glad I didn't."

Hanna nodded, trying to look thoughtful. Who were these people kidding? She wondered if they were secretly dying to get some.

"Sean, how about you?" Candace asked. "You were saying last week that you and your girlfriend had differing opinions about sex. How's that going?"

Hanna felt heat rise to her cheeks. She. Could. *Not.* Believe. It.

"Fine," Sean mumbled.

"Are you sure? Did you have a talk with her, like we discussed?"

"Yes," Sean said curtly.

A long silence followed. Hanna wondered if they knew that "her" was . . . her.

Candace went around the room asking the others to speak about their temptations: Had anyone gotten horizontal with a boyfriend or girlfriend? Had anyone made out? Had anyone watched Skinamax? *Yes, yes, yes!* Hanna ticked off in her head—even though she knew they were all V Club no-no's.

A few other kids asked sex questions—most were trying to figure out what counted as "a sexual experience," and what they should avoid. "All of it," Candace deadpanned. Hanna was flabbergasted—she'd figured V Club banned intercourse, but not the whole sexual menu. Finally, the meeting adjourned, and the V Club kids got out of their chairs to stretch. Cans of soda, paper cups, a plate of Oreos, and a bag of Terra Yukon Golds were on a table off to the side. Hanna stood up, slid the straps of her purple wedges back around her ankles, and stretched her arms in the air. She couldn't help but notice that Sean was staring at her exposed abs. She gave him a flirty smile, then walked over.

"Hey," she said.

"Hanna . . ." He ran his hand through his close-cropped hair, looking uncomfortable. When he cut it last spring, Hanna said it made him look a little like Justin Timberlake, only less skanky. In response, Sean had done an awful but also cute rendition of "Cry Me a River." That was back when he was fun. "What are you doing?" he asked.

She fluttered her hand to her throat. "What do you mean?"

"I just . . . I don't know if you should be here."

"Why?" she fumed. "I have every right to be here, just like everyone. I just wanted to apologize, all right? I've been trying to chase you down in school, but you keep running away from me."

"Well, it's complicated, Hanna," Sean said.

Hanna was about to ask what was so complicated when Candace put her hands on both their shoulders. "I see you two know each other!"

"That's right," Hanna chirped, momentarily burying her irritation.

"We're so happy to have you, Hanna." Candace beamed. "You'd be a very positive role model for us."

"Thanks." Hanna felt a little thrill. Even if it was V Club, she wasn't often embraced like this. Not by her third-grade tennis coach, not by her friends, not by her teachers, certainly not by her parents. Perhaps V Club was her calling. She pictured herself as the spokeswoman of V Club. Maybe it was like being Miss America, except instead of a crown, she'd get a fabulous V Club ring. Or maybe a V Club bag. A cherry-monogrammed Louis Vuitton clutch with a hand-painted *V*.

"So, do you think you'll join us next week?" Candace asked.

Hanna looked at Sean. "Probably."

"Wonderful!" Candace cried.

She left Hanna and Sean alone again. Hanna sucked in her stomach, wishing she hadn't hogged down a Good Humor chocolate éclair bar she'd impetuously bought from the Y's ice cream truck before the meeting. "So, you talked about me here, huh?"

Sean shut his eyes. "I'm sorry she mentioned that."

"No, it's all right," Hanna interrupted. "I didn't realize how much all this . . . meant to you. And I really like some of the stuff they were saying. About, um, the person being someone you love. I'm all for that. And everyone seems really sweet." She felt surprised the words were coming out of her mouth. She actually kind of meant them.

Sean shrugged. "Yeah, it's okay."

Hanna frowned, surprised by his apathy. Then she sighed and raised her eyes. "Sean, I'm really sorry about what happened. About . . . about the car. I just . . . I don't really know how to apologize. I just feel so stupid. But I can't deal with you hating me."

Sean was quiet. "I don't hate you. Things came out kind of harsh on Friday. I think we were both in weird places. I mean, I don't think you should've done what you did, but . . ." He shrugged. "You're volunteering at the clinic, right?"

"Uh-huh." She hoped her nose didn't wrinkle up in disgust.

He nodded a few times. "I think that's really good. I'm sure you'll brighten the patients' day."

Hanna felt her cheeks flush with gratitude, but his sweetness didn't surprise her. Sean was a textbook good, compassionate guy—he gave money to homeless people in Philly, recycled his old cell phones, and never badmouthed anyone, even celebrities who existed to be made fun of. It had been one of the reasons she'd first come to love Sean back in sixth grade when she still was a chubby loser.

But just last week, Sean *had* been hers. She'd come a long way from being a loserish girl who did Ali's gossipy dirty work, and she couldn't let a little drunken error in judgment at a field party ruin their relationship. Although . . . there was something—or *someone*—else that might ruin their relationship.

I can RUIN you.

"Sean?" Hanna's heart pounded. "Have you gotten any weird texts about me?"

"Texts?" Sean repeated. He cocked his head. "No . . ."

Hanna bit her fingernail. "If you do," she said, "don't believe them."

"All right." Sean smiled at her. Hanna felt electric.

"So," she said after a pause. "Are you still going to Foxy?"

Sean looked away. "I guess. Probably with a bunch of guys or whatever."

"Save me a dance," she purred, and squeezed his hand. She loved the way his hands felt–solid, warm, and masculine. It made her so happy to touch him that maybe she *could* give up sex until marriage. She and Sean would stay constantly vertical, cover their eyes at sex scenes, and avoid Victoria's Secret in the mall. If that was what it took to be with the only boy she'd ever kind of, well, *loved*, then maybe Hanna could make that sacrifice.

Or maybe, if the way Sean was eyeing her midriff again was any indication, she could talk him out of it.

11

DIDN'T EMILY'S MOTHER EVER TEACH HER NOT TO GET IN STRANGERS' CARS?

Emily twisted the dial on the Fresh Fields' gumball machine. It was Wednesday after swim practice, and she was picking up stuff for dinner for her mom. She hit the gumball machine every time she came into Fresh Fields, and had made a game out of it: if she got a yellow gumball, something good would happen to her. She looked at the gumball in her palm. It was green.

"Hey." Someone stood over her.

Emily looked up. "Aria. Hey."

As usual, Aria clearly wasn't afraid to stand out with her outfit. She wore a neon blue puffy vest that accentuated her arresting, ice-blue eyes. And although she wore the school's standard-issue uniform skirt, she'd hiked it up well above her knees and paired it with black leggings and funky royal blue ballet flats. Her black hair was up in a high, cheerleader-style ponytail. It completely worked, and most of the guys in the Fresh Fields parking lot under seventy-five were staring at her.

Aria leaned closer. "You holding up okay?"

"Yeah. You?"

Aria shrugged. She gave a surreptitious glance around the parking lot, which was full of eager cart boys pushing stray carts into the corral. "You haven't gotten any—"

"Nope." Emily avoided Aria's eyes. She'd deleted Monday's text from A—the one about her new love—so it was *almost* as if it hadn't happened. "You?"

"Nada." Aria shrugged. "Maybe we're in the clear."

We're not, Emily wanted to say. She chewed on the inside of her cheek.

"Well, you can call me anytime." Aria took a step toward the soda cases.

Emily left the store, a cold sweat covering her body. Why was she the only one who'd heard from A, anyway? Was A singling her out?

She put the grocery bag into her backpack, unlocked her bike, and pedaled out of the parking lot. As she turned onto a side street that was nothing but miles of white-picket farm fencing, she felt the teensiest hint of fall in the air. Fall in Rosewood always reminded Emily that it was the start of swimming season. That was usually a good thing, but this year, Emily felt uneasy. Coach Lauren had made the captain announcement yesterday after the Rosewood Tank ended. All the girls had mobbed Emily to congratulate her, and when she'd told her parents, her mom had gotten teary-eyed. Emily knew she should feel happy—things were back to normal. Except she felt like *she'd* already irrevocably changed.

"Emily!" someone called behind her.

She twisted around to see who was calling her, and her bike's front wheel skidded on a wet patch of leaves. All of a sudden, she found herself on the ground.

"Oh my God, are you okay?" a voice called.

Emily opened her eyes. Standing over her was Toby Cavanaugh. He had the hood of his parka up, so his face looked shadowed and hollow.

She yelped. Yesterday's incident in the locker room hallway kept coming back to her. Toby's face, his frustrated expression. How he'd just *looked* at Ben, and Ben had backed off. And was it a coincidence that he'd been coming through the hall at that moment, or had he been following her? She thought of A's note. *Although most of us have totally changed* . . . Well, Toby certainly had.

Toby crouched down. "Let me help you."

Emily pushed the bike off herself, cautiously moved her legs, then pulled up her pant leg to inspect the long, harsh scrape on her shin. "I'm fine."

"You dropped this back there." Toby handed Emily her lucky change purse. It was made of pink patent leather and had a monogrammed *E* on the front; Ali had given it to Emily a month before she went missing.

"Um, thanks." Emily took it from him, feeling uneasy.

Toby frowned at the scrape. "That looks kind of bad.

You want to get into my car? I think I have some Band-Aids. . . ."

Emily's heart pounded. First she'd gotten that note from A, then Toby had rescued her in the locker room, now this. Why was he at Tate, anyway? Wasn't he supposed to be in Maine? And she'd always wondered if Toby knew about The Jenna Thing and why he'd confessed. "Really. I'm okay," she said, her voice rising.

"Can I at least drive you somewhere?"

"No!" Emily yelped. Then she noticed how much blood was gushing out of her leg. She despised seeing blood. Her arms started to feel limp.

"Emily?" Toby asked her. "Are you . . . ?"

Emily's vision warped. She couldn't faint right now. She had to get away from Toby. *Although most of us have totally changed* . . . And then everything went black.

When she woke up, she was lying in the backseat of a small car. A bunch of mini Band-Aids crisscrossed the scrape on her leg. She looked around woozily, trying to get her bearings, when she noticed who was driving.

Toby twisted around. "Boo."

Emily screamed.

"Whoa!" Toby paused at a stoplight and held his hands in the air, a gesture that said, *Don't shoot!* "Sorry. I was just playing."

Emily sat up. The backseat was filled with stuff: empty Gatorade bottles, spiral-bound notebooks, textbooks,

beat-up sneakers, and a pair of gray sweats. Toby's seat
cushion had worn off in places, revealing a core of ratty
blue foam. A Grateful Dead dancing bear air freshener
hung from the rearview mirror. The car didn't smell
fresh, though. It smelled sharp and acrid. "What are you
doing?" Emily screeched. "Where are we going?"

"You passed out," Toby said calmly. "From the
blood, maybe. I didn't know what to do, so I lifted you
up and put you in my car. I stuck your bike in my trunk."

Emily glanced at her feet; there was her backpack.
Toby picked her up? Like, in his arms? She felt so
freaked, she felt like she was going to faint again. Looking
around, she didn't recognize the woodsy road they were
on. They could be *anywhere*.

"Let me out," Emily cried. "I can bike from here."

"But there isn't a shoulder. . . ."

"Seriously. Pull over."

Toby pulled over to the grassy hump and faced her.
The corners of his mouth drooped down and his eyes widened in concern. "I didn't mean . . ." He ran his hand over
his chin. "What was I supposed to do? Leave you there?"

"Yes," Emily said.

"Well, um, I'm sorry then." Toby got out of the car,
walked to her side, and opened her door. A lock of dark
hair fell over his eyes. "At school, I volunteered for the
EMS unit. I kind of want to rescue everything now. Even,
like, roadkill."

Emily looked down the country road and noticed the

giant Applegate Horse Farm waterwheel. They weren't in the middle of nowhere. They were a mile from her house.

"C'mon," Toby said. "I'll help you out."

Maybe she was overreacting. There were a lot of people who'd really changed—take any of Emily's old friends, for instance. It didn't mean Toby was definitely A. She unclenched her grip on the seat cushion. "Um, you can drive me. If you want."

He stared at her for a minute. One side of his mouth curled up into an almost-smile. The expression on his face said, *Um, okay, crazy girl*, but he didn't say it.

He got back in the driver's seat, and Emily quietly inspected him. Toby really *had* transformed. His formerly creepy-looking dark eyes now just looked deep and brooding. And he actually spoke. Coherently. The summer after sixth grade, Emily and Toby went to the same swim camp, and Toby would stare at Emily unashamedly, then pull his cap over his eyes and hum. Even then, Emily wished she could ask him the billion-dollar question: Why had he taken the blame for blinding his stepsister, when he hadn't?

The night it happened, Ali came inside the house and told them that everything was fine, that no one had seen her. Everyone was too scared to sleep at first, but Ali scratched everyone's backs, calming them down. The next day, when Toby confessed, Aria asked Ali if she'd known he was going to do that all along—how else could she have been so chill? "I just had this vibe we'd be okay," Ali explained.

Over time, Toby's confession had just become one of those life mysteries they'd never understand—like why Brad and Jen *really* got divorced, what was on the Rosewood Day girls' bathroom floor the day the janitorial worker screamed, why Imogen Smith missed so much school in sixth grade (because it definitely wasn't mono), or like . . . who killed Ali. Maybe Toby felt guilty about something else, or wanted to get out of Rosewood? Or maybe he did have a firework in the tree house and shot it by mistake.

Toby steered into Emily's street. A rambling, bluesy song played on his stereo, and he drummed the steering wheel with his palms. She thought of how he'd saved her from Ben yesterday. She wanted to thank him, but what if he asked more about it? What would Emily say? *Oh, he was pissed because I was French-kissing a girl.*

Emily finally thought of a safe question. "So, you're at Tate now?"

"Yep," he answered. "My parents said if I got in, I could go. And I did. It's nice being close to home. I get to see my sister—she's at school in Philadelphia."

Jenna. Emily's whole body, including her toes, tensed. She tried not to show any reaction, and Toby stared straight ahead, seemingly unaware that she was nervous. "And, um, where were you before? Maine?" Emily asked, making it sound like she didn't know he'd been at the

Manning Academy for Boys, which, according to her Google research, was on Fryeburg Road in Portland.

"Yup." Toby slowed down to let two little kids on Rollerblades cross the street. "Maine was pretty cool. The best thing about it was EMS."

"Did you . . . did you see anyone die?"

Toby met her eyes in the rearview mirror again. Emily had never noticed they were actually dark blue. "Nope. But this old lady willed me her dog."

"Her *dog*?" Emily couldn't help but laugh.

"Yep. I was with her in the ambulance and visited her in the ICU. We talked about her dog, and I said I loved dogs. When she died, her lawyer found me."

"So . . . did you keep the dog?"

"She's at my house now. She's really sweet, but about as old as the lady was."

Emily giggled, and something inside her began to thaw. Toby seemed sort of . . . normal. And *nice*. Before she could say anything else, they were at her house.

Toby parked the car and pulled Emily's bike out of the trunk. As she took the handlebars from him, their fingers touched. A little spark went through her. Toby looked at Emily for a moment, and she looked down at the sidewalk. Eons ago, she'd pressed her hand into the freshly poured concrete. Now, the handprint looked way too small ever to have been hers.

Toby climbed into the driver's seat. "So I'll see you tomorrow?"

Emily's head shot up. "W-Why?"

Toby turned the ignition. "It's the Rosewood-Tate meet. Remember?"

"Oh," Emily answered. "Of course."

As Toby pulled away, she felt her heart slow down. For some crazy reason, she'd thought Toby wanted to ask her out on a date. *But c'mon,* she told herself as she walked up the front steps to her house. This was Toby. The two of them together was about as likely as . . . as, well, Ali still being alive. And for the first time since she'd disappeared, Emily had finally given up hoping for that.

12

NEXT TIME, STASH EMERGENCY COVER-UP IN YOUR PURSE

"¿Cuándo es?" a voice said in her ear. *"What time is it? Time for Spencer to die!"*

Spencer shot up. The dark, familiar figure that had been looming over her face had vanished. Instead, she was in a clean, white bedroom. There were Rembrandt etchings and a poster of the human musculature system on the bedroom wall. On TV, Elmo was teaching kids how to tell time in Spanish. The cable box said 6:04, and she assumed it was A.M.: out the window, she saw that the sun was just coming up, and she could smell fresh bagels and scrambled eggs wafting up from the street.

She looked next to her, and it all made sense. Wren slept on his back, one arm thrown over his face, his chest bare. Wren's father was Korean and his mother was British, so his skin was this perfect, golden shade. There was a scar above his lip; he had freckles across his nose, and shaggy blue-black hair, and smelled like Adidas deodorant and Tide. The thick silver ring he wore on his right pointer finger glinted in the morning sun. He pulled his arm off his face and opened his gorgeous almond-shaped eyes.

"Hey." He slowly grabbed Spencer around her waist and pulled her toward him.

"Hey," she whispered, hanging back. She could still hear the voice from her dream: *It's time for Spencer to die!* It was Toby's voice.

Wren frowned. "What's wrong?"

"Nothing," Spencer said quietly. She pressed her fingers to the base of her neck and felt her pulse race. "Just . . . bad dream."

"You want to share?"

Spencer hesitated. She wished she could. Then she shook her head.

"Well, then. C'mere."

They spent a few minutes kissing, and Spencer got a relieved, grateful rush. Everything was going to be all right. She was safe.

This was the first time Spencer had slept—*and* stayed over—in a guy's bed. Last night, she'd sped into Philly, parked on the street, and hadn't even bothered with the Club; her parents were probably planning on repossessing her car, anyway. She and Wren had fallen into bed immediately and hadn't gotten up since except to answer the door for the Chinese takeout delivery boy. Later on, she called and left a message on her parents' machine that she was staying the night at her hockey friend Kirsten's house. She felt silly, trying to be all responsible when she was really being so *irresponsible*, but whatever.

For the first time since her first A note, she'd slept like a baby. It was partly because she was in Philadelphia and not Rosewood, *next door* to Toby, but it was also because of Wren. Before they went to sleep, they'd talked about Ali—their friendship, what it had been like when Ali went missing, that someone had killed her—for an hour. He'd also let her choose the "crickets chirping" sound on the sound machine, even though it was his second-least favorite noise, after "babbling brook."

Spencer began kissing him more forcefully now, and slid out of his oversize Penn T-shirt, which she was wearing as a nightgown. Wren traced her naked collarbone, then pushed himself up onto his hands and knees. "Do you want to . . . ?" he asked.

"I think so," Spencer whispered.

"Are you *sure*?"

"Uh-huh." She wriggled out of her underwear. Wren pulled his shirt over his head. Spencer's heart pounded. She was a virgin, and was as discriminating about sex as she was about everything else in her life—she had to do it with the perfect person.

But Wren *was* the right person. She knew she was passing the Point of No Return—if her parents found out, they'd never pay for anything ever, ever again. Or pay attention to her. Or send her to college. Or feed her, possibly. So what? Wren made her feel safe.

One *Sesame Street*, one *Dragon Tales*, and a half an *Arthur* later, Spencer rolled onto her back, staring blissfully at the ceiling. So much for going slow. Then she propped herself up on her elbows and looked at the clock. "Shit," she whispered. It was seven-twenty. School started at eight; she was going to miss first period at the very least.

"I have to go." She leaped out of bed and surveyed her plaid skirt, blazer, undies, cami, and boots, all in a haphazard pile on the floor. "*And* I'm going to have to go home."

Wren sat on the bed, watching her. "Why?"

"I can't wear the same outfit two days in a row."

Wren was obviously trying not to laugh at her. "But it's a uniform, right?"

"Yes, but I wore this *camisole* yesterday. And these boots."

Wren chuckled. "You're so lovably anal."

Spencer ducked her head at the word *love*.

She quickly showered, rinsing her head and body. Her heart was still pounding. She felt overcome with nerves, anxious that she was late for school, troubled by the Toby nightmare, but totally blissed about Wren. When she came out of the shower, Wren was sitting on the bed. The apartment smelled like hazelnut coffee. Spencer reached for Wren's hand and slowly slid his silver ring off his

finger and put it on her thumb. "It looks good on me."
When she looked at him, Wren wore a small, unreadable
smile. "What?" Spencer asked.

"You're just . . ." Wren shook his head and shrugged.
"It's hard for me to remember you're still in high school.
You're just so . . . together."

Spencer blushed. "I'm really not."

"No, you are. It's like . . . you actually seem more
together than—"

Wren stopped, but Spencer knew he'd been going to
say, *More together than Melissa.* She felt herself swell with
satisfaction. Melissa might have won the fight for their
parents, but Spencer had won the battle for Wren. And
that was the one that mattered.

Spencer strode up her house's long, brick-paved driveway. It was now 9:10 A.M., and second period at
Rosewood Day had already started. Her father would be
long gone to work by now, and with any luck, her mom
would be at the stables.

She opened the front door. The only sound was the
hum of the refrigerator. She tiptoed up to her room,
reminding herself that she'd have to forge a tardy slip
from her mother—and then realizing that she'd never
had to forge a tardy slip before. Every year, Spencer
earned Rosewood Day's perfect-attendance and punc-
tuality awards.

"Hey."

Spencer screamed and whirled around, her schoolbag slipping from her hands.

"Jesus." Melissa stood in the doorway. "Calm down."

"W-Why aren't you in class?" Spencer asked, her nerves vibrating.

Melissa wore dark pink velour sweatpants and a faded Penn T-shirt, but her blunt-cut, chin-length blond hair was held back by a navy blue headband. Even when Melissa relaxed, she still managed to look uptight. "Why aren't *you* in class?"

Spencer ran her hand along the back of her neck, finding it sweaty. "I . . . I forgot something. I had to come back."

"Ah." Melissa gave her a mysterious smile. Chills ran up Spencer's spine. She felt like she was on the edge of a cliff, about to topple over. "Well, I'm actually glad you're here. I've thought about what you said on Monday. I'm sorry about everything too."

"Oh," was all Spencer could think to say.

Melissa lowered her voice. "I mean, we really should be nicer to each other. Both of us. Who knows what might happen in this crazy world? Look at what happened to Alison DiLaurentis. It makes what we're fighting about seem sort of petty."

"Yeah," Spencer murmured. It was sort of an odd comparison to make.

"Anyway, I talked to Mom and Dad about it, too. I think they're coming around."

"Oh." Spencer ran her tongue over her teeth. "Wow. Thanks. That means a lot."

Melissa beamed at her in response. There was a long pause, and then Melissa took another step into Spencer's bedroom, leaning up against a cherry highboy dresser. "Sooooo . . . what's going on with you? You going to Foxy? Ian asked me, but I don't think I'm going to go. I'm probably too old."

Spencer paused, completely thrown off guard. Was Melissa up to something? These weren't the types of things they usually talked about. "I . . . uh . . . I don't know."

"Damn." Melissa smirked. "I hope you're going with the guy who gave you *that*." She pointed at Spencer's neck.

Spencer ran to her mirror and saw a huge, purple hickey near her collarbone. Her hands fluttered frantically to her neck. Then she noticed she was still wearing Wren's thick silver ring.

Melissa used to *live* with Wren—had she recognized it? Spencer yanked the ring off her finger and shoved it into her underwear drawer. Her pulse raged at her temples.

The phone rang, and Melissa picked it up in the hall. Within seconds, her head was back inside Spencer's room. "It's for you," she whispered. "A boy!"

"A . . . *boy*?" Was Wren stupid enough to call? Who else would it be, at nine-fifteen on a Thursday morning? Spencer's mind scattered in twenty directions. She took the phone. "Hello?"

"Spencer? It's Andrew. Campbell." He let out a nervous laugh. "From school."

Spencer glanced at Melissa. "Um, hey," she croaked. For a split second, she couldn't even recall who Andrew Campbell *was*. "What's up?"

"Just wanted to see if you have that flu going around. I didn't see you at the student council meeting this morning. You're never, um, not in student council."

"Oh." Spencer swallowed hard. She glanced at Melissa, who stood expectantly in the doorway. "Well, yeah, but I . . . I'm better now."

"I just wanted to say that I offered to pick up your homework for your classes," Andrew said. "Since we're in all the same ones." His voice echoed; it sounded like he was calling from the gym locker room. Andrew would be just the type to duck out of gym. "For calc, we have a bunch of end-of-chapter problem sets."

"Oh. Well, thanks."

"And do you maybe want to go over some notes for the essays? McAdam says it's a huge percentage of our grade."

"Um, sure," Spencer answered. Melissa caught Spencer's eye and gave her a hopeful, excited look. *Hickey?* she mouthed, pointing at Spencer's neck and then at the phone.

Spencer's brain felt like it was plodding through yogurt. Then, suddenly, she had an idea. She cleared her throat. "Actually, Andrew . . . do you have a date for Foxy?"

"Foxy?" Andrew repeated. "Um, I don't know. I guess I didn't have any pla—"

"Do you want to come with me?" Spencer interrupted.

Andrew laughed; it sounded like a hiccup. "Seriously?"

"Um, yeah," Spencer said, her eyes on her sister.

"Well, yeah!" Andrew said. "That'd be great! What time? What should I wear? Are you going out with any friends beforehand? Are there any after-parties?"

Spencer rolled her eyes. Leave it to Andrew to ask questions, like he was going to be quizzed on it. "We'll figure it out," Spencer said, turning to the window.

Then she hung up, feeling winded, as if she'd sprinted miles and miles for field hockey. When she turned back to her door, Melissa was gone.

13

A CERTAIN ENGLISH TEACHER IS
SUCH AN UNRELIABLE NARRATOR

On Thursday, Aria hesitated in the AP English classroom
doorway when Spencer walked by. "Hey." Aria grabbed
her arm. "Have you gotten any . . . ?"

Spencer's eyes darted back and forth, sort of like those
of the big lizards Aria had seen on display at the Paris
Zoo. "Um, no," she said. "But I'm really late, so . . . " She
ran down the hall. Aria bit down hard on her lip. *Okay.*

Someone put a hand on her shoulder. She let out a
little shriek and dropped her water bottle. It clunked to
the floor and started rolling.

"Whoa. Just trying to get by."

Ezra stood behind her. He'd been absent from school
on Tuesday and Wednesday, and Aria had wondered if he'd
resigned. "Sorry," she mumbled, her cheeks bright red.

Ezra had on the same rumpled corduroys he'd worn
last week, a tweedy jacket with a tiny hole in the elbow,
and Merrill lace-ups. Up close, he smelled faintly like the

Seda France ylang-ylang and saffron-scented "man candle" Aria remembered from his living room mantel. She'd visited his apartment just six days ago, but it felt like two lifetimes had passed since then.

Aria tiptoed into the classroom behind him. "So, were you sick?" she asked.

"Yes," Ezra aswered. "I had the flu."

"Sorry to hear that." Aria wondered if she was going to get the flu too.

Ezra looked at the empty classroom and walked closer to her. "So. Listen. How about a fresh start?" His face was businesslike.

"Um, okay," Aria croaked.

"We have a year to get through," Ezra added. "So we'll forget this happened?"

Aria swallowed. She knew their relationship was wrong, but she still had feelings for Ezra. She'd bared her soul to him, and she couldn't do that with just anyone. And he was so different. "Of course," she said, although she didn't entirely believe it. They'd had a real . . . connection.

Ezra nodded slightly. Then, ever so slowly, he reached out and put his hand on the back of Aria's neck. Tingles ran up her spine. She held her breath until he brought his hand back to his side and walked away.

Aria took a seat at her desk, her mind churning. Was that some sort of sign? He had *said* forget it, but it hadn't *felt* that way.

Before she could decide if she should say anything to Ezra, Noel Kahn slid into the seat across from Aria and poked her with his Montblanc pen. "So, I hear you're cheating on me, Finland."

"What?" Aria sat up, alert. Her hand fluttered to her neck.

"Sean Ackard was asking about you. You know he's with Hanna though, right?"

Aria poked the backs of her teeth with her tongue. "Sean . . . Ackard?"

"He's not with Hanna anymore," James Freed interrupted, sliding into his seat in front of Noel. "Mona told me Hanna dumped him."

"So, you like Sean?" Noel pushed his wavy black hair out of his eyes.

"No," Aria said automatically. Although she kept coming back to the conversation she'd had with Sean in his car on Tuesday. It had felt good to talk to someone about things.

"Good," Noel said, brushing a hand across his forehead. "I was worried."

Aria rolled her eyes.

Hanna sauntered into the room just as the bell rang, putting her oversize Prada bag on her desk and sinking dramatically into her chair. She gave Aria a tight smile.

"Hey." Aria felt a little shy. In school, Hanna seemed awfully closed off.

"Hey, Hanna, are you with Sean Ackard anymore?" Noel asked loudly.

Hanna stared at him. Her eyelid twitched. "It wasn't working between us. Why?"

"No reason," Aria butted in quickly. Although she wondered why Hanna had broken up with him. They were two peas in a typical Rosewood pod.

Ezra clapped his hands. "All right," he said. "In addition to the books we're reading as a class, I want to do an extra side project on unreliable narrators."

Devon Arliss raised her hand. "What does *that* mean?"

Ezra strode around the room. "Well, the narrator tells us the story in a book, right? But what if . . . the narrator isn't telling us the truth? Maybe he's telling his skewed version of the story to get you on his side. Or to scare you. Or maybe he's crazy!"

Aria shivered. That made her think of A.

"I'm going to assign each of you a book," Ezra said. "In a ten-page paper, you are to make the case for and against its narrator being unreliable."

The class groaned. Aria rested her head in her palm. Maybe A wasn't entirely reliable? Maybe A didn't really know anything but was just *trying* to convince them otherwise. Who was A, anyway? She looked around the classroom, at Amber Billings, poking her finger through a tiny hole in her stockings; at Mason Byers, secretly checking the Phillies scores on his cell phone, using his notebook as a shield; and at Hanna, writing down what

Ezra was saying with her purple-ink feather pen. Could any of these people be A? Who could know about Ezra, her parents . . . *and* The Jenna Thing?

A groundskeeper zoomed by on a John Deere mower outside the window, and Aria jumped. Ezra was still talking about lying narrators, pausing to take a sip out of his mug. He shot Aria the tiniest smile, and her heart began to thrum.

James Freed leaned over, poked Hanna, and gestured to Ezra. "So, I hear Fitz gets some serious ass," he whispered, loud enough for Aria—and the rest of her row—to hear.

Hanna looked at Ezra and wrinkled her nose. "Him? Ew."

"Apparently he's got this girlfriend in New York, but he's on a different Hollis girl every week," James went on.

Aria straightened up. *Girlfriend?*

"Where'd you hear that?" Noel asked James.

James grinned. "You know Ms. Polanski? The bio student teacher? She told me. She hangs out with us at the smoking corner sometimes."

Noel gave James a high five. "Dude, Ms. Polanski is *hot.*"

"Seriously," James answered. "You think I could take her to Foxy?"

Aria felt like someone had just thrown her into a bonfire. A *girlfriend?* Friday night, he'd said he hadn't dated anybody in a long time. Aria remembered noticing his bachelorish frozen dinners for one, his eight thousand books but one drinking glass, and his sad, dead spider plants. It didn't *look* like he had a girlfriend.

James could have his facts wrong, but she doubted it. Aria bubbled with anger. Years ago, she might've thought only typical Rosewood boys were players, but she'd learned a lot about boys in Iceland. Sometimes the most unassuming boys were the sketchiest. No girl would look at Ezra—sensitive, rumpled, sweet, caring Ezra—and distrust him. He reminded Aria of someone. Her father.

Aria suddenly felt sick. She stood up, grabbed the hall pass from the peg, and strode out the door.

"Aria?" Ezra called, sounding concerned.

She didn't stop. In the girls' room, she rushed to the sink, dispensed pink soap into her hands, and scrubbed the spot on her neck Ezra had touched. She was walking back to class when her cell phone chimed. She pulled it out of her bag and pressed *read*.

Naughty, naughty Aria! You should know better than to go after a teacher, anyway. It's girls like you who break up perfectly happy families. —A

Aria froze. She was in the middle of the empty front hallway. When she heard a noise, she whirled around. She was facing the glass trophy case, which had been transformed into an Alison DiLaurentis temple. Inside were various candids from Rosewood Day classes—teachers always took tons of pictures throughout the year, and the school typically presented them to parents when their child graduated. There was Ali as a gap-toothed kindergartner at her old school; there she was dressed up as a pilgrim for their fourth-grade play. There was even some of her schoolwork, like an Under the Sea diorama from third grade and an illustration of the circulatory system from fifth.

A square of hot pink caught Aria's eye. Someone had stuck a Post-it note on the memorial's glass. Aria's eyes widened.

P.S. Wondering who I am, aren't you? I'm closer than you think. —A

14

EMILY'S PERFECTLY FINE WITH TAKING ALI'S SLOPPY SECONDS

"Say *butterfly*!" crowed Scott Chin, Rosewood Day's yearbook photographer. It was Thursday afternoon, and the swim team was in the natatorium for team photos before the Tate meet started. Emily had been on swim teams for so long, she didn't even think about having her picture taken in a bathing suit.

She posed with her hands on the starting block and tried to smile. "Gorgeous!" Scott cried, pursing his pink lips. A lot of kids at school speculated about whether Scott was gay. Scott never outwardly admitted it, but he didn't do anything to dispel the rumors, either.

As Emily maneuvered across the deck to her duffel bag, she noticed Tate Prep's team strolling to their bleachers. Toby was in the middle of the pack, wearing a blue Champion sweatshirt and rolling his shoulders back and forth to warm up.

Emily held her breath. She'd been thinking about

Toby ever since he rescued her yesterday. She couldn't imagine Ben ever having picked her up like that—he'd have worried that lifting her might pull his shoulder muscles and compromise his race today. And thinking about Toby had triggered something else, too: a memory of Ali that Emily had nearly forgotten.

It was one of the last times Emily was ever alone with Ali. She'd never forget that day—clear blue sky, all the flowers had bloomed, there were bees everywhere. Ali's tree house smelled like Kool-Aid, sap, and cigarette smoke—Ali had pilfered a Parliament from her older brother's pack. She grabbed Emily's hands. "You *can't* tell the others this," she said. "I've started secretly seeing this older guy, and it's a-*maz*-ing."

Emily's smile drooped. Every time Ali told her about a guy she liked, a little piece of her heart cracked off.

"He's *so* hot," Ali went on. "I almost want to go sort of far with him."

"What do you mean?" Emily had never heard anything so horrifying in her life. "Who is he?"

"I can't tell." Ali smiled slyly. "You guys would *freak*."

And then, because Emily couldn't stand it any longer, she leaned forward and kissed Ali. There was a singular, wonderful moment; then Ali pulled away and laughed. Emily tried to pass it off like she was just playing . . . and then they went to their separate houses to have dinner.

She'd thought about the kiss so many times, she'd hardly remembered what had come before it. But now

that Toby was back and he was so cute . . . it got Emily
thinking that maybe Ali's guy had been Toby? Who else
would've made them freak?

Ali liking Toby sort of made sense. At the end of
seventh grade, she'd been on a bad-boy kick, talking
about how she wanted to go out with someone who was
"like, *bad*." Being sent to reform school qualified as bad,
and maybe Ali saw something in Toby that no one else
did. Emily thought maybe she could see that same something, now. And, slightly bizarre as it was, the possibility
that Ali had liked Toby made Toby seem that much
more attractive to Emily. What was good enough for Ali
was certainly good enough for her.

As soon as the swim meet broke for the diving competition, Emily pulled her flip-flops out of her Rosewood
Day swimming tote, preparing to walk over to Toby. Her
fingers bumped against her cell phone, tucked under
her towel. It was blinking; she'd missed seven calls
from Maya.

Emily's throat tightened. Maya had called, IM'ed,
texted, and e-mailed her all week, and Emily hadn't
responded. With every new missed phone call, she felt
more confused. Part of her wanted to find Maya in
school and run her hand through her soft, curly hair. To
climb on the back of her bike and ditch school. Kissing
Maya had felt dangerously good. But part of her wished
Maya would just . . . disappear.

Emily stared at her cell phone window, a lump in her

throat. Then, slowly, she snapped it shut. It kind of felt like the time when she was eight and decided to throw away Bee-Bee, her security blanket. *Big girls don't need blankies,* she'd told herself, but it had been awful to close the trash can's lid with Bee-Bee inside.

She took a deep breath and headed for Tate's bleachers. On her way there, she glanced over her shoulder, looking for Ben. He was over on Rosewood Day's side, slapping Seth's shoulder with his Sammy towel. Since the Tank on Tuesday, Ben had stayed out of Emily's way, acting like she didn't exist. It was certainly better than attacking her, but it made her paranoid that he was saying stuff about her behind her back. She kind of wanted Ben to see her right now, just as she approached Toby. *Look! I'm talking to a guy!*

Toby had laid his towel on the natatorium tile and had headphones over his ears and an iPod on his lap. His hair was slicked back from his face, and the royal blue sweats he wore over his Speedo—which Emily hadn't been brave enough to peek at during his first event—made his eyes look even bluer.

When he saw Emily, he brightened. "Hey. Told you I'd see you here, didn't I?"

"Yeah." Emily smiled shyly. "So, um, I just wanted to say thanks. For helping me yesterday. *And* the day before."

"Oh. Well, it was nothing."

Just then, Scott appeared with his yearbook camera. "Gotcha!" he cried, and snapped a picture. "I can see the

caption now: 'Emily Fields, flirting with the enemy!'"
Then he said to Emily in a lower voice, "Although I
thought he wasn't your type."

Emily looked at Scott questioningly. What was *that*
supposed to mean? But he fluttered away. When she
turned to Toby again, he was playing with his iPod, so
she started back for her team's side. She'd taken three
steps when Toby called out, "Hey, you want to get
some air?"

Emily paused. Quickly, she glanced at Ben. Still not
paying any attention. "Um, all right," she decided.

They walked through the Rosewood Day natatorium's
double doors, past a bunch of kids waiting for the late
buses, and sat down on the edge of the Founder's Day
fountain. Water gushed out of the top in a long, shim-
mering plume. It was cloudy out, though, so the water just
looked dull and white instead of sparkly. Emily stared at
a bunch of pennies on the fountain's shallow, shiny bottom. "On the last day of school, seniors push their favorite
teacher into this fountain," she told him.

"I know," Toby said. "I used to go here, remember?"

"Oh." Emily felt like a moron. Of course he did. And
then they sent him away.

Toby pulled a package of chocolate chip cookies out
of his bag. He held them out to Emily. "Want one?
Pre-race snack?"

Emily shrugged. "Maybe half."

"Good for you," Toby said, handing her one. He

looked away. "It's funny how it's totally different between guys and girls. Guys want to out-eat each other. Even guys I know that are older. Like my shrink, in Maine? One time, at his house, we had a shrimp-eating contest. He beat me by six shrimp. And he's, like, at least thirty-five."

"Shrimp." Emily shuddered. Because she didn't want to ask the obvious—*You had a shrink?*—she asked, "What happened after your, um, shrink ate all that?"

"He threw up." Toby skimmed the surface of the water with his fingertips. The fountain water smelled even more like chlorine than the pool did.

Emily ran her hands over her knees. She wondered if he had a shrink for the same reason he'd taken the blame for The Jenna Thing.

A luxury bus pulled into the Rosewood Day parking lot. Slowly, members of the Rosewood Day band trooped off, still in their uniforms—red jackets with braided trim, flared tuxedo pants, the drum major in a goofy furry hat that looked like it would be really hot and uncomfortable to wear. "You, um, talk a lot about Maine," Emily said. "Are you happy to be in Rosewood again?"

Toby raised an eyebrow. "Are *you* happy to be in Rosewood?"

Emily frowned. She watched as a squirrel ran circles around one of the oak trees. "I don't know," she said quietly. "Sometimes I feel kind of wrong here. I used to be normal, but now . . . I don't know. I feel like I should be one way, but I'm not."

Toby stared at her. "I hear that." He sighed. "There are all these perfect people here. And . . . it's like, if you're not one of them, then you're messed up. But I think, inside, the flawless-looking people are just as messed up as we are."

He turned his gaze to Emily, and her insides turned over. She felt like her thoughts and secrets were 72-point-font newspaper headlines, and Toby could read all of them. But Toby was also the first person who'd expressed something close to how she felt about things. "I feel pretty messed up most of the time," she said quietly.

Toby looked like he didn't believe her. "How are you messed up?"

A clap of thunder exploded overhead. Emily slid her hands inside her warm-up jacket sleeves. *I'm messed up because I don't know who I am or what I want,* she wanted to say. But instead, she looked directly at him and blurted, "I love storms."

"Me too," he answered.

And then, slowly, Toby leaned forward and kissed her. It was very soft and tentative, just a little whisper across her mouth. When he pulled back, Emily touched her lips with her fingers, like the kiss might still be on her lips.

"What was that for?" she whispered.

"I don't know," Toby said. "Should I not have . . . ?"

"No," Emily whispered. "It was nice." Her first thought was, *I just kissed a boy Ali might have kissed.* Her second was that maybe it was messed up of her to have even thought that.

"Toby?" a voice interrupted them. A man in a leather jacket stood under the natatorium awning, hands on his hips. It was Mr. Cavanaugh. Emily recognized him from summer swim team, years ago . . . and from the night Jenna got hurt. Her shoulder muscles tightened. If Mr. Cavanaugh was here, was Jenna? Then she remembered that Jenna was at school in Philadelphia. Hopefully.

"What are you doing out here?" Mr. Cavanaugh put his hand outside the awning, feeling the rain, which had just begun to fall. "Your relay's soon."

"Oh." Toby jumped off the wall. He smiled at Emily. "You going back in too?"

"In a sec," Emily said weakly. If she tried to use her legs right now, they might not work. "Good luck with your race."

"Okay." Toby's eyes lingered on her for another moment. He looked ready to say something else, but he broke away, falling into step with his dad.

Emily sat on the stone wall for a few minutes, the rain soaking through her jacket. She felt strangely fizzy, like she was carbonated. What had just happened? When her Nokia announced that she had a text, she flinched and dug it out of her jacket pocket. Her heart sank. It was who she thought it was.

Emily, how about this picture of you for the yearbook
instead?

She clicked on the attachment. It was a shot of Emily
and Maya from Noel's photo booth. They were looking
into each other's eyes longingly, inches from kissing.
Emily's mouth fell open. She remembered hitting the
button in the booth to start the photos—but hadn't Maya
taken them when they left?

You wouldn't want this to get around, would you? said the
line of text under the photo.

And—of course—it was signed, *A.*

15

SHE STEALS FOR YOU, AND THIS IS HOW YOU REPAY HER

Mona emerged from the Saks dressing room in a square-necked, sheer green Calvin Klein dress. Its full skirt fanned out as she twirled. "What do you think?" she asked Hanna, who was standing at the racks right outside.

"Gorgeous," Hanna murmured. Under the dressing room's fluorescent lights, she could tell Mona wasn't wearing a bra.

Mona posed in the three-way mirror. She was so skinny, sometimes she dipped down to an enviable size zero. "I think this might be better with your coloring." She pulled at one of the straps. "You want to try?"

"I don't know," Hanna said. "It's kind of see-through."

Mona frowned. "Since when do you care?"

Hanna shrugged and looked through a rack of Marc Jacobs blazers. It was Thursday evening, and they were at the designer department of Saks in the King James Mall, frantically searching for Foxy dresses. A lot of prep school and out-of-college-but-living-in-the-estate-with-the-'rents girls attended, and it was important to find a dress that five other girls wouldn't be wearing.

"I want to look classy," Hanna answered. "Like Scarlett Johansson."

"Why?" Mona asked. "She's got a big ass."

Hanna pursed her lips. When she said *classy*, she meant *subtle*. Like those girls in those diamond ads who looked sweet but had the words *fuck me* airbrushed into a strand of their hair. Sean needed to be so entranced by Hanna's virtue, he'd reject his V Club vows and tear her underwear off.

Hanna picked up a pair of peep-toe, camel-colored Miu Miu shoes from the sale shelf just outside the dressing room. "I love these." She held one up for Mona to see.

"Why don't you . . . ?" Mona nudged her chin down to Hanna's bag.

Hanna dropped them back on the shelf. "No way."

"Why not?" Mona whispered. "Shoes are the easiest. You know that." When Hanna hesitated, Mona clucked her tongue. "You're still freaked about Tiffany?"

Instead of answering, Hanna pretended to be interested in a pair of metallic Marc Jacobs sling-backs.

Mona pulled a few more things off the racks and went back into the changing room. Seconds later, she emerged empty-handed. "This place blows. Let's try Prada."

They walked through the mall, Mona typing on her

Sidekick. "I'm asking Eric what color flowers he's getting me," she explained. "Maybe I'll match my dress to them."

Mona had decided to go to Foxy with Noel Kahn's brother, Eric, who she'd hung out with a few times this week already. The Kahn boys were always a safe Foxy date—they were good-looking and rich, and society photographers loved them. Mona tried to coax Hanna into asking Noel, but she'd waited too long. Noel had asked Celeste Richards, who went to the Quaker boarding school—a surprise, since everyone thought Noel had a thing for Aria Montgomery. Hanna didn't care, though. If she wasn't going with Sean, she wasn't going with anyone.

Mona looked up from her texting. "Which spray-on tan place do you think is better, Sun Land or Dalia's? Celeste and I might go to Sun Land tomorrow, but I think they make you look orange."

Hanna shrugged, feeling a pang of jealousy. Mona should've been going tanning with her, not Celeste. She was about to answer, when her own phone rang. Her heart sped up a little. Whenever her phone rang, she thought of A.

"Hanna?" It was her mom. "Where are you?"

"I'm out shopping," Hanna answered. Since when did her mom care?

"Well, you need to go home. Your father is stopping over."

"What? Why?" Hanna glanced at Mona, who was checking out the cheapo sunglasses at an esplanade kiosk.

She hadn't told Mona that her dad had visited on Monday. It was too weird to talk about.

"He just . . . He needs to pick something up," her mom said.

"Like what?"

Ms. Marin let out a flustered snort. "He's coming over to get some financial paperwork we need to settle before he gets married. Is that enough explanation for you?"

A prickly sweat gathered on the back of Hanna's neck. One, because her mom had mentioned what she hated to think about—that her dad was getting *married* to Isabel, and he would be Kate's *father*. And two, she'd sort of thought her dad might be stopping by to see her, specifically. Why should she go home if he was coming for another reason? It would look like she didn't have a life. She checked her reflection in the Banana Republic window. "When's he coming?" she asked.

"He'll be here in an hour." Her mother abruptly hung up. Hanna snapped her phone closed and cradled it between her hands, feeling its warmth seep into her palms.

"Who was *that*?" Mona singsonged, linking her arm through Hanna's.

"My mom," Hanna said distractedly. She wondered if she'd have enough time to shower when she got home; she reeked of all the different perfumes she'd sampled at Neiman Marcus. "She wants me to go home."

"Why?"

"Just . . . because."

Mona stopped and eyed Hanna carefully. "Han. Your mom doesn't just randomly call to summon you home."

Hanna stopped. They were standing in front of the entrance to Year of the Rabbit, the mall's upscale Chinese bistro, and the overpowering smell of hoisin sauce wafted into her nostrils. "Well, it's because . . . my dad's coming over."

Mona frowned. "Your dad? I thought he was—"

"He's not," Hanna said quickly. When Mona and Hanna became friends, Hanna told Mona that her father was dead. She'd vowed never to speak to him again, so it wasn't exactly a lie. "We weren't in touch for a really long time," she explained. "But I saw him the other day, and he has business in Philly or whatever. He's not coming over today because of me. I don't know why my mom wants me there."

Mona put one hand on her hip. "Why didn't you tell me before?"

Hanna shrugged.

"So when did this happen?"

"I don't know. Monday?"

"Monday?" Mona sounded hurt.

"Girls!" interrupted a voice. Hanna and Mona looked up. It was Naomi Zeigler. She and Riley Wolfe were coming out of Prada, black shopping bags slung over their perfectly spray-tanned shoulders.

"Are you shopping for Foxy?" Naomi asked. Her

blond hair was as lustrous as ever and her skin glowed irritatingly, but Hanna couldn't help note that her BCBG dress was last season's. Before she could answer, Naomi added, "Don't bother with Prada. We bought the only good stuff."

"Maybe we've already *got* dresses," Mona said stiffly.

"Hanna, you're going, too?" Riley widened her brown eyes and tossed her shiny red hair. "I thought maybe since you aren't with Sean . . ."

"I wouldn't miss Foxy," Hanna said haughtily.

Riley put her hand on her hip. She was wearing black leggings, a frayed denim shirt, and a fugly black-and-white striped sweater. Recently there had been a paparazzi shot of Mischa Barton wearing the exact same outfit. "Sean's so beautiful," Riley purred. "I think he got even cuter over the summer."

"He's totally gay," Mona said quickly.

Riley didn't look worried. "I bet I can get him to change his mind."

Hanna clenched her fists.

Naomi brightened. "So, hey, Hanna, the Y is awesome, huh? You'll have to take the Pilates class with me. The instructor, Oren? *Gorgeous.*"

"Hanna doesn't go to the Y," Mona interrupted. "We go to Body Tonic. The Y is a shithole."

Hanna swiveled from Mona to Naomi, her stomach fluttering.

"You don't go to the Y?" Naomi made the most

innocent face she could. "I'm confused. Didn't I see you there yesterday? Outside the elliptical room?"

Hanna grabbed Mona's arm. "We're late for something." She dragged her away from the Prada store, back in the direction of Saks.

"What was that all about?" Mona asked, skirting gracefully around a horsey woman laden with shopping bags.

"Nothing. I just can't stand her."

"Why were you at the Y yesterday? You told me you were seeing the dermatologist."

Hanna stopped. She'd known seeing Naomi before V Club was trouble. "I . . . I had something to do there."

"What?"

"I can't tell you."

Mona frowned, then whirled around. She took determined, stiff steps into Burberry. Hanna caught up with her. "Look, I just can't. I'm sorry."

"I'm sure you are." Mona started digging through her purse and pulled out the camel-colored Miu Mius from Saks. They weren't in their box, and the security tag had been ripped off them. She dangled them in front of Hanna's face. "I was *going* to give these to you as a present. But forget it."

Hanna's mouth fell open. "But . . ."

"That thing with your dad happened three days ago, and you never told me about it," Mona said. "And now you're lying to me about what you're doing after school."

"It's not like that at all . . ." Hanna stuttered.

"It looks that way to me." Mona frowned. "What else are you lying about?"

"I'm sorry," Hanna squeaked. "I just . . ." She looked down at her shoes and took a deep breath. "You want to know why I was at the Y? Fine. I went to Virginity Club."

Mona's eyes widened. Her cell phone rang in her bag, but she made no motion to get it. "Now I *hope* you're lying."

Hanna shook her head. She felt a little nauseated; Burberry smelled way too much like its new perfume.

"But . . . why?"

"I want Sean back."

Mona burst out laughing. "You told me you ended it with Sean at Noel's party."

Hanna glanced into Burberry's window and nearly had a heart attack. Was her butt really that chunky? She suddenly had the same proportions as dorky, fat Hanna of the past. She gasped, looked away, and looked again. Normal Hanna stared back. "No," she told Mona. "He ended it with me."

Mona didn't laugh, but she didn't try to comfort Hanna, either. "Is that why you were at his dad's clinic, too?"

"No," Hanna said quickly, forgetting that she'd seen Mona there. Then, realizing that she might have to tell Mona the *real* reason, she backtracked. "Well, yeah. Sort of."

Mona shrugged. "Well, I sort of heard Sean broke up with you from somewhere else, anyway."

"*What?*" Hanna hissed. "From who?"

"Maybe in gym. I don't remember." Mona shrugged. "Maybe Sean started it."

Hanna's eyesight blurred. She doubted Sean had told . . . but maybe A had.

Mona considered her. "I thought you wanted to lose your virginity, not prolong it."

"I just wanted to see what it was like," Hanna said softly.

"And?" Mona pursed her lips mischievously. "Give me the dirt. I bet it was hilarious. What did you talk about? Did you chant? Sing? What?"

Hanna frowned and then turned away. Normally, she'd have told Mona everything. Except it stung that Mona was laughing at her, and she didn't want to give her the satisfaction. Candace had so plaintively said, *This is a safe space*. Right now, Hanna didn't feel she had the right to give up anyone's secrets, not when it looked like A was giving up hers. And why, if Mona had heard a rumor about her, hadn't she said anything? Weren't they supposed to be best friends? "None of that, really," she murmured. "It was pretty boring."

Mona's face had held a look of expectation; now it wilted in disappointment. She and Hanna stared at each other. Then Mona's cell rang and she looked away.

"Celeste?" Mona said when she answered. "Hey!"

Hanna chewed nervously on her lips and looked at her Gucci bracelet watch. "I have to go," she whispered to Mona, gesturing toward the mall's east exit. "My dad . . ."

"Hold on," Mona said into her phone. She covered the receiver with her hands, rolled her eyes at the Miu Miu shoes, and shoved them at Hanna. "Just take these. I actually kind of hate them."

Hanna backed away, holding the stolen shoes by their straps. All of a sudden, she kind of hated them too.

16

NICE, NORMAL, FAMILY NIGHT
AT THE MONTGOMERYS'

That night, Aria sat on her bed, knitting a stuffed owl out of mohair yarn. The owl was brown and boyish-looking; she'd started it the week before, thinking she would give it to Ezra. Now, that obviously wasn't happening, so she wondered . . . maybe she'd give it to Sean? How weird was that?

Before Ali went missing, she kept trying to set Aria up with Rosewood boys, saying, "Just go over and *talk* to him. It's not hard." But for Aria, it *was* hard. She got around a Rosewood boy and froze, blurting out the first idiotic thing that came out of her mouth—which, for some reason, was often about math. And she *hated* math. By the time she'd finished seventh grade, only one guy had spoken to her outside of class: Toby Cavanaugh.

And that had been scary. It was just a few weeks before Ali went missing, and Aria had signed up for a weekend arts camp, and who should show up in her workshop but *Toby*. Aria was astounded—wasn't he supposed to be in boarding school . . . forever? But apparently, his school broke for summer vacation earlier than Rosewood Day's did, and there he was. He sat in the corner, hair over his face, snapping a rubber band against his wrist.

Their drama teacher, a wispy, frizzy-haired woman who wore a lot of tie-dye, made everyone do a drama exercise: They paired up and shouted a phrase to each other over and over, getting into a rhythm. The phrase was supposed to change organically. They had to go around the room, partnering with everyone, and Aria soon found herself in front of Toby. The phrase for that day was, *It never snows in the summer.*

"It never snows in the summer," Toby said.

"It never snows in the summer," Aria said back to him.

"It never snows in the summer," Toby repeated. His eyes were sunken and his nails were bitten down to the quick. Aria felt twitchy standing this close to him. She couldn't help thinking about Toby's ghoulish face in Ali's window just before they hurt Jenna. And how the paramedics pulled Jenna down the tree house ladder, nearly dropping her. And how, a few days later, when they were at the Firework Safety Benefit, she overheard her health teacher, Mrs. Iverson, say, "If I were that boy's father, I wouldn't just send him to boarding school. I'd send him to *jail.*"

And then the phrase did change. It became, *I know*

what you did last summer. Toby was the one to say it first, but Aria shouted it back a few times before she realized what it really meant.

"Oh, like the movie!" the teacher cried, clapping her hands.

"Yep," Toby said, and smiled at Aria. A real smile, too, not a sinister one, which made her feel worse. When she told Ali what had happened, Ali sighed. "Aria, Toby's, like, mentally deranged. I heard he practically drowned up in Maine, swimming in a frozen creek, trying to take a picture of a moose."

But Aria never went back to drama class.

She thought again about A's Post-it. *Wondering who I am? I'm closer than you think.*

Could A be Toby? Had he sneaked into Rosewood Day and stuck that Post-it on Ali's case? Had any of her friends seen it? Or perhaps A was in one of her classes. Her English class would make the most sense—the timing of most of her notes revolved around them. But who? Noel? James Freed? Hanna?

Aria paused on Hanna. She'd wondered about her before—Ali could have told Hanna about her parents. And Hanna was part of The Jenna Thing.

But why?

She flipped through the Rosewood Day facebook—the directory that had just come out today of all her class-mates' names and phone numbers—and found Sean's picture. His hair was sportily short, and he was bronzed like he'd spent the summer on his dad's yacht. The boys Aria dated in Iceland were pale and floppy-haired, and if they had boats, they were kayaks that they used to paddle to the Snaefellsjokull glacier.

She dialed Sean's number but got his voice mail. "Hey, Sean," she said, hoping her voice wasn't too singsongish. "It's Aria Montgomery. I, um, I was just calling to say hi, and, um, I have a philosopher recommendation for you. It's Ayn Rand. She's like, super-complex but really readable. Check it out."

She gave him her cell number and IM screen name, hung up, and wanted to delete the message. Sean probably had tons of non-spastic Rosewood girls calling.

"Aria!" Ella called from the bottom of the stairs. "Dinner!"

She threw her phone on her bed and slowly walked downstairs. Her ears pricked up at a strange beeping noise coming from the kitchen. Was that . . . the oven timer? But that was impossible. Their kitchen was done in a retro-1950s style, and the stove was an authentic Magic Chef from 1956. Ella rarely used it because she was afraid it was so old, it might set the house on fire.

But to Aria's surprise, Ella did have something in the oven, and her brother and father were at the table. This was the first time since the weekend that her whole family had been together. Mike had spent the past three nights at various lacrosse boys' houses, and her dad, well, he'd been so busy "teaching."

A roast chicken, a bowl of mashed potatoes, and a dish of green beans sat in the middle of the table. All the plates and utensils matched, and there were even *place mats*. Aria tensed. It seemed way too normal . . . especially for her family. Something must be wrong. Had someone died? Had A told?

But her parents seemed untroubled. Her mom pulled a tray of rolls from the oven—which, miraculously, wasn't on fire—and her dad sat quietly, flipping the op-ed pages of the *New York Times*. He was always reading: at the table, at Mike's sporting events, even while driving.

Aria turned to her dad, whom she'd hardly seen since Monday at the Victory bar. "Hey, Byron," she said.

Her father gave Aria a genuine smile. "Hello, Monkey." He sometimes called her Monkey; he used to call her Hairy Ape, too, until she told him to stop. He always looked like he'd just rolled out of bed: He wore holey, thrift-store T-shirts, Philadelphia 76ers boxers or plaid pajama pants, and old shearling-lined slippers. His dark brown bushy hair was always crazy messy, too. Aria thought he resembled a koala bear.

"And hey, Mike!" Aria said brightly, ruffling his hair. Mike recoiled. "Don't freaking touch me!"

"Mike," Ella said, pointing at him with one of the chopsticks that usually secured the bun in her brownish-black hair.

"I was just being nice." Aria stopped herself from shooting Mike a standard sarcastic retort. Instead, she sat down, unfolded her embroidered floral napkin onto her lap, and picked up a Bakelite-handled fork. "The chicken smells *really* good, Ella."

Ella spooned potatoes onto everyone's plates. "It was just one of those things from the deli counter."

"Since when do you think chicken smells good?" Mike snarled. "You don't eat it."

That was true. Aria had been a vegetarian ever since her second week in Iceland, when Hallbjorn, her first boyfriend, bought her a snack from a food cart that she thought was a hot dog. It was to die for, but after she ate it, he told her it was puffin meat. Ever since then, whenever meat was in front of her, she always imagined a cute baby puffin's face. "Well, still," Aria said. "I *do* eat potatoes." She shoved a steaming hot spoonful into her mouth. "And *these* are awesome."

Ella furrowed her brow. "They're just instant. You know I can't cook."

Aria knew she was trying too hard. But if she was a model daughter instead of her sarcastic, grumbling self, Byron might realize what he was missing.

She turned again to Byron. Aria didn't want to hate her dad. There were tons of good things about him—he always listened to her problems, he was smart, he made her Get Well Soon fudge brownies when she had the flu. She'd tried to come up with logical, non-romantic reasons why the Meredith thing had happened. She didn't want to think he loved someone else, or that he was trying to break up the family. It was hard, though, not to take it personally.

As she took a spoonful of green beans, Ella's cell phone, which was sitting on the kitchen island, began to ring. Ella looked at Byron. "Should I get that?"

Byron frowned. "Would someone be calling you at dinnertime?"

"Maybe it's Oliver from the gallery."

Suddenly, Aria felt her throat constrict. *What if it's A?*

The phone rang again. Aria stood up. "I'll answer it."

Ella wiped her mouth and pushed back her chair. "No, I should get it."

"No!" Aria rushed to the island. The phone rang a third time. "I . . . um . . . it's . . ."

She flailed her arms wildly, trying to think. Out of ideas, she grabbed the phone and flung it into the living room. It skidded across the floor, stopped against the couch, and stopped ringing. The Montgomerys' cat, Polo, padded up and tapped the phone with his striped paw.

When Aria turned back around, her family was staring at her. "What is the matter with you?" Ella asked.

"I just . . ." Aria was damp with sweat, and her whole body throbbed with her heartbeat. Mike crossed his hands behind his head. *Fuh-REEK*, he mouthed.

Ella swished by her to the living room and crouched to look at the phone's screen. Her crinkle skirt grazed the floor, picking up dust. "It *was* Oliver."

At the same time, Byron stood up. "I have to be going."

"Going?" Ella's voice caught. "But we just started eating."

Byron carried his empty plate to the sink. He had always been the fastest eater on the planet, even faster than Mike. "I have stuff to do in my office."

"But . . ." Ella clasped her hands at her small waist. They all watched helplessly as Byron disappeared up the stairs and then came down about a half a minute later in rumpled gray pants and a blue button-down. His hair was still completely uncombed. He grabbed his worn leather briefcase and keys. "See you in a little while."

"Can you pick up orange juice?" Ella cried, but Byron shut the front door without answering.

A second later, Mike stormed out of the kitchen without putting his plate in the sink. He grabbed his jacket and lacrosse stick and wormed his feet into his sneakers without untying them. "Now, where are *you* going?" Ella asked.

"Practice," Mike snapped. He had his head way down and was chewing on his lip, like he was trying to keep from crying. Aria wanted to run up to her brother and hug him and try to figure out what to do here, except she felt stuck, as if grouted to the checkerboard ceramic tiles on the kitchen floor.

Mike slammed the door, making the whole house

shake. A few seconds of silence passed, then Ella raised her gray eyes to Aria. "Everyone's leaving us."

"No, they're not," Aria said quickly.

Her mother went back to the table and stared at the remaining chicken on her plate. After a few seconds of pondering, she laid a napkin over it, uneaten, and turned back to Aria. "Has your father seemed strange to you?"

Aria felt her mouth go dry. "About what?"

"I don't know." Ella traced her finger around the porcelain dinner plate's edge. "It seems like something's bothering him. Maybe it's about teaching? He seems so busy. . . ."

Aria knew she should say something, but the words felt gummed up in her stomach, like she needed a toilet plunger or a vacuum to suck them out. "He hasn't said anything about that, no." It wasn't exactly a lie.

Ella stared at her. "You'd tell me if he had, right?"

Aria bent her head down, pretending she had something in her eye. "Of course."

Ella rose and cleared the rest of the stuff off the table. Aria stood there, useless. This was her chance . . . and she was just standing here. Like a sack of potatoes.

She wandered up to her room and sat down at her desk, not sure what to do with herself. Downstairs, she could hear the beginning strains of *Jeopardy!*. Perhaps she should go back down and hang out with Ella. Except what she really wanted to do was cry.

Her Instant Messenger made the bloopy noise of a

new message. Aria went over to it, wondering if maybe it was Sean. But . . . it wasn't.

A A A A A A: Two choices: Make it go away or tell your mom. I'm giving you till the stroke of midnight Saturday night, Cinderella. Or else. —A

A creaking sound made her jump. Aria whirled around and saw that her cat had nosed her bedroom door open. She petted him absentmindedly, reading the IM again. And again. And again.

Or else? And *make it go away?* How was she supposed to do that?

Her computer made another *bloop*. The IM window flashed.

A A A A A A: Not sure how? Here's a hint: Strawberry Ridge Yoga Studio. 7:30 a.m. Tomorrow. Be there.

17

DADDY'S LITTLE GIRL
HAS A SECRET

Hanna stood six inches from her bedroom mirror, closely inspecting herself. It must've been a freak reflection at the mall—here, she looked normal and thin. Although . . . were her pores looking a little bigger? Were her eyes slightly crossed?

Nervous, she opened her bureau drawer and pulled out a giant bag of salt-and-pepper kettle chips. She shoved a big handful into her mouth, chewed, then stopped. Last week, A's notes had led her into the horrible binge/purge cycle all over again—even though she'd refrained from the habit for years. She *wouldn't* start doing this again. And especially not in front of her father.

She rolled up the bag and looked out the window again. Where *was* he? Nearly two hours had passed since her mom called her at the mall. Then she saw a forest-green Range Rover turn into her driveway, which was a winding, wooded, quarter-mile-long road. The car easily maneuvered around the driveway's twists and turns in a way that only someone who had lived there could. When Hanna was younger, she and her dad used to sled on the driveway. He taught her how to lean into each turn so she wouldn't tip.

When the doorbell rang, she jumped. Her miniature pinscher, Dot, started to bark, and the bell rang again. Dot's barking became more high-pitched and frenzied, and the bell rang for the third time. "Coming!" Hanna growled.

"Hey," her father said as she flung open the door. Dot began to dance around his heels. "Hello there." He reached down to pick up the tiny dog.

"Dot, no!" Hanna commanded.

"No, he's fine." Mr. Marin petted the miniature pinscher's little nose. Hanna had gotten Dot shortly after her dad left.

"So." Her father lingered on the porch awkwardly. He wore a charcoal gray business suit and a red and blue tie, as if he'd just come from a meeting. Hanna wondered if he wanted to come in. She felt funny inviting her dad into his own house. "Should I . . . ?" he started.

"Do you want to . . . ?" Hanna said at the same time. Her father laughed nervously. Hanna wasn't sure if she wanted to hug him. Her father took a step toward her, and she took a step back, bumping into the door. She tried to make it look like she'd meant to do it. "Just come in," she said, the annoyance in her voice showing.

They stood in the foyer. Hanna felt her father's eyes on her. "It's really nice to see you," he said.

Hanna shrugged. She wished she had a cigarette or something to do with her hands. "Yeah, well. So do you want the financial thingie? It's right here."

He squinted, ignoring her. "I meant to ask you the other day. Your hair. You did something different with it. It's . . . Is it shorter?"

She smirked. "It's *darker*."

He pointed. "Bingo. And you don't have your glasses on!"

"I got LASIK." She stared him down. "Two years ago."

"Oh." Her father put his hands in his pockets.

"You make it sound like it's a bad thing."

"No," her father answered quickly. "You just look . . . different."

Hanna crossed her arms. When her parents decided to divorce, Hanna thought it was because she got fat. And clumsy. And ugly. Meeting Kate had just felt like more proof. He'd found his replacement daughter, and he'd traded up.

After the Annapolis disaster, her father tried to stay in touch. At first, Hanna complied, having a couple of moody, one-word phone conversations. Mr. Marin tried to tease out what was wrong, but Hanna was too embarrassed to talk about it. Eventually, the length of time between conversations became longer and longer . . . and then they stopped happening altogether.

Mr. Marin strolled down the foyer, his feet creaking on the wood floor. Hanna wondered if he was assessing what was the same and what had changed. Did he notice the black-and-white photo of Hanna and her dad that hung above the Mission-style hall table had been removed? And that the lithograph of a woman going through the yoga sun salutations—a print Hanna's father *hated*, but Hanna's mom loved—hung in its place?

Her dad flopped on the living room couch, even though no one ever used the living room. *He* never used to use the living room. It was dark, way too stuffy, had ugly Oriental rugs, and smelled like Endust. Hanna didn't know what else to do, so she followed him in and sat down on the claw-foot ottoman in the corner.

"So. How are you doing, Hanna?"

She curled her legs underneath her. "I'm all right."

"Good."

Another ocean of silence. She heard Dot's tiny toenails tick across the kitchen floor, and his little tongue lap up water from his dish. She wished for an interruption—a phone call, the fire alarm going off, even another text from A—anything to take her away from this awkwardness.

"And how are you?" she finally asked.

"Not too bad." He picked up a tasseled pillow from the couch and held it out at arm's length. "These things were always so ugly."

Hanna agreed with him, but what, were the pillows at Isabel's house *perfect*?

Her father looked up. "Remember that game you used to play? You put the pillows on the floor and jumped from one to the other, because the floor was lava?"

"Dad." Hanna wrinkled her nose and hugged her knees even tighter.

He squeezed the pillow. "You could play that for hours."

"I was six."

"Remember Cornelius Maximilian?"

She looked up. His eyes were twinkling. "Dad . . ."

He threw the pillow up in the air and caught it. "Should I not talk about him? Has it been too long?"

She stuck her chin stiffly into the air. "Probably."

Inside, though, she cracked a tiny smile. Cornelius Maximilian was this inside joke they made up after they saw *Gladiator*. It had been a big treat for Hanna to go to a gory, R-rated movie, except she'd been only ten, and all the blood traumatized her. She was positive she wouldn't be able to sleep that night, so her father made up Cornelius to make her feel better. He was the only dog—a poodle, they thought, although sometimes they changed him to a Boston terrier—mighty enough to fight in the gladiator ring. He beat the tigers, he beat the other scary gladiators. He could do anything, including bring the dead gladiators back to life.

They made up a whole Cornelius character, talking about what he did on his off days, what sorts of studded collars he liked to wear, how he needed a girlfriend. Sometimes, Hanna and her father would reference

Cornelius around her mother, and she'd say, "What? Who?" even though they'd explained the joke a thousand times. When Hanna got Dot, she considered naming him Cornelius, but it would've been too sad.

Her father sat back on the couch. "I'm sorry that things are like this."

Hanna pretended to be interested in her French manicure. "Like what?"

"Like . . . with us." He cleared his throat. "I'm sorry I haven't been in touch."

Hanna rolled her eyes. This was way too after-school special for her. "No biggie."

Mr. Marin drummed his fingers on the coffee table. It was obvious he was really squirming. Good. "So why'd you steal your boyfriend's dad's car, anyway? I asked your mom if she knew, but she didn't."

"It's complicated," Hanna said quickly. Talk about ironic: when they first divorced, Hanna tried to think of ways she could get her parents to talk again so they'd fall back in love—like Lindsay Lohan's twin characters did in *The Parent Trap*. Turned out all she'd needed to do was get arrested a few times.

"Come on," Mr. Marin coaxed. "Did you guys break up? Were you upset?"

"I guess."

"He ended things?"

Hanna gulped miserably. "How'd you know?"

"If he's giving you up, maybe he wasn't worth it."

Hanna couldn't believe he just said that. In fact, she didn't believe it. Maybe she'd misheard. Maybe she'd been listening to her iPod too loud.

"Have you been thinking about Alison?" her father asked.

Hanna looked at her hands. "I guess. Yeah."

"It's pretty unbelievable."

Hanna gulped again. All of a sudden, she felt like she was going to cry. "I know."

Mr. Marin leaned back. The couch made a strange farting sound. It was something her dad might have commented on years ago, but now he kept quiet. "You know what my favorite memory of Alison is?"

"What?" Hanna asked quietly. She prayed he wasn't going to say, *That time you girls came to Annapolis and she bonded with Kate.*

"It was summer. I guess you guys were going into seventh grade or so. I took you and Alison to Avalon for the day. Do you remember that?"

"Vaguely," Hanna said. She recalled that she'd eaten too much saltwater taffy, that she looked fat in her bikini and Ali looked perfectly skinny in hers, and that a surfer boy invited Ali to a bonfire party, but she ditched him at the last minute.

"We were sitting on the beach; there were a girl and a boy a few blankets over. You guys knew the girl from school—but she wasn't anyone you typically hung around with. She had some sort of water bottle contraption strapped to her back that she sucked through with a straw. Ali talked to her brother and ignored her."

Suddenly, Hanna remembered it perfectly. It was common to run into people from Rosewood at the Jersey Shore—and that girl had actually been *Mona*. The boy was Mona's cousin. Ali thought he was cute, so she went over to talk to him. Mona seemed ecstatic that Ali was even in her vicinity, but all Ali did was turn to Mona and say, "Hey, my guinea pig drinks water from a bottle like that."

"*That's* your favorite memory?" Hanna blurted. She'd blocked it out; she was pretty sure Mona had too.

"I'm not done," her father said. "Alison walked down to the edge of the beach with the boy, but you stayed behind and talked to the girl, who looked just crushed that Alison had left. I don't know what you said, but you were nice to her. I was really proud of you."

Hanna wrinkled her nose. She doubted she was nice—she just probably wasn't straight-up mean. After The Jenna Thing happened, Hanna didn't savor teasing quite as much.

"You were always so nice to everyone," her father said.

"No, I wasn't," she said quietly.

She remembered how she used to talk about Jenna: *You wouldn't believe this girl, Dad,* she said. *She tried out for the same part Ali wants in the musical, and you should've heard her sing. She was like a* cow. Or, *Jenna Cavanaugh might've gotten every question right on the health test and done twelve pull-ups in gym for the Presidential Fitness test, but she's* still *a loser.*

Her father had always been a good listener, as long as he knew she didn't say mean things to people's faces. Which had made what he asked a few days after Jenna's accident, as they were driving to the store, that much more devastating. He'd turned to her and said, out of no where, *Wait. That girl that was blinded? She's the one who sings like a cow, right?* He looked as if he'd made the connection. Hanna, too terrified to answer, faked a coughing fit and then changed the subject.

Her father stood up and walked over to the living room's baby grand piano. He lifted the lid, and dust sifted into the air. When he pressed down a key, a tinny sound came out. "I guess your mother told you that Isabel and I are getting married?"

Hanna's heart sank. "Yeah, she said something like that."

"We were thinking next summer, except that Kate won't be able to make it then. She's going to a pre-college summer program in Spain."

Hanna bristled at Kate's name. *Poor baby has to go to Spain.*

"We'd like you to be at the wedding as well," her father added. When Hanna didn't respond, her dad kept talking. "If you could. I know it's kind of weird. If it is, we should talk about it. I'd rather have you talk to me than steal cars."

Hanna sniffed. How dare her father think stealing

stuff boiled down to him and his stupid marriage! But then she stopped. *Did* it? "I'll think about it," she said.

Her father ran his hands along the edge of the piano bench. "I'm staying in Philly all weekend, and Saturday, I've booked us for dinner at Le Bec-Fin."

"Really?" Hanna cried, despite herself. Le Bec-Fin was a famous French restaurant in downtown Philadelphia that she'd wanted to eat at for years. Spencer's and Ali's families used to drag them there, and they'd whine about it. It was so snotty, they said, the menu wasn't even in English, and it was full of old ladies in hideous furs that had heads and faces. But to Hanna, Le Bec-Fin sounded totally glamorous.

"And I booked you a suite at the Four Seasons," her father went on. "I know you're supposed to be in trouble, but your mother said it was okay."

"Seriously?" Hanna clapped her hands. She adored staying in fancy hotels.

"It has a pool." He smiled coyly. Hanna used to get really excited when they stayed in hotels with pools. "You could come early Saturday afternoon for a swim."

Suddenly, Hanna's face fell. Saturday was . . . Foxy. "Can we do Sunday instead?"

"Well, no. It has to be Saturday."

Hanna chewed on her lip. "Then I can't."

"Why?"

"I just . . . there's this dance thing. It's sort of . . . important."

Her father folded his hands. "Your mom's letting you go to a dance after . . . after what you did? I thought you were grounded."

Hanna shrugged. "I bought the tickets way in advance. They were expensive."

"It would mean a lot to me if you came," her father said softly. "I'd love a weekend with you."

Her dad looked genuinely *upset*. Almost like he was going to cry. She wanted a weekend with him, too. He'd remembered the molten lava floor, how she used to talk about Le Bec-Fin, and how much she adored ritzy hotels with pools. She wondered if he shared inside jokes like that with Kate. She didn't want him to. She wanted to be special.

"I guess I can blow it off," she finally answered.

"Great." Her father smiled back.

"For Cornelius Maximilian's sake," she added, giving him a shy look.

"Even better."

Hanna watched as her father got into his car and drove slowly down the driveway. A warm, buzzing feeling filled her body. She was so happy, she didn't even think about digging out the bag of kettle chips that she'd thrown back into the pantry. Instead, she felt like dancing through the house.

When she heard her BlackBerry buzzing upstairs, she snapped back to attention. There was so much to do. She had to tell Sean she wasn't going to Foxy. She had to call and tell Mona, too. She had to dig up a fabulous outfit to wear to Le Bec-Fin—maybe that pretty Theory belted dress she hadn't had a chance to wear yet?

She ran upstairs, opened the BlackBerry, and frowned. It was . . . a text.

Four simple words:

Hanna. Marin. Blinded. Jenna.

What would Daddy think about you if he knew that?

I'm watching you, Hanna, and you'd better do what I say. —A

18

SURROUND YOURSELF WITH NORMAL, AND MAYBE YOU'LL BE NORMAL TOO

"You're so lucky you get to go to Foxy for free," Emily's older sister Carolyn said. "You really should take advantage of it."

It was Friday morning, and Emily and Carolyn were outside on the driveway, waiting for their mom to drive them to early-morning swim practice. Emily turned to her sister, running her hand through her hair. As captain, she got free Foxy tickets, but it seemed weird to party so soon after Ali's funeral. "It's not like I'm going to go. I have no one to go with. Ben and I aren't together anymore, so . . ."

"Go with a friend." Carolyn smeared ChapStick over her thin, naturally pink lips. "Topher and I would love to go, but I'd have to spend all my baby-sitting money just on a ticket. So we're going to have movie night at his house instead."

Emily glanced at her sister. Carolyn was a senior and

looked just like Emily, with reddish-blond, chlorine-dried hair, freckles across her cheeks, pale eyelashes, and a strong, compact, swimmer's body. When Emily was named captain, she worried that Carolyn would be jealous—she *was* older. But Carolyn seemed completely fine with the whole thing. Secretly, Emily would have loved to see her wig out about something. Just once.

"Oh hey!" Carolyn perked up. "I saw a funny picture of you yesterday!"

Emily's field of vision narrowed. "Picture?" she repeated hoarsely. She thought of the photo booth picture A had texted her yesterday. A had spread it around. It was starting.

"Yeah, it's from the Tate meet yesterday?" Carolyn reminded her. "You look . . . I don't know. Ambushed. You have this funny expression on your face."

Emily blinked. The picture Scott took. With Toby. Her muscles relaxed. "Oh," she said.

"Emily?"

Emily looked up and made a tiny, inaudible gasp. Maya stood a few feet away from them on the street, straddling her blue Trek mountain bike. Her curly, brownish-black hair was clipped out of her face, and she'd rolled up the sleeves of her white denim jacket. There were dark circles under her eyes. It seemed weird, seeing her at such an early hour of the morning.

"Hey," Emily squeaked. "Um, what's up?"

"This was the only place I thought I could actually catch you." Maya gestured to Emily's house. "You haven't said a word to me since, like, Monday."

Emily glanced over her shoulder at Carolyn, who was now rooting through the front pocket of her purple North Face backpack. She thought again of A's note. *How* could A have gotten those pictures? Didn't Maya have them . . . or had there been others?

"I'm sorry," Emily said to Maya. She didn't know what to do with her hands, so she placed them on top of her mailbox, which was a miniaturized version of her house. "I've been sort of busy."

"Yep, sure looks that way."

The bitterness in Maya's voice made the hair on the back of Emily's neck rise. "W-What do you mean?" Emily snapped.

But Maya merely looked blank and sad. "I . . . I just mean you haven't called me back."

Emily pulled the strings of her red hoodie. "Let's go over here," she murmured, walking to the edge of her property under a weeping willow tree. All she wanted was some simple privacy, so Carolyn wouldn't listen in, but unfortunately, it was kind of sexy under the tree's thick, concealing branches. The light was a very pale green, and Maya's skin looked so . . . dewy. She looked like a wood sprite.

"I have a question for you, actually," Emily whispered, trying to block out all sexy-wood-sprite thoughts. "You know those pictures of us, from the photo booth?"

"Uh-huh." Maya was leaning so close, Emily could almost feel the tips of her hair grazing her cheek. It felt, suddenly, like she'd grown a billion extra nerve endings, and they were all tingling.

"Has anyone seen them?" Emily whispered.

It took Maya a minute to respond. "No . . ."

"Are you sure?"

Maya cocked her head, birdlike, and grinned. "But I'll show them around, if you want. . . ." When she saw Emily cringe, the teasing sparkle in her eyes dimmed. "Wait. Is this why you're avoiding me? You thought I actually *did* show them around?"

"I don't know," Emily mumbled, running her foot along one of the willow's big exposed roots. Her heart was beating so fast, she was pretty sure it was setting some sort of new world record.

Maya reached out and took Emily's chin in her hand, tilting it up so that Emily would look at her. "I wouldn't do that. I want to keep them for myself."

Emily jerked her chin away. This could *not* happen in her front yard. "There's something else you should know. I've . . . I've met someone."

Maya tilted her head. "What kind of someone?"

"His name's Toby. He's really nice. And . . . and I think I like him."

Maya blinked in disbelief, as if Emily had told her she'd fallen in love with a goat.

"And I think I might ask him to Foxy," Emily went on.

The idea had just occurred to Emily, but it felt okay. She liked that Toby wasn't perfect and didn't bother to try. And if she tried hard enough, she could almost forget the complication that he was Jenna's stepbrother. And if she took a boy to Foxy, it would negate those photos from Noel's party and prove to everyone she wasn't gay.

Er, right?

Maya clucked her tongue. "But isn't Foxy tomorrow? What if he has plans?"

Emily shrugged. She was pretty sure Toby didn't.

"And anyway," Maya went on. "I thought you said Foxy was too expensive."

"I was, um, named the captain of the swim team. So I get to go for free."

"Wow," Maya said, after a pause. It was as if Emily could *smell* Maya's disappointment, like it was a phero-mone. Maya had been the person to convince Emily to quit swimming. "Well, congrats, I guess."

Emily stared at her burgundy Vans. "Thanks," she said, even though Maya clearly hadn't meant it nicely. She could feel Maya waiting for her to look up and say, *Silly. I'm just kidding.* Emily felt a surge of irritation. Why did Maya have to make this so difficult? Why couldn't they just be normal friends?

Maya sniffed loudly, then pushed through the tree's branches, back into Emily's yard. Emily followed, only to realize that her mother was at the front door. Mrs. Fields's close-cropped hair was stiff and blown out, and she had her *Don't mess with me, I'm in a hurry* look on her face.

When she noticed Maya, she paled. "Emily, time to go," she barked.

"Sure thing," Emily chirped. She had *not* wanted her mom to see this. She turned back to Maya, who now stood next to her bike at the curb.

Maya was staring at her. "You can't change who you are, Emily," she said in a loud voice. "I hope you know that."

Emily felt her mother and Carolyn staring at her. "I don't know what you're talking about," she cried just as loudly.

"Emily, you're going to be late," Mrs. Fields warned.

Maya gave Emily a parting look, then pedaled furiously down the street. Emily swallowed hard. She felt so ambivalent. On one hand, she was angry at Maya for confronting her—here, in her yard, in front of Carolyn and her mom. On the other, she had the same feeling she did when she was seven years old and had accidentally let go of the Mickey Mouse–shaped balloon she'd begged her parents to buy her at Disney World. She'd watched it float into the sky until it was no longer visible. She'd thought about it for the rest of the trip until her mom said, *It's just a balloon, sweetie! And it's your fault you let go of it!*

She trudged back to the Volvo and gave Carolyn the front seat without a fight. As they pulled out of the driveway, Emily glanced at Maya, now a tiny dot in the distance, then took a deep breath and put her hands on the back of her mother's seat.

"Guess what, Mom. I'm going to ask a boy to the charity thing tomorrow."

"What charity thing?" Mrs. Fields murmured, in a voice that said, *I'm not happy with you right now.*

"Foxy." Carolyn announced, fiddling with the radio. "The annual thing that the news covers. It's so big, some girls get plastic surgery for it."

Mrs. Fields pursed her lips. "I'm not sure I want you going to that."

"But I get to go for free. Because I'm captain."

"You *have* to let her go, Mom," Carolyn urged. "It's *soooo* glamorous."

Mrs. Fields glanced at Emily in the rearview mirror. "Who's the boy?"

"Well, his name is Toby. He used to go to our school, but now he goes to Tate," Emily explained, leaving out where Toby had been for the past three years—and *why.* Luckily, her mother didn't memorize every detail about every Rosewood kid Emily's age, like some mothers did. Carolyn didn't appear to remember the name, either— Carolyn never remembered scandals, not even juicy Hollywood ones. "He's really sweet, and he's a really good swimmer. Way faster than Ben."

"That Ben was nice," Mrs. Fields murmured.

Emily gritted her teeth. "Yeah, but Toby is much,

much nicer." She also wanted to add, *And don't worry, he's white,* but she didn't have the nerve.

Carolyn twisted around in her seat. "Is it the boy in that picture I saw of you?"

"Yeah." Emily said quietly.

Carolyn turned to their mother. "He's *good.* He beat Topher in the 200 free."

Mrs. Fields gave Emily a little smile. "You're supposed to be grounded, but after all the circumstances of this week, I suppose you can go. But no plastic surgery."

Emily frowned. It was just the sort of ridiculous, over-the-top thing her mother would worry about. Last year, Mrs. Fields saw a *20/20* program on crystal meth and how it was everywhere, even in private schools, and she banned Sudafed from the house, as if Emily and Carolyn were going to start up a mini meth lab in their bedroom. She let out a half-laugh. "I'm not going to get—"

But Mrs. Fields started chuckling and caught Emily's eye in the mirror. "I'm only kidding." She nodded to Maya's receding figure, now at the opposite end of their street, and added, "It's nice to see you making new friends."

19

WATCH OUT FOR GIRLS
WITH BRANDING IRONS

The Strawberry Ridge Yoga Studio was in a converted barn on the other side of Rosewood. On her bike ride there, Aria passed a tobacco-colored covered bridge and the row of Hollis art department houses, charmingly ramshackle Colonials that were spatter-painted various shades of purple, pink, and blue. She crammed her bike into the rack in front of the yoga studio; it was already full of other bikes, all bearing MEAT IS MURDER and PETA stickers on their frames.

She paused in the yoga studio's lobby and looked at the scruffy, makeupless girls and hairy, limber boys. Was she crazy to take A's instructions—*Strawberry Ridge Yoga Studio. Be there*—literally? And was she ready to see Meredith? Perhaps A was baiting her. Perhaps A was *here*.

Aria had seen Meredith only three times before: first when Meredith came over to her dad's student-teacher cocktail party, then when she caught Meredith and her dad in the car together, and finally the other day at the Victory, but she'd have recognized her anywhere. Now Meredith was paused in front of the studio's closet, dragging down mats, blankets, blocks, and straps. Her brown hair was up in a messy ponytail and there was that pink spiderweb tattoo on the inside of her wrist.

Meredith noticed Aria and smiled. "You're new, right?" She met Aria's eyes, and for a terrifying second Aria was certain Meredith knew who she was. But then she broke eye contact, leaning over to pop a CD into the portable stereo. Indian sitar music swam out. "Have you done Ashtanga before?"

"Um, yes," Aria answered. She noticed a big sign on the table that said INDIVIDUAL CLASSES $15, and fished out a ten and a five and laid them on the desk, wondering how A knew Meredith was here—and if A really was here.

Meredith smirked. "And I guess you know the secret, huh?"

"W-What?" Aria whispered, her heart pounding. *"Secret?"*

"You brought your own mat." Meredith pointed to the red yoga mat under Aria's arm. "So many new people come here and use the studio's mats. You didn't hear it from me, but you could scrape off the foot fungus on our mats and make cheese."

Aria tried to smile. She'd brought her own yoga mat to classes ever since she first went with Ali in seventh grade. Ali always used to tell her that community yoga mats gave you STDs.

Meredith squinted at her. "You look familiar. Are you in my drawing class?"

Aria shook her head, suddenly aware that the place smelled like a mixture of feet and incense. This was the sort of yoga studio Ella would go to. In fact, perhaps Ella already *had*.

"What's your name?"

"Um, Alison," Aria said quickly. It wasn't as if she had the most common name in the world, and she was afraid Byron might have mentioned it to Meredith. Which made her pause. *Would* Byron talk about Aria to Meredith?

"You look like this girl in the drawing class I TA for," Meredith said. "But class just started. I get everyone confused."

Aria picked up a leaflet for a seminar on Getting to Know Your Chakras. "So, you're a grad student?"

Meredith nodded. "Getting my MFA."

"What is your, um, medium?"

"Well, I do all sorts of stuff. Painting. Drawing." Meredith looked behind Aria and waved at someone else coming in. "But I recently got into branding."

"What?"

"Branding. I weld these custom-made branding irons together to make words, and then I burn the words on big blocks of wood."

"Wait, so the brands are like cattle brands?"

Meredith ducked her head. "I try to explain it, but most people think I'm crazy."

"No," Aria said quickly. "It's cool."

Meredith glanced at the clock on the wall. "We have a couple minutes. I can show you some photos." She reached into a striped cloth bag that sat next to her and pulled out her cell phone. "Just scroll through these, here. . . ."

The photos were of blond slabs of wood. A few just had single letters on them, and a few said short things, like *catch me* and *control freak*. The letters were a little strangely shaped, but looked really cool charred into the wood. Aria flipped to the next photo. It was a longer slab that said, *To err is human, but it feels divine.*

Aria looked up. "Mae West."

Meredith brightened. "It's one of my favorite quotes."

"Same." Aria handed her back the phone. "These are really cool."

Meredith smiled. "Glad you like 'em. I might have a show in a couple months."

"I'm sur . . ." Aria clamped her lips together. She was about to say, *I'm surprised.* She hadn't expected Meredith to be like this. When Aria imagined Meredith, only uncool attributes had come to mind. Imaginary Meredith #1 studied art history and worked for a stuffy, stale gallery somewhere on the Main Line that sold Hudson River School landscapes to rich old ladies.

Imaginary Meredith #2 listened to Kelly Clarkson, loved *Laguna Beach*, and, if encouraged, would lift her shirt to get on *Girls Gone Wild*. Never did Aria think she'd be arty. Why would Byron need an artist? He had Ella.

As Meredith greeted another yoga student, Aria moved into the main studio room. It had high ceilings, exposing the barn's wooden rafters; shiny, caramel-colored wood floors; and large, Indian-print sheets hanging everywhere. Most people had already sat down on their mats and were lying on their backs. It was weirdly silent.

Aria looked around the room. A girl with a brown ponytail and large thighs was doing a backbend. A lanky guy moved from downward dog into child's pose, breathing forcefully through his nose. A blond girl in the corner did a seated twist. When she faced forward, Aria's stomach dropped. "*Spencer?*" she blurted.

Spencer paled and pushed herself onto her knees. "Oh," she said. "Aria. Hey."

Aria swallowed hard. "What are you doing here?"

Spencer looked at her crazily. "Yoga?"

"No, I know that, but . . ." Aria shook her head. "I mean, did someone tell you to come here, or . . . ?"

"No . . ." Spencer narrowed her eyes suspiciously. "Wait. What do you mean?"

Aria blinked. *Wondering who I am? I'm closer than you think.*

She looked from Spencer to Meredith, who was chatting with someone in the lobby, then back to Spencer.

The wheels in her head started to turn. Something about this felt really, really messed up.

Her heart pounded as she backed out of the main room. She rushed to the door, bumping up against a tall, bearded guy in a leotard. Outside, the world was maddeningly impassive to her panic—the birds chirped, the pines swayed, a woman walked by with a baby carriage, talking on her cell phone.

As Aria flung herself toward the bike rack and unlocked her bike, a hand squeezed down on her arm. Hard. Meredith was standing next to her, giving her a very fixed stare. Aria's mouth fell open. She gasped loudly.

"You aren't staying?" Meredith asked.

Aria shook her head. "I . . . um . . . family emergency." She jerked her bike free and started pedaling away.

"Wait!" Meredith screamed. "Let me give you your money back!"

But Aria was already halfway down the block.

20

LAISSEZ-FAIRE MEANS "HANDS OFF," BTW

Friday in AP econ, Andrew Campbell leaned across the aisle and tapped the top of Spencer's notebook. "So, I can't remember. Limo or car to Foxy?"

Spencer rolled her pencil between her fingers. "Um, car, I guess."

It was a tough one. Normally, Promzilla that she was, Spencer always insisted on a limo. And she wanted her family to think she was taking tomorrow's date with Andrew seriously. Only, she felt so tired. Having a brand-new boyfriend was wonderful, but it was tough to try to see him *and* remain Rosewood Day's most ambitious student. Last night, she'd done homework until 2:30 A.M. She'd fallen asleep this morning at yoga—after Aria had so bizarrely run out. Maybe Spencer should have mentioned her note from A, but Aria bolted before she could. She'd dozed off again in study hall. Maybe she could go to the nurse's office and sleep on the little cot for a bit?

Andrew didn't have time to ask any more questions. Mr. McAdam had given up on his battle with the overhead projector—it happened every class—and was now standing at the board. "I'm looking forward to reading everyone's essay questions on Monday," he boomed. "And I have a surprise. If you can e-mail your essays to me by tomorrow, you'll get five points extra credit to reward you for beginning them early."

Spencer blinked, puzzled. She pulled out her Sidekick and checked the date. When had it become Friday? She scrolled to Monday. There it was. Econ essays due.

She hadn't started on them. She hadn't even *thought* about them. After the credit card fiasco Tuesday, Spencer had meant to get McAdam's supplemental books at the library. Except then Wren happened, and the B minus didn't matter as much. Nothing did.

She'd spent Wednesday night at Wren's house. Yesterday, after sneaking into school after third period, she ditched hockey and sneaked into Philly again, taking SEPTA this time instead of driving, because she figured it would be quicker. Except . . . her train stalled. By the time she got into Thirtieth Street station, she only had forty-five minutes before she had to turn around to get home for dinner. So Wren had met her there and they'd made out on a secluded bench behind the concourse's flower stand, emerging flushed with kisses and smelling like lilacs.

She noticed that the first ten cantos of *The Inferno* translated for Italian VI were also due Monday. And a three-page English paper on Plato. A calculus exam. Auditions for *The Tempest*, Rosewood Day's first play of the year, were Monday. She put her head on her desk.

"Ms. Hastings?"

Startled, Spencer looked up. The bell had rung, everyone else had filed out, and she was alone. Squidward stood over her. "Sorry to wake you," he said icily.

"No . . . I really wasn't . . ." Spencer mustered, gathering up her things. But it was too late. Squidward was already erasing notes off the board. She noticed he was slowly shaking his head, as if she were hopeless.

"All right," Spencer whispered. She was sitting at her computer, books and papers around her. Slowly, she mouthed the first essay question again.

Explain Adam Smith's concept of an "invisible hand" in a laissez-faire economy, and give a modern-day example.

Okaaay.

Normally, Spencer would have read the AP econ assignment *and* Adam Smith's book cover to cover, marked the appropriate pages, and made an outline for the answer. But she hadn't. She had no idea what laissez-faire even meant. Was it something to do with supply and demand? What was invisible about it? She typed a few key words into Wikipedia, but the theories were complex and unfamiliar. So were her pages of class notes; she didn't remember writing any of them down.

She'd slaved over school for eleven long, arduous years—twelve, if you counted Montessori school before kindergarten. Just this once, couldn't she write some lame, B-minus paper and make up the grade later in the semester?

But grades were more important than ever. Yesterday, as she and Wren were wrenched from each other at the train station, he suggested she should graduate at the end of this year and apply to Penn. Spencer immediately warmed to the idea, and in the last few minutes before her train pulled up, they'd fantasized about the apartment they'd share, how they'd have separate corners of the room for studying, and how they would get a cat—Wren had never had one when he was young, because his brother was allergic.

The idea had blossomed in Spencer's head on the train ride home, and as soon as she was back in her bedroom, she checked to see if she had enough credits to graduate from Rosewood and downloaded an application to Penn. It was kind of sticky since Melissa went to Penn too, but it was a big school, and Spencer figured they'd never run into each other.

She sighed and glanced at her Sidekick. Wren had told her he'd call today between five and six, and it was now six-thirty. It bothered Spencer when people didn't do what they said they would. She skimmed her phone's missed-calls log, to see if his number was there. She called her voice mail to see if her phone wasn't getting reception. No new messages.

Finally, she tried Wren's number. Voice mail again. Spencer threw her phone over on her bed and looked at her questions again. Adam Smith. Laissez-faire. Invisible hands. Big, strong, doctorly, British hands. All over her body.

She fought the temptation to try Wren again. It seemed too high school—ever since Wren remarked that Spencer seemed so grown-up, she'd started to question her every action. Her cell phone's default ringtone was "My Humps" by Black Eyed Peas; did Wren see it as ironic, as she did, or simply adolescent? What about the lucky stuffed monkey key chain she'd pinned on her backpack? And would an older girl have paused when Wren plucked a single tulip from the flower stand when the florist wasn't looking and handed it to Spencer without paying, thinking they were going to get in trouble?

The sun started to sink into the trees. When her dad poked his head into her room, Spencer jumped. "We're eating soon," he told her. "Melissa's not joining us tonight."

"All right," Spencer answered. These were the first non-hostile words he'd said to her in days.

Light reflected off her dad's platinum Rolex. His face looked almost . . . repentant. "I picked up some of those cinnamon buns you like. I'm heating them up a little."

Spencer blinked. As soon as he said it, she could smell them in the oven. Her dad knew the cinnamon rolls from the Struble Bakery were Spencer's favorite food in the world. The bakery was a hike from his law office and he rarely had time to get them. It was clearly a sticky-bun olive branch.

"Melissa tells us you're taking someone to Foxy," he said. "Anyone we know?"

"Andrew Campbell," Spencer answered.

Mr. Hastings raised an eyebrow. "Class president Andrew Campbell?"

"Yes." It was a touchy subject. Andrew had beat out Spencer for the post; her parents had seemed devastated that she'd lost. Melissa had been class president, after all.

Mr. Hastings looked pleased. Then he lowered his eyes. "Well, it's good that you're . . . I mean, I'm glad this mess is over."

Spencer hoped her cheeks weren't bright red. "Um . . . what does Mom think?"

Her dad gave her a little smile. "She'll come around." He patted the door frame, then continued down the hall. Spencer felt guilty and weird. The cinnamon buns baking downstairs almost smelled like they were burning.

Her cell phone rang, startling her. She dove for it.

"Hey there." Wren sounded happy and boisterous when she picked up, which instantly irritated Spencer. "What's up?"

"Where have you been?" Spencer demanded.

Wren paused. "Some school friends and I are hanging out before our shift today."

"Why didn't you call earlier?"

Wren paused. "It was loud in the bar." His voice became distant, annoyed.

Spencer clenched up her fists. "I'm sorry," she said. "I think I'm a little stressed."

"Spencer Hastings, stressed?" She could tell Wren was smiling. "Why?"

"Econ paper," she sighed. "It's impossible."

"Ugh," Wren said. "Blow it off. Come meet me."

Spencer paused. Her notes were scattered haphazardly across her desk. On the floor was this week's quiz. The B minus glowed like a neon sign. "I can't."

"All right," Wren groaned. "So tomorrow, then? Can I have you all day?"

Spencer bit the inside of her cheek. "I can't tomorrow, either. I . . . I have to go to this benefit thing. I'm going with this boy from school."

"A *date*?"

"Not really."

"Why didn't you ask me?"

Spencer frowned. "It's not like I *like* him. He's just this kid from school. But, I mean, I won't, if you don't want me to."

Wren chuckled. "I'm just giving you a hard time. Go to your charity thing. Have a blast. We can hang out on Sunday." Then he said he had to run—he needed to get to his shift at the hospital. "Good luck with your work," he added. "I'm sure you'll figure it out."

Spencer stared wistfully at the CALL ENDED window on her phone's screen. Their conversation had lasted a whopping one minute and forty-six seconds. "Of course I'll figure it out," she whispered to the phone. With about a week's extension.

As she passed her computer, she noticed a new e-mail at the top of her inbox. It had come in about five minutes ago, while she was talking to her father.

Want the easy A? I think you know where to find it. —A

Spencer's stomach tightened. She glanced out the window, but there was no one on her lawn. Then she stuck her head outside, checking to see if someone had installed a surveillance camera or put in a mini microphone. But all she saw was her house's grayish-brown stone exterior.

Melissa kept her high school papers on the family computer. She was as anal as Spencer, and saved everything. Spencer wouldn't even have to ask Melissa for permission to look at the papers—they were on the shared drive.

But how the hell did A know that?

It *was* tempting. Except . . . no. Anyway, Spencer doubted A wanted to help her. Was this an elaborate trap? Could A *be* Melissa?

"Spencer?" her mother called from downstairs. "Dinner!"

Spencer minimized the e-mail and walked absent-mindedly to the door. The thing was, if she took Melissa's paper, she'd have time to finish her other homework *and* see Wren. She could switch some words . . . use the thesaurus. . . . She'd never do it again.

Her computer made another *ting*, and she turned back.

P.S. You hurt me, so I'm going to hurt you. Or maybe I should hurt a certain new boyfriend instead? You guys better watch out—I'll show up when you least expect it.

—A

21

SOME SECRET ADMIRER . . .

Friday afternoon, Hanna sat on the soccer bleachers, watching the Rosewood Day boys' team battle Lansing Prep. Only she couldn't really focus. Her normally manicured fingernails were ragged, the skin around her thumbs was bleeding from nervous picking, and her eyes had become so red from sleeplessness, it looked like she had pinkeye. She should have been hiding at home. Sitting on the bleachers was way too public.

I'm watching you, A had said. *You'd better do what I say.*

But maybe it was like what politicians said about terrorist attacks: If you holed up in your house, afraid they were going to strike, it would mean the terrorists had won. She would sit here and watch soccer, like she had all last year and the year before that.

But then Hanna looked around. That someone really, truly knew about The Jenna Thing—and was poised to

blame *her*—terrified her. And what if A really did tell her
dad? Not now. Not when things might be getting better.

She craned her neck for the millionth time toward
the commons, looking for Mona. Watching the boys'
games was a little Hanna-Mona tradition; they mixed
SoCo with syrupy Diet Dr Peppers from the concession
stand and yelled sexy insults at the away team. But Mona
was AWOL. Since their weird fight at the mall yesterday,
Hanna and Mona hadn't spoken.

Hanna caught a glimpse of a blond ponytail and
a loose red braid and cringed. Riley and Naomi had
arrived, and had climbed up to a spot not that far away
from Hanna. Today, both girls carried matching patent
leather Chanel bags and wore obviously brand-spanking-
new swingy tweed coats, as if it were actually a chilly
fall day and not still a summery seventy-five degrees.
When they looked in Hanna's direction, Hanna quickly
pretended to be fascinated with the soccer game, even
though she had no idea what the score was.

"Hanna looks fat in that outfit," she overheard
Riley whisper.

Hanna felt her cheeks heat up. She stared at the way
her cotton C&C California top gently stretched against
her midsection. She probably was getting fatter, with all
the nervous eating she'd been doing this week. It was just
that she was really trying to resist the urge to throw it all
up—although, that was what she wanted to do right now.

The teams broke for halftime, and the Rosewood

Day boys trotted to their bench. Sean flopped down on the grass and started massaging his calf. Hanna saw her chance and clomped down the bleacher's metallic seats. Yesterday, after A texted her, she hadn't called Sean to tell him she wasn't going to Foxy. She'd been too shell-shocked.

"Hanna," Sean said, seeing her standing over him. "Hey." He looked beautiful today as usual, despite his shirt being sweat-stained and his face a teensy bit unshaven. "How are you?"

Hanna sat down next to him, tucking her legs under her and arranging her pleated uniform skirt around her so all the soccer players couldn't see her undies. "I'm . . ." She swallowed hard, trying not to burst into tears. *Losing my mind. Being tortured by A.* "So, um, listen." She clasped her hands together. "I'm not going to Foxy."

"Really?" Sean cocked his head. "Why not? Are you okay?"

Hanna ran her hands through the closely cropped, sweet-smelling soccer field grass. She'd told Sean the same story she'd told Mona—that her father had died. "It's . . . complicated. But, um, I thought I should tell you."

Sean unfastened the Velcro on his shin guard and then tightened it up again. For a brief second, Hanna got a glimpse of his perfect, sinewy calves. For whatever reason, she thought they were the sexiest part of his body. "I might not go, either," he said.

"Really?" she asked, startled.

Sean shrugged. "All my friends are going with dates. I'd be the odd guy out."

"Oh." Hanna moved her legs out of the way so the soccer coach, who was staring at his clipboard, could pass by. She resisted smacking herself. Did that mean Sean had thought of her as his date?

Sean shaded his eyes and stared at her. "Are you all right? You seem . . . sad."

Hanna cupped her hands over her bare knees. She needed to talk to someone about A. Except there was no way. "I'm just tired." She sighed.

Sean touched Hanna's wrist lightly. "Listen. Maybe some night next week, let's get dinner. I don't know. . . . We probably should talk about stuff."

Hanna's heart did a tiny leap. "Sure. That sounds nice."

"Cool." Sean smiled, standing up. "See you later, then."

The band started playing the Rosewood Day fight song, signaling that the team's break was over. Hanna climbed back to the top of the bleachers, feeling a little better. As she returned to her seat, Riley and Naomi were looking at her curiously.

"Hanna!" Naomi cried, when Hanna met her gaze. "Hi!"

"Hey," Hanna said, mustering up as much fake-sweetness as she could.

"Were you talking to Sean?" Naomi ran her hand through her blond ponytail. She was always obsessively petting her hair. "I thought you guys had a bad breakup."

"It wasn't a bad breakup," Hanna said. "We're still friends . . . and whatever."

Riley let out a little laugh. "And *you* broke up with him, right?"

Hanna's stomach lurched. Had someone said something? "That's right."

Naomi and Riley exchanged a look. Then Naomi said, "Are you going to Foxy?"

"Actually, no," Hanna said haughtily. "I'm meeting my father at Le Bec-Fin."

"Ooh." Naomi winced. "I heard Le Bec-Fin was, like, the place people take people when they don't want to be seen."

"No, it's not." Heat rose to Hanna's face. "It's, like, the best restaurant in Philly." She started to panic. Had Le Bec-Fin changed?

Naomi shrugged, her face impassive. "It's just what I've heard, is all."

"Yeah." Riley widened her brown eyes. "Everyone knows that."

Suddenly, Hanna noticed a piece of paper sitting next to her on the bleachers. It was folded in the shape of an airplane and weighed down with a rock.

"What's that?" Naomi called. "Origami?"

Hanna unfolded the airplane and turned it over.

Hi again, Hanna! I want you to read Naomi and Riley the sentences below just as they're written. No cheating! And

if you don't, everyone will know the truth about you-know-
what. That includes Daddy. —A

Hanna stared at the paragraph below, written in rounded, unfamiliar handwriting. "No," she whispered, her heart starting to pound. What A had written would ruin her flawless rep forever:

I tried to get in Sean's pants at Noel's party, but he dumped me instead. And, oh yeah, I make myself throw up at least three times a day.

"Hanna, did you get a *luuuuve* letter?" Riley cooed. "Is it from a secret admirer?"

Hanna glanced at Naomi and Riley, in their short-ened pleated skirts and wedge heels. They both stared at her like wolves, as if they could smell her weakness. "Did you see who put this here?" she asked, but they looked at her blankly and shrugged.

Next she looked around the soccer bleachers, at every clump of kids, every parent, even at Lansing's bus driver in the parking lot, leaning against the back of the bus smoking a cigarette. Whoever was doing this to her had to be *here*, right? They would have to know Riley and Naomi were sitting near her.

She looked at the note again. She couldn't say this to them. There was no way.

But then she thought about the final time her dad asked her about Jenna's accident. He'd sat down on her bed and spent a long time staring at the knitted socktopus Aria had made for her. "Hanna," he finally said. "I'm worried about you. Promise me you guys weren't playing with fireworks the night that girl was blinded."

"I . . . I didn't touch the fireworks," Hanna whispered. It wasn't a lie.

Down on the soccer field, two Lansing boys were giving each other high fives. Somewhere under the bleachers, someone lit up a joint; its skunky, mossy smell wafted into Hanna's nostrils. She crumpled up the piece of paper, stood up, and, stomach churning, walked over to Naomi and Riley. They looked up at her, bemused. Riley's mouth hung open. Her breath, Hanna noticed, stunk like someone who was on Atkins.

"Itriedtogetinseanspantsatnoelspartybuthedumpedmeinstead," Hanna blurted out. She took a deep breath. The part wasn't even exactly *true*, but whatever. "AndImakemyselfbarfthreetimesaday."

The words came out in a fast, unintelligible jumble, and Hanna turned swiftly around. "*What* did she say?" she heard Riley whisper, but she certainly wasn't going to turn around and make herself clearer.

She stomped down the bleachers, ducking around someone's mother who was carrying a precarious tray of Cokes and popcorn. She looked for someone—*anyone*—who might be looking back. But nothing. Not a single person was giggling or whispering. Everyone was just watching the Rosewood Day soccer boys advance toward Lansing's goal.

But A had to be here. A had to be watching.

22

YOU CAN'T HANDLE THE TRUTH

Friday evening, Aria shut off the radio in her bedroom. For the past hour, the local DJ had gone on and on about Foxy. He made it sound as if Foxy were a shuttle launch or a presidential inauguration, not just some silly benefit.

She listened to the sounds of her parents walking around the kitchen. There wasn't the usual cacophony of noise—NPR on the radio, CNN or PBS on the kitchen TV, or a classical or experimental jazz CD playing on the kitchen stereo. All Aria heard were pots and pans clanging. Then a crash. "Sorry," Ella said curtly. "It's fine," Byron answered.

Aria turned back to her laptop, feeling more and more crazed by the second. Since her Meredith-stalk had been cut short, she was now researching her online. Once you started Web-stalking someone, it was hard to stop. Aria had Meredith's last name—Stevens—from a Strawberry Ridge Yoga schedule she found online, so she searched

Google for Meredith's phone number. She thought maybe she'd try to call to tell her, kindly, to stay away from Byron. But then she found her address and wanted to see how far away Meredith lived, so she mapped it on MapQuest. From there, it got nuts. She looked at a hypertext paper Meredith had done in her freshman year of college on William Carlos Williams. She hacked into Hollis's student portal to see Meredith's grades. Meredith was on Friendster, Facebook, *and* MySpace. Her favorite movies were *Donnie Darko*; *Paris, Texas*; and *The Princess Bride*, and her interests were quirky things like snow globes, tai chi, and magnets.

In a parallel universe, Aria and Meredith could have been *friends*. It made it even harder to do what A asked in Aria's last text message: *make it go away.*

It felt like A's threat was burning a hole in her Treo, and whenever she thought about seeing not only Meredith but *Spencer* in the yoga studio that morning, she felt uneasy. What was Spencer doing there? Did Spencer know something?

Back in seventh grade, Aria had told Ali about seeing Toby at her drama workshop while she, Ali, and Spencer were hanging out at Spencer's pool. "He doesn't know anything, Aria," Ali had answered, calmly applying more sunscreen. "Chill out."

"But how can you be sure?" Aria had protested. "What about that person I saw outside the tree house that night? Maybe they told Toby! Maybe it *was* Toby!"

Spencer frowned, then glanced at Alison. "Ali, maybe you should just—"

Ali cleared her throat loudly. "Spence," she said, sort of as a warning.

Aria looked back and forth at them, confused. Then she blurted out the question she'd wanted to ask for a while: "What were you guys whispering about the night of her accident? When I woke up and you were in the bathroom?"

Ali cocked her head. "We weren't whispering."

"Ali, we *were*," Spencer hissed.

Ali gave her another sharp look, then turned back to Aria. "Look, we weren't talking about Toby. Besides"— she gave Aria a little smile—"don't you have bigger things to worry about right now?"

Aria bristled. Just days before, Aria and Ali had caught her father with Meredith.

Spencer tugged Ali's arm. "Ali, I really think you should tell—"

Ali held up her hand. "Spence, I swear to God."

"You swear to God *what*?" Spencer shrieked. "You think this is easy?"

After Aria saw Spencer at the yoga studio this morning, she'd considered tracking her down in school and talking to her. Spencer and Ali had covered something up, and maybe it was tangled in A. But . . . she felt afraid. She thought she'd known her old friends inside and out. But now that she knew they all had dark secrets they didn't want to share . . . maybe she'd never really known them at all.

Aria's cell phone rang, breaking her out of the memory. Startled, she dropped it into a pile of dirty T-shirts she'd been meaning to wash. She grabbed it.

"Hey," said a boy's voice on the other end. "It's Sean."

"Oh!" Aria exclaimed. "What's up?"

"Not much. Just got back from a soccer game. What are you doing tonight?"

Aria wiggled with glee. "Um . . . nothing, really."

"Wanna hang out?"

She heard another clatter downstairs. Then her father's voice. "I'm going." The front door slammed. He wasn't even going to have dinner with them. *Again.*

She put her mouth back to the phone. "How about right now?"

Sean parked his Audi in a desolate lot and led Aria up an embankment. To their left was a chain-link fence, to their right a sloping path. Above them were the elevated train tracks, and below them was all of Rosewood. "My brother and I found this place years ago," Sean explained.

He spread his cashmere sweater on the grass and gestured for her to sit. Then he pulled a chrome thermos out of his backpack and handed it to her. "Want some?" Aria could smell the Captain Morgan through the little space in the lid.

She took a greedy swig, then looked at him crookedly.

His face was so chiseled and his clothes fit so perfectly, but he didn't have the same *I'm hot and I know it* air about him that other typical Rosewood boys did. "You come here a lot?" she asked.

Sean shrugged and sat down next to her. "Not a lot. But sometimes."

Aria had assumed Sean and his typical Rosewood boy crowd drove around partying all night, or sneaked their parents' beer at someone's empty house while playing Grand Theft Auto on PlayStation. And there would be a soak in a hot tub to cap off the night, of course. Pretty much everyone in Rosewood had a hot tub in their backyard.

The town lights twinkled below. Aria could see Hollis's spire, which was lit up in ivory at night. "This is amazing," she sighed. "I can't believe I've never found this place."

"Well, we used to live not far from here." Sean smiled. "My brother and I rode all over these woods on our dirt bikes. We also used to come here and play Blair Witch."

"Blair Witch?" Aria repeated.

He nodded. "After the movie came out, we were obsessed with making our own ghost movies."

"I did that too!" Aria cried, so excited she laid her hand on Sean's arm. She quickly pulled it away. "Except I did mine in my backyard."

"You still have the videos?" Sean asked.

"Yep. You?"

"Uh-huh." Sean paused. "Maybe you could come see them some time."

"I'd like that." She smiled. Sean was starting to remind her of the *croque-monsieur* she once ordered in Nice. At first glance, it looked like a plain, cookie-cutter grilled cheese, nothing special. But when she bit into it, the cheese was Brie and there were chopped-up portabello mushrooms hidden underneath. There was a lot more to it than it had appeared.

Sean leaned back on his elbows. "One time, my brother and I came here and caught this couple having sex."

"Really?" Aria giggled.

Sean took the mug from her. "Yeah. And they were so into it, they didn't see us at first. I backed up really slowly but then tripped over some rocks. They totally freaked."

"I'm sure." She shivered. "God, that would be awful."

Sean poked her in the arm. "What, you've never done it in public?"

Aria looked away. "Nah."

They were quiet for a moment. Aria wasn't sure how she felt. Uneasy, sort of. But also . . . a little buzzy. It felt like something was going to happen. "So, um, remember that secret you told me, in your car?" she asked. "The one about not wanting to be a virgin?"

"Yeah."

"Why do you . . . why do you think you feel that way?"

Sean leaned back on his elbows. "I started going to V Club because everybody was rushing to have sex, and I wanted to see why the people at V Club decided not to."

"And?"

"Well, I think they're mostly scared. But also, I think they want to find the right person. Like, someone they can be completely honest and themselves with."

He paused. Aria hugged her knees to her chest. She wished—just a little—that Sean would say, *And Aria, I think you're the right person.* She sighed. "I had sex, once."

Sean put the mug in the grass and looked at her.

"In Iceland, a year after I moved there," she admitted. It felt strange to say it out loud. "It was this boy I liked. Oskar. He wanted to, and so did I, but . . . I don't know." She pushed her hair out of her face. "I didn't love him or anything." She paused. "You're the first person I ever told."

They were quiet for a while. Aria felt her heart thumping against her chest. Someone far below was grilling; she could smell the charcoal and the burgers. She heard Sean swallow and shift his weight, moving a little closer. She moved a little closer, too, feeling nervous.

"Go to Foxy with me," Sean blurted out.

Aria cocked her head. "F-Foxy?"

"The benefit thing? You dress up? Dance?"

She blinked. "I know what Foxy is."

"Unless you're going with someone else. And we could go as friends, of course."

Aria felt a tiny twinge of disappointment when he

used the word *friends*. A second ago, she'd thought they were going to kiss. "You haven't asked anyone already?"

"No. That's why I asked you."

Aria sneaked a peek at Sean. Her eyes kept gravitating toward the little cleft in his chin. Ali used to call them "butt chins," but it was actually pretty cute. "Um, yeah, okay."

"Cool." Sean grinned. Aria grinned back. Except . . . something made her wilt. *I'm giving you till the stroke of midnight Saturday night, Cinderella. Or else.* Saturday was tomorrow.

Sean noticed her expression. "What is it?"

Aria swallowed. Her whole mouth tasted like rum. "I met the woman my dad's fooling around with yesterday. Sort of by accident." She took a deep breath. "Or not by accident at all. I wanted to ask her what was going on, but I couldn't. I'm just afraid my mom's going to . . . to catch them together." Tears came to her eyes. "I don't want my family to fall apart."

Sean held her for a while. "Couldn't you try talking to the girl again?"

"I don't know." She stared at her hands. They were shaking. "I mean, I have this whole speech for her figured out in my head. I just want her to know my side." She arched her back and looked up at the sky, as if the universe might give her the answer. "But maybe it's a stupid idea."

"It's not. I'll go with you. For moral support."

She looked up. "You . . . you *would*?"

Sean glanced out over the trees. "Right now, if you want."

Aria quickly shook her head. "I couldn't right now. I left my, um, script at home."

Sean shrugged. "Do you remember what you want to say?"

"I guess," Aria said faintly. She looked out over the trees. "It's not far, actually. . . . She lives right over this hill. In Old Hollis." She knew this from stalking Meredith on Google Earth.

"C'mon." Sean extended his hand. Before she could think too much about it, they were scampering down the grassy hill, past Sean's car.

They crossed the street into Old Hollis, the student neighborhood that was full of crumbling, spooky Victorian houses. Old VWs, Volvos, and Saabs lined the curbs. For a Friday night, the neighborhood was absolutely empty. Perhaps there was some big event in Hollis elsewhere. Aria wondered if Meredith would even be home; she sort of hoped that she wouldn't be.

Halfway down the second block, Aria stopped at a pink house that had four pairs of running shoes airing out on the porch and a chalk drawing of what looked like a penis on the driveway. It was only fitting that Meredith lived here. "I think this is it."

"You want me to wait here?" Sean whispered.

Aria pulled her sweater around her. It was suddenly

freezing. "I guess." Then she grabbed Sean's arm. "I can't do this."

"Sure you can." Sean put his hands on her shoulders. "I'll be right here, okay? Nothing's going to happen to you. I promise."

Aria felt a rush of gratitude. He was so . . . sweet. She leaned forward and gently kissed Sean on the lips; as she pulled away, he looked stunned. "Thank you," she said.

She walked up Meredith's cracked front steps slowly, the rum coursing through her veins. She'd drunk three-quarters of Sean's thermos, while he'd only taken a few gentlemanly sips. As she rang the bell, she steadied herself against one of the porch's columns for balance. Tonight was not the night to be wearing her wobbly sling-backs from Italy.

Meredith flung open the door. She wore terry-cloth short-shorts and a white T-shirt with a drawing of a banana on it—it was the cover to some old album, Aria just couldn't remember what. And she seemed bigger tonight. Less lithe and more muscular, like the ass-kicking chicks on that show, *Rollergirls*. Aria felt puny.

Meredith's eyes brightened with recognition. "Alison, right?"

"Actually, it's Aria. Aria Montgomery. I'm Byron Montgomery's daughter. I know everything that's going on. I want it to stop."

Meredith's eyes widened. She took a deep breath, then exhaled slowly through her nose. Aria almost thought dragonlike steam was going to come out. "You do, huh?"

"That's right," Aria wavered, realizing she was slurring her speech. *Thassright.* And her heart was beating so loud, she wouldn't have been surprised if her skin was pulsating.

Meredith raised an eyebrow. "It's none of your business." She stuck her head out on the porch and looked around suspiciously. "How did you find out where I lived?"

"Look, you're destroying everything," Aria protested. "And I just want it to stop. Okay? I mean . . . this is hurting everyone. He's still married . . . and he has a family."

Aria winced to herself at the pathetic edge to her voice and how her perfectly crafted speech had slipped from her grasp.

Meredith crossed her arms over her chest. "I do know all that," she answered, starting to shut the door. "And I'm sorry. I really am. But we're in love."

23

NEXT STOP, GREATER
ROSEWOOD JAIL

Late Saturday afternoon, a few hours before Foxy, Spencer
sat at her computer. She'd just addressed an e-mail to
Squidward and attached her essays. *Just send it,* she told
herself. She closed her eyes, clicked the mouse, and,
when she opened them, her work had been sent.

Well, it was *sort of* her work.

She hadn't cheated. Really. Well, maybe she had.
But who could blame her? After A's message came in
last night, she'd spent the whole night calling Wren, but
his phone kept going to voice mail. And she'd left five
messages for him, each of them becoming more frantic.
She'd put on her shoes twelve separate times, ready to
drive into Philadelphia to see if Wren was okay, but
then talked herself out of it. The one time her Sidekick
chimed, she dove for it, but it was just a classwide e-mail
from Squidward, reminding everyone of the proper
annotation style for the essay questions.

When someone put their hand on Spencer's shoulder, she screamed.

Melissa stepped back. "Whoa! Sorry! Just me!"

Spencer righted herself, breathing hard. "I . . ." She surveyed her desk. *Shit.* There was a slip of paper that said, *Gynecologist, Tuesday, 5 P.M. Ortho Tri-Cyclen?* And she had Melissa's old history essays on her computer screen. She kicked the computer hard drive's on/off switch with her foot, and the monitor went black.

"You stressed?" Melissa asked. "Lots of homework before Foxy?"

"Kinda." Spencer quickly shoved all of her desk's random papers into neat piles.

"Wanna borrow my lavender neck pillow?" Melissa asked. "It's a stress reliever."

"That's all right," Spencer answered, not even daring to look at her sister. *I stole your paper and your boyfriend,* she thought. *You shouldn't be nice to me.*

Melissa pushed her lips together. "Well, not to make you more stressed, but there's a cop downstairs. He says he wants to ask you some questions."

"*What?*" Spencer cried.

"It's about Alison." Melissa said. She shook her head, making the ends of her hair swing. "They shouldn't make you talk about it—the *week* of her memorial. It's sick."

Spencer tried not to panic. She stared at herself in the mirror, smoothing down her blond hair and dabbing concealer under her eyes. She pulled on a white button-down blouse and skinny khaki pants. There. She looked trustworthy and innocent.

But her whole body was shaking.

Sure enough, there was a cop standing in the living room but looking into her father's second office, where he kept his vintage guitar collection. When the cop turned around, Spencer realized that he wasn't the one she'd spoken to at the funeral. This guy was young. And he looked familiar, like she might've seen him somewhere else.

"Are you Spencer?" he asked.

"Yes," she said quietly.

He stuck out his hand. "I'm Darren Wilden. I've just been assigned to Alison DiLaurentis's murder case."

"Murder," Spencer repeated.

"Yes," Officer Wilden said. "Well, we're investigating it as a murder."

"Okay." Spencer tried to sound even and mature. "Wow."

Wilden motioned for Spencer to sit down on her living room couch; then he sat opposite her on the chaise. She realized where she knew him from: Rosewood Day. He'd gone there when she was in sixth grade, and he'd earned a reputation as a badass. One of Melissa's nerdy friends, Liana, had a crush on him, and once made Spencer deliver a secret admirer note to him at the espresso bar where he worked. Spencer recalled thinking that Darren had biceps the size of Chunky Soup cans.

Now he was staring at her. Spencer felt her nose itch, and the grandfather clock made a few loud ticks. Finally, he said, "Is there anything you'd like to tell me?"

Fear shot through her chest. "Tell you?"

Wilden sat back. "About Alison."

Spencer blinked. Something about this felt wrong. "She was my best friend," she managed. Her palms felt sweaty. "I was with her the night she went missing."

"Right." Wilden looked at a notepad. "That's in our files. You talked to someone at the police station after she went missing, right?"

"Yes. Twice."

"Right." Wilden clasped his hands together. "Are you sure you told them *everything*? Was there someone who hated Alison? Maybe the officer asked you all these questions before, but since I'm new, maybe you could refresh my memory."

Spencer's brain stalled. Truthfully, lots of girls had hated Ali. *Spencer* even hated Ali sometimes, especially the way she always could manipulate her, and how she'd threatened to point the finger at Spencer for The Jenna Thing if she ever told what she knew. And secretly, it was kind of a relief when Ali disappeared. Ali gone and Toby away at school meant their secret was hidden for good.

She swallowed hard. She wasn't sure what this cop knew. A could have tipped the cops off that she was hiding something. And it was brilliant—if Spencer told him, *Yes, I do know someone who hated Ali,* really *hated her enough to kill her,* she'd have to confess her involvement in The Jenna Thing. If she said nothing and protected herself, A still might punish her friends . . . and Wren.

You hurt me, so I'm going to hurt you.

Sweat prickled on the back of her neck. But then there was more: What if Toby was back to hurt her? What if he and A were working together? What if he was A? But if he was—and he killed Ali—would he go to the cops and incriminate himself? "I'm pretty sure I told them everything," she finally said.

There was a long, long pause. Wilden stared at Spencer. Spencer stared at Wilden. It made Spencer think about the night after The Jenna Thing happened. She'd dozed into a fitful, paranoid sleep, her friends quietly crying around her. But all of a sudden, she was awake again. The cable box clock said 3:43 A.M., and the room was still. She felt unhinged, and found Ali, sleeping sitting up on the couch with Emily's head in her lap. "I can't do this," she said, shaking her awake. "We should turn ourselves in."

Ali got up, led Spencer into the hall bathroom, and sat down on the edge of the tub. "Get a grip, Spence," Ali said. "You can't spaz if the police ask us questions."

"The *police*?" Spencer shrieked, her heart picking up speed.

"*Shhh,*" Ali whispered. She drummed her nails against the tub's porcelain edge. "I'm not saying the police are definitely going to talk to us, but we have to make a plan in case they *do*. All we need is a solid story. An alibi."

"Why can't we just tell them the truth?" Spencer asked. "Exactly what you saw Toby do, and that it surprised you so much, you set the firework off by accident?"

Ali shook her head. "It's better my way. We keep Toby's secret, he keeps ours."

A knock on the door made them stand up. "Guys?" a voice called. It was Aria.

"Fair enough," Wilden finally said, breaking Spencer from her memory. He handed her a business card. "Call me if you think of anything, all right?"

"Of course," Spencer whimpered.

Wilden put his hands on his hips and looked around the room. At the Chippendale furniture; the exquisite stained-glass window; the heavy, framed art on the walls; and her father's prized George Washington clock that had been in the family since the 1800s. Then he canvassed Spencer, from the diamond studs in her ears to the delicate Cartier watch on her wrist to her blond highlights, which cost $300 every six weeks. The smug little smile on his face seemed to say, *You seem like a girl who has a lot to lose.*

"You going to that benefit tonight?" he asked, making her jump. "Foxy?"

"Um, yeah," Spencer said quietly.

"Well." Wilden gave her a little salute. "Have fun." His voice was totally normal, but she could've sworn the look on his face said, *I'm not through with you yet.*

24

$250 GETS YOU DINNER, DANCING . . . AND A WARNING

Foxy was held in Kingman Hall, an old English countryside mansion built by a man who'd invented some new-fangled milking machine in the early 1900s. In fourth grade, when they learned about the hall in the All About Pennsylvania social studies unit, Emily nicknamed it "Moo Mansion."

As the check-in girl scrutinized their invites, Emily looked around. The place had a labyrinthine garden in its front yard. Gargoyles leered from the arches of the mansion's stately front. Ahead of her was the tent where the actual event was being held. It was lit up with fairy lights and full of people.

"Wow." Toby came up beside her. Beautiful girls swished by them toward the tent, wearing elaborate, custom-made dresses and carrying bejeweled bags. Emily looked down at her own dress—it was a simple, strapless pink sheath Carolyn had worn to prom last year. She'd done her hair herself, put on a lot of Carolyn's ultra-girly Lovely perfume—which made her sneeze—and was wearing earrings for the first time in a while, poking them forcefully through the holes in her ears that had almost closed up. Even with all that, she still felt plain next to everyone else.

Yesterday, when Emily called Toby to ask him to Foxy, he'd sounded so surprised—but really excited. She was psyched, too. They would go to Foxy, share another kiss, and who knew? Maybe become a couple. In time, they would visit Jenna at her school in Philadelphia, and Emily would somehow make it all up to her. She'd foster Jenna's next Seeing Eye dog. She'd read to her all the books that hadn't yet come out in Braille. Maybe, in time, Emily would confess her involvement in Jenna's accident.

Or maybe not.

Except now that she was at Foxy, something just felt . . . wrong. Emily's body kept feeling hot, then cold, and her stomach kept clenching up in pain. Toby's hands felt too scratchy, and she'd been so nervous, they'd barely said anything to each other on the way over. Foxy itself didn't seem to be very calming, either; everyone was so stiff and poised. And Emily was sure someone was watching her. As she inspected every girl's made-up, glossy face and every guy's scrubbed, handsome one, she wondered, *Are you A?*

"Smile!" A flashbulb popped in Emily's face, and she let out a little scream. When the spots faded from her eyes, a blond girl in a merlot-red dress with a press badge over her right boob and a digital camera slung over her shoulder was laughing at her. "I was just taking photos for the *Philadelphia Inquirer*," she explained. "Wanna try that again, without the freaked expression this time?" Emily clutched Toby's arm and tried to look happy, except her expression was more of a petrified grimace.

After the press girl whirled away, Toby turned to Emily. "Is something wrong? You seemed so relaxed in front of a camera before."

Emily stiffened. "When have you seen me in front of a camera?"

"The Rosewood versus Tate?" Toby reminded her. "That crazy yearbook kid?"

"Oh, right." Emily breathed out.

Toby's eyes followed a waiter scurrying around with a drink tray. "So, is this your scene?"

"God, no!" Emily said. "I've never been to anything like this in my life."

He looked around. "Everyone looks so . . . so plastic. I used to want to kill most of these people."

A sharp, startled frisson passed through Emily. It was the same sort of feeling she'd felt when she woke up in the back of Toby's car. When Toby noticed her face, he quickly smiled. "Not *literally*." He squeezed her hand. "You're much prettier than all the girls here."

Emily flushed. Only she was finding that her insides didn't turn upside down when he said it or when he touched her. They *should*. Toby looked hot. Gorgeous, actually, in his black suit and black wingtips, with his hair pushed back off his angular, square-jawed face. Every girl was checking him out. When he'd shown up on her porch, even mild-mannered Carolyn had squealed, "He's so cute!"

But when he held her hand, as much as she wanted it to feel like something, it felt like nothing. It was like holding hands with her sister.

Emily tried to relax. She and Toby made their way into the tent, got two virgin piña coladas, and joined a bunch of kids on the dance floor. There were only a handful of girls who were trying to dance in that über-sexy, hands-above-the-head, I'm getting my moves down for MTV Spring Break way. Most everyone else was just jumping around, singing along to Madonna. Technicians were setting up a karaoke machine in the corner, and girls were writing down the songs they wanted to sing.

Emily broke away to go to the bathroom, leaving the tent and walking through a sexy, candlelit hallway paved in rose petals. Girls passed her, arm and arm, whispering and giggling. Emily discreetly checked out her chest; she'd never worn a strapless dress before and was certain it was going to fall down and expose her boobs to the world.

"Want a reading?"

Emily looked over. A dark-haired woman dressed in a silky, paisley-print dress sat at a small table under a huge portrait of Horace Kingman, the milking-machine inventor himself. She wore a ton of bracelets on her left arm and a large snake brooch at her throat. A deck of cards sat next to her along with a little sign at the edge of the table: THE MAGIC OF THE TAROT.

"That's okay," Emily told her. The tarot reader was so . . . public. Out here in the open, in the middle of the hall.

The woman extended a long fingernail toward her. "You need one, though. Something's going to happen to you tonight. Something life-changing."

Emily stiffened. *"Me?"*

"Yes, you. And the date you brought? He's not the one you want. You must go to the one you really love."

Emily's mouth fell open, and her mind began to race.

The tarot reader looked as if she was about to say something else, but Naomi Zeigler pushed past Emily and sat down at the table. "I met you here last year," Naomi gushed, leaning excitedly on her elbows. "You gave me the best reading ever."

Emily slunk away, her mind churning. Something was going to happen to her tonight? Something . . . *life-changing*? Maybe Ben was going to tell everyone. Or Maya was going to tell everyone. A was going to show everyone those pictures. Or A had told Toby. . . about Jenna. It could be anything.

Emily splashed cold water on her face and exited the bathroom. As she made the turn for the tent, she bumped into someone's back. As soon as she saw who it was, her body tensed.

"Hey," Ben said in a mock-friendly tone, drawing the word out. He wore a charcoal suit and had a small white gardenia pinned to his lapel.

"H-Hey," Emily stammered. "I didn't know you were coming."

"I was going to say the same thing to you." Ben leaned down. "I like your date." He put *date* in air quotes. "I saw you with him at yesterday's Tate meet, too. How much did you have to pay him to come here with you?"

Emily pushed past him. She strode down the shadowy hall, noting that this would *not* be the best time to trip in her heels. Ben's footsteps rang out behind her. "Why are you running away?" he singsonged.

"Leave me alone." She didn't turn around.

"Is that dude your bodyguard? First he protects you at swimming, now here. Only where is he now? Or did you only rent him to walk in with you, so everybody wouldn't think you were a big lesbo?" Ben let out a little snicker.

"Ha ha." Emily whirled around to face him. "You're funny."

"Yeah?" Ben shoved her up against the wall. Just like that. He pinned her wrists back and pressed his body to hers. "Is this funny?"

Ben's actions were forceful and his body was heavy.

Just feet away, kids swept past them toward the bathrooms. Didn't they *see*? "Stop it," Emily mustered.

His rough hand reached for the hem of her dress. He poked Emily's kneecap, then slid his hand up her leg. "Just tell me that you like this," he said in her ear. "Or I'll tell everyone you're a dyke."

Tears came to Emily's eyes. "Ben," she whispered, pressing her legs together. "I'm not a dyke."

"Then say you like it," Ben growled. His hand squeezed her bare thigh.

Ben was getting closer and closer to her underwear. When they were dating, they hadn't even gotten this far. Emily bit her lip so hard, she was certain she drew blood. She was about to give in and tell him she liked it, just so he'd stop, but fury slashed through her. Let Ben think what he wanted. Let him tell the whole school. No way could he do this to her.

She pressed her body up against the wall for leverage. Then she brought up her knee and angled it toward Ben's crotch. Hard.

"*Uff!*" Ben stepped away, holding his groin. A tiny, babyish wail came out of his mouth. "What did you . . . ?" he gasped.

Emily straightened her dress. "Stay away from me." Anger coursed through her like a drug. "I swear to God."

Ben staggered backward and hit the far wall. His knees buckled, and he slid down until he was sitting on the floor. "Bad, bad move."

"Whatever," Emily said, then turned to walk away. She took long, fast, confident strides. She wouldn't let him see how upset she was. That she was on the verge of tears.

"Hey." Someone gently grabbed Emily's arm. When Emily's eyes focused, she realized it was Maya.

"I just saw the whole thing," Maya whispered, nudging her chin to where Ben was still crouched. "Are you okay?"

"Yeah," Emily said quickly. But her voice caught. She tried to hold it together, but she couldn't. She leaned against the wall and covered her face with her hands. If she just counted to ten, she could get through this. *One . . . two . . . three . . .*

Maya touched Emily's arm. "I'm so sorry, Em."

"Don't be," Emily managed, her face still covered. *Eight . . . nine . . . ten.* She took her hands away and straightened up. "I'm fine."

She paused, looking at Maya's ivory geisha-style dress. She looked so much prettier than all of the blond, French-twisted, Chanel clones she'd seen on her way in. She ran her hands along the sides of her own dress, wondering if Maya was checking her out too. "I . . . I should probably get back to my date," Emily stammered.

Maya took a tiny step to the side. Only Emily couldn't move an inch.

"I have a secret for you before you go," Maya said.

Emily came closer and Maya leaned into Emily's ear. Her lips didn't touch it, but they were so close. Tingles shot up Emily's back, and she heard herself breathe in sharply. It wasn't right to respond this way, but she just . . . *couldn't* . . . help it.

Go to the one you really love.

"I'll wait for you," Maya whispered, her voice a little sad and a lot sexy. "However long it takes."

25

THE SURREAL LIFE, STARRING HANNA MARIN

Saturday night, Hanna rode the elevator up to her suite at the Philadelphia Four Seasons, feeling taut, loose, and glowing. She'd just had a lemongrass body wrap, an 80-minute massage, and a Kissed by the Sun tanning treatment, all in a row. The pampering had made her feel *slightly* less stressed. That, and being away from Rosewood . . . and A.

Hopefully she was away from A.

She unlocked the door to their two-bedroom suite and strode inside. Her father was sitting on the couch in the front room. "Hey." He stood up. "How was it?"

"Wonderful." Hanna beamed at him, overcome with both happiness and sadness at once. She wanted to tell him how grateful she felt that they were back together—and yet, she knew her future with him hung in the balance—A's balance. Hopefully, blurting out stuff to Naomi and Riley yesterday would keep her safe, but what if it didn't?

Maybe she should just tell him the truth about Jenna, before A got to him first.

She pressed her lips together and looked at the carpet bashfully. "Well, I have to shower really fast if we're going to make it to Le Bec-Fin."

"Just a sec." Her dad stood up. "I have another surprise for you."

On instinct, Hanna looked at her dad's hands, hoping he was holding a gift for her. Maybe it was something to make up for all those lame birthday cards. But the only thing in his hand was his cell phone.

Then came a knock on the door to the adjoining suite. "Tom? Is she here?"

Hanna froze, feeling the blood drain from her head. She knew that voice.

"Kate and Isabel are here," her father whispered excitedly. "They're coming to Le Bec-Fin with us, and then we're all going to see *Mamma Mia!*. Didn't you say Thursday that you wanted to see that?"

"Wait!" Hanna blocked him before he got to the door. "*You* invited them?"

"Yes." Her father looked at her crazily. "Who else would have?"

A, Hanna thought. It seemed like A's style. "But I thought it was going to just be you and me."

"I never said that."

Hanna frowned. Yes, he had. Hadn't he?

"Tom?" Kate's voice called. Hanna was relieved that

Kate called her dad Tom, and not Daddy, but she tightened her grip on her dad's wrist.

Her father hesitated at the door, his eyes flickering back and forth awkwardly. "But, I mean, Hanna, they're already here. I thought this would be nice."

"Why . . . ?" *Why would you think that?* Hanna wanted to ask. *Kate makes me feel like shit and you ignore me when she's here. This is why I haven't spoken to you in years!*

But there was so much confusion and disappointment on her father's face. He'd probably been planning this for days. Hanna stared at the tassels on the Oriental rug. Her throat felt clogged, as if she'd just swallowed something enormous.

"I guess you should let them in, then," she mumbled.

When her father opened the door, Isabel cried out with glee, as if they'd been separated by whole galaxies, not just states. She was still overly thin and too tan, and Hanna's eyes went immediately to the rock on her left hand. It was a three-carat Tiffany Legacy ring—Hanna knew the catalogue backward and forward.

And Kate. She was more beautiful than ever. Her diagonal-striped slip dress had to be a size two, and her straight chestnut hair was even longer than a few years ago. She gracefully placed her Louis Vuitton purse on the hotel room's little dining table. Hanna seethed. Kate probably never tripped in her new Jimmy Choos or slid on the hardwood floors after the cleaning lady waxed them.

Kate's face looked pinched, like she was really pissed

to be here. When she noticed Hanna, however, her puckered look softened. She looked Hanna up and down—from her structured Chloé jacket to her strappy sling-backs—and then she smiled.

"Hey, Hanna," Kate said, her surprise obvious. "Wow." She put her hand on Hanna's shoulder but luckily didn't hug her. If she had, she'd have found out how badly Hanna was trembling.

"Everything looks so good," Kate breathed, staring at her menu.

"Indeed," Mr. Marin echoed. He flagged down the waiter and ordered a bottle of pinot grigio. Then he gazed warmly at Kate, Isabel, and Hanna. "I'm glad we can all be here. Together."

"It's really lovely to see you again, Hanna," Isabel cooed.

"Yeah," Kate echoed. "It totally is."

Hanna stared down at her dainty silverware. It was surreal to see them again. And not the cool, Zac-Posen-kaleidoscopic-dress sort of surreal, but nightmarish surreal, like when that Russian guy in the book Hanna had to read for English last year woke up and found he'd turned into a roach.

"Darling, what are you going to get?" Isabel asked her with her hand over Hanna's father's. She still couldn't believe her father was into Isabel. She was so . . . plain. And way too tan. Cute if you were a model, fourteen years old, or from Brazil—not if you were a middle-aged woman from Maryland.

"Hmm," Mr. Marin said. "What's *pintade*? Is it fish?"

Hanna flipped through the menu's pages. She had no idea what she could eat. Everything was either fried or in cream sauce.

"Kate, will you translate?" Isabel leaned in Hanna's direction. "Kate's fluent."

Of course she is, Hanna thought.

"We spent last summer in Paris," Isabel explained, looking at Hanna. Hanna ducked behind the wine list. They went to Paris? Her father, too? "Hanna, do you study languages?" Isabel asked.

"Um." Hanna shrugged. "I took a year of Spanish."

Isabel pursed her lips. "What's your favorite subject in school?"

"English?"

"Mine too!" Kate exclaimed.

"Kate got her school's top English prize last year," Isabel bragged, looking very proud.

"Mom," Kate whined. She looked at Hanna and mouthed, *Sorry.*

Hanna still couldn't believe how Kate's pissed-off look had melted when she'd seen Hanna. Hanna had *made* that look before. Like the time in ninth grade when her English teacher volunteered her to show around Carlos, the Chilean exchange student. Hanna stormed resentfully to the front office to greet him, certain that

Carlos was going to be a dork and bring down her cool quotient. When she got to the office and saw a tall, wavy-haired, green-eyed boy who looked like he'd been playing beach volleyball since birth, she stood up a little straighter and discreetly checked her breath. Kate probably thought they shared some sort of cute-girl bond.

"Do you do any extracurriculars?" Isabel asked her. "Sports?"

Hanna shrugged. "Not really." She'd forgotten that Isabel was one of *those* mothers: All she talked about were Kate's honors classes, languages, awards, extracurriculars, and so on. It was yet another thing Hanna couldn't compete with.

"Don't be so modest." Her father poked Hanna in the shoulder. "You have plenty of extracurriculars."

Hanna looked at her dad blankly. What, like stealing?

"The burn clinic?" he prompted. "And your mom said you joined a support group?"

Hanna's mouth fell open. In a moment of weakness, she'd told her mom about going to V Club, sort of to say, *See? I actually have morals.* She couldn't believe her mom had told her dad. "I . . ." she stuttered. "It's nothing."

"It's not nothing." Mr. Marin pointed his fork at her.

"*Dad,*" Hanna hissed.

The others looked at her expectantly. Isabel's bulgy eyes widened. Kate had the tiniest whisper of a smirk on her face, but her eyes looked sympathetic. Hanna eyed the bread basket. *Screw it,* she thought, and shoved a whole roll into her mouth.

"It's an abstinence club, okay?" she blurted out, her mouth full of dough and poppy seeds. Then she stood up. "Thanks a lot, Dad."

"Hanna!" Her father pushed his chair back and stood up halfway, but Hanna kept walking. Why had she bought into his little *I'd love a weekend with you* story? It was just like the last time, when her father called Hanna a piggy. And to think what she'd risked to be here—she'd told those bitches she puked three times a day! That wasn't even true anymore!

She shoved through the bathroom door, slammed into a stall, and knelt down in front of the toilet. Her stomach gurgled, and she felt the urge to take care of it. *Calm down,* she told herself, staring dizzily at her reflection in the toilet's water. *You can get through this.*

Hanna stood up again, her jaw trembling, tears threatening to spill from her eyes. If only she could stay in this bathroom for the rest of the night. Let them have Hanna's special weekend without her. Her cell phone rang. Hanna pulled it out of her purse to silence it. Then her stomach dropped. She had an e-mail from a familiar garbled address.

Since you followed my orders so nicely yesterday, consider this a gift: Get to Foxy, now. Sean's there with another girl. —A

She was so startled, she nearly dropped the phone on the bathroom's marble floor.

She dialed Mona. They still weren't speaking—Hanna hadn't even told Mona she wasn't going to Foxy—and Mona didn't answer. Hanna hung up, so frustrated she threw her phone against the door. Who could Sean be with? Naomi? Some V Club bitch?

She burst noisily out of the stall, making an old lady washing her hands at the sink jump. When Hanna came around the corner for the door, she skidded to a halt. Kate was sitting on the chaise lounge, applying pale, salmon-colored lipstick. Her long, slender legs were crossed and she looked super-poised.

"Everything okay?" Kate raised her deep blue eyes to Hanna. "I came to check."

Hanna stiffened. "Yeah. I'm fine."

Kate twisted up her mouth. "No offense to your dad, but sometimes he can say the most inappropriate things. Like this one time I was going out on this date with this guy. We were leaving the house, and your dad goes, 'Kate? I see you wrote OB on the grocery list. What is that? What aisle can I find it in?' I was mortified."

"God." Hanna felt a twinge of sympathy. That sounded like her dad, all right.

"Hey, it doesn't matter," Kate said gently. "He didn't mean anything."

Hanna shook her head. "It's not that." She glanced up at Kate. Oh, what the hell. Maybe they *did* have a pretty-girl bond. "It's . . . it's my ex. I got a text that he's at this benefit thing called Foxy with another girl."

Kate frowned. "When did you break up?"

"Eight days ago." Hanna sat down on the chaise. "I'm half tempted to go back there right now and kick his ass."

"Why don't you?"

Hanna slumped back in the couch. "I wish, but . . ." She motioned toward the door leading back to the restaurant.

"Listen." Kate stood up and puckered for the mirror. "Why don't you blame that support group thing you're in? Say that one of the people in it called you and said she was feeling really 'weak,' and you're her buddy, so you have to talk her down."

Hanna raised an eyebrow. "You know an awful lot about support groups."

Kate shrugged. "I have a couple friends who've been through rehab."

Okaaay. "I don't think it's a good idea."

"I'll cover for you, if you want," Kate offered.

Hanna eyed her in the mirror. "Really?"

Kate looked back at her meaningfully. "Let's just say I owe you one."

Hanna flinched. Something told her Kate was talking about that time in Annapolis. It made her feel squirmy—that Kate remembered, and that she recognized that she'd been mean. At the same time, it gave her a certain satisfaction.

"Besides," Kate said, "your dad said we'd be seeing a lot more of each other. Might as well start it off right."

Hanna blinked. "He said he . . . he wants to see me more?"

"Well, you *are* his daughter."

Hanna played with the heart-shaped charm on her Tiffany necklace. It gave her a little thrill, hearing Kate say that. Maybe she'd overreacted at the dinner table.

"What—it'll take you two hours, tops?" Kate asked.

"Probably less than that." All she wanted to do was take SEPTA to Rosewood and curse the bitch out. She opened her hobo bag to see if she had train fare. Kate stood above her and pointed to something at the purse's bottom. "What's that?"

"This?" As soon as Hanna pulled it out, she wanted to stuff it back in. It was the Percocet she'd stolen from the burn clinic on Tuesday. She'd forgotten.

"Can I have one of those?" Kate whispered excitedly. Hanna looked at her cross-eyed. "Serious?"

Kate gave Hanna a naughty look. "I need *something* to help me get through this musical your dad's dragging us to."

Hanna handed over a packet. Kate pocketed the pills, then turned on her heel and strode confidently out of the bathroom. Hanna followed, her mouth open in awe.

That was the most surreal thing of the night. Maybe if she had to see Kate again, it wouldn't be a fate worse than death. It might even be . . . *fun.*

26

AT LEAST SHE DOESN'T
HAVE TO SING BACKUP

By the time Spencer and Andrew got to Foxy, the place was mobbed. The valet line was twenty cars long, the wanna-bes who hadn't been invited swarmed around the entrance, and the main tent was jammed with kids at tables, around the bar, and on the dance floor.

As Andrew made his way back from the drinks table, Spencer checked her cell phone again. *Still* no calls from Wren. She paced around the cross-shaped marble pattern on the dining hall's floor, wondering why she was here. Andrew had come to pick her up, and, despite all her anxiety, Spencer had put her drama club skills to use and fooled her family into thinking they were an item—giving Andrew a little kiss near the lips when she saw him, graciously accepting his flowers, posing for a picture, her cheek pressed to his. Andrew had seemed giddily flustered, which helped all the more with the ruse.

Now she had no use for him, but unfortunately he

didn't know that. He kept introducing Spencer to every-one—people they both *knew*—as his date. What she really wanted to do was to go into a quiet room and think. She needed to untangle what that cop, Wilden, knew, and what he didn't. If Toby was A *and* Ali's killer, he wouldn't be talking with the police. But what if Toby wasn't A . . . and A *had* told the police something?

"I think they're doing karaoke." Andrew pointed at the stage. Sure enough, some girl was belting out "I Will Survive." "Want to sing something?"

"I don't think so," Spencer said anxiously, fiddling with the pin of her corsage. She looked around for the fiftieth time for her old friends, hoping they would appear. She felt she had to warn them about Toby—*and* the cops. A had told her not to, but maybe she could do it in code.

"Well, maybe you'll do one with me?" Andrew coaxed.

Spencer turned to him. Andrew looked just like one of her family's labradoodles, begging for table scraps. "Didn't I just say I didn't want to?"

"Oh." Andrew fiddled with his paisley tie. "Sorry."

In the end, she agreed to sing backup for Christina Aguilera's "Dirrty"—so asinine that squeaky-clean Andrew chose to sing *that* song—because it was easier that way. Now Mona Vanderwaal and Celeste What's-her-name—she went to the Quaker school—were onstage singing "Total Eclipse of the Heart." They already seemed tipsy, holding each other's arms for balance, and repeatedly dropping their suede mini bags on the floor.

"We're going to be way better than them," Andrew said. He was standing too close. Spencer felt his hot, Orbit gum–minty breath and bristled. Wren breathing heavily on her neck was one thing, but Andrew was quite another. If she didn't get some air right now, she might pass out. "I'll be back," she murmured to Andrew, and fumbled toward the door.

As soon as she passed through the terrace's French doors, her phone vibrated. She flinched. When she looked at the LED screen, her heart lifted. *Wren.*

"Are you all right?" Spencer said as she answered. "I was so worried!"

"You've left twelve messages," Wren replied. "What's going on?"

Spencer could feel the stress seeping out of her and her shoulders relaxing. "I . . . I didn't hear from you, and I thought . . . Why didn't you check your voice mail?"

Wren cleared his throat, sounding a little uncomfortable. "I was busy. That's all."

"But I thought you were—"

"What?" Wren said, sort of laughing. "In a gutter? C'mon, Spence."

"But . . ." Spencer paused, trying to figure out how to explain. "I just had a weird feeling."

"Well, I'm fine." Wren paused. "Are *you* fine?"

"Yeah," Spencer answered, smiling a little. "I mean,

I'm here at my lame-ass dance, with my lame-ass date, and I'd rather be with you, but I'm so much better now. I'm glad you're okay."

When she hung up, she was so relieved, she wanted to run up and kiss a random person on the terrace—like Adriana Peoples, the Catholic school girl who was sitting on the Dionysus statue, smoking a clove. Or Liam Olsen, the ice hockey player who was fondling his date. Or Andrew Campbell, who was standing behind her, looking forlorn and useless. When it registered in Spencer's brain that Andrew was, well, *Andrew*, her stomach clenched.

"Um, hey," she said haltingly. "How . . . how long have you been standing there?"

But by the dejected look on Andrew's face, Spencer realized he'd been standing there just long enough. "Listen," she said, sighing. She might as well just cut this off at its nerve center. "The truth is, Andrew, I hope you don't think anything's going to happen between us. I have a boyfriend."

At first, Andrew looked stunned. Then hurt, then embarrassed, then angry. The emotions passed so quickly over his face, it was like watching a sunset in time-lapse photography. "I know," he said, pointing to her Sidekick. "I heard your conversation."

Of course you did. "I'm sorry," Spencer answered. "But I—"

Andrew held up his hand to stop her. "So why bring me and not him? Is he some guy your parents don't want you to date? So you come with me, thinking you have them totally fooled?"

"No," Spencer said quickly, feeling a twinge of discomfort. Was she that transparent, or was Andrew just a lucky guesser? "It's . . . it's hard to explain. I thought we could have fun. I didn't mean to hurt you."

A lock of hair fell over Andrew's eyes. "You could've fooled me." He turned for the door.

"Andrew!" Spencer cried. "Wait!" As she watched him disappear through the crowd of kids, a cold, uneasy feeling washed over her. She'd definitely picked the wrong boy as her fake date. It would've been better to go with Ryan Vreeland, who was in the closet, or Thayer Anderson, who was too into basketball to date girls seriously.

She ran into the main tent and looked around; she at least owed Andrew an apology. The whole place was lit by candles, however, so it was hard to find anyone. She could just make out Noel and the Quaker school girl on the dance floor, sneaking drinks out of Noel's flask. Naomi Zeigler and James Freed were now onstage, singing some Avril Lavigne song Spencer couldn't stand. Mason Byers and Devon Arliss leaned in to kiss. Kirsten Cullen and Bethany Wells whispered in the corner.

"Andrew?" she called.

Then Spencer noticed Emily across the room. She wore a strapless pink dress and had a pink pashmina thrown over her shoulders. Spencer took a few steps toward her, but then noticed her date standing next to her, his hand on her arm. Just as Spencer squinted to get a better look, the guy turned his head and noticed her. He had dark, denim-blue eyes, the same exact color they'd been in her dream.

Spencer gasped and stepped back.

I'll show up when you least expect it.

It was Toby.

27

ARIA IS AVAILABLE BY PRESCRIPTION ONLY

Aria leaned against the Foxy bar and ordered a cup of black coffee. It was so crowded in this tent that the lining of her polka-dotted dress was already drenched with sweat. And she'd only been here for twenty minutes.

"Hey." Her brother sidled up next to her. He wore the same gray suit he'd worn to the funeral and polished black shoes that belonged to Byron.

"Hey," Aria squeaked, surprised. "I . . . I didn't know you were coming." By the time she'd gotten out of the shower to get ready for Foxy, the house was empty. In a moment's confusion, she'd thought her family had abandoned her.

"Yeah. I came with . . ." Mike whirled around and pointed to a thin, pale girl Aria recognized from Noel Kahn's party the week before. "Hot, huh?"

"Yeah." Aria downed her coffee in three gulps and

noticed that her hands were shaking. This was her fourth cup in an hour.

"So where's Sean?" Mike asked. "That's who you're here with, right? Everyone's talking about it."

"They are?" Aria asked faintly.

"Yeah. You're like the new It couple."

Aria didn't know whether to laugh or cry. She could just picture some of the Rosewood Day girls gossiping about her and Sean. "I don't know where he is."

"Why? Did the It couple break up already?"

"No . . ." The truth was, Aria was sort of hiding from Sean.

Yesterday, after Meredith told Aria that she and Byron were in love, Aria had run back to Sean and burst into tears. Never in a gazillion years had she expected Meredith to say what she said. Now that Aria knew the truth, she felt helpless. Her family was doomed. For ten minutes, she'd wailed into Sean's shoulder, *What am I going to doooooo?* Sean calmed her down enough to take her home and even walked her up to her room, put her into bed, and laid her favorite stuffed animal, Pigtunia, on the pillow beside her.

As soon as Sean left, Aria threw back the covers and paced. She peeked into the bedroom. Her mom was there, sleeping peacefully . . . alone. But Aria couldn't wake her. When she woke up a few hours later, she went to her bedroom again, steeling herself to *just do it*, but this time, Byron was in bed beside Ella. He lay on his side, with his arm slung over Ella's shoulder.

Now why would you cuddle, if you were in love with someone else?

In the morning, when Aria awoke from her one big hour of sleep, her eyes were puffy and her skin had broken out in little red bumps. She felt hungover, and as she ran over the night's events, she crawled back under her duvet in shame. Sean had *tucked her in*. She'd blown *snot* on his shoulder. She'd wailed like an insane person. What better way to lose the guy you like than slobber all over him? When Sean picked her up for Foxy—amazing that he'd even shown up at all—he immediately wanted to talk about last night, but Aria shrugged him off, saying she felt much better. Sean looked at her sort of funny, but was smart enough not to ask questions. And now she was dodging him.

Mike leaned up against the wooden Foxy bar, bobbing his head when the DJ put on Franz Ferdinand. There was a self-satisfied little smile on his face—Aria knew he felt like the man for scoring a Foxy ticket, since he was only a sophomore. But she was his sister, and she could see pain and sadness underneath. It was like when they were little and hanging out at the community pool, and Mike's friends were calling him a homo because he was wearing white swim trunks that had turned pinkish in the wash. Mike tried to take it like a man, but later, during adult swim, Aria caught him secretly crying by the baby pool.

She wanted to say something to make him feel better. About how she was sorry for what she was going to have to tell Ella—Aria was going to tell her mom that night when she got home, no excuses—and that none of this was his fault, and if their family fell apart, it would still be okay. Somehow.

But she knew what would happen if she tried. Mike would just run away.

Aria grabbed her coffee and strode away from the bar. She just needed to be moving. "Aria," called a voice behind her. She turned. Sean was about six feet away, near one of the tables. He looked upset.

Panicked, Aria put her drink down and dashed toward the women's bathroom. One of her chunky wedges slid right off her foot. Jamming it back on, she kept pushing forward, only to get stuck at a wall of kids. She tried to elbow her way through, but no one was moving.

"Hey." Sean was right next to her.

"Oh," Aria yelled over the music, trying to act nonchalant. "Hi."

Sean took Aria by the arm and led her into the parking lot, which was the one place at Foxy that was empty. Sean retrieved his keys from the valet. He helped Aria into his car and drove to an empty spot farther down the driveway.

"What's going on with you?" Sean demanded.

"Nothing." Aria stared out the window. "I'm fine."

"No, you're not. You're like . . . a zombie. It's freaking me out."

"I just . . ." Aria ran the strand of pearls she'd worn as a bracelet up and down her wrist. "I don't know. I don't want to bother you."

"Why not?"

She shrugged. "Because you don't want to hear it. You must think I'm a complete freak. Like, I'm super-obsessed with my parents. It's all I've talked about."

"Well . . . it sort of has been. But I mean–"

"I wouldn't be mad," she interrupted, "if you wanted to dance with other girls and whatever. There are some really cute girls here."

Sean blinked, his face blank. "But I don't want to dance with anyone else."

They were quiet. The bass line of Kanye West's "Gold Digger" pumped out of the tent.

"You thinking about your parents?" Sean asked quietly.

She nodded. "I guess. I have to tell my mom tonight."

"Why do *you* have to tell her?"

"Because . . ." Aria couldn't tell him about A. "It has to be me. This can't go on any longer."

Sean sighed. "You put a lot of pressure on yourself. Can't you take a night off?"

At first, Aria felt defensive, but then she leaned back. "I really think you should go back in there, Sean. You shouldn't let me ruin your night."

"Aria . . ." Sean let out a frustrated sigh. "Stop it."

Aria made a face. "I just don't think it's going to work out for us."

"Why?"

"Because . . ." She paused, trying to figure out what she wanted to say. Because she wasn't the typical Rosewood girl? Because whatever Sean liked about her, there was so much else about her *not* to like? She felt like she was one of those wonder drugs that were always advertised on TV. The narrator would go through paragraphs of how the drug had helped millions of people, but at the very end of the commercial, he'd say really quietly that side effects include heart palpitations and an oily discharge. With her, it'd be like, *Cool, kooky girl . . . but family baggage may result in psycho outbursts and randomly blowing snot on your expensive shirts.*

Sean carefully put his hand over Aria's. "If you're scared that I'm freaked about last night, I'm not. I really like you. I sort of like you more *because* of last night."

Tears came to Aria's eyes. "Really?"

"Really."

He pressed his forehead to hers. Aria held her breath. Finally, their lips touched. Then again. Harder, this time.

Aria pressed her mouth to his and grabbed the back of his neck, pulling him closer. His body felt so warm and right. Sean ran his hands up Aria's waist. All at once, they were biting each other's bottom lips, their hands scratching up and down each other's backs. Then they broke away, breathing heavily and staring into each other's eyes.

They dove back for each other. Sean pulled at the zipper on Aria's dress. He flung off his jacket and threw it into the backseat, and she pawed at the buttons on his shirt. She kissed Sean's gorgeous ears and ran her hands inside his shirt, to his smooth, bare skin. He circled her waist with his hands as best he could, his body at an awkward angle on the cramped Audi seat. Sean tilted the seat back, lifted Aria up, and brought her to him. The knobs of her spine grated against the steering wheel.

She arched her neck as Sean kissed her throat. When she opened her eyes, she saw something—a yellow piece of paper under the windshield wiper. At first she thought it was some sort of flyer—maybe a kid advertising some after-Foxy party—but then she noticed the big, bulky words, written sloppily in black Sharpie marker.

Don't forget! Stroke of midnight!

She jerked away from Sean.

"What is it?" he asked.

She pointed at the note, her hands shaking. "Did you write that?" It was a stupid question, though: She already knew the answer.

28

IT'S NOT A PARTY
WITHOUT HANNA MARIN

As her taxi pulled up to Kingman Hall, Hanna threw twenty bucks at the cabdriver, an older, balding guy who seemed to have a sweating problem. "Keep it," she said. She slammed the door and ran for the entrance, her stomach roiling. She'd bought a bag of Cool Ranch Doritos at the train station in Philly and had maniacally scarfed down the whole thing in five frantic minutes. Bad move.

To her right was the Foxy check-in table. A whippet-thin girl with close-cropped blond hair and tons of eyeliner was collecting tickets and checking off names in her book. Hanna hesitated. She had no idea where her ticket was, but if she tried to bargain her way in, they'd just tell her to go home. She narrowed her eyes at the Foxy tent, which glowed like a birthday cake. There was no way she was letting Sean get away with this. She was getting into Foxy, whether Eyeliner Girl liked it or not.

Taking a deep breath, Hanna sprinted at top speed past the check-in table. "Hey!" she heard the girl call. "Wait!"

Hanna hid behind a column, her heart beating fast. A beefy bouncer in a tux ran by her, then stopped and looked around. Frustrated and confused, he shrugged and said something into his walkie-talkie. Hanna felt a little satisfied thrill. Sneaking in gave her the same rush as stealing.

Foxy was a blur of kids. She couldn't remember it ever being this packed. Most of the girls on the dance floor had taken their shoes off, and they held them in the air as they spun. There was an equally enormous crowd by the bar, and more kids were gathered in line by what looked like a karaoke booth. By the looks of the neatly set, empty tables, they hadn't served dinner yet.

Hanna grabbed the elbow of Amanda Williamson, a Rosewood Day sophomore who always tried to say hi to Hanna in the halls. Amanda's face lit up. "*Heyyy*, Hanna!"

"Have you seen Sean?" Hanna barked.

A surprised look crossed Amanda's face; then she shrugged. "I'm not sure. . . ."

Hanna pressed on, her heart pounding. Maybe he wasn't here. She switched directions, nearly colliding with a waiter carrying a huge tray of cheese. Hanna grabbed an enormous chunk of cheddar and shoved it in her mouth. She swallowed without even tasting it.

"Hanna!" Naomi Zeigler, dressed in a gold sheath and looking very faux-tanned, cried. "How fun! You're here! I thought you said you weren't coming!"

Hanna frowned. Naomi was clutching James Freed. She pointed to both of them. "You guys came together?" Hanna had thought maybe Naomi was Sean's date.

Naomi nodded. Then she leaned forward. "Are you looking for Sean?" She shook her head, awestruck. "It's all *everyone's* been talking about. I seriously can't believe it."

Hanna's heart sped up. "So Sean's here?"

"He's here, all right." James ducked, pulled a Coke bottle full of a suspicious-looking clear liquid from his inside jacket pocket, and dumped it into his orange juice. He took a sip and smiled.

"I mean, they're so *different*," Naomi mused. "You said you guys were still friends, right? Did he tell you why he asked her?"

"Lay off." James nudged Naomi. "She's sexy."

"*Who?*" Hanna screamed. Why did everyone know about this but her?

"There they are." Naomi pointed across the room.

It was as if the sea of kids parted and a huge spotlight beamed down from the ceiling. Sean was in the corner by the karaoke machine, hugging a tall girl in a black-and-white polka-dotted dress. He had his head crooked around her neck, and her hands were dangerously close to his butt. Then the girl turned her head, and Hanna saw the familiar elfin, exotic features, and that trademark blue-black hair. *Aria*.

Hanna screamed.

"Oh my God, I can't believe you didn't know." Naomi put a consoling arm around Hanna's shoulder.

Hanna shook her off and stormed across the room, right up to Aria and Sean, who were hugging. Not dancing, just hugging. *Freaks*.

After Hanna stood there for a few seconds, Aria opened one eye, then the other. She made a little gasping noise. "Um, hey, Hanna."

Hanna stood there, quivering with rage. "You . . . you *bitch*."

Sean stepped defensively in front of Aria. "Hold up. . . ."

"Hold *up*?" Hanna's voice danced up the scale. She pointed at Sean; she was so angry, her finger was shaking. "You . . . you told me you weren't coming because your friends were all bringing dates, and you didn't want to!"

Sean shrugged. "Things changed."

Hanna's cheeks stung, as if he'd slapped her. "But we're going on a *date* this week!"

"We're going out to *dinner* this week," Sean corrected. "As friends." He smiled at her like she was a slow kindergartner. "We broke up last Friday, Hanna. Remember?"

Hanna blinked. "And, what, you're with *her*?"

"Well . . ." Sean looked at Aria. "Yeah."

Hanna clutched her hand to her stomach, certain she

was going to puke. This had to be a joke. Sean and Aria made about as much sense as a fat girl wearing skinny leggings.

Then she noticed Aria's dress. The side zipper was undone, revealing half of Aria's lacy black strapless bra. "Your boob's hanging out," she growled, pointing.

Aria quickly looked down, folded her arms over her chest, and zipped her dress up.

"Where'd you get that dress, anyway?" Hanna asked. "Luella for Target?"

Aria straightened her back. "Actually, yeah. I thought it was cute."

"God." Hanna rolled her eyes. "You're such a martyr." She looked at Sean. "Actually, I guess you guys have that in common. Did you know Sean's pledged to be a virgin till he's thirty, Aria? He might've tried to feel you up, but he's never going to go all the way. He's made a sacred *promise*."

"Hanna!" Sean shushed her.

"I personally think it's because he's gay. What do you think?"

"Hanna . . ." Now there was a pleading tone in Sean's voice.

"What?" Hanna challenged. "You're a liar, Sean. And an asshole."

When Hanna looked around, she saw that a group of kids had gathered. The ones who were always invited to the parties, the ones who were interchangeably hooking up.

The girls who weren't *quite* cool enough, the overweight boys everyone kept around only because they were funny, the rich kids who spent oodles of money on everyone because they were cute or interesting or manipulative. They were hungrily eating this up. The whispers had already started.

Hanna took a final look at Sean, but instead of saying anything else, she fled.

At the girls' bathroom, she marched straight to the front of the line. As someone was coming out of a stall, Hanna shoved her way in. "Bitch!" someone screamed, but Hanna didn't care. Once the door was shut, she leaned over the toilet and got rid of the Doritos and everything else she'd eaten that night. When she was done, she sobbed.

The looks on everyone's faces. The *pity*. And Hanna had cried in front of people. It had been one of Hanna and Mona's first rules after they reinvented themselves: Never, *ever* let anyone see you cry. And more than any of that, she just felt so naïve. Hanna had really believed Sean was going to take her back. She'd thought by going to the burn clinic and V Club, she was making a difference, but all this time . . . he'd been thinking of someone else.

When she finally pushed open the door, the bathroom was empty. It was so quiet, she could hear water dripping into the mosaic-tiled basin. Hanna glanced at herself in the mirror, to see how bad she looked. When she did, she gasped.

A very different Hanna stared back. This Hanna was chubby, with poopy brown hair and bad skin. She had braces with pink rubber bands, and her eyes were narrowed from squinting because she didn't want to wear her glasses. Her tan blazer strained against her pudgy arms, and her blouse buckled at the bra line.

Hanna covered her eyes in horror. *It's A,* she thought. *A's doing this to me.*

Then, she thought of A's note: *Get to Foxy now. Sean's there with another girl.* If A had known Sean was at Foxy with another girl, then it meant . . .

A was at Foxy.

"Hey."

Hanna jumped and whirled around. Mona stood in the doorway. She looked gorgeous in a slinky black dress Hanna didn't recognize from their shopping expedition. Her pale hair was swept back from her face, and her skin shimmered. Embarrassed—she probably had puke on her face—Hanna made a beeline back to the stall.

"Wait." Mona caught her arm. When Hanna whirled back around, Mona looked earnest and concerned. "Naomi said you weren't coming tonight."

Hanna peeked at herself in the mirror again. Her reflection showed the eleventh-grade Hanna, not the seventh-grade one. Her eyes were a bit red, but otherwise she looked fine.

"It's Sean, isn't it?" Mona asked. "I just got here

and saw him with *her*." She lowered her head. "I'm so sorry, Han."

Hanna shut her eyes. "I feel like such an ass," she admitted.

"You're not. *He's* the ass."

They looked at each other. Hanna felt a rush of regret. Mona's friendship meant so much to her, and she'd been letting everything else get in the way. She couldn't remember why they were fighting. "I'm so sorry, Mon. About everything."

"*I'm* sorry," Mona said. And then they hugged, squeezing extra hard.

"Oh my God, there you are."

Spencer Hastings strode across the bathroom's marble floor and pulled Hanna out of the hug. "I need to talk to you."

Hanna pulled away, annoyed. "What? Why?"

Spencer glanced shifty-eyed at Mona. "I can't tell you right here. You have to come with me."

"Hanna doesn't have to go anywhere." Mona took Hanna's arm and pulled her close.

"This time, she does." Spencer's voice rose. "It's an emergency."

Mona clamped down on Hanna's arm. She had the same forbidding expression from the other day, at the mall—the look that said, *If you keep one more secret from me, I swear, that's it between us.* But Spencer looked terrified. Something felt wrong. *Very* wrong.

"I'm sorry," Hanna said, touching Mona's hand. "I'll be right back."

Mona dropped her arm. "Fine," she said angrily, walking to the mirror to inspect her makeup. "Take your time."

29

LET IT ALL OUT

Spencer wordlessly led Hanna out of the bathroom and past a clump of kids. Then she noticed Aria standing near the bar, alone. "You're coming too."

Hanna dropped Spencer's hand. "I'm not going anywhere she's going."

"Hanna, you told everyone you dumped Sean!" Aria protested. "In English?"

Hanna crossed her arms over her chest. "It didn't mean I wanted you to come here with him. It didn't mean I wanted you to *steal* him."

"I'm not stealing anything!" Aria screamed, raising her fist. Spencer worried for a second that Aria might try to hit Hanna and inserted her body between the two of them.

"That's *it*," she said. "Just stop it. We have to find Emily." Before they could protest, she dragged them past the ice sculptures, the karaoke line, and the jewelry auction tables. Spencer had just seen Emily not twenty minutes ago, but now Emily was gone. She passed Andrew, sitting at a long, candlelit table with his friends. He noticed her, then quickly turned back to his friends and barked out a loud, fake laugh, obviously for her benefit. Spencer felt a twinge of remorse. But she couldn't deal with him now.

Tightening her grip on the girls' hands, she strode past the tables out to the terrace. Kids were gathered around the fountain, dipping their bare feet, but still no Emily. By the giant statue of Pan, Hanna started to moan. "I have to go."

"You can't go yet." Spencer pushed Aria and Hanna back into the dining room. "This is important for all of us. We have to find Emily."

"Why is that so important?" Hanna wailed. "Who the hell cares?"

"Because." Spencer stopped. "She's here with Toby."

"So?" Aria asked.

Spencer took a deep breath. "I think . . . I think maybe Toby's going to try to hurt her. I think he wants to hurt all of us."

The girls looked shocked. "Why?" Aria demanded, her hands on her hips.

Spencer looked at the ground. Her stomach felt tight. "I think A is Toby."

"What makes you think that?" Aria looked angry.

"A sent me a note," she admitted. "It says we're all in danger."

"You got a note?" Hanna shrieked. "I thought we were going to tell each other!"

"I know." Spencer stared at her pointy Louboutins. Back inside the tent, some of the boys were having a break-dancing contest. Noel Kahn was trying to do a kickworm, and Mason Byers was doing some sort of butt-spin. Wasn't this supposed to be a *civilized* function? "I didn't know what to do. I . . . I actually got two notes. The first one said that it would be better if I *didn't* tell you guys. But the second one really sounded like it was Toby . . . and now Toby's here with Emily, and–"

"Wait, the first note said we were in trouble, and you did nothing?" Hanna asked. She didn't sound angry, exactly, just confused.

"I wasn't sure it was for real," Spencer said. She ran her hand through her hair. "I mean, if I'd known–"

"You know, I got a note too," Aria said softly.

Spencer blinked at her. "You did? Was it about Toby too?"

"No . . ." Aria seemed to consider her words. "Spencer, why were you at that yoga studio Friday?"

"Yoga studio?" Spencer narrowed her eyes. "What does that have to do with . . . ?"

"It was a *little* too much of a coincidence," Aria went on.

"What are you talking about?" Spencer cried.

Hanna interrupted. "Aria, was your note about Sean?"

"*No.*" Aria turned to Hanna and creased her brow.

"Well, I'm *sorry!*" Hanna spat. "I got a text from A, too, and it *was* about Sean! It said that he was at Foxy with another girl . . . *you!*"

"You guys . . ." Spencer warned, not wanting to get into this argument again. Then she knit her eyebrows together. "Wait. When did you get a text, Hanna?"

"Earlier tonight."

"So, that means . . ." Aria pointed at Hanna. "If your note from A said Sean was at Foxy with me, it meant A saw us. Which means—"

"A is at Foxy. I know," Hanna finished, giving Aria a tight smile.

Spencer's heart pounded. It was really happening. A was here . . . and A was Toby.

"Come on." Spencer led them into the long, narrow hall that led to the auction room. By day, the hall was stuffy and very Philadelphia, with tons of Mission end tables, oily portraits of grumpy, rich men, and creaky wood floors, but by night, each table held an aromatherapy candle, and the wainscoting was decorated with different-colored lights. As the girls paused under a blue bulb, they looked like corpses.

"Run this by me again, Spencer," Aria said slowly. "Your first note said that you shouldn't tell us. But shouldn't tell us what? That you got a note? That A was Toby?"

"No . . ." Spencer turned to face them. "I wasn't supposed to tell you what I knew. About The Jenna Thing."

Horror crossed the girls' faces. *Here it comes,* Spencer thought. She took a deep breath. "The truth is . . . Toby saw Ali light that firework. He's known all along."

Aria stepped back and bumped into a table. A piece of pottery wavered, then fell off, shattering all over the wood floor. No one moved to clean it up.

"You're lying," Hanna whispered.

"I wish I was."

"What do you mean, *Toby saw*?" Aria's voice was quivery. "Ali said he didn't."

Spencer wrung her hands together. "He told me he saw. Me and Ali, actually."

Her friends blinked at her, stunned.

"The night Jenna got hurt, when I ran out to see what was going on, Toby came up to Ali and me. He said he saw Ali . . . do it." Spencer's voice was trembling. She'd had nightmares so many times about this very moment; it was surreal to be *in it*.

"Ali stepped in," she went on. "She told Toby she'd seen him do something . . . *awful* . . . and she was going to tell everyone. The only way she wouldn't was if Toby took the blame. Before Toby ran off he said, *I'll get you.* But the next day, he confessed."

Spencer ran her hand along the back of her neck. Saying this out loud transported her right back to that night. She could smell the sulfur from the lit firework, and the freshly mown grass. She could see Ali, her blond hair pulled back in a ponytail, wearing the pearl teardrop earrings she'd gotten for her eleventh birthday. Tears came to her eyes.

Spencer swallowed and continued. "The second note A sent me said, *You hurt me, so I'm going to hurt you*, and that he was going to show up when we least expected it. A cop came to my house this morning, too, asking me about Ali again, and this cop was *grilling* me, acting like I knew something I shouldn't. I thought Toby might've been behind it. Now he's brought Emily here. I'm afraid he might hurt her."

It took Aria and Hanna a long time to respond. Finally, Aria's hands started shaking. A deep red patch crept up her neck into her cheeks. "Why didn't you tell us before?" She squinted uncertainly at Spencer, searching for words. "I mean, there was that time, in seventh grade, when I was *alone* with Toby, at that drama thing! He could've hurt me . . . or all of us . . . and if he really hurt Ali, we could've helped save her!"

"I feel sick," Hanna moaned distantly.

Tears ran down Spencer's cheeks. "I wanted to tell you guys, but I was scared."

"What did Ali say to blackmail Toby so he wouldn't tell?" Aria demanded.

"Ali wouldn't say," Spencer lied. She felt superstitious about telling Toby's secret, as if as soon as she said it, a bolt of lightning would descend through the skylight . . . or Toby would appear, supernaturally having heard everything.

Aria stared at her hands. "Toby's known *all along*," she repeated again.

"And now he's . . . back." Hanna looked positively green.

"He's not only back," Spencer said. "He's *here*. And he's A."

Aria grabbed Hanna's arm. "Come on."

"Where are you going?" Spencer called nervously. She didn't want Aria out of her sight.

Aria turned halfway around. "We have to find Emily," she said angrily. She picked up the hem of her dress and started running.

30

CORNFIELDS ARE THE SCARIEST PLACE IN ROSEWOOD

Emily had shoved herself into a little back alcove on the Kingman Hall terrace and was quietly watching all of the Foxy smokers. The girls in their frilly, pastel dresses, the boys in their elegant suits. But who was she watching *more*? She wasn't sure. She shut her eyes tight, then opened them fast, and the first person she noticed was Tara Kelley, a Rosewood Day senior. She had bright red hair and beautiful, pale skin. Emily gritted her teeth and shut her eyes again. When she opened them, she saw Ori Case, the hot football player. A *guy*. There.

But then she couldn't help but notice Rachel Firestein's thin, giraffelike arms. Chloe Davis made a sexy, teasing face at her date, Chad Something-or-other, that made her mouth look adorable. Elle Carmichael tilted her chin just so. Emily caught a whiff of someone's Michael Kors perfume and had never smelled anything so yummy in her life. Except, maybe, for banana gum.

It couldn't be true. It *couldn't*.

"What are you doing?"

Toby stood above her. "I . . ." Emily stuttered.

"I've been looking all over for you. Are you all right?"

Emily took stock: She was hiding in an alcove on a freezing-cold balcony, using her pashmina as a cloaking device, and doing a deranged peek-a-boo to test herself whether she liked boys or girls. She turned her eyes to Toby. She wanted to explain what had just happened. With Ben, with Maya, with the tarot reader—everything. "You might hate me for asking this, but . . . do you mind if we leave?"

Toby smiled. "I was *hoping* you'd ask that." He pulled Emily up by her wrists.

On their way out, Emily noticed Spencer Hastings standing on the edge of the dance floor. Spencer's back was to Emily, and Emily considered going up and saying hello. Then Toby pulled on her hand, and she decided against it. Spencer might ask her something about A, and she was in no mood to talk about any of *that* right now.

As they pulled out of the parking lot, Emily rolled down the window. The night smelled delicious, like pine needles and oncoming rain. The moon was huge and full, and thick clouds began to roll in. It was so quiet outside, Emily could hear the car's tires slapping along the pavement.

"You sure you're okay?" Toby asked.

Emily jumped a little. "Yeah, I'm fine." She glanced at

Toby. He told her he'd bought a new suit for this, and now she was making him go home three hours early. "I'm sorry the night sucked."

"It's cool." Toby shrugged.

Emily turned over the little Tiffany box that sat in her lap. She'd plucked one off the table right before she left the tent, figuring she might as well get her parting gift.

"So nothing happened?" Toby asked. "You're so quiet."

Emily blew air out of her cheeks. She watched three different cornfields roll by before she answered. "I was accosted by a tarot card reader."

Toby frowned, not understanding.

"She just said that something was going to happen to me tonight. Something, um, life-changing." Emily tried to muster up a laugh. Toby opened his mouth to say something, then quickly shut it.

"Thing was, it kind of came true," Emily said. "I ran into that guy, Ben. The one who was in the hallway at the Tank, who was . . . you know. Anyway, he tried . . . I don't know. I guess he tried to hurt me."

"*What?*"

"It's okay. I'm all right. He just . . ." Emily's chin trembled. "I don't know. Maybe I deserved it."

"Why?" Toby clenched his teeth. "What did you do?"

Emily picked at the gift's white bow. Raindrops began to spatter the windshield. She took a deep breath. Was she really going to say this out loud? "Ben and I used to date. When we were still together, he caught me kissing someone else. A girl. He was calling me a dyke, and when I tried to tell him that I wasn't, he tried to make me prove it. Like kiss him and . . . whatever. That's what was happening when you came into the locker room hall."

Toby shifted in his seat uncomfortably.

Emily ran her hands along the white gardenia Toby had given her as a corsage. "The thing is, maybe I *am* a dyke. I mean, I did, like, *love* Alison DiLaurentis. But I thought it was only Ali I loved, not that I was a lesbian. Now . . . now I don't know. Maybe Ben's right. Maybe I *am* gay. Maybe I should just deal with it."

Emily couldn't believe all that had just spilled from her mouth. She turned to Toby. His mouth was a fixed, impassive line. She thought maybe that if there was a time to admit that he'd been Ali's boyfriend, now would be it. Instead, he said quietly, "Why are you so afraid to admit that?"

"Because!" Emily laughed. Wasn't it obvious? "Because I don't want to *be* . . . you know. Gay." And then, in a quieter voice: "Everyone would make fun of me."

They rolled up to a deserted two-way stop sign. Instead of pausing and rolling through, Toby put the car into park. Emily was puzzled. "What are we doing?"

Toby took his hands off the steering wheel and stared at Emily for a long time. So long, Emily began to feel uncomfortable. He seemed upset. She touched the back of her neck, then turned away and looked out the window. The road was silent and dead and paralleled yet another cornfield, one of Rosewood's biggest. The rain was coming down harder now, and because Toby didn't turn on the windshield wipers, everything was blurry. She wished, suddenly, for civilization. For a car to drive by. A house to appear. A gas station. Something. Was Toby upset because he liked her, and she'd just come halfway out of the closet? Was Toby *homophobic*? This was what she would have to deal with, if she really thought she was gay. People would probably do this to her every day of her life.

"You've never been on that end of it, have you?" Toby finally asked. "You've never had anyone make fun of you."

"N-No . . ." She searched Toby's face, trying to understand his question. "I guess not. Well, not until Ben, anyway." Thunder cracked overhead, and she jumped. Then she saw a zigzag of lightning, slashing across the sky a few miles ahead of them. It lit things up for a moment, and Emily could see Toby frowning, picking at a button on his jacket.

"Seeing all those people tonight just made me realize how hard it used to be, living in Rosewood," he said. "People used to really hate me. But tonight, everyone was so nice—all these people who used to make fun of me. It was sickening. It was like it had never happened." He wrinkled his nose. "Do they not realize what assholes they were?"

"I guess not," Emily said, feeling uneasy.

Toby glanced at her. "I saw one of your old friends there. Spencer Hastings." Lightning flashed again, making Emily jump. Toby smiled crookedly. "You guys were such a clique, back then. You really let people have it. Me . . . my sister . . ."

"We didn't mean to," Emily said, on instinct.

"Emily." Toby shrugged. "You did. And why not? You were the most popular girls in school. You *could*." His voice was sharply sarcastic.

Emily tried to smile, hoping that this was a joke. Only Toby didn't smile back. Why were they talking about *this*? Weren't they supposed to be talking about Emily being gay? "I'm sorry. We just . . . We were so stupid. We did what Ali wanted us to do. And I mean, I thought you were over that, since you and Ali got together that next year—"

"*What?*" Toby interrupted sharply.

Emily backed against the window. Her chest burned with adrenaline. "You . . . you weren't fooling around with Ali in, um, seventh grade?"

Toby looked horrified. "It was hard for me even to *see* her," he said quietly. "Now it's hard for me even to hear her name." He put his palms to his forehead and let out a huge breath. When he faced her again, his eyes were dark. "Especially after . . . after what she did."

Emily stared at him. Lightning flashed again, and a stiff wind kicked up, making the cornstalks sway. They looked like hands, desperately reaching out for something.

"Wait, what?" She laughed, hoping–praying–she'd heard him wrong. Praying that she'd blink, and the night would right itself and go back to being normal.

"I think you heard me," Toby said in a flat, emotionless tone. "I know you were friends and you loved her and whatever, but personally, I'm glad that bitch is dead."

Emily felt like someone had sucked all the oxygen out of her body. *Something's going to happen to you tonight. Something life-changing.*

You really let people have it. Me . . . my sister . . .

It's hard for me even to hear her name. Especially after what she did . . .

AFTER WHAT SHE DID.

I'm glad that bitch is dead.

Toby . . . *knew?*

A crack started to form in her brain. He *did* know. She was sure of it, more certain than she'd ever been of anything in her life. Emily felt as if she'd always known this, that it had been right in front of her face, but she'd been trying to just ignore it. Toby knew what they'd done to Jenna, but A hadn't told him. He'd known for a very long time. And he must have hated Ali for it. He must have hated all of them, if he knew they were all involved.

"Oh my God," Emily whispered. She pulled at the door handle, gathering her dress in her hands as she stepped out of the car. The rain hit her immediately and felt like needles. Of course there was something suspicious about Toby being friendly to her. He wanted to ruin Emily's life.

"Emily?" Toby unbuckled his seat belt. "Where are you—"

Then she heard the engine roar. Toby was driving down the road toward her, the passenger door wide open. She looked right and left, and then, hoping she knew where she was, she dove into the cornfield, not even caring that she was getting absolutely soaked.

"Emily!" Toby called again. But Emily kept running.

Toby killed Ali. Toby was A.

31

LIKE HANNA WOULD STEAL AN AIRPLANE—SHE DOESN'T EVEN KNOW HOW TO FLY!

Hanna pushed her way through crowds of kids, hoping to see Emily's familiar reddish-blond hair. She found Spencer and Aria by the oversize windows, talking to Gemma Curran, one of Emily's swimming teammates.

"She was here with that guy from Tate, right?" Gemma pursed her lips and tried to think. "I'm pretty sure I saw them leave."

Hanna exchanged uneasy glances with her friends. "What are we going to do?" Spencer whispered. "It's not like we have any idea where they're going."

"I tried calling her," Aria said. "But her phone just kept ringing."

"Oh my God," Spencer said, her eyes filling up with tears.

"Well, what did you expect?" Aria said through her

teeth. "You're the one who let this happen." Hanna couldn't remember Aria ever being this angry.

"I know," Spencer repeated. "I'm sorry."

A huge *boom* interrupted them. Everyone looked outside to see the trees blowing sideways and rain coming down in sheets. "Shit," Hanna heard a girl say next to her. "My dress is going to be ruined."

Hanna faced her friends. "I know someone who can help us. A cop." She looked around, half-expecting Officer Wilden, the guy who'd arrested Hanna for stealing a Tiffany bracelet and Mr. Ackard's car *and* who'd gotten it on with her mom—to be at Foxy tonight. But the guys guarding the exits and the jewelry auction were the Foxhunting League's private security team—only if something devastating happened would they call in the cops. Last year, a Rosewood Day senior drank too much and ran off with a David Yurman bracelet that was up for auction, and even then they'd only left a tactful message on the boy's family's voice mail, saying that they'd like it back by the next day.

"We can't go to the *cops*," Spencer hissed. "The way the one cop was acting with me this morning, I wouldn't be surprised if they thought *we* killed Ali."

Hanna stared up at the giant crystal chandelier on the ceiling. A couple kids were tossing their napkins at it, trying to get the crystals to swing. "But I mean, your note pretty much says, *I'm gonna hurt you*, right? Isn't that enough?"

"It's signed *A*. And it said that *we* hurt him. How would we explain that?"

"But how do we make sure she's all right?" Aria asked, pulling up her polka-dotted dress. Hanna noted bitterly that the side zipper was still partially down.

"Maybe we should drive by her house," Spencer suggested.

"Sean and I could go right now," Aria volunteered.

Hanna's jaw dropped. "You're telling *Sean* about this?"

"No," Aria shouted, over the swells of Natasha Bedingfield and the pounding rain. Hanna could even see it fogging up the hall's skylight, thirty feet above their heads. "I won't tell him anything. Or I don't know how I'll explain it. But he won't know."

"So are you and Sean going to any after-parties?" Hanna pried.

Aria looked at her crazily. "You think I'd go to an after-party after all this?"

"Yeah, but if this hadn't happened, would you have gone?"

"Hanna." Spencer put her cool, thin hand on Hanna's shoulder. "Let it go."

Hanna gritted her teeth, grabbed a glass of champagne from a waitress's tray, and belted it down. She *couldn't* let it go. It wasn't possible.

"You check out Emily's house," Spencer said to Aria. "I'll keep calling her."

"What if we drive by Emily's and Toby is with her?"

Aria asked. "Do we confront him? I mean . . . if he *is* A . . . ?"

Hanna exchanged an uneasy glance with the others. She wanted to kick Toby's ass—how had he found out about Kate? Her father? Her arrests? How Sean had broken up with her and that she made herself puke? How dare he try to bring her down! But she was also afraid. If Toby was A—if he knew—then he really would want to hurt them. It made . . . sense.

"We should just concentrate on making sure Emily's safe," Spencer said. "How about, if we don't hear from her soon, we call the police and leave an anonymous tip. We could say we saw Toby hurt her. We wouldn't have to get into the specifics."

"If the cops come looking for him, he'll know it was us," Hanna reasoned. "And then what if he tells them about Jenna?" She could picture herself in juvenile hall, wearing an orange jumpsuit and talking to her father through a wall of glass.

"Or what if he comes after us?" Aria asked.

"We'll have to find her before that happens," Spencer interrupted.

Hanna looked at the clock. Ten-thirty. "I'm out." She strode toward the door. "I'll call you, Spencer." She didn't say anything to Aria. She couldn't even *look* at Aria. Or the giant hickey on her neck.

As she was leaving, Naomi Zeigler grabbed her hand. "Han, about what you said to me yesterday at the soccer game." She had the large-eyed, empathetic look of a talk-show host. "There are bulimia support groups. I could help you find one."

"Fuck off," Hanna said, and brushed past her.

By the time Hanna collapsed on the Philadelphia-bound SEPTA train, totally soaked from running from the cab to the train, her head felt heavy. In every reflection, a shadowy chimera of her seventh-grade self winked back. She shut her eyes.

When she opened her eyes again, the train had stalled. All the lights were out, except for the emergency glow-in-the-dark exit signs. Only, they didn't say EXIT anymore. They said WATCH IT.

To her left, Hanna saw miles of forest. The moon shone full and clear over the treetops. But hadn't it been pouring just minutes ago? The train paralleled Route 30 on the other side. The road was usually packed with traffic, but now, not a single car waited at the intersection. As she craned her neck down the aisle to see how the others were reacting to SEPTA's breakdown, she noticed that all the passengers were asleep.

"They're not asleep," a voice said. "They're dead."

Hanna jumped. It was Toby. His face was blurry, but she knew it was him. Slowly, he rose from his seat and walked over to her.

The train blew its whistle, and Hanna was jolted awake. The fluorescent lights were as bright and unflattering as ever; the train chugged toward the city; and outside, lightning crackled and danced. When she looked out the window, she saw a tree branch snap off and careen to the ground. Two white-haired old ladies in the seat ahead of her kept commenting on the lightning, saying, "Oh, goodness! That was a big one!"

Hanna pulled her knees up to her chest. Nothing like an earth-shattering confession about Toby Cavanaugh to rock your world. And make you paranoid as hell.

She wasn't sure how to take the news. She didn't react to things right away, like Aria did; she had to mull them over. She was angry at Spencer for not telling, yes. And terrified about Toby. But at the moment, her only overwhelming thoughts were about Jenna. Did she know, too? Had she known all along? Did she know that Toby had killed Ali?

Hanna had actually seen Jenna after her accident—just once, and she'd never told the others. It was just a few weeks before Ali went missing, and she'd thrown an impromptu party in her backyard. All of Rosewood Day's popular kids came—even some older girls from Ali's field hockey team. For the first time ever, Hanna was having a real conversation with Sean; they were talking about the movie *Gladiator*. Hanna was talking about how scary the movie was when Ali sauntered up beside them.

At first Ali gave Hanna a look that said, *Hooray! You're finally talking to him!* But then, when Hanna said, "When my dad and I came out of the theater, oh my God, I was so scared, I went straight to the bathroom and threw up," Ali nudged Hanna's side. "You've had some trouble with that lately, haven't you?" she joked.

Hanna paled. "*What?*" This wasn't long after the Annapolis thing happened.

Ali made sure she had Sean's attention. "This is Hanna," she said, and stuck her finger down her throat, gagged, and then giggled. Sean didn't laugh, however; he looked back and forth at them, seeming uncomfortable and confused. "I, um, have to . . ." he muttered, and slipped away to his friends.

Hanna turned to Ali, horrified. "*Why* did you do that?"

"Oh, Hanna," Ali said, whirling away. "Can't you take a joke?"

But Hanna couldn't. Not about that. She stomped to the other side of Ali's wraparound deck, heaving deep, angry breaths. When she looked up, she found herself staring right into Jenna Cavanaugh's face.

Jenna was standing at the edge of her property, wearing big sunglasses and carrying a white cane. Hanna's throat seized up. It was like seeing a ghost. *She really is blind,* Hanna thought. She sort of thought it hadn't actually happened.

Jenna stood very still on the curb. If she could have seen, she would have been looking at the big hole in Ali's side yard that they were digging for her family's twenty-seat gazebo—the exact spot where, years later, workers would find Ali's body. Hanna stared at her for a long time, and Jenna stared blankly back. Then it hit her. Back there, with Sean, Hanna had taken Jenna's place, and Ali had taken Hanna's. There was no reason for Ali to tease Hanna except that she *could*. The realization struck Hanna so forcefully, she had to grab onto the railing for balance.

She looked at Jenna again. *I'm so sorry,* she mouthed. Jenna, of course, didn't respond. She couldn't see.

Hanna was never so happy to see the lights of Philadelphia—she was finally far away from Rosewood and Toby. She still had time to get back to the hotel before her father, Isabel, and Kate returned from *Mamma Mia!*, and perhaps she could take a bubble bath. Hopefully there was something good in the minibar, too. Something strong. Perhaps she'd even tell Kate what happened and they'd order room service and kill a big bottle of something together.

Wow. *That* was a thought Hanna never imagined would cross her mind.

She slid her room card into the door, pulled it open, slumped inside, and . . . nearly bumped into her father. He was standing in front of the door, talking on his cell phone. "Oh!" she screamed.

Her father whirled around. "She's here," he said into the phone, then slapped it shut. He eyed Hanna coolly. "Well. Welcome back."

Hanna blinked. Beyond her father were Kate and

Isabel. Just . . . sitting there, on the couch, reading the Philadelphia tourist magazines that came with the room. "Hey," she said cautiously. Everyone was staring at her. "Did Kate tell you? I had to—"

"Go to Foxy?" Isabel interrupted.

Hanna's mouth fell open. Another bolt of lightning outside made her jump. She turned desperately to Kate, who had her hands haughtily folded in her lap and her head raised high. Had she . . . had she *told*? The look on her face said yes.

Hanna felt like she'd been dropped on her head. "It . . . it was an emergency."

"I'm sure it was." Her father put his hands flat on the table. "I can't believe you even came back. We thought you were going to pull another all-nighter . . . steal another car, maybe. Or . . . or who knows? Steal someone's airplane? Assassinate the president?"

"Dad . . ." Hanna pleaded. She'd never seen her father like this. His shirt was untucked, the ends of his socks weren't taut against his toes, and there was a smudge behind his ear. And he was *raving*. He never used to yell like this. "I can explain."

Her father pressed the heels of his hands to his forehead. "Hanna . . . can you explain this, too?" He reached into his pocket for something. Slowly, he unfurled his fingers, one by one. Inside, was the little foil packet of Percocet. Unopened.

As Hanna lunged for it, he snapped his hand closed like a clamshell. "Oh, no, you don't."

Hanna pointed at Kate. "She took those from me. She wanted them!"

"You gave them to me," Kate said evenly. She had this knowing, *gotcha* look on her face, a look that said, *Don't even think you're worming your way into our lives.* Hanna hated herself for being so stupid. Kate hadn't changed. Not a bit.

"What were you doing with pills in the first place?" her father asked. Then he held up his hand. "No. Forget it. I don't want to know. I . . ." He squeezed his eyes shut. "I don't know you anymore, Hanna. I really don't."

A dam inside Hanna broke. "Well, of course you don't!" she screamed. "You haven't bothered to speak to me for almost four fucking years!"

A hush fell over the room. Everyone seemed afraid to move. Kate's hands were flat against her magazine. Isabel froze, one finger bizarrely at her earlobe. Her father opened his mouth to speak, but then shut it again.

There was a knock on the door, and everyone jumped.

Ms. Marin was on the other side, looking uncharacteristically disheveled: Her hair was wet and stringy, she didn't have much makeup on, and she was wearing a simple T-shirt and jeans, a far cry from the put-together ensembles she usually wore to Wawa.

"You're coming with me." She narrowed her eyes at Hanna but didn't even glance at Isabel or Kate. Hanna wondered fleetingly if this was the first time everyone was meeting. When her mother saw the Percocet in Mr. Marin's hand, she paled. "He told me about *that* on the way here."

Hanna looked over her shoulder at her father, but he had his head down. He didn't look disappointed exactly. He just looked . . . sad. Hopeless. Ashamed. "Dad . . ." she squeaked desperately, wrenching away from her mom. "I don't have to go, do I? I want to stay. Can't I tell you what's going on with me? I thought you wanted to know."

"It's too late," her father said mechanically. "You're going home with your mother. Maybe she can talk some sense into you."

Hanna had to laugh. "You think *she's* going to talk sense into me? She's . . . she's sleeping with the cop who arrested me last week. She's been known to come home at two A.M. on school nights. If I'm sick and have to stay home from school, she tells me it's okay to call up the front office and just pretend I'm her, because she's too busy, and—"

"Hanna!" her mother screamed, clamping her fingers around Hanna's arm.

Hanna's brain was so scrambled, she had no idea whether telling her dad this stuff was helping or hurting her. She just felt so *duped*. By everyone. She was sick of people walking all over her. "There are so many things I wanted to tell you, but I can't. Please let me stay. *Please.*"

The only thing that wavered in her father was a tiny muscle, up by his neck. Otherwise, his face was stony and impassive. He took a step closer to Isabel and Kate. Isabel took his hand.

"Good night, Ashley," he said to Hanna's mother. To Hanna, he said nothing at all.

32

EMILY GOES TO BAT

Emily sobbed with relief when she discovered her house's side door was open. She threw her soaked body into the laundry room, nearly bursting into tears at the insulated, untroubled domesticity of everything: her mother's BLESS THIS MESS! cross-stitch above the washer and dryer; the neat row of detergent, bleach, and fabric softener on the little shelf; her father's green rubber gardening boots by the door.

The phone rang; it sounded like a scream. Emily grabbed a towel from the laundry pile, wrapped it around her shoulders, and tentatively picked up the cordless extension. "Hello?" Even the sound of her own voice seemed scary.

"Emily?" came a familiar gravelly voice on the other end.

Emily frowned. "Spencer?"

"Oh my God." Spencer sighed. "We've been looking for you. Are you all right?"

"I . . . I don't know," Emily said shakily. She'd run crazily through the cornfield. The rain had created rivers of mud between the rows. One of her shoes had fallen off, but she'd kept going, and now the bottom of her dress and her legs were filthy. The field butted up to the woods behind her house, and she'd torn through those, too. She'd slid twice on wet grass, scraping up her elbow and hip, and once, lightning hit a tree just twenty feet from her, violently snapping branches to the ground. She knew it was dangerous to be out there in a storm, but she couldn't stop, afraid Toby was right behind her.

"Emily. Stay where you are," Spencer instructed. "And stay away from Toby. I'll explain everything later, but for right now, just lock your door and—"

"I think Toby's A," Emily interrupted, her voice a scratchy, trembling whisper. "And I think he killed Ali."

There was a pause. "I know. So do I."

"What?" Emily cried. A crack of thunder radiated through the sky, making Emily cower. Spencer didn't answer. The line was dead.

Emily put the phone on top of the dryer. Spencer *knew*? It made Emily's revelation even more real—and much, much scarier.

Then, she heard a voice. "Emily! Emily?"

She froze. It sounded like it was coming from the kitchen. She sprinted in there and saw Toby looking in, his hands pressed against her sliding glass door. The rain had soaked through his suit and matted down his hair, and he was shivering. His face was in the shadows.

Emily screamed.

"Emily!" Toby said again. He tried the door handle, but Emily quickly latched it.

"Go away," she hissed. He could . . . he could burn down their house. Break in. Suffocate Emily while she slept. If he could kill Ali, he was capable of anything.

"I'm getting soaked," he called to her. "Let me in."

"I . . . I can't talk to you. Please, Toby, *please*. Just leave me alone."

"Why did you run away from me?" Toby looked confused. He had to yell, too, because it was raining so hard. "I'm not sure what happened in the car. I was just . . . I was just sort of messed up from seeing all those people. But that was all years ago. I'm sorry."

The sweetness in his voice made it even worse. He tried the handle again, and Emily shouted, "No!" Toby stopped, and Emily looked around frantically for something that could be a weapon. A heavy, ceramic chicken plate. A dull kitchen knife. Perhaps she could root around in the cabinets and find the griddle. . . . "Please." Emily was trembling so badly, her legs were wobbly. "Just go away."

"Let me at least give you back your purse. It's in my car."

"Just put it in my mailbox."

"Emily, don't be ridiculous." Toby started pounding angrily on the door. "Just get over here and let me in!"

Emily picked up the heavy chicken plate on the kitchen table. She held it out in front of her with both hands, like a shield. "Go away!"

Toby pushed his soaked hair off his face. "The stuff I said to you in the car . . . it came out all wrong. I'm sorry if I said something that—"

"It's too late," Emily interrupted. She squeezed her eyes shut. All she wanted was to open her eyes again and for all this to be a dream. "I know what you did to her."

Toby stiffened. "Wait. *What?*"

"You heard me," Emily said. "I. Know. What. You. Did. To. Her."

Toby's mouth fell open. The rain fell harder, making his eyeballs look like hollow pits. "How could you know about that?" his voice wobbled. "No one . . . no one knew. It was . . . it was a long time ago, Emily."

Emily's mouth dropped open. What, did he think he was so sly that he could get *away* with it? "Well, I guess your secret's out."

Toby started to pace back and forth across her deck, running his fingers through his hair. "But, Emily, you don't understand. I was so *young*. And . . . and confused. I wish I hadn't done it. . . ."

Emily felt a huge tug of regret. She didn't want Toby to be Ali's killer. The sweet way he'd helped her out of his car, how he'd defended her in front of Ben, how lost and vulnerable he'd looked when Emily glanced at him, standing alone on the Foxy dance floor. Maybe he really was sorry for what he'd done. Maybe he'd just been confused.

But then Emily thought about the night Ali went missing. It had been so beautiful out, the perfect kickoff to what was going to be a perfect summer. They were planning to go to the Jersey Shore the following weekend, had tickets to the No Doubt concert in July, and Ali was going to throw a huge thirteenth birthday party in August. All that was gone the instant Ali stepped out of Spencer's family's barn.

Toby might have come up to her from behind. Maybe he hit her with something. Maybe he said things to her. When he threw her into the hole, he must have . . . covered her up with dirt so no one would find her. Was that how it went? And after Toby hurt her, had he just gotten on his bike and ridden home? Had he returned to Maine for the rest of the summer? Had he watched everyone searching on the news with a bowl of microwave popcorn in his lap, like it was a movie on HBO?

I'm glad that bitch is dead. Emily had never heard anything so horrible in her life.

"Please," Toby cried. "I can't go through all this again. And neither can—"

He couldn't even finish his sentence. Then, suddenly, he covered his face with his hands and ran away, back into the woods in her backyard.

All was quiet. Emily looked around. The kitchen was

spotless—her parents had gone away this weekend to Pittsburgh to visit Emily's grandmother, and her mother always cleaned maniacally before she went. Carolyn was still out with Topher.

She was all alone.

Emily sprinted to the front door. It was locked, but she pulled the chain across for extra protection. She twisted the dead bolt to make sure it was secure. Then she remembered the garage door: The mechanical part of it had broken, and her dad had been lazy about fixing it. Someone strong enough could lift up the garage door himself.

And then she realized. Toby had her purse. Which meant . . . he had her *keys*.

She picked up the phone in the kitchen and dialed 911. But the phone didn't even ring. She hung up and listened for a dial tone, but there was none. Emily felt her knees weaken. The storm must have knocked out the phone lines.

She remained frozen in the hallway for a few seconds, her jaw trembling. *Had Toby dragged Ali by her hair? Had she still been alive when he tossed her into that hole?*

She ran into the garage and looked around. In the corner was her old baseball bat. It felt strong and heavy in her hands. Satisfied, she slid out to the front porch, locked the door behind her with the spare key from the kitchen, and settled gently into the porch swing in the shadows, the bat in her lap. It was freezing outside, and she could see a giant spider building a web in the other corner of the porch. Spiders always terrified her, but she had to be brave. She wouldn't let Toby hurt her, too.

33

WHO'S THE NAUGHTY SISTER NOW?

The next morning, Spencer came back into her bedroom after taking a shower and noticed the window was open. As in, seriously hoisted up about two feet, screen and all. The curtains fluttered in the breeze.

She ran to the window, her throat tight. Although she'd calmed down after she reached Emily last night, this was odd. The Hastingses *never* opened the screens, because moths could fly in and ruin the expensive rugs. She jerked the window down, then nervously checked under her bed and in her closet. No one.

When her Sidekick buzzed, she nearly jumped out of her silk pajama pants. She found her phone buried in her Foxy dress, which she'd stripped off last night and left in a pile on the floor—something the old Spencer Hastings would never have done. It was an e-mail from Squidward.

Dear Spencer, Thank you for turning in your essay
questions early. I've read them, and I'm very pleased.
See you Monday. —Mr. McAdam

Spencer slumped back down on her bed, her heart
beating slowly but forcefully.

Out her bedroom window, she could see that it was a
beautiful, crisp September Sunday. The aroma of apples
hung in the air. Her mother, wearing a straw hat and
rolled-up jeans, strolled to the end of the driveway with
her gardening shears to prune back the bushes.

She couldn't deal with all this . . . this pleasantness.
She grabbed her Sidekick and speed-dialed Wren's number. Perhaps they could start their date early. She needed
out of Rosewood. The phone rang a few times; then
there was a clatter and a clunk. It took a few seconds for
Wren to say hello. "It's me," Spencer sobbed.

"Spencer?" Wren sounded groggy.

"Yeah." Her mood shifted to irritation. Did he not
recognize her voice?

"Could I call you back?" Wren yawned. "I'm sort
of . . . I'm still sleeping."

"But . . . I need to talk with you."

He sighed.

Spencer softened. "I'm sorry. Can you *please* talk to
me right now?" She paced around the room. "I need to
hear a friendly voice."

Wren was quiet. Spencer even checked her Sidekick's

LED screen to make sure they were still connected. "Look," he finally said. "This isn't the easiest thing to say, but . . . I don't think this is going to work out."

Spencer rubbed her ears. "What?"

"I thought this would be okay." Wren sounded numb. Robotic, almost. "But I think you're too young for me. I just . . . I don't know. We seem to be in really different places."

The room blurred, then tilted. Spencer grasped the phone so hard, her knuckles turned white. "Wait. *What?* We were just together the other day, and it was fine then!"

"I know. But . . . God, this isn't that easy . . . I've started seeing someone else."

For a few seconds, Spencer's brain shut down. She had no idea how to respond. She was pretty sure she wasn't even breathing. "But I had sex with you," she whispered.

"I know. I'm sorry. But I think this is for the best."

The best . . . for who? In the background, Spencer heard Wren's coffeemaker beep that brewing had finished. "Wren . . ." Spencer pleaded. "Why are you doing this?"

But he had already hung up.

Her phone flashed CALL ENDED. Spencer held it at arm's length.

"Hey!"

Spencer jumped. Melissa stood in Spencer's doorway. In her yellow J. Crew tissue tee and orange Adidas shorts, she looked like a ball of sunshine. "How'd it go?"

Spencer blinked. "Huh?"

"Foxy! Was it fun?"

Spencer tried to mask her swirling emotions. "Um, yeah. It was great."

"Did they have an ugly jewelry auction this year? How was Andrew?"

Andrew. She'd meant to explain everything to Andrew, but Toby had gotten in the way. Spencer had left Foxy shortly after she found out Emily was okay, hailing one of the town cars that were chugging in Kingman Hall's circular drive. Her parents had reinstated her credit cards, so she could actually pay for the trip home.

It made her squeamish to imagine how Andrew felt today. They might even be feeling the same way—blindsided, rushed. But that was silly, really. Spencer and Wren had had something serious. . . . Andrew was delusional if he'd thought he and Spencer were honestly together.

Her eyes widened. Was *she* delusional, thinking that she was honestly with Wren? What kind of jerk dumps you over the phone, anyway?

Melissa sat next to her on her bed, expectantly awaiting an answer.

"Andrew was good." Spencer's brain felt gummy. "He was very, um, chivalrous."

"What was for dinner?"

"Um, squab," Spencer lied. She didn't have a clue.

"And was it romantic?"

Spencer quickly tried to conjure up some cute scenes

with Andrew. Sharing the appetizer. Drunkenly dancing to Shakira. She caught herself. What was the point? It didn't matter anymore.

The clouds started to move out of her brain. Melissa was sitting here, so sweetly trying to make an effort to patch things up. The way she'd taken an interest in Foxy, the way she'd urged their parents to forgive her . . . and Spencer had repaid her by stealing Wren and ripping off her old econ paper. Even Melissa didn't deserve this.

"I have something to tell you," Spencer blurted out. "I . . . I saw Wren."

Melissa barely flinched, so Spencer pressed forward. "This whole week. I've gone to his new apartment in Philly, we've talked on the phone, everything. But . . . I think it's over now." She curled into the fetal position, armoring herself for when Melissa started to hit her. "You can hate me. I mean, I wouldn't blame you. You can go tell Mom and Dad to kick me out of the house."

Melissa quietly held Spencer's preppy seersucker pillow to her chest. It took a long time for her to answer. "It's all right. I won't tell them anything." Melissa leaned back. "I actually have something to tell *you*. You remember Friday night, when you couldn't reach Wren? You left five messages?"

Spencer stared at her. "H-How do you know that?"

Melissa gave her a tight, satisfied smile. A smile that suddenly made everything all too clear. *I've been seeing someone else,* Wren had said. *It can't be,* Spencer thought.

"Because Wren wasn't in Philly," Melissa answered nonchalantly. "He was here, in Rosewood. With me." She got up off the bed and pushed her hair behind her ears, and Spencer saw the hickey on Melissa's neck, practically in the same spot where Spencer's had been. Melissa couldn't have been more deliberate if she'd circled it with a Sharpie.

"And he *told* you?" she managed. "You knew, all this time?"

"No, I only found out last night." Melissa ran her hand over her chin. "Let's just say I got an anonymous tip from a concerned individual."

Spencer gripped her bedspread. *A.*

"Anyway," Melissa lilted, "I was with Wren last night, too, when you were at Foxy." She tilted her head down at Spencer, giving her the same haughty look she used to make when they played Queen, back when they were little. The rules of Queen never changed: Melissa was always Queen, and Spencer always had to do what she said. *Make my bed, loyal subject,* Melissa would say. *Kiss my feet. You're mine forever.*

Melissa took a step toward the door. "But I decided this morning. I haven't told him yet, but Wren's really *not* for me. So I'm never going to see him again." She paused, considered her words, then smirked. "And by the looks of things, I guess you won't be seeing him ever again, either."

34

SEE? DEEP DOWN, HANNA REALLY IS A GOOD GIRL

The first thing Hanna heard on Sunday morning was someone singing that Elvis Costello song "Alison."

"ALLLLLison, I know this world is KILLING you!" It was a guy, his voice loud and grating like a lawn mower. Hanna threw her covers back. Was it the TV? Was it someone outside?

When she stood up, her head felt like it was full of cotton candy. She saw the Chloé jacket she'd worn last night thrown over her desk chair, and everything came flooding back to her.

After her mom retrieved her from the Four Seasons, they'd driven home in stony silence. When they pulled into the driveway, Ms. Marin jammed the Lexus into park and stormed crookedly into the house, drunk with anger. When Hanna got to the door, her mom slammed it in her face, and there was a loud, solid *clunk*. Hanna stood back, stunned. Okay, so she'd outed her mom's worst parenting faux pas, and that was probably a bad move. But was her mom seriously locking her out?

Hanna pounded on the door, and Ms. Marin opened it a crack. Her eyebrows were drawn together. "Oh, I'm sorry. You want to come in?"

"Y-Yes," Hanna squeaked.

Her mother guffawed. "You're completely willing to insult and disrespect me in front of your father, but you're not too proud to live here?"

Hanna had made some sort of blubbering attempt at an apology, but her mom stormed away. She did, however, leave the door open. Hanna had scooped up Dot and run to her room, too traumatized to even cry.

"Ohhhhh, ALLLLLison . . . I know this world is KILLLing YOU!"

Hanna tiptoed to her door. The singing was coming from inside the house. Her legs started to shake. Only a crazy person would be stupid enough to sing that "Alison" song in Rosewood right now. The cops would probably arrest you just for humming it in public.

Was it *Toby*?

She straightened her yellow camisole and stepped into the hall. At the same moment, the hall bathroom door opened and a guy stepped out.

Hanna put her hand to her mouth. The guy had a towel—*her* white, fluffy, Pottery Barn towel—wrapped around his waist. His blackish hair stood up in peaks. A silent scream got stuck in Hanna's throat.

And then he turned around and faced her. Hanna took a step back. It was Darren Wilden. *Officer* Darren Wilden.

"Whoa." Wilden froze. "Hanna."

It was hard not to gawk at his perfectly formed abs. He was definitely not a cop who ate too many Krispy Kremes. "Why were you *singing* that?" she finally asked.

Wilden looked embarrassed. "Sometimes I don't notice I'm singing."

"I thought you were . . . " Hanna trailed off. What the hell was Wilden *doing* here? But then she realized. Of course. Her mom. She smoothed down her hair, not feeling any calmer. What if it had been Toby? What would she have done? She would probably be dead.

"Do you . . . do you need to get in here?" Wilden gestured bashfully at the steamy bathroom. "Your mom's in hers."

Hanna was too stunned to respond. Then, before she knew exactly what she was saying, she blurted out, "I have something to tell you. Something important."

"Oh?" A droplet of water fell off a strand of Wilden's hair onto the floor.

"I think I know something about . . . about who killed Alison DiLaurentis."

Wilden raised an eyebrow. "Who?"

Hanna licked her lips. "Toby Cavanaugh."

"Why do you think that?"

"I . . . I can't tell you why. You just have to take my word for it."

Wilden frowned and leaned against the doorjamb, still half-naked. "You're going to have to give me a little more than that. You could be giving me the name of some guy who broke your heart, for revenge."

In that case, I'd have told you Sean Ackard, Hanna thought bitterly. She didn't know what to do. If she told Wilden about The Jenna Thing, her dad would hate her. Everyone in Rosewood would talk. She and her friends would go to juvie.

But keeping the secret from her dad—and the rest of Rosewood—didn't really matter anymore. Her whole life was ruined, and besides, she was the one who'd really hurt Jenna. That night might've been an accident, but Hanna had hurt her plenty of times on purpose.

"I'll tell you," she said slowly, "but I don't want anyone else to get in trouble. Only . . . only me, if someone has to. Okay?"

Wilden held up his hand. "It doesn't matter. We checked out Toby when Alison first disappeared. He has an airtight alibi. Couldn't have been him."

Hanna gaped. "He has an alibi? *Who?*"

"I can't disclose that." Wilden looked stern for a moment, but then the corners of his mouth curled up into a smile. He pointed at Hanna's A&F moose-printed flannel pants. "You look cute in your jammies."

Hanna curled her toes into the carpet. She'd always hated the word *jammies.* "Wait, are you *sure* Toby's innocent?"

Wilden was about to respond, but his walkie-talkie, which was perched on the edge of the bathroom sink, made a crackling sound. He turned and grabbed it, keeping one hand on the towel around his waist. "Casey?"

"There's another body," a crackling voice answered. "And it's . . ." The transmission turned to static.

Hanna's heart started pounding again. *Another body?*

"Casey." Wilden was buttoning up his police shirt. "Can you repeat that? Hello?" Fuzz was all he got in reply. He noticed Hanna still standing there. "Go to your room."

Hanna bristled. The nerve of him, trying to speak to her like he was her father! "What about another body?" she whispered.

Wilden put the walkie-talkie back on the counter, whipped on his pants, and tore the towel off his lower half, tossing it on the bathroom floor just like Hanna often did. "Just calm down," he said, his friendliness all gone. He put his gun in his holster and clomped down the stairs.

Hanna followed him. Spencer had called last night to tell her that Emily was okay—but what if she'd been mistaken? "Is it a girl's body? Do you know?"

Wilden flung the front door open. In the driveway next to her mom's champagne-colored Lexus was his squad car. ROSEWOOD PD was printed, loud and clear, on the side panel. Hanna gawked. Had that been here all night? Could the neighbors see it from the road?

Hanna followed Wilden to his car. "Can you at least tell me where the body *is*?"

He whirled around. "I can't tell you that."

"But . . . you don't understand–"

"Hanna." Wilden didn't let her finish. "Tell your mom I'll call her later." He swung into his car and put the siren on. If the neighbors didn't know he'd been there before, they sure did now.

35

SPECIAL DELIVERY

Sunday at 11:52 A.M., Aria sat on her bed, staring at her red-painted fingernails. She felt slightly disoriented, as if she were forgetting something . . . something *huge*. Like those dreams she sometimes had where it was June, and she just realized she hadn't gone to math class the whole year and was going to flunk out.

And then she remembered. Toby was A. And today was Sunday. Her time was up.

It scared her to put a name and face to A's wrath—and that Ali and Spencer *had* been covering something up, something that could be really, *really* serious. Aria still had no idea how Toby had found out about Byron and Meredith, but if Aria caught them together twice, others could have seen them together, too—including Toby.

She'd meant to tell Ella about everything last night. When Sean dropped her off at home, he asked repeatedly if he should come in with her. But Aria told him no—she had to do what she was going to do alone. The house had been dark and still, the only sound the groaning of the dishwasher on high-scrub mode. Aria had fumbled for the foyer lights, then tiptoed into the dark, empty kitchen. Usually, her mother was up at least until 1 or 2 A.M. on Saturday nights, doing Sudoku puzzles or having discussions with Byron at the table over decaf coffee. But the table was spotless; she could see dried sponge swirls on its surface.

Aria had bounded up to her parents' bedroom, wondering if Ella had fallen asleep early. Their door was wide open. The bed was unmade, but there was no one in it. The master bathroom was empty, too. Then Aria noticed that the Honda Civic her parents shared wasn't in the driveway.

So she waited at the foot of the steps for them to come home, anxiously checking her watch every thirty seconds as it ticked to midnight. Her parents were possibly the only people in the universe who didn't have cell phones, so she couldn't call them. That meant Toby couldn't call them, either . . . or had he found another way to get in touch?

And then . . . she'd woken up here, in her bed. Someone must have carried her in, and Aria, who slept like the dead, hadn't noticed a thing.

She listened to the sounds downstairs. Drawers opening and closing. The wood floor groaning under someone's feet. Pages of the newspaper turning. Were there two parents down there, or just one? She tiptoed down the stairs, a billion different scenarios going through her head. Then she saw them: tiny red droplets, all over the entrance hall floor. They made a trail from the kitchen straight to the front door.

It looked like blood.

Aria ran for the kitchen. Toby had told her mother, and Ella, in a rage, had killed Byron. Or Meredith. Or Toby. Or everyone. Or Mike had killed them. Or . . . or Byron had killed Ella. When she got to the kitchen, she stopped.

Ella was at the table alone. She wore a wine-colored blouse, high heels, and makeup, as if she were ready to go out somewhere. The *New York Times* was folded to the crossword puzzle, but instead of letters filling in the squares, the page was scribbled over in thick, black ink. Ella stared straight ahead, sort of randomly toward the kitchen window, pushing the tines of a fork into the heel of her hand.

"Mom?" Aria croaked, stepping closer. Aria could see now that the blouse was wrinkled and her makeup looked smudged. It was almost like she'd slept in her clothes . . . or hadn't slept at all.

"Mom?" Aria asked again, her voice tinged with fear. Finally, her mother slowly looked over. Ella's eyes were heavy and swimming. She shoved the fork farther into her palm. Aria wanted to reach out and take it away, but she was afraid. She'd never seen her mom like this. "What's going on?"

Ella swallowed. "Oh . . . you know."

Aria swallowed hard. "What's the . . . the red stuff in the hall?"

"Red stuff?" Ella asked soullessly. "Oh. Maybe it's paint. I threw out some art supplies this morning. I threw out a lot of stuff this morning."

"Mom." Aria could feel tears come to her eyes. "Is something wrong?"

Her mother looked up. Her movements were slow, like she was underwater. "You knew for almost four years."

Aria stopped breathing. "What?" she whispered.

"Are you *friends* with her?" Ella asked, still in the same, dead voice. "She's not that much older than you. And I heard you went to her yoga studio the other day."

"*What?*" Aria whispered. *Yoga studio?* "I don't know w-what you mean!"

"Of course you do." Ella gave her the saddest smile Aria had ever seen. "I got a letter. At first I didn't believe it, but I confronted your father. And to think I thought he was distant because of work."

"*What?*" Aria backed up. Spots formed in front of her eyes. "You got a *letter*? When? Who sent it?"

But by the cold, vacant way Ella looked at her, Aria knew exactly who'd sent it. A. *Toby*. And he'd told her everything.

Aria put her hands on her forehead. "I'm so sorry," she said. "I . . . I wanted to tell you, but I was so afraid and–"

"Byron's gone," Ella said, almost flip. "He's with the girl." She let out a little snicker. "Maybe they're doing *yoga* together."

"I'm sure we could get him to come back." Aria choked on tears. "I mean, he has to, right? We're his family."

At that precise second, the cuckoo clock struck twelve. The clock had been a gift from Byron to Ella on their twentieth wedding anniversary last year in Iceland; Ella was really into it because it was rumored to have belonged to Edvard Munch, the famous Norwegian painter who painted *The Scream*. She'd carefully carried it home with her on the plane, constantly peeling back the bubble wrap to make sure it was okay. Now, they had to listen to twelve chirps and see that stupid bird pop out of his wooden house twelve times. Each chirp sounded more and more accusatory. Instead of *cuckoo*, the bird singsonged, *You knew. You knew. You knew.*

"Oh, Aria," Ella scolded. "I don't think he's coming back."

"Where's the letter?" Aria asked, snot running down her face. "Can I see it? I don't know who would do this to us . . . who would ruin things like this."

Ella stared at her. Her eyes were teary and huge, too. "I threw the letter away. But it doesn't matter who sent it. What matters is that it's *true*."

"I'm so sorry." Aria kneeled next to her, drinking in

the funny, familiar way her mom smelled—like turpen-
tine, newspaper ink, sandalwood incense, and, strangely,
scrambled eggs. She put her head on her mother's
shoulder, but Ella shook her away. "Aria," she said
sharply, standing up. "I can't be near you right now."

"What?" Aria cried.

Ella wasn't looking at her but instead was staring at
her left hand, which, Aria abruptly noticed, didn't have
a wedding ring on it anymore.

She pushed past Aria, floating, ghostlike, into the
hall and tracking the red paint all the way up the stairs.
"Wait!" Aria screamed, following her. She scrambled up
the stairs but tripped over a muddy pair of Mike's lacrosse
cleats, banged her knee, and slid two steps down. "Damn
it," she spat, gripping the carpet with her fingernails. She
pushed herself up and reached the landing, panting with
rage. Her mother's bedroom door was closed. So was the
door to the bathroom. Mike's bedroom door was open,
except Mike wasn't there. *Mike,* Aria thought, her heart
breaking all over again. Did he know?

Her cell phone started to ring. Dazed, she went into
her bedroom to find it. Her brain felt wild. She was still
panting. She almost wanted the call to be from A—Toby—
just so she could chew him out. But it was just Spencer.
Aria stared at the number, fuming. It didn't matter that
Spencer wasn't A—she might as well be. If Spencer had
turned in Toby back in seventh grade, he would never
have told Ella, and her family would be intact.

She snapped her phone open but didn't speak. She just sat there, taking deep, heaving breaths. "Aria?" Spencer called cautiously.

"I have nothing to say to you," Aria ground out. "You've ruined my life."

"I know," Spencer answered quietly. "It's just . . . Aria, I'm sorry. I didn't want to keep the Toby secret from you. But I didn't know what to do. Can't you see it from my perspective?"

"No," Aria said thickly. "You don't understand. You've *ruined my life*."

"Wait, what do you mean?" Spencer sounded worried. "What . . . what happened?"

Aria put her head in her hands. It was too exhausting to explain. And she *could* see things from Spencer's perspective. Of course she could. What Spencer was saying was hauntingly close to what Aria had said to Ella, three minutes ago. *I didn't want to keep this from you. I didn't know what to do. I didn't want to hurt you.*

She sighed and wiped her nose. "Why are you calling?"

"Well . . ." Spencer paused. "Have you heard from Emily this morning?"

"No."

"Shit," Spencer whispered.

"What's the matter?" Aria sat up straighter. "I thought you said last night that you got a hold of her, and she was at home."

"Well, she was. . . ." Aria heard Spencer swallow. "I'm sure it's nothing, but my mom was just driving by Emily's neighborhood, and there are three police cars in her driveway."

36

JUST ANOTHER SLOW
NEWS DAY IN ROSEWOOD

Emily lived in an older, modest neighborhood with a lot of retired residents, and everyone was out on their porches or in the middle of the street, concerned over the three police cars in the Fieldses' driveway and by the ambulance that had just roared away. Spencer pulled up to the curb and spotted Aria. She was still in her polka-dotted dress from Foxy.

"I just got here," Aria said as Spencer approached. "But I can't find out anything. I've asked a bunch of people what's going on, but no one knows."

Spencer looked around. There were plenty of police dogs, police officers, EMS people, and even a Channel 4 news van—it had probably just driven over from the DiLaurentis house. She felt like all the police officers were looking at her.

And then Spencer started to shake. This was her fault. Completely her fault. She felt sick. Toby had warned her that people would get hurt, yet she'd done nothing. She'd been so absorbed in Wren—and look how that had turned out. She couldn't even think about Wren right now. Or Melissa. Or them together. It made her feel like there were worms crawling through her veins. Something had happened to Emily, and she'd had the chance to stop it. The police had been sitting in her living room. Even A had warned her.

Suddenly, Spencer noticed Emily's sister Carolyn standing in the driveway, talking to some cops. One of the officers leaned down and whispered something in her ear. Carolyn's face crumpled, like she was crying. She ran back into the house.

Aria's posture wavered a little, like she was about to faint. "Oh God, Emily's . . ."

Spencer swallowed hard. "We don't know anything yet."

"I can just feel it, though," Aria said, her eyes full of tears. "A—Toby—his threats." She paused, pushing away a strand of hair that had gotten in her mouth. Her hands shook badly. "We're next, Spencer. I know it."

"Where are Emily's parents?" Spencer asked in a loud voice, trying to drown out everything Aria just said. "Wouldn't they be here if Emily were . . . " She didn't want to say the word *dead*.

A Toyota Prius barreled crookedly up the road and parked behind Spencer's Mercedes. Hanna got out. Or, it was a girl who *resembled* Hanna. She hadn't bothered changing out of a pair of flannel pajama pants, and her long, normally stick-straight dark auburn hair was kinky and stuffed into a half-up, half-down bun. Spencer hadn't seen her look so un-put together in years.

Hanna spied them and ran over. "What's going on? Is it—"

"We don't know," Spencer interrupted.

"You guys, I found something out." Hanna slipped off her sunglasses. "I talked to a cop this morning, and . . ."

Another news van pulled up and Hanna stopped talking. Spencer recognized the woman from Channel 8 news. She took a couple steps closer to the girls, her cell phone to her ear. "So the body was found outside this morning?" she said, looking at a clipboard. "Okay, thanks."

The girls exchanged a pleading look. Then Aria took the others' hands and they strode across Emily's lawn, treading straight through a flower bed. They were a few feet from Emily's front door when a police officer stepped in their path.

"Hanna, I told you to stay out of this," the cop said.

Spencer gulped. It was Wilden, the guy who'd come by her house yesterday. Her heart started to pound.

Hanna tried to push him aside. "Don't tell me what to do!" The officer grabbed Hanna by the shoulders, and she started to squirm. "Get off me!"

Spencer quickly gripped Hanna around her tiny waist.

"Try to calm her down," Wilden said to Spencer. Then he noticed who she was. "Oh," he breathed. He looked confused, then curious. "Miss Hastings."

"We just want to know what happened to Emily," Spencer tried to explain, her insides roiling. "She's . . . she's our friend."

"You guys should all go home." Wilden crossed his arms over his chest.

Suddenly, the front door opened . . . and Emily stepped out.

She was barefoot and pale, and holding a glass of water in an old McDonald's Muppet mug. Spencer was so relieved to see her, she actually cried out. A vulnerable, pained noise escaped from her throat.

The girls rushed over to her. "Are you all right?" Hanna asked.

"What happened?" Aria said at the same time.

"What's going on?" Spencer gestured to the crowd of people.

"Emily . . ." Wilden put his hands on his hips. "Maybe you should see your friends later. Your parents said you were supposed to stay inside."

But Emily shook her head, almost irritated. "No, it's okay."

Emily led them right past the cop to her side yard. They stood practically in a rosebush up against the side of the house, so they'd have a little privacy. Spencer took a good look at Emily. She had dark circles under her eyes, and there were scratches all over her legs, but otherwise, she looked fine. "What happened?" Spencer asked.

Emily took a huge breath. "A mountain biker found Toby's body in the woods behind my house this morning. I guess . . . I guess he OD'd on pills or something."

Spencer's heart stopped. Hanna gasped. Aria went pale. "What? *When?*" she asked.

"It was sometime during the night," Emily said. "I was going to call you, except that cop's watching me like a hawk." Her jaw was trembling. "My parents are visiting my grandmother this weekend." She tried to smile, but it warped into a grimace, and then her face collapsed into a sob.

"It's all right," Hanna comforted her.

"He was acting crazy last night," Emily said, wiping her face with her shirt. "He took me home from Foxy, and one minute, it was totally normal, and the next, he was telling me how much he hated Ali. He said he couldn't forgive Ali for what she did, and that he was glad she's dead."

"Oh my God." Spencer covered her eyes. It was all true.

"That's when I realized—Toby *knew*," Emily went on, her pale, freckly hands fluttering. "He must have found out what Ali did, and . . . and I think he killed her."

"Wait a second," Hanna interrupted, holding up her hand. "I don't think he—"

"Shhh." Spencer put her hand lightly on Hanna's tiny

wrist. Hanna looked like she wanted to say something, but Spencer was afraid that if Emily stopped, she wouldn't be able to finish.

"I ran away from him—the whole way to my house," Emily said. "When I got inside, Spencer called, but we got cut off. Then . . . then Toby was at my back door. I told him that I knew what he'd done, and I was going to tell the police. He acted all amazed that I'd figured it out."

Emily seemed winded by all that talking. "You guys— how did Toby know?"

Spencer's stomach dropped. The phone lines had gone down before she could explain the truth of The Jenna Thing to Emily last night. She wished she didn't have to tell Emily now—she seemed so fragile. It had been bad enough telling Aria and Hanna—but the truth was going to shatter Emily's world.

Aria and Hanna were looking at Spencer expectantly, so Spencer steeled herself. "He always knew," she said. "He saw Ali do it. Only, Ali blackmailed him into taking the blame. She made me keep the secret." She paused for a breath and noticed that Emily wasn't reacting the way she thought she would. She was standing there, completely calm, as if she were listening to a geography lecture. It kind of put Spencer off balance. "So, um, when Ali went missing, I always thought that maybe, I don't know . . ." She looked up toward the sky, realizing that what she was about to say was true. "I thought maybe Toby had something to do with it, but I was too scared to say anything. But then he came back for her funeral . . . and my A notes referenced the Toby secret. The last one said, *You hurt me, so I'm going to hurt you.* He wanted revenge on all of us. He must have known we were all involved."

Emily was still standing there so calmly. Then, slowly, her shoulders started to shake. She shut her eyes. At first, Spencer thought she was crying, but then she realized she was laughing.

Emily threw her head back, laughing louder. Spencer glanced at Aria and Hanna uneasily. Emily had obviously lost it. "Em . . ." she prodded gently.

When Emily brought her head back down, her bottom lip was trembling. "Ali promised us that no one knew what we'd done."

"Guess she lied," Hanna said flatly.

Emily's eyes flickered searchingly back and forth. "But how could she lie to us like that? What if Toby decided to tell?" She shook her head. "This . . . this happened when we were all inside Ali's house, watching at her front door?" Emily asked. "That very same night?"

Spencer nodded solemnly.

"And Ali came back inside and said everything was fine, and when none of us could sleep except for her, she comforted us by scratching our backs?"

"Yes." Tears came to Spencer's eyes. Of course Emily remembered every detail.

Emily stared off into space. "And she gave us these." She held up her arm. The bracelet Ali had made them—to symbolize the secret—was tightly knotted around her wrist. Everyone else had taken theirs off.

Emily's legs buckled, and she fell to the grass. Then she started tearing at the bracelet around her wrist, trying get it off, but the strings were old and tough. "Damn it," Emily said, collapsing her fingers together to make her wrist smaller so she could yank the bracelet off without untying it. Then she went at it with her teeth, but it wouldn't budge.

Aria put her hand on Emily's shoulder. "It's all right."

"I just can't believe any of it." She wiped her eyes, giving up on the bracelet. Emily pulled up a fistful of grass. "And I can't believe I went to Foxy with Ali's . . . *killer*."

"We were so scared for you," Spencer whispered.

Hanna waved her arms around. "You guys, that's what I've been trying to tell you. Toby's *not* Ali's killer."

"Huh?" Spencer frowned. "What are you talking about?"

"I . . . I spoke to that cop this morning." Hanna pointed toward Wilden, who was talking to the news team. "I told him about Toby . . . how I thought he killed Ali. He said they checked him out, like, years ago. Toby's not even a suspect."

"He definitely did it." Emily stood back up. "Last night, when I told him I knew what he'd done, he got really panicked and begged me not to tell the cops."

Everyone looked at one another, confused. "So you think the cops are just wrong?" Hanna fiddled with the heart-shaped charm on her bracelet.

"Wait a minute," Emily said slowly. "Spencer, what was Ali blackmailing him about? How did she get Toby to take the blame for . . . for Jenna?"

"Spencer said Ali wouldn't tell her," Aria answered.

Spencer felt a tight, nervous feeling come over her. *It's better my way,* Ali had said. *We keep Toby's secret, he keeps ours.*

But Toby was dead. Ali was dead. It didn't matter, now. "I do know," she said quietly.

Then Spencer noticed someone coming around the side yard, and her heart sped up. It was Jenna Cavanaugh.

She was dressed in a black T-shirt and skinny black jeans, and her black hair was piled up on her head. Her skin was still a brilliant, snowy white, but her face was half-hidden by oversized sunglasses. She held a white cane in one hand and the harness to her golden retriever in the other. He led Jenna to the edge of the group.

Spencer was pretty sure she was about to faint. Either that or start crying again.

Jenna and her dog stopped right next to Hanna. "Is Emily Fields here?"

"Yes," Emily whispered. Spencer could hear the fear in her voice. "Right here."

Jenna turned in the direction of Emily's voice. "This is yours." She held out a pink satin purse. Emily took it very carefully, as if it were made of glass. "And there's something you should read." Jenna reached in her pocket for a wrinkled piece of paper. "It's from Toby."

37

STRING BRACELETS
ARE SO OUT, ANYWAY

Emily pushed her hair behind her ears and looked at Jenna. The sunglasses she wore stretched from her cheekbones to above her eyebrows, but Emily could just make out a few pinkish, wrinkled scars—burn scars—on her forehead.

She thought of that night. The way Ali's house had smelled like an Aveda peppermint candle. The way Emily's mouth tasted like salt-and-vinegar chips. How her feet rubbed against the grooves in the DiLaurentises' living room wood floor as she stood at the window, watching Ali run across the Cavanaughs' lawn. The *boom* of the firework, the paramedics climbing up the tree house ladder, how Jenna's mouth made a rectangle, she was crying so hard.

Jenna handed her the dirty, wrinkled piece of paper. "They found this with him," she said, her voice cracking on the word *him*. "He wrote things to all of us. Your part is somewhere in the middle."

The paper was actually the Foxy auction list; Toby had scrawled something on the back. Seeing the way Toby's words didn't stay between the lines, that he'd barely used any capital letters, and that he'd signed the note *Toby* in wobbly cursive made Emily clench up inside. Although she'd never seen Toby's handwriting before, it seemed to bring him to life beside her. She could smell the soap he used, feel his big hand holding her smaller one. This morning, she'd awakened not on the porch swing but in her bed. The doorbell was ringing. She stumbled down the stairs, and there was a guy in bike shorts and a helmet at her door. "Can I use your phone?" he asked. "It's an emergency."

Emily had stared at him woozily, not awake. Carolyn appeared behind her, and the cyclist started to explain himself. "I was just riding through your woods, and I found this boy, and first I thought he was sleeping, but . . ."

He'd paused, and Carolyn's eyes had widened. She ran in to get her cell phone. Meanwhile, Emily stood on the porch, trying to make sense of what was happening. She thought about Toby at her window last night. How he'd violently banged on the sliding glass door, then bolted for the woods.

She looked at the cyclist. "This boy in the woods, was he trying to hurt you?" she whispered, her heart pounding. It was horrifying that Toby really *had* camped out in her woods all night. What if he'd come up onto her porch after Emily had dozed off?

The cyclist hugged his helmet to his chest. He looked about Emily's dad's age, with green eyes and a salt-and-pepper beard. "No," he said gently. "He was . . . *blue.*"

And now, this: a letter. A suicide note.

Toby had seemed so tortured, sprinting into the woods. Had he taken the pills right then? Or could Emily have stopped him? And was Hanna right—was Toby *not* Ali's killer?

The world started spinning. She felt a strong hand on the small of her back. "Whoa," Spencer whispered. "It's okay."

Emily straightened herself and looked at the letter. Her friends leaned in, too. There, right in the middle, was her name.

Emily, three years ago, I promised Alison DiLaurentis I'd keep a secret for her if she kept a secret for me. She promised that secret would never get out, but I guess it has. I've tried to deal with it—and to forget it—and when we became friends, I thought I could. . . . I thought I'd changed—and that my life had changed. But I guess you can't ever really change who you are. What I did to Jenna was the biggest mistake I've ever made. I was young and confused and stupid, and I never meant to hurt her. And I can't live with it anymore. I'm done.

Emily folded the note back up, the paper quaking in her hands. It didn't make sense—*they* were the ones who'd hurt Jenna, not Toby—what was he talking about? She handed it back to Jenna. "Thank you."

"You're welcome."

As Jenna turned to leave, Emily cleared her throat. "Wait," she croaked. "Jenna."

Jenna stopped. Emily swallowed hard. Everything Spencer just told her about Toby knowing and Ali lying, everything Toby had said last night, all the guilt she'd carried about Jenna for so many years . . . it all bubbled over.

"Jenna, *I* should apologize to you. We were . . . we used to be so mean. The stuff we did . . . the names, whatever . . . It wasn't funny."

Hanna stepped forward. "She's totally right. It wasn't funny at all." Emily hadn't seen Hanna look so tortured in a long time. "And you didn't deserve it," she added.

Jenna stroked her dog's head. "It's okay," she answered. "I'm over it."

Emily sighed. "But it's not okay. It's not okay at all. I . . . I never knew what being . . . teased because you're different . . . felt like. But now I do." She tensed her shoulder muscles, hoping it would keep her from crying. Part of her wanted to tell everyone what she was struggling with. But she held back. This wasn't the right time. There was more she wanted to say, too, but how could she? "And I'm sorry about your accident, too. I never got to tell you."

She wanted to add, *I'm sorry for what we accidentally did,* but she was too afraid.

Jenna's chin trembled. "It's not your fault. And anyway, it's not the worst thing that happened to me." She pulled on her dog's collar and walked back to the front yard.

The girls were quiet until Jenna was out of earshot.

"What could be worse than being blinded?" Aria whispered.

"There was something worse," Spencer interrupted. "The thing that Ali knew . . ."

Spencer had that look on her face again—like she had a lot to say, but she didn't want to say any of it. She sighed. "Toby used to . . . touch . . . Jenna," she whispered. "That's what he was doing, the night of Jenna's accident. That's why Ali misaimed the firework into the tree house."

When Ali got to Toby's tree house, Spencer explained, she saw Toby in the window and lit the firework. And then . . . she saw Jenna was there, too. There was something strange about Jenna's expression, and her shirt was unbuttoned. Then Ali saw Toby go over to Jenna and put his hand on her neck. He moved his other hand under Jenna's shirt and on top of the bra. He slid a strap off her shoulder. Jenna looked terrified.

Ali said she was so shocked, she bumped the firework out of position. The spark sped rapidly up the wick, and the rocket launched. Then there was a bright, confusing flash. Glass shattered. Someone screamed . . . and Ali ran.

"When Toby came up to us and told Ali he'd seen her, Ali told Toby she'd seen *him* . . . fooling around with Jenna," Spencer said. "The only way she wouldn't tell Toby's parents was if Toby admitted to lighting the firework himself. Toby agreed." She sighed. "Ali made me promise not to tell what Toby had done, along with everything else."

"Jesus," Aria whispered. "So Jenna must've been *happy* Toby was sent away."

Emily had no idea how to respond. She turned to look at Jenna, who was standing across the lawn with her mom, talking to a reporter. What must that have felt like, having your stepbrother do that to you? It had been bad enough when Ben went at her—what if she had to live with him? What if he was part of her family?

But it tore her up inside, too. Doing that to your step-sister was horrible, but it was also . . . pathetic. Of course Toby had just wanted to get past it now, to get on with his life. And he had been . . . until Emily scared him into thinking it was all coming back to haunt him.

She felt so horrified, she covered her face with her hands and took huge, gulping breaths. *I ruined Toby's life,* she thought. *I killed him.*

Her friends let her cry for a while—they were all crying, too. When Emily was reduced to dry, shuddering sobs, she looked up. "I just can't believe it."

"I can." Hanna said. "Ali only cared about herself. She was the queen of manipulation."

Emily looked at her, surprised. Hanna shrugged. "My seventh-grade secret? The one only Ali knew? Ali tortured me with it. Any time I didn't go along with something she wanted me to do, Ali threatened to tell you guys—and everyone else."

"She did that to you, too?" Aria sounded surprised. "There were times when she'd say something about my secret that made it so . . . *obvious*." She lowered her eyes. "Before Toby . . . took those pills, he outed that secret about me. The secret Ali knew, and the one A—*Toby*—was threatening me about."

Everyone sat up straighter. "What was it?" Hanna asked.

"It was . . . just this family thing." Aria's lip trembled. "I can't talk about it now."

Everyone was quiet for a while, thinking. Emily stared at the birds fluttering in and out of her dad's feeder. "It makes perfect sense that Toby was A," Hanna whispered. "He didn't kill Ali, but he still wanted revenge."

Spencer shrugged. "I hope you're right."

It was calm and bright back inside Emily's house. Her parents weren't home yet, but Carolyn had just made microwave popcorn, and the whole house smelled like it. To Emily, microwave popcorn always smelled better than it tasted, and despite her lack of appetite, her stomach growled. She thought, *Toby will never smell microwave popcorn again.*

Neither would Ali.

She glanced through her bedroom window toward the front yard. Just hours ago, Toby had been standing there, pleading with Emily not to tell the cops. And to think, what he'd meant was *Please don't tell them what I did to Jenna.*

Emily thought about Ali again. How Ali had lied to them about everything.

The funny but sad thing about all of it was that Emily was pretty sure she'd started loving Ali the night of Jenna's accident, after the ambulances left and Ali came back inside. Ali was so calm and protective, so self-assured and wonderful. Emily had been freaking out, but Ali was there to make her feel better.

"It's all right," Ali had cooed to her, scratching Emily's back, her fingers making large, slow circles. "I promise you. It'll be okay. You have to believe me."

"But how can it be okay?" Emily sobbed. "How do you know?"

"Because I just do."

Then Ali took Emily and laid her down on the couch, propping Emily's head in her lap. Ali's hands began to softly rake her scalp. It felt spookily good. So good, Emily forgot where she was, or how scared she felt. Instead, she was . . . transported.

Ali's movements got slower and slower, and Emily began to fall asleep. What happened next, Emily would never forget. Ali bent down and kissed Emily's cheek. Emily froze, jolted awake. Ali did it again. It felt so good.

She sat back up and started scratching Emily's head again. Emily's heart beat madly.

The rational part of Emily's brain put the incident out of her mind, figuring Ali had meant it in a comforting way. But the emotional part of her let the feeling bloom like the tiny capsules her parents put in her Christmas stocking that slowly formed big, spongy shapes in hot water. That was when Emily's love for Ali took hold, and without that night, maybe it never would have happened at all.

Emily sat down on her bed, staring abstractly out the window. She felt empty, like someone had scooped her insides right out like a jack-o'-lantern.

Her room was very quiet; the only sound was of the ceiling fan's blades whapping around. Emily opened the top drawer of her desk and found a pair of old left-handed scissors. She placed the blades between the strings of the bracelet Ali had made for her so many years ago, and in one swift chop, she cut it off. She didn't quite want to throw the bracelet away, but she didn't want to leave it on the floor where she could see it, either. In the end, she pushed it far under her bed with the edge of her foot.

"Ali," she whispered, tears running down her face. *"Why?"*

A buzzing across the room startled her. Emily had hung the pink bag Jenna returned to her on her bedroom doorknob. She could see her phone glowing through its thin fabric. Slowly, she got up and retrieved her purse. By the time she pulled her phone out, it had stopped ringing.

ONE NEW TEXT MESSAGE, her little Nokia said. Emily felt her heart speed up.

> Poor, confused Emily. I bet you could use a big warm girl hug right now, huh? Don't get too comfortable. It's not over until I say it is. —A

ACKNOWLEDGMENTS

There are a lot of people to thank for *Flawless*. First and foremost, the Alloy Entertainment crew, for all of their hard work and perseverance to make these books great: the inimitable Josh Bank, who can harness his inner teenage girl better than anyone I know. Ben Schrank, whose editorial guidance and oddly witty banter I will sorely miss. Les Morgenstein, for his "Eureka!" plot ideas . . . and because he buys us cookies. And last but not least, thanks to my editor, Sara Shandler, who can talk about dogs for hours, who makes great parrot noises, and who is a big reason this book makes sense.

My appreciation also to the extraordinary people at HarperCollins: Elise Howard, Kristin Marang, Farrin Jacobs, and the rest of the Harper team. All of your unflagging enthusiasm for the Pretty Little Liars series has been wonderful.

As always, thanks and love to Bob and Mindy Shepard, for teaching me at a young age that the most important things in life are to be silly, to be happy with what you do, and to always write fake information on restaurant comment cards. You're lovely parents and always have been—combining only the good qualities of Emily's, Spencer's, Aria's, and Hanna's. Thanks to Ali and to Ali's demonic, striped, I-love-to-bite cat, Polo.

Kisses to Grammar, Pavlov, Kitten, Sparrow, Chloe, Rover, Zelda, Riley, and Harriet. I'm so happy to have my cousin Colleen around, because she throws great parties, has friends who read my books, and comes up with the best drinking games. And, as usual, all of my love to Joel for, among other things, scratching my back, dealing with me when I make no sense, eating icing out of the can, and watching catty, girly shows on TV with me and even discussing them afterward.

I'd also like to acknowledge my late grandfather, Charles Vent. He was sort of my inspiration for Hanna—he had a little habit of "taking things without paying for them." But seriously, he was one of the most loving and creative people I was lucky enough to know, and I always thought he deserved a little bit of fame, even if it's in the acknowledgments page of a book.

WHAT HAPPENS NEXT . . .

Did you really believe I was Toby? Puh-lease. I would have killed myself too. I mean, honestly—ew. He totally had it coming. Karma's a bitch, and so am I—just ask Aria, Emily, Hanna, and Spencer. . . .

Let's start with Aria. The girl's so busy getting busy, I can barely keep track of her boyfriends. First Ezra, now Sean, and I have more than a sneaking suspicion she's not done with Ezra yet. That's the irritating thing about arty girls; they can never make up their minds. I guess I'll just have to help little Aria out and make the choice for her. I'm sure she's just going to loooove that.

Then there's Emily. Sweet, clueless Emily. Alison and Toby would probably say that kissing Emily is pretty much the kiss of death. But . . . oops . . . they can't say anything—they're dead. I guess Em should watch where she puts her poisonous little lips. She's two for two, and superstitious Emily knows better than anyone that bad things always happen in threes.

Lonely wittle Hannakins. Sean dumped her. Her dad dumped her. And her mom probably would if she could. Being unpopular kinda makes you want to throw up, huh? Or is that just Hanna? At least she has her BFF, Mona, to hold her hair back. Wait a second, no she doesn't. I wish I could tell you it couldn't get any worse for Hanna, but no one likes a liar. Least of all me.

Finally, there's Spencer: Sure, the little overachiever knows her SAT words by heart, but her memory's kinda fuzzy when it comes to the night Alison disappeared. Don't worry, she's about to get a refresher course courtesy of yours truly. Look at me—so eleemosynary! That's SAT for "nice"!

If you were as smart as me, you'd probably have figured out who I am by now. OMG, not being a genius must be so annoying. And I can't help you with that one—I've got my hands full with four pretty little liars at the moment. But since you've been so patient, I'll give you one hint: Spencer may have a 4.0, but I've got As to my name, too. Kisses! —A

Photo by Daniel Snyder

SARA SHEPARD is the author of the #1 *New York Times* bestselling series Pretty Little Liars. She graduated from New York University and has an MFA in Creative Writing from Brooklyn College. Sara recently moved back to Philadelphia's Main Line from Arizona, where her new series, The Lying Game, is set.

For exclusive information
on your favorite authors and artists,
visit www.authortracker.com.